The Tom Swift Omnibus #2

The Tom Swift Omnibus #2
By Victor Appleton

Wilder Publications, LLC.
PO Box 3005
Radford VA 24143-3005

ISBN 10: 1-60459-099-8
ISBN 13: 978-1-60459-099-9

First Edition

10 9 8 7 6 5 4 3 2 1

Tom Swift and His Submarine Boat
(Or under the Ocean for Sunken Treasure)

Tom Swift and His Electric Runabout
(Or the Speediest Car on the Road)

Tom Swift and His Wireless Message
(Or the Castaways of Earthquake Island)

Tom Swift and His Submarine Boat
(or Under the Ocean for Sunken Treasure)

TABLE OF CONTENTS:

NEWS OF A TREASURE WRECK

There was a rushing, whizzing, throbbing noise in the air. A great body, like that of some immense bird, sailed along, casting a grotesque shadow on the ground below. An elderly man, who Was seated on the porch of a large house, started to his feet in alarm.

"Gracious goodness! What was that, Mrs. Baggert?" he called to a motherly-looking woman who stood in the doorway. "What happened?"

"Nothing much, Mr. Swift," was the calm reply "I think that was Tom and Mr. Sharp in their airship, that's all. I didn't see it, but the noise sounded like that of the Red Cloud."

"Of course! To be sure!" exclaimed Mr. Barton Swift, the well-known inventor, as he started down the path in order to get a good view of the air, unobstructed by the trees. "Yes, there they are," he added. "That's the airship, but I didn't expect them back so soon. They must have made good time from Shopton. I wonder if anything can be the matter that they hurried so?"

He gazed aloft toward where a queerly-shaped machine was circling about nearly five hundred feet in the air, for the craft, after Swooping down close to the house, had ascended and was now hovering just above the line of breakers that marked the New Jersey seacoast, where Mr. Swift had taken up a temporary residence.

"Don't begin worrying, Mr. Swift," advised Mrs. Baggert, the housekeeper. "You've got too much to do, if you get that new boat done, to worry."

"That's so. I must not worry. But I wish Tom and Mr. Sharp would land, for I want to talk to them."

As if the occupants of the airship had heard the words of the aged inventor, they headed their craft toward earth. The combined aeroplane and dirigible balloon, a most wonderful traveler of the air, swung around, and then, with the deflection rudders slanted downward, came on with a rush. When near the landing place, just at the side of the house, the motor was stopped, and the gas, with a hissing noise, rushed into the red aluminum container. This immediately made the ship more buoyant and it landed almost as gently as a feather.

No sooner had the wheels which formed the lower part of the craft touched the ground than there leaped from the cabin of the Red Cloud a young man.

"Well, dad!" he exclaimed. "Here we are again, safe and sound. Made a record, too. Touched ninety miles an hour at times--didn't we, Mr. Sharp?"

"That's what," agreed a tall, thin, dark-complexioned man, who followed Tom Swift more leisurely in his exit from the cabin. Mr. Sharp, a veteran aeronaut, stopped to fasten guy ropes from the airship to strong stakes driven into the ground.

"And we'd have done better, only we struck a hard wind against us about two miles up in the air, which delayed us," went on Tom. "Did you hear us coming, dad?"

"Yes, and it startled him," put in Mrs. Baggert. "I guess he wasn't expecting you."

"Oh, well, I shouldn't have been so alarmed, only I was thinking deeply about a certain change I am going to make in the submarine, Tom. I was day-dreaming, I think, when your ship whizzed through the air. But tell me, did you find everything all right at Shopton? No signs of any of those scoundrels of the Happy Harry gang having been around?" and Mr. Swift looked anxiously at his son.

"Not a sign, dad," replied Tom quickly. "Everything was all right. We brought the things you wanted. They're in the airship. Oh, but it was a fine trip. I'd like to take another right out to sea."

"Not now, Tom," said his father. "I want you to help me. And I need Mr. Sharp's help, too. Get the things out of the car, and we'll go to the shop."

"First I think we'd better put the airship away," advised Mr. Sharp. "I don't just like the looks of the weather, and, besides, if we leave the ship exposed we'll be sure to have a crowd around sooner or later, and we don't want that."

"No, indeed," remarked the aged inventor hastily. "I don't want people prying around the submarine shed. By all means put the airship away, and then come into the shop."

In spite of its great size the aeroplane was easily wheeled along by Tom and Mr. Sharp, for the gas in the container made it so buoyant that it barely touched the earth. A little more of the powerful vapor and the Red Cloud would have risen by itself. In a few minutes the wonderful craft, of which my readers have been told in detail in a previous volume, was safely housed in a large tent, which was securely fastened.

Mr. Sharp and Tom, carrying some bundles which they had taken from the car, or cabin, of the craft, went toward a large shed, which adjoined the house that Mr. Swift had hired for the season at the seashore. They found the lad's father standing before a great shape, which loomed up dimly in the semi-darkness of the building. It was like an immense cylinder, pointed at either end, and here and there were openings, covered with thick glass, like immense, bulging eyes. From the number of tools and machinery all about the place, and from the appearance of the great cylinder itself, it was easy to see that it was only partly completed.

"Well, how goes it, dad?" asked the youth, as he deposited his bundle on a bench. "Do you think you can make it work?"

"I think so, Tom. The positive and negative plates are giving me considerable trouble, though. But I guess we can solve the problem. Did you bring me the galvanometer?"

"Yes, and all the other things," and the young inventor proceeded to take the articles from the bundles he carried.

Mr. Swift looked them over carefully, while Tom walked about examining the submarine, for such was the queer craft that was contained in the shed. He noted that some progress had been made on it since he had left the seacoast several days before to make a trip to Shopton, in New York State, where the Swift home was located, after some tools and apparatus that his father wanted to obtain from his workshop there.

"You and Mr. Jackson have put on several new plates," observed the lad after a pause.

"Yes," admitted his father. "Garret and I weren't idle, were we, Garret?" and he nodded to the aged engineer, who had been in his employ for many years.

"No; and I guess we'll soon have her in the water, Tom, now that you and Mr. Sharp are here to help us," replied Garret Jackson.

"We ought to have Mr. Damon here to bless the submarine and his liver and collar buttons a few times," put in Mr. Sharp, who brought in another bundle. He referred to an eccentric individual Who had recently made an airship voyage with himself and Tom, Mr. Damon's peculiarity being to use continually such expressions as: "Bless my soul! Bless my liver!"

"Well, I'll be glad when we can make a trial trip," went on Tom. "I've traveled pretty fast on land with my motor- cycle, and we certainly have hummed through the air. Now I want to see how it feels to scoot along under water."

"Well, if everything goes well we'll be in position to make a trial trip inside of a month," remarked the aged inventor. "look here, Mr. Sharp, I made a change in the steering gear, which I'd like you and Tom to consider."

The three walked around to the rear of the odd-looking structure, if an object shaped like a cigar can be said to have a front and rear, and the inventor, his son, and the aeronaut were soon deep in a discussion of the technicalities connected with under-water navigation.

A little later they went into the house, in response to a summons from the supper bell, vigorously rung by Mrs. Baggert. She was not fond of waiting with meals, and even the most serious problem of mechanics was, in her estimation, as nothing compared with having the soup get cold, or the possibility of not having the meat done to a turn.

The meal was interspersed with remarks about the recent airship flight of Tom and Mr. Sharp, and discussions about the new submarine. This talk went on even after the table was cleared off and the three had adjourned to the sitting- room. There Mr. Swift brought out pencil and paper, and soon he and Mr. Sharp were engrossed in calculating the pressure per square inch of sea water at a depth of three miles.

"Do you intend to go as deep as that?" asked Tom, looking up from a paper he was reading.

"Possibly," replied his father; and his son resumed his perusal of the sheet.

"Now," went on the inventor to the aeronaut, "I have another plan. In addition to the positive and negative plates which will form our motive power, I am going to install forward and aft propellers, to use in case of accident."

"I say, dad! Did you see this?" suddenly exclaimed Tom, getting up from his chair, and holding his finger on a certain place in the page of the paper.

"Did I see what?" asked Mr. Swift.

"Why, this account of the sinking of the treasure ship."

"Treasure ship? No. Where?"

"Listen," went on Tom. "I'll read it: 'Further advices from Montevideo, Uruguay, South America, state that all hope has been given up of recovering the steamship Boldero, which foundered and went down off that coast in the recent gale. Not only has all hope been abandoned of raising the vessel, but it is feared that no part of the three hundred thousand dollars in gold bullion which she carried will ever be recovered. Expert divers who were taken to the scene of the wreck state that the depth of water, and the many currents existing there, due to a submerged shoal, preclude any possibility of getting at the hull. The bullion, it is believed, was to have been used to further the interests of a certain revolutionary faction, but it seems likely that they will have to look elsewhere for the sinews of war. Besides the bullion the ship also carried several cases of rifles, it is stated, and other valuable cargo. The crew and what few passengers the Boldero carried were, contrary to the first reports, all saved by taking to the boats. It appears that some of the ship's plates were sprung by the stress in which she labored in a storm, and she filled and sank gradually.' There! what do you think of that, dad?" cried Tom as he finished.

"What do I think of it? Why, I think it's too bad for the revolutionists, Tom, of course."

"No; I mean about the treasure being still on board the ship. What about that?"

"Well, it's likely to stay there, if the divers can't get at it. Now, Mr. Sharp, about the propellers--"

"Wait, dad!" cried Tom earnestly.

"Why, Tom, what's the matter?" asked Mr. Swift in some surprise.

"How soon before we can finish our submarine?" went on Tom, not answering the question.

"About a month. Why?"

"Why? Dad, why can't we have a try for that treasure? It ought to be comparatively easy to find that sunken ship off the coast of Uruguay. In our submarine we can get close up to it, and in the new diving suits you invented we can get at that gold bullion. Three hundred thousand dollars! Think of it, dad! Three hundred thousand dollars! We could easily claim all of it, since the owners have abandoned it, but we would be satisfied with half. Let's hurry up, finish the submarine, and have a try for it."

"But, Tom, you forget that I am to enter my new ship in the trials for the prize offered by the United States Government."

"How much is the prize if you win it?" asked Tom.

"Fifty thousand dollars."

"Well, here's a chance to make three times that much at least, and maybe more. Dad, let the Government prize go, and try for the treasure. Will you?"

Tom looked eagerly at his father, his eyes shining with anticipation. Mr. Swift was not a quick thinker, but the idea his son had proposed made an impression on him. He reached out his hand for the paper in which the young inventor had seen the account of the sunken treasure. Slowly he read it through. Then he passed it to Mr. Sharp.

"What do you think of it?" he asked of the aeronaut

"There's a possibility," remarked the balloonist "We might try for it. We can easily go three miles down, and it doesn't lie as deeply as that, if this account is true. Yes, we might try for it. But we'd have to omit the Government contests."

"Will you, dad?" asked Tom again.

Mr. Swift considered a moment longer.

"Yes, Tom, I will," he finally decided. "Going after the treasure will be likely to afford us a better test of the submarine than would any Government tests. We'll try to locate the sunken Boldero."

"Hurrah!" cried the lad, taking the paper from Mr. Sharp and waving it in the air. "That's the stuff! Now for a search for the submarine treasure!"

FINISHING THE SUBMARINE

"What's the matter?" cried Mrs. Baggert, the housekeeper, hurrying in from the kitchen, where she was washing the dishes. "Have you seen some of those scoundrels who robbed you, Mr. Swift? If you have, the police down here ought to--"

"No, it's nothing like that," explained Mr. Swift. "Tom has merely discovered in the paper an account of a sunken treasure ship, and he wants us to go after it, down under the ocean."

"Oh, dear! Some more of Captain Kidd's hidden hoard, I suppose?" ventured the housekeeper. "Don't you bother with it, Mr. Swift. I had a cousin once, and he got set in the notion that he knew where that pirate's treasure was. He spent all the money he had and all he could borrow digging for it, and he never found a penny. Don't waste your time on such foolishness. It's bad enough to be building airships and submarines without going after treasure." Mrs. Baggert spoke with the freedom of an old friend rather than a hired housekeeper, but she had been in the family ever since Tom's mother died, when he was a baby, and she had many privileges.

"Oh, this isn't any of Kidd's treasure," Tom assured her. "If we get it, Mrs. Baggert, I'll buy you a diamond ring."

"Humph!" she exclaimed, as Tom began to hug her in boyish fashion. "I guess I'll have to buy all the diamond rings I want, if I have to depend on your treasure for them," and she went back to the kitchen.

"Well," went on Mr. Swift after a pause, "if we are going into the treasure-hunting business, Tom, we'll have to get right to work. In the first place, we must find out more about this ship, and just where it was sunk."

"I can do that part," said Mr. Sharp. "I know some sea captains, and they can put me on the track of locating the exact spot. In fact, it might not be a bad idea to take an expert navigator with us. I can manage in the air all right, but I confess that working out a location under water is beyond me."

"Yes, an old sea captain wouldn't be a bad idea, by any means," conceded Mr. Swift. "Well, if you'll attend to that detail, Mr. Sharp, Tom, Mr. Jackson and I will finish the submarine. Most of the work is done, however, and it only remains to install the engine and motors. Now, in regard to the negative and positive electric plates, I'd like your opinion, Tom."

For Tom Swift was an inventor, second in ability only to his father, and his advice was often sought by his parent on matters of electrical construction, for the lad had made a specialty of that branch of science.

While father and son were deep in a discussion of the apparatus of the submarine, there will be an opportunity to make the reader a little better acquainted with them. Those of you who have read the previous volumes of this series do not need to be told who Tom Swift is. Others, however, may be glad to have a proper introduction to him.

Tom Swift lived with his father, Barton Swift, in the village of Shopton, New York. The Swift home was on the outskirts of the town, and the large house was surrounded by a number of machine shops, in which father and son, aided by Garret Jackson, the engineer, did their experimental and constructive work. Their house was not far from Lake Carlopa, a fairly large body of water, on which Tom often speeded his motor

In the first volume of this series, entitled "Tom Swift and His Motor-Cycle," it was told how be became acquainted with Mr. Wakefield Damon, who suffered an accident while riding one of the speedy machines. The accident disgusted Mr. Damon with motor-cycles, and Tom secured it for a low price. He had many adventures on it, chief among which was being knocked senseless and robbed of a valuable patent model belonging to his father, which he was taking to Albany. The attack was committed by a gang known as the Happy Harry gang, who were acting at the instigation of a syndicate of rich men, who wanted to secure control of a certain patent turbine engine which Mr. Swift had invented.

Tom set out in pursuit of the thieves, after recovering from their attack, and had a strenuous time before he located them.

In the second volume, entitled "Tom Swift and His Motor- Boat," there was related our hero's adventures in a fine craft which was recovered from the thieves and sold at auction. There was a mystery connected with the boat, and for a long time Tom could not solve it. He was aided, however, by his chum, Ned Newton, who worked in the Shopton Bank, and also by Mr. Damon and Eradicate Sampson, an aged colored whitewasher, who formed quite an attachment for Tom.

In his motor-boat Tom had more than one race with Andy Foger, a rich lad of Shopton, who was a sort of bully. He had red hair and squinty eyes, and was as mean in character as he was in looks. He and his cronies, Sam Snedecker and Pete Bailey, made trouble for Tom, chiefly because Tom managed to beat Andy twice in boat races.

It was while in his motor-boat, Arrow, that Tom formed the acquaintance of John Sharp, a veteran balloonist. While coming down Lake Carlopa on the way to the Swift home, which had been entered by thieves, Tom, his father and Ned Newton, saw a balloon on fire over the lake. Hanging from a trapeze on it was Mr. Sharp, who had made an ascension from a fair ground. By hard work on the part of Tom and his friends the aeronaut was saved, and took up his residence with the Swifts.

His advent was most auspicious, for Tom and his father were then engaged in perfecting an airship, and Mr. Sharp was able to lend them his skill, so that the craft was soon constructed.

In the third volume, called "Tom Swift and His Airship," there was set down the doings of the young inventor, Mr. Sharp and Mr. Damon on a trip above the clouds. They undertook it merely for pleasure, but they encountered considerable danger, before they completed it, for they nearly fell into a blazing forest once, and were later fired at by a crowd of excited people. This last act was to effect their capture, for they were taken for a gang of bank robbers, and this was due directly to Andy Foger.

The morning after Tom and his friends started on their trip in the air, the Shopton Bank was found to have been looted of seventy-five thousand dollars. Andy Foger at once told the police that Tom Swift had taken the money, and when asked how he knew this, he said he had seen Tom hanging around the bank the night before the vault was burst open, and that the young inventor had some burglar tools in his possession. Warrants were at once sworn out for Tom and Mr. Damon, who was also accused of being one of the robbers, and a reward of five thousand dollars was offered.

Tom, Mr. Damon and Mr. Sharp sailed on, all unaware of this, and unable to account for being fired upon, until they accidentally read in the paper an account of their supposed misdeeds. They lost no time in starting back home, and on, the way got on the track of the real bank robbers, who were members of the Happy Harry gang.

How the robbers were captured in an exciting raid, how Tom recovered most of the stolen money, and how he gave Andy Foger a deserved thrashing for giving a false clue was told of, and there was an account of a race in which the Red Cloud (as the airship was called) took part, as well as details of how Tom and his friends secured the reward, which Andy Foger hoped to collect.

Those of you who care to know how the Red Cloud was constructed, and how she behaved in the air, even during accidents and when struck by lightning, may learn by reading the third volume, for the airship was one of the most successful ever constructed.

When the craft was finished, and the navigators were ready to start on their first long trip, Mr. Swift was asked to go with them. He declined, but would not tell why, until Tom, pressing him for an answer, learned that his father was planning a submarine boat, which he hoped to enter in some trials for Government prizes. Mr. Swift remained at home to work on this submarine, while his son and Mr. Sharp were sailing above the clouds.

On their return, however, and after the bank mystery had been cleared up, Tom and Mr. Sharp, aided Mr. Swift in completing the submarine, until, when the present story opens, it needed but little additional work to make the craft ready for the water.

Of course it had to be built near the sea, as it would have been impossible to transport it overland from Shopton. So, before the keel was laid, Mr. Swift rented a large cottage at a seaside place on the New Jersey coast and there, after, erecting a large shed, the work on the Advance, as the under-water ship was called, was begun.

It was soon to be launched in a large creek that extended in from the ocean and had plenty of water at high tide. Tom and Mr. Sharp made several trips back and forth from Shopton in their airship, to see that all was safe at home and occasionally to get needed tools and supplies from the shops, for not all the apparatus could be moved from Shopton to the coast.

It was when returning from one of these trips that Tom brought with him the paper containing an account of the wreck of the Boldero and the sinking of the treasure she carried.

Until late that night the three fortune-hunters discussed various matters.

"We'll hurry work on the ship," said Mr. Swift it length. "Tom, I wonder if your friend, Mr. Damon, would care to try how it seems under Water? He stood the air trip fairly well."

"I'll write and ask him," answered the lad. "I'm sure he'll go."

Securing, a few days later, the assistance of two mechanics, whom he knew he could trust, for as yet the construction of the Advance was a secret, Mr. Swift prepared to rush work on the submarine, and for the next three weeks there were busy times in the shed next to the seaside cottage. So busy, in fact, were Tom and Mr. Sharp, that they only found opportunity for one trip in the airship, and that was to get some supplies from the shops at home.

"Well," remarked Mr. Swift one night, at the close of a hard day's work, "another week will see our craft completed. Then we will put it in the water and see how it floats, and whether it submerges as I hope it does. But come on, Tom. I want to lock up. I'm very tired to-night."

"All right, dad," answered the young inventor coming from the darkened rear of the shop. "I just want to--"

Ne paused suddenly, and appeared to be listening. Then he moved softly back to where he had come from.

"What's the matter?" asked his father in a whisper. "What's up, Tom?"

The lad did not answer Mr. Swift, with a worried look on his face, followed his son. Mr. Sharp stood in the door of the shop.

"I thought I heard some one moving around back here," went on Tom quietly.

"Some one in this shop!" exclaimed the aged inventor excitedly. "Some one trying to steal my ideas again! Mr. Sharp, come here! Bring that rifle! We'll teach these scoundrels a lesson!"

Tom quickly darted hack to the extreme rear of the building. There was a scuffle, and the next minute Tom cried out:

"What are you doing here?"

"Ha! I beg your pardon," replied a voice. "I am looking for Mr. Barton Swift."

"My father," remarked Tom. "But that's a queer place to look for him. He's up front. Father, here's a man who wishes to see you," he called.

"Yes, I strolled in, and seeing no one about I went to the rear of the place," the voice went on. "I hope I haven't transgressed."

"We were busy on the other side of the shop, I guess," replied Tom, and he looked suspiciously at the man who emerged from the darkness into the light from a window. "I beg your pardon for grabbing you the way I did," went on the lad, "but I thought you were one of a gang of men we've been having trouble with."

"Oh, that's all right," continued the man easily. "I know Mr. Swift, and I think he will remember me. Ah, Mr. Swift, how do you do?" he added quickly, catching sight of Tom's father, who, with Mr. Sharp, was coming to meet the lad.

"Addison Berg!" exclaimed the aged inventor as he saw the man's face more plainly. "What are you doing here?"

"I came to see you," replied the man. "May I have a talk with you privately?"

"I—I suppose so," assented Mr. Swift nervously. "Come into the house."

Mr. Berg left Tom's side and advanced to where Mr. Swift was standing. Together the two emerged from the now fast darkening shop and went toward the house.

"Who is he?" asked Mr. Sharp of the young inventor in a whisper.

"I don't know," replied the lad; "but, whoever he is, dad seems afraid of him. I'm going to keep my eyes open."

Mr. Berg Is Astonished

Following his father and the stranger whom the aged inventor had addressed as Mr. Berg, Tom and Mr. Sharp entered the house, the lad having first made sure that Garret Jackson was on guard in the shop that contained the sub marine.

"Now," said Mr. Swift to the newcomer, "I am at your service. What is it you wish?"

"In the first place, let me apologize for having startled you and your friends," began the man. "I had no idea of sneaking into your workshop, but I had just arrived here, and seeing the doors open I went in. I heard no one about, and I wandered to the back of the place. There I happened to stumble over a board—"

"And I heard you," interrupted Tom.

"Is this one of your employees?" asked Mr. Berg in rather frigid tones.

"That is my son," replied Mr. Swift.

"Oh, I beg your pardon." The man's manner changed quickly. "Well, I guess you did hear me, young man. I didn't intend to hark my shins the way I did, either. You must have taken me for a burglar or a sneak thief."

"I have been very much bothered by a gang of unscrupulous men," said Mr. Swift, "and I suppose Tom thought it was some of them sneaking around again."

"That's what I did," added the lad. "I wasn't going to have any one steal the secret of the submarine if I could help it."

"Quite right! Quite right!" exclaimed Mr. Berg. "But my purpose was an open one. As you know, Mr. Swift, I represent the firm of Bentley & Eagert, builders of submarine boats and torpedoes. They heard that you were constructing a craft to take part in the competitive prize tests of the United States Government, and they asked me to come and see you to learn when your ship would be ready. Ours is completed, but we recognize that it will be for the best interests of all concerned if there are a number of contestants, and my firm did not want to send in their entry until they knew that you were about finished with your ship. How about it? Are you ready to compete?"

"Yes," said Mr. Swift slowly. "We are about ready. My craft needs a few finishing touches, and then it will be ready to launch."

"Then we may expect a good contest on your part," suggested Mr. Berg.

"Well," began the aged inventor, "I don't know about that."

"What's that?" exclaimed Mr. Berg.

"I said I wasn't quite sure that we would compete," went on Mr. Swift. "You see, when I first got this idea for a submarine boat I had it in mind to try for the Government prize of fifty thousand dollars."

"That's what we want, too," interrupted Mr. Berg with a smile.

"But," went on Tom's father, "since then certain matters have come up, and I think, on the whole, that we'll not compete for the prize after all."

"Not compete for the prize?" almost shouted the agent for Bentley & Eagert. "Why, the idea! You ought to compete. It is good for the trade. We think we have a very fine craft, and probably we would beat you in the tests, but—"

"I wouldn't be too sure of that," put in Tom. "You have only seen the outside of our boat. The inside is better yet."

"Ah, I have no doubt of that," spoke Mr. Berg, "but we have been at the business longer than you have, and have had more experience. Still we welcome competition. But I am very much surprised that you are not going to compete for the prize, Mr. Swift. Very much surprised, indeed! You see, I came down from Philadelphia to arrange so that we could both enter our ships at the same time. I understand there is another firm of submarine boat builders who are going to try for the prize, and I want to arrange a date that will he satisfactory to all. I am greatly astonished that you are not going to compete."

"Well, we were going to," said Mr. Swift, "only we have changed our minds, that's all. My son and I have other plans."

"May I ask what they are?" questioned Mr. Berg.

"You may," exclaimed Tom quickly; "but I don't believe we can tell you. They're a secret," he added more cordially.

"Oh, I see," retorted Mr. Berg. "Well, of course I don't wish to penetrate any of your secrets, but I hoped we could contest together for the Government prize. It is worth trying for I assure you—fifty thousand dollars. Besides, there is the possibility of selling a number of submarines to the United States. It's a fine prize."

"But the one we are after is a bigger one," Cried Tom impetuously, and the moment he had spoken the wished he could recall the words.

"Eh? What's that?" exclaimed Mr. Berg. "You don't mean to say another government has offered a larger prize? If I had known that I would not have let my firm enter into the competition for the bonus offered by the United States. Please tell me."

"I'm sorry," went on Tom more soberly. "I shouldn't have spoken. Mr. Berg, the plans of my father and myself are such that we can't reveal them now. We are going to try for a prize, but not in competition with you. It's an entirely different matter."

"Well, I guess you'll find that the firm of Bentley & Eagert are capable of trying for any prizes that are offered," boasted the agent. "We may be competitors yet."

"I don't believe so," replied Mr. Swift

"We may," repeated Mr. Berg. "And if we do, please remember that we will show no mercy. Our boats are the best."

"And may the best boat win," interjected Mr. Sharp. "That's all we ask. A fair field and no favors."

"Of course," spoke the agent coldly. "Is this another son of yours?" he asked.

"No but a good friend," replied the aged inventor. "No, Mr. Berg, we won't compete this time. You may tell your firm so."

"Very good," was the other's stiff reply. "Then I will bid you good night. We shall carry off the Government prize, but permit me to add that I am very much astonished, very much indeed, that you do not try for the prize. From what I have seen of your submarine you have a very good one, almost as good, in some respects, as ours. I bid you good night," and with a bow the man left the room and hurried away from the house.

TOM IS IMPRISONED

"Well, I must say he's a cool one," remarked Tom, as the echoes of Mr. Berg's steps died away. "The idea of thinking his boat better than ours! I don't like that man, dad. I'm suspicious of him. Do you think he came here to steal some of our ideas?"

"No, I hardly believe so, my son. But how did you discover him?"

"Just as you saw, dad. I heard a noise and went back there to investigate. I found him sneaking around, looking at the electric propeller plates. I went to grab him just as he stumbled over a hoard. At first I thought it was one of the old gang. I'm almost sure he was trying to discover something."

"No, Tom. the firm he works for are good business men, and they would not countenance anything like that. They are heartless competitors, however, and if they saw a legitimate chance to get ahead of me and take advantage, they would do it. But they would not sneak in to steal my ideas. I feel sure of that. Besides, they have a certain type of submarine which they think is the best ever invented, and they would hardly change at this late day. They feel sure of winning the Government prize, and I'm just as glad we're not going to have a contest."

"Do you think our boat is better than theirs?"

"Much better, in many respects."

"I don't like that man Berg, though," went on Tom.

"Nor do I," added his father. "There is something strange about him. He was very anxious that I should compete. Probably he thought his firm's boat would go so far ahead of ours that they would get an extra bonus. But I'm glad he didn't see our new method of propulsion. That is the principal improvement in the Advance over other types of submarines. Well, another week and we will be ready for the test."

"Have you known Mr. Berg long, dad?"

"Not very. I met him in Washington when I was in the patent office. He was taking out papers on a submarine for his firm at the same time I got mine for the Advance. It is rather curious that he should come all the way here from Philadelphia. merely to see if I was going to compete. There is something strange about it, something that I can't understand."

The time was to come when Mr. Swift and his son were to get at the bottom of Mr. Berg's reasons, and they learned to their sorrow that he had penetrated some of their secrets.

Before going to bed that night Tom and Mr. Sharp paid a visit to the shed where the submarine was resting on the ways, ready for launching. They found Mr. Jackson on guard and the engineer said that no one had been around. Nor was anything found disturbed.

"It certainly is a great machine," remarked the lad as he looked up at the cigar-shaped bulk towering over his head. "Dad has outdone himself this trip."

"It looks all right," commented Mr. Sharp. "Whether it will work is another question."

"Yes, we can't tell until it's in the water," con ceded Tom. "But I hope it does. Dad has spent much time and money on it."

The Advance was, as her name indicated, much in advance of previous submarines. There was not so much difference in outward construction as there was in the means of propulsion and in the manner in which the interior and the machinery were arranged.

The submarine planned by Mr. Swift and Tom jointly, and constructed by them, with the aid of Mr. Sharp and Mr. Jackson, was shaped like a Cigar, over one hundred feet long and twenty feet in diameter at the thickest part. It was divided into many compartments, all water-tight, so that if one or even three were flooded the ship would still be useable.

Buoyancy was provided for by having several tanks for the introduction of compressed air, and there was an emergency arrangement so that a collapsible aluminum container could be distended and filled with a powerful gas. This was to be used if, by any means, the ship was disabled on the bottom of the ocean. The container could be expanded and filled, and would send the Advance to the surface.

Another peculiar feature was that the engine-room, dynamos and other apparatus were all contained amidships. This gave stability to the craft, and also enabled the same engine to operate both shafts and propellers, as well as both the negative forward electrical plates, and the positive rear ones.

These plates were a new idea in submarine construction, and were the outcome of an idea of Mr. Swift, with some suggestions from his son.

The aged inventor did not want to depend on the usual screw propellers for his craft, nor did he want to use a jet of compressed air, shooting out from a rear tube, nor yet a jet of water, by means of which the creature called the squid shoots himself along. Mr. Swift planned to send the Advance along under water by means of electricity.

Certain peculiar plates were built at the forward and aft blunt noses of the submarine. Into the forward plate a negative charge of electricity was sent, and into the one at the rear a positive charge, just as one end of a horseshoe magnet is positive and will repel the north end of a compass needle, while the other pole of a magnet is negative and will attract it. In electricity like repels like, while negative and positive have a mutual attraction for each other.

Mr. Swift figured out that if he could send a powerful current of negative electricity into the forward plate it would pull the boat along, for water is a good conductor of electricity, while if a positive charge was sent into the rear plate it would serve to push the submarine along, and he would thus get a pulling and pushing motion, just as a forward and aft propeller works on some ferry boats.

But the inventor did not depend on these plates alone. There were auxiliary forward and aft propellers of the regular type, so that if the electrical plates did not work, or got out of order, the screws would serve to send the Advance along.

There was much machinery in the submarine There were gasolene motors, since space was too cramped to allow the carrying of coal for boilers. There were dynamos, motors and powerful pumps. Some of these were for air, and some for water. To sink the submarine below the surface large tanks were filled with water. To insure a more sudden descent, deflecting rudders were also used, similar to those on an airship. There were also special air pumps, and one for the powerful gas, which was manufactured on board.

Forward from the engine-room was a cabin, where meals could be served, and where the travelers could remain in the daytime. There was also a small cooking galley, or kitchen, there. Back of the engine-room were the sleeping quarters and the storerooms. The submarine was steered from the forward compartment, and here were also levers, wheels and valves that controlled all the machinery, while a number of dials showed in which direction they were going, how deep they were, and at what speed they were moving, as well as what the ocean pressure was.

On top, forward, was a small conning, or observation tower, with auxiliary and steering and controlling apparatus there. This was to be used when the ship was moving along on the surface of the ocean, or merely with the deck awash. There was a small flat deck surrounding the conning tower and this was available when the craft was on the surface.

There was provision made for leaving the ship when it was on the bed of the ocean. When it was desired to do this the occupants put on diving suits, which were provided with portable oxygen tanks. Then they entered a chamber into which water was admitted until it was equal in pressure to that outside. Then a steel door was opened, and they could step out. To re-enter the ship the operation was reversed. This was not a new feature. In fact, many submarines to-day use it

At certain places there were thick bull's-eye windows, by means of which the under-water travelers could look out into the ocean through which they were moving. As a defense against the attacks of submarine monsters there was a steel, pointed ram, like a big harpoon. There were also a bow and a stern electrical gun, of which more will be told later.

In addition to ample sleeping accommodations. there were many conveniences aboard the Advance. Plenty of fresh water could be carried, and there was an apparatus for distilling more from the sea water that surrounded the travelers. Compressed air was carried in large tanks, and oxygen could be made as needed. In short, nothing that could add to the comfort or safety of the travelers had been omitted. There was a powerful crane and windlass, which had been installed when Mr. Swift thought his boat might be bought by the Government. This was to be used for raising wrecks or recovering objects from the bottom of the ocean. Ample stores and provisions were to be carried and, once the travelers were shut up in the

Advance, they could exist for a month below the surface, providing no accident occurred.

All these things Tom and Mr. Sharp thought of as they looked over the ship before turning in for the night. The craft was made immensely strong to withstand powerful pressure at the bottom of the ocean. The submarine could penetrate to a depth of about three miles. Below that it was dangerous to go, as the awful force would crush the plates, powerful as they were.

"Well, we'll rush things to-morrow and the next day," observed Tom as he prepared to leave the building. "Then we'll soon see if it works."

For the next week there were busy times in the shop near the ocean. Great secrecy was maintained, and though curiosity seekers did stroll along now and then, they received little satisfaction. At first Mr. Swift thought that the visit of Mr. Berg would have unpleasant results, for he feared that the agent would talk about the craft, of which he had so unexpectedly gotten a sight. But nothing seemed to follow from his chance inspection, and it was forgotten.

It was one evening, about a week later, that Tom was alone in the shop. The two mechanics that had been hired to help out in the rush had been let go, and the ship needed but a few adjustments to make it ready for the sea.

"I think I'll just take another look at the water tank valves," said Tom to himself as he prepared to enter the big compartments which received the water ballast. "I want to be sure they work properly and quickly. We've got to depend on them to make us sink when we want to, and, what's more important, to rise to the surface in a hurry. I've got time enough to look them over before dad and Mr. Sharp get back."

Tom entered the starboard tank by means of an emergency sliding door between the big compartments and the main part of the ship. This was closed by a worm and screw gear, and once the ship was in the water would seldom be used.

The young inventor proceeded with his task, carefully inspecting the valves by the light of a lantern he carried. The apparatus seemed to be all right, and Tom was about to leave when a peculiar noise attracted his attention. It was the sound of metal scraping on metal, and the lad's quick and well-trained ear told him it was somewhere about the ship.

He turned to leave the tank, but as he wheeled around his light flashed on a solid wall of steel back of him. The emergency outlet had been closed! He was a prisoner in the water compartment, and he knew, from past experience, that shout as he would, his voice could not be heard ten feet away. His father and Mr. Sharp, as he was aware, had gone to a nearby city for some tools, and Mr. Jackson, the engineer, was temporarily away. Mrs. Baggert, in the house, could not hear his cries.

"I'm locked in!" cried Tom aloud. "The worm gear must have shut of itself. But I don't see how that could be. I've got to get out mighty soon, though, or I'll smother. This tank is airtight, and it won't take me long to breath up all the oxygen there is here. I must get that slide open."

He sought to grasp the steel plate that closed the emergency opening. His fingers slipped over the smooth, polished surface. He was hermetically sealed up—a captive! Blankly he set his lantern down and leaned hopelessly against the wall of the tank.

"I've got to get out," he murmured.

As if in answer to him he heard a voice on the outside, crying:

"There, Tom Swift! I guess I've gotten even with you now! Maybe next time you won't take a reward away from me, and lick me into the bargain. I've got you shut up good and tight, and you'll stay there until I get ready to let you out."

"Andy Foger!" gasped Tom. "Andy Foger sneaked in here and turned the gear. But how did he get to this part of the coast? Andy Foger, you let me out!" shouted the young inventor; and as Andy's mocking laugh came to him faintly through the steel sides of the submarine, the imprisoned lad beat desperately with his hands on the smooth sides of the tank, vainly wondering how his enemy had discovered him.

MR. BERG IS SUSPICIOUS

Not for long did the young inventor endeavor to break his way out of the water-ballast tank by striking the heavy sides of it. Tom realized that this was worse than useless. He listened intently, but could hear nothing. Even the retreating footsteps of Andy Foger were inaudible.

"This certainly is a pickle!" exclaimed Tom aloud. "I can't understand how he ever got here. He must have traced us after we went to Shopton in the airship the last time. Then he sneaked in here. Probably he saw me enter, but how could he knew enough to work the worm gear and close the door? Andy has had some experience with machinery, though, and one of the vaults in the bank where his father is a director closed just like this tank. That's very likely how he learned about it. But I've got to do something else besides thinking of that sneak, Andy. I've got to get out of here. Let's see if I can work the gear from inside."

Before he started, almost, Tom knew that it would be impossible. The tank was made to close from the interior of the submarine, and the heavy door, built to withstand the pressure of tons of water, could not be forced except by the proper means.

"No use trying that," concluded the lad, after a tiring attempt to force back the sliding door with his hands. "I've got to call for help."

He shouted until the vibrations in the confined space made his ears ring, and the mere exertion of raising his voice to the highest pitch made his heart beat quickly. Yet there came no response. He hardly expected that there would be any, for with his father and Mr. Sharp away, the engineer absent on an errand, and Mrs. Baggert in the house some distance off, there was no one to hear his calls for help, even if they had been capable of penetrating farther than the extent of the shed, where the under-water craft had been constructed.

"I've got to wait until some of them come out here," thought Tom. "They'll be sure to release me and make a search. Then it will be easy enough to call to them and tell them where I am, once they are inside the shed. But—" He paused, for a horrible fear came over him. "Suppose they should come—too late?" The tank was airtight. There was enough air in it to last for some time, but, sooner or later, it would no longer support life. Already, Tom thought, it seemed oppressive, though probably that was his imagination.

"I must get out!" he repeated frantically. "I'll die in here soon."

Again he tried to shove back the steel door. Then he repeated his cries until be was weary. No one answered him. He fancied once he could hear footsteps in the shed, and thought, perhaps, it was Andy, come back to gloat over him. Then Tom knew the red-haired coward would not dare venture back. We must do Andy the justice to say that he never realized that he was endangering

Tom's life. The bully had no idea the tank was airtight when he closed it. He had seen Tom enter and a sudden whim came to him to revenge himself.

But that did not help the young inventor any. There was no doubt about it now—the air was becoming close. Tom had been imprisoned nearly two hours, and as he was a healthy, strong lad, he required plenty of oxygen. There was certainly less than there had been in the tank. His head began to buzz, and there was a ringing in his ears.

Once more he fell upon his knees, and his fingers sought the small projections of the gear on the inside of the door He could no more budge the mechanism than a child could open a burglar-proof vault.

"It's no use," he moaned, and he sprawled at full length on the floor of the tank, for there the air was purer. As he did so his fingers touched something. He started as they closed around the handle of a big monkey wrench. It was one he had brought into the place with him. Imbued with new hope be struck a match and lighted his lantern, which he had allowed to go out as it burned up too much of the oxygen. By the gleam of it he looked to see if there were any bolts or nuts he could loosen with the wrench, in order to slide the door back. It needed but a glance to show him the futility of this.

"It's no go," he murmured, and he let the wrench fall to the floor. There was a ringing, clanging sound, and as it smote his ears Tom sprang up with an exclamation.

"That's the thing!" he cried. "I wonder I didn't think of it before. I can signal for help by pounding on the sides of the tank with the wrench. The blows will carry a good deal farther than my voice would." Every one knows how far the noise of a boiler shop, with hammers falling on steel plates, can be heard; much farther than can a human voice.

Tom began a lusty tattoo on the metal sides of the tank. At first he merely rattled out blow after blow, and then, as another thought came to him, he adopted a certain plan. Some time previous, when he and Mr. Sharp had planned their trip in the air, the two had adopted a code of signals. As it was difficult in a high wind to shout from one end of the airship to the other, the young inventor would sometimes pound on the pipe which ran from the pilot house of the Red Cloud to the engine-room. By a combination of numbers, simple messages could be conveyed. The code included a call for help. Forty-seven was the number, but there had never been any occasion to use it.

Tom remembered this now. At once he ceased his indiscriminate hammering, and began to beat out regularly— one, two, three, four—then a pause, and seven blows would be given. Over and over again he rang out this number—forty seven—the call for help.

"If Mr. Sharp only comes back he will hear that, even in the house," thought poor Tom "Maybe Garret or Mrs. Baggert will hear it, too, but they won't know what it means. They'll think I'm just working on the submarine."

It seemed several hours to Tom that he pounded out that cry for aid, but, as he afterward learned, it was only a little over an hour. Signal after signal he sent vibrating from the steel sides of the tank. When one arm tired he would use the other. He grew weary, his head was aching, and there was a ringing in his ears; a ringing that seemed as if ten thousand bells were jangling out their peals, and he could barely distinguish his own pounding.

Signal after signal he sounded. It was becoming like a dream to him, when suddenly, as he paused for a rest, he heard his name called faintly, as if far away.

"Tom! Tom! Where are you?"

It was the voice of Mr. Sharp. Then followed the tones of the aged inventor.

"My poor boy! Tom, are you still alive?"

"Yes, dad! In the starboard tank!" the lad gasped out, and then he lost his senses. When he revived he was lying on a pile of bagging in the submarine shop, and his father and the aeronaut were bending over him.

"Are you all right, Tom?" asked Mr. Swift.

"Yes—I—I guess so," was the hesitating answer. "Yes," the lad added, as the fresh air cleared his head. "I'll be all right pretty soon. Have you seen Andy Foger?"

"Did he shut you in there?" demanded Mr. Swift.

Tom nodded.

"I'll have him arrested!" declared Mr. Swift "I'll go to town as soon as you're in good shape again and notify the police."

"No, don't," pleaded Tom. "I'll take care of Andy myself. I don't really believe he knew how serious it was. I'll settle with him later, though."

"Well, it came mighty near being serious," remarked Mr. Sharp grimly. "Your father and I came back a little sooner than we expected, and as soon as I got near the house I heard your signal. I knew what it was in a moment. There were Mrs. Baggert and Garret talking away, and when I asked them why they didn't answer your call they said they thought you were merely tinkering with the machinery. But I knew better. It's the first time we ever had a use for 'forty- seven,' Tom."

"And I hope it will be the last," replied the young inventor with a faint smile. "But I'd like to know what Andy Foger is doing in this neighborhood."

Tom was soon himself again and able to go to the house, where he found Mrs. Baggert brewing a big basin of catnip tea, under the impression that it would in some way be good for his. She could not forgive herself for not having answered his signal, and as for Mr. Jackson, he had started for a doctor as soon as he learned that Tom was shut up in the tank. The services of the medical man were canceled by telephone, as there was no need for him, and the engineer came back to the house.

Tom was fully himself the next day, and aided his father and Mr. Sharp in putting the finishing touches to the Advance. It was found that some alteration was required in the auxiliary propellers, and this, much to the regret of the young inventor, would necessitate postponing the trial a few days.

"But we'll have her in the water next Friday." promised Mr. Swift.

"Aren't you superstitious about Friday?" asked the balloonist.

"Not a bit of it," replied the aged inventor. "Tom," he added, "I wish you would go in the house and get me the roll of blueprints you'll find on my desk."

As the lad neared the cottage he saw, standing in front of the place, a small automobile. A man had just descended from it, and it needed but a glance to show that he was Mr. Addison Berg.

"Ah, good morning, Mr. Swift," greeted Mr. Berg. "I wish to see your father, but as I don't wish to lay myself open to suspicions by entering the shop, perhaps you will ask him to step here."

"Certainly," answered the lad, wondering why the agent had returned. Getting the blueprints, and asking Mr. Berg to sit down on the porch, Tom delivered the message.

"You come back with me, Tom," said his father. "I want you to be a witness to what he says. I'm not going to get into trouble with these people."

Mr. Berg came to the point at once.

"Mr. Swift," he said, "I wish you would reconsider your determination not to enter the Government trials. I'd like to see you compete. So would my firm."

"There is no use going over that again," replied the aged inventor. "I have another object in view now than trying for the Government prize. What it is I can't say, but it may develop in time—if we are successful," and he looked at his son, smiling the while.

Mr. Berg tried to argue, but it was of no avail Then he changed his manner, and said:

"Well, since you won't, you won't, I suppose. I'll go back and report to my firm. Have you anything special to do this morning?" he went on to Tom.

"Well, I can always find something to keep me busy," replied the lad, "but as for anything special—"

"I thought perhaps you'd like to go for a trip in my auto," interrupted Mr. Berg. "I had asked a young man who is stopping at the same hotel where I am to accompany me, but he has unexpectedly left, and I don't like to go alone. His name was—let me see. I have a wretched memory for names, but it was something like Roger or Moger."

"Foger!" cried Tom. "Was it Andy Foger?"

"Yes, that was it. Why, do you know him?" asked Mr. Berg in some surprise.

"I should say so," replied Tom. "He was the cause of what might have resulted in something serious for me," and the lad explained about being imprisoned in the tank.

"You don't tell me!" cried Mr. Berg. "I had no idea he was that kind of a lad. You see, his father is one of the directors of the firm by whom I am employed. Andy came from home to spend a few weeks at the seaside, and stopped at the same hotel that I did. He went off yesterday afternoon, and I haven't seen him since, though he promised to go for a ride with me. He must have come over here and entered your shop unobserved. I remember now he asked me where the submarine was being built that was going to compete with our firm's, and

I told him. I didn't think he was that kind of a lad. Well, since he's probably gone back home, perhaps you will come for a ride with me, Tom."

"I'm afraid I can't go, thank you," answered the lad. "We are very busy getting our submarine in shape for a trial. But I can imagine why Andy left so hurriedly. He probably learned that a doctor had been summoned for me, though, as it happened, I didn't need one. But Andy probably got frightened at what he had done, and left. I'll make him more sorry, when I meet him."

"Don't blame you a bit," commented Mr. Berg. "Well, I must be getting back."

He hastened out to his auto, while Tom and his father watched the agent.

"Tom, never trust that man," advised the aged inventor solemnly.

"Just what I was about to remark," said his son. "Well, let's get back to work. Queer that he should come here again, and it's queer about Andy Foger."

Father and son returned to the machine shop, while Mr. Berg puffed away in his auto. A little later, Tom having occasion to go to a building near the boundary line of the cottage property which his father had hired for the season, saw, through the hedge that bordered it, an automobile standing in the road. A second glance showed him that it was Mr. Berg's machine. Something had gone wrong with it, and the agent had alighted to make an adjustment.

The young inventor was close to the man, though the latter was unaware of his presence.

"Hang it all!" Tom heard Mr. Berg exclaim to himself. "I wonder what they can be up to? They won't enter the Government contests, and they won't say why. I believe they're up to some game, and I've got to find out what it is. I wonder if I couldn't use this Foger chap?"

"He seems to have it in for this Tom Swift," Mr. Berg went on, still talking to himself, though not so low but that Tom could hear him. "I think I'll try it. I'll get Andy Foger to sneak around and find out what the game is. He'll do it, I know."

By this time the auto was in working order again, and the agent took his seat and started off.

"So that's how matters lie, eh?" thought Tom. "Well, Mr. Berg, we'll be doubly on the lookout for you after this. As for Andy Foger, I think I'll make him wish he'd never locked me in that tank. So you expect to find out our 'game,' eh, Mr. Berg? Well, when you do know it, I think it will astonish you. I only hope you don't learn what it is until we get at that sunken treasure, though."

But alas for Tom's hopes. Mr. Berg did learn of the object of the treasure-seekers, and sought to defeat them, as we shall learn as our story proceeds.

TURNING THE TABLES

When the young inventor informed his father what he had overheard Mr. Berg saying, the aged inventor was not as much worried as his son anticipated.

"All we'll have to do, Tom," he said, "is to keep quiet about where we are going. Once we have the Advance afloat, and try her out, we can start on our voyage for the South American Coast and search for the sunken treasure. When we begin our voyage under water I defy any one to tell where we are going, or what our plans are. No, I don't believe we need worry about Mr. Berg, though he probably means mischief."

"Well, I'm going to keep my eyes open for him and Andy Foger," declared Tom.

The days that followed were filled with work. Not only were there many unexpected things to do about the submarine, but Mr. Sharp was kept busy making inquiries about the sunken treasure ship. These inquiries had to he made carefully, as the adventurers did not want their plans talked of, and nothing circulates more quickly than rumors of an expedition after treasure of any kind.

"What about the old sea captain you were going to get to go with us?" asked Mr. Swift of the balloonist one afternoon. "Have you succeeded in finding one yet?"

"Yes; I am in communication with a man think will be just the person for us. His name is Captain Alden Weston, and he has sailed all over the world. He has also taken part in more than one revolution, and, in fact, is a soldier of fortune. I do not know him personally, but a friend of mine knows him, and says he will serve us faithfully. I have written to him, and he will he here in a few days."

"That's good. Now about the location of the wreck itself. Have you been able to learn any more details?"

"Well, not many. You see, the Boldero was abandoned in a storm, and the captain did not take very careful observations. As nearly as it can be figured out the treasure ship went to the bottom in latitude forty-five degrees south, and longitude twenty-seven east from Washington. That's a pretty indefinite location, but I hope, once we get off the Uruguay coast, we can better it. We can anchor or lay outside the harbor, and in the small boat we carry go ashore and possibly gain more details. For it was at Montevideo that the shipwrecked passengers and sailors landed."

"Does Captain Weston know our object?" inquired Tom.

"No, and I don't propose to tell him until we are ready to start," replied Mr. Sharp. "I don't know just how he'll consider a submarine trip after treasure, but if I spring it on him suddenly he's less likely to back out. Oh, I think he'll go."

Somewhat unexpectedly the next day it was discovered that certain tools and appliances were needed for the submarine, and they had been left in the house at Shopton, where Eradicate Sampson was in charge as caretaker during the absence of Mr. Swift and his son and the housekeeper.

"Well, I suppose we'll have to go back after them," remarked Tom. "We'll take the airship, dad, and make a two- days' trip of it. Is there anything else you want?"

"Well, you might bring a bundle of papers you'll find in the lower right hand drawer of my desk. They contain some memoranda I need."

Tom and Mr. Sharp had become so used to traveling in the airship that it seemed no novelty to them, though they attracted much attention wherever they went. They soon had the Red Cloud in readiness for a flight, and rising in the air above the shop that contained the powerful submarine, a craft utterly different in type from the aeroplane, the nose of the airship was pointed toward Shopton.

They made a good flight and landed near the big shed where the bird of the air was kept. It was early evening when they got to the Swift homestead, and Eradicate Sampson was glad to see them.

Eradicate was a good cook, and soon had a meal ready for the travelers. Then, while Mr. Sharp selected the tools and other things needed, and put them in the airship ready for the start back the next morning, Tom concluded he would take a stroll into Shopton, to see if he could see his friend, Ned Newton. It was early evening, and the close of a beautiful day, a sharp shower in the morning having cooled the air.

Tom was greeted by a number of acquaintances as he strolled along, for, since the episode of the bank robbery, when he had so unexpectedly returned with the thieves and the cash, the lad was better known than ever.

"I guess Ned must be home" thought our hero as he looked in vain for his chum among the throng on the streets. "I've got time to take a stroll down to his house."

Tom was about to cross the street when he was startled by the sound of an automobile horn loudly blown just at his side. Then a voice called:

"Hey, there! Git out of the way if you don't want to be run over!"

He looked up, and saw a car careening along. At the wheel was the red-haired bully, Andy Foger, and in the tonneau were Sam Snedecker and Pete Bailey.

"Git out of the way," added Sam, and he grinned maliciously at Tom.

The latter stepped back, well out of the path of the car, which was not moving very fast. Just in front of Tom was a puddle of muddy water. There was no necessity for Andy steering into it, but he saw his opportunity, and a moment later one of the big pneumatic tires had plunged into the dirty fluid, spattering it all over Tom, some even going as high as his face.

"Ha! ha!" laughed Andy. "Maybe you'll get out of my way next time, Tom Swift."

The young inventor was almost speechless from righteous anger. He wiped the mud from his face, glanced down at his clothes, which were all but ruined, and called out:

"Hold on there, Andy Foger! I want to see you!" for he thought of the time when Andy had shut him in the tank.

"Ta! ta!" shouted Pete Bailey.

"See you later," added Sam.

"Better go home and take a bath, and then sail away in your submarine," went on Andy. "I'll bet it will sink."

Before Tom could reply the auto had turned a corner. Disgusted and angry, he tried to sop up some of the muddy water with his handkerchief. While thus engaged he heard his name called, and looked up to see Ned Newton.

"What's the matter? Fall down?" asked his chum.

"Andy Foger," replied Tom.

"That's enough," retorted Ned. "I can guess the rest. We'll have to tar and feather him some day, and ride him out of town on a rail. I'd kick him myself, only his father is a director in the bank where I work, and I'd be fired if I did. Can't afford any such pleasure. But some day I'll give Andy a good trouncing, and then resign before they can discharge me. But I'll be looking for another job before I do that. Come on to my house, Tom, and I'll help you clean up."

Tom was a little more presentable when he left his chum's residence, after spending the evening there, but he was still burning for revenge against Andy and his cronies. He had half a notion to go to Andy's house and tell Mr. Foger how nearly serious the bully's prank at the sub marine had been, but be concluded that Mr. Foger could only uphold his son. "No, I'll settle with him myself," decided Tom.

Bidding Eradicate keep a watchful eye about the house, and leaving word for Mr. Damon to be sure to come to the coast if he again called at the Shopton house, Tom and Mr. Sharp prepared to make their return trip early the next morning.

The gas tank was filled and the Red Cloud arose in the air. Then, with the propellers moving at moderate speed, the nose of the craft was pointed toward the New Jersey coast.

A few miles out from Shopton, finding there was a contrary wind in the upper regions where they were traveling, Mr. Sharp descended several hundred feet. They were moving over a sparsely settled part of the country, and looking down, Tom saw, speeding along a highway, an automobile.

"I wonder who's in it?" he remarked, taking down a telescope and peering over the window ledge of the cabin. The next moment he uttered a startled exclamation.

"Andy Foger, Sam Snedecker and Pete Bailey!" he cried. "Oh, I wish I had a bucket of water to empty on them."

"I know a better way to get even with them than that," said Mr. Sharp.

"How?" asked Tom eagerly.

"I'll show you," replied the balloonist. "It's a trick I once played on a fellow who did me an injury. Here, you steer for a minute until I get the thing fixed, then I'll take charge."

Mr. Sharp went to the storeroom and came back with a long, stout rope and a small anchor of four prongs. It was carried to be used in emergencies, but so far had never been called into requisition. Fastening the grapple to the cable, the balloonist said:

"Now, Tom, they haven't seen you. You stand in the stern and pay out the rope. I'll steer the airship, and what I want you to do is to catch the anchor in the rear of their car. Then I'll show you some fun."

Tom followed instructions. Slowly he lowered the rope with the dangling grapple. The airship was also sent down, as the cable was not quite long enough to reach the earth from the height at which they were. The engine was run at slow speed, so that the noise would not attract the attention of the three cronies who were speeding along, all unconscious of the craft in the air over their heads. The Red Cloud was moving in the same direction as was the automobile.

The anchor was now close to the rear of Andy's car. Suddenly it caught on the tonneau and Tom called that fact to Mr. Sharp.

"Fasten the rope at the cleat," directed the balloonist.

Tom did so, and a moment later the aeronaut sent the airship up by turning more gas into the container. At the same time he reversed the engine and the Red Cloud began pulling the touring car backward, also lifting the rear wheels clear from the earth.

A startled cry from the occupants of the machine told Tom and his friend that Andy and his cronies were aware something was wrong. A moment later Andy, looking up, saw the airship hovering in the air above him. Then he saw the rope fast to his auto. The airship was not rising now, or the auto would have been turned over, but it was slowly pulling it backward, in spite of the fact that the motor of the car was still going.

"Here! You let go of me!" cried Andy. "I'll have you arrested if you damage my car."

"Come up here and cut the rope." called Tom leaning over and looking down. He could enjoy the bully's discomfiture. As for Sam and Pete, they were much frightened, and cowered down on the floor of the tonneau.

"Maybe you'll shut me in the tank again and splash mud on me!" shouted Tom.

The rear wheels of the auto were lifted still higher from the ground, as Mr. Sharp turned on a little more gas. Andy was not proof against this.

"Oh! oh!" he cried. "Please let me down, Tom. I'm awful sorry for what I did! I'll never do it again! Please, please let me down! Don't You'll tip me over!"

He had shut off his motor now, and was frantically clinging to the steering wheel.

"Do you admit that you're a sneak and a coward?" asked Tom, "rubbing it in."

"Yes, yes! Oh, please let me down!"

"Shall we?" asked Tom of Mr. Sharp.

"Yes," replied the balloonist. "We can afford to lose the rope and anchor for the sake of turning the tables. Cut the cable."

Tom saw what was intended. Using a little hatchet, he severed the rope with a single blow. With a crash that could be heard up in the air where the Red Cloud hovered, the rear wheels of the auto dropped to the ground. Then came two loud reports.

"Both tires busted!" commented Mr. Sharp dryly, and Tom, looking down, saw the trio of lads ruefully contemplating the collapsed rubber of the rear wheels. The tables had been effectually turned on Andy Foger. His auto was disabled, and the airship, with a graceful sweep, mounted higher and higher, continuing on its way to the coast.

MR. DAMON WILL GO

"Well, I guess they've had their lesson," remarked Tom, as he took an observation through the telescope and saw Andy and his cronies hard at work trying to repair the ruptured tires. "That certainly was a corking good trick."

"Yes," admitted Mr. Sharp modestly. "I once did something similar, only it was a horse and wagon instead of an auto. But let's try for another speed record. The conditions are just right."

They arrived at the coast much sooner than they had dared to hope, the Red Cloud proving herself a veritable wonder.

The remainder of that day, and part of the next, was spent in working on the submarine.

"We'll launch her day after to-morrow," declared Mr. Swift enthusiastically. "Then to see whether my calculations are right or wrong."

"It won't be your fault if it doesn't work," said his son. "You certainly have done your best."

"And so have you and Mr. Sharp and the others, for that matter. Well, I have no doubt but that everything will be all right, Tom."

"There!" exclaimed Mr. Sharp the next morning, as he was adjusting a certain gage. "I knew I'd forget something. That special brand of lubricating oil. I meant to bring it from Shopton, and I didn't."

"Maybe I can get it in Atlantis," suggested Tom, naming the coast city nearest to them. "I'll take a walk over. It isn't far."

"Will you? I'll be glad to have you," resumed the balloonist. "A gallon will be all we'll need."

Tom was soon on his way. He had to walk, as the roads were too poor to permit him to use the motor-cycle, and the airship attracted too much attention to use on a short trip. He was strolling along, when from the other side of a row of sand dunes, that lined the uncertain road to Atlantis, he heard some one speaking. At first the tones were not distinct, but as the lad drew nearer to the voice he heard an exclamation.

"Bless my gold-headed cane! I believe I'm lost. He said it was out this way somewhere, bet I don't see anything of it. If I had that Eradicate Sampson here now I'd—bless my shoelaces I don't know what I would do to him."

"Mr. Damon! Mr. Damon!" cried Tom. "Is that you?"

"Me? Of course it's me! Who else would it be?" answered the voice. "But who are you. Why, bless my liver! If it isn't Tom Swift!" he cried. "Oh, but I'm glad to see you! I was afraid I was shipwrecked! Bless my gaiters, how are you, anyhow? How is your father? How is Mr. Sharp, and all the rest of them?"

"Pretty well. And you?"

"Me? Oh, I'm all right; only a trifle nervous. I called at your house in Shopton yesterday, and Eradicate told me, as well as he could, where you were located. I had nothing to do, so I thought I'd take a run down here. But what's this I hear about you? Are you going on a voyage?"

"Yes."

"In the air? May I go along again? I certainly enjoyed my other trip in the Red Cloud. What is, all but the fire and being shot at. May I go?"

"We're going on a different sort of trip this time," said the youth.

"Where?"

"Under water."

"Under water? Bless my sponge bath! You don't mean it!"

"Yes. Dad has completed the submarine he was working on when we were off in the airship, and it will be launched the day after to-morrow."

"Oh, that's so. I'd forgotten about it. He's going to try for the Government prize, isn't he? But tell me more about it. Bless my scarf-pin, but I'm glad I met you! Going into town, I take it. Well, I just came from there, but I'll walk back with you. Do you think—is there any possibility —that I could go with you? Of course, I don't want to crowd you, but—"

"Oh, there'll be plenty of room," replied the young inventor. "In fact, more room than we had in the airship. We were talking only the other day about the possibility of you going with us, but we didn't think you'd risk it."

"Risk it? Bless my liver! Of course I'll risk' it! It can't be as bad as sailing in the air. You can't fall, that's certain."

"No; but maybe you can't rise," remarked Tom grimly.

"Oh, we won't think of that. Of course, I'd like to go. I fully expected to be killed in the Red Cloud, but as I wasn't I'm ready to take a chance in the water. On the whole, I think I prefer to be buried at sea, anyhow. Now, then, will you take me?"

"I think I can safely promise," answered Tom with a smile at his friend's enthusiasm.

The two were approaching the city, having walked along as they talked. There were still some sand dunes near the road, and they kept on the side of these, nearest the beach, where they could watch the breakers.

"But you haven't told me where you are going," went on Mr. Damon, after blessing a few dozen objects. "Where do the Government trials take place?"

"Well," replied the lad, "to be frank with you, we have abandoned our intention of trying for the Government prize."

"Not going to try for it? Bless my slippers! Why not? Isn't fifty thousand dollars worth striving for? And, with the kind of a submarine you say you have, you ought to be able to win."

"Yes, probably we could win," admitted the young inventor, "but we are going to try for a better prize."

"A better one? I don't understand."

"Sunken treasure," explained Tom. "There's a ship sunk off the coast of Uruguay, with three hundred thousand dollars in gold bullion aboard. Dad and I are going to try to recover that in our submarine. We're going to start day after to-morrow, and, if you like, you may go along."

"Go along! Of course I'll go along!" cried the eccentric man. "But I never heard of such a thing. Sunken treasure! Three hundred thousand dollars in gold! My, what a lot of money! And to go after it in a submarine! It's as good as a story!"

"Yes, we hope to recover all the treasure," said the lad. "We ought to be able to claim at least half of it."

"Bless my pocketbook!" cried Mr. Damon, but Tom did not hear him. At that instant his attention was attracted by seeing two men emerge from behind the sand dune near which he and Mr. Damon had halted momentarily, when the youth explained about the treasure. The man looked sharply at Tom. A moment later the first man was joined by another, and at the sight of him our hero could not repress an exclamation of alarm. For the second man was none other than Addison Berg.

The latter glanced quickly at Tom, and then, with a hasty word to his companion, the two swung around and made off in the opposite direction to that in which they had been walking.

"What's the matter?" asked Mr. Damon, seeing the young inventor was strangely affected.

"That—that man," stammered the lad.

"You don't mean to tell me that was one the Happy Harry gang, do you?"

"No. But one, or both of those men, may prove to be worse. That second man was Addison Berg, and he's agent for a firm of submarine boat builders who are rivals of dad's. Berg has been trying to find out why we abandoned our intention of competing for the Government prize."

"I hope you didn't tell him."

"I didn't intend to," replied Tom, smiling grimly, "but I'm afraid I have, however He certainly overheard what I said. I spoke too loud. Yes, he must have heard me. That's why he hurried off so."

"Possibly no harm is done. You didn't give the location of the sunken ship."

"No; but I guess from what I said it will be easy enough to find. Well, if we're going to have a fight for the possession of that sunken gold, I'm ready for it. The Advance is well equipped for a battle. I must tell dad of this. It's my fault."

"And partly mine, for asking you such leading questions in a public place," declared Mr. Damon. "Bless my coat-tails, but I'm sorry! Maybe, after all, those men were so interested in what they themselves were saying that they didn't understand what you said."

But if there had been any doubts on this score they would have been dissolved had Tom and his friend been able to see the actions of Mr. Berg and his companion a little later. The plans of the treasure-hunters had been revealed to their ears.

ANOTHER TREASURE EXPEDITION

While Tom and Mr. Damon continued on to Atlantis after the oil, the young inventor lamenting from time to time that his remarks about the real destination of the Advance had been overheard by Mr. Berg, the latter and his companion were hastening back along the path that ran on one side of the sand dunes.

"What's your hurry?" asked Mr. Maxwell, who was with the submarine agent. "You turned around as if you were shot when you saw that man and the lad. There didn't appear to be any cause for such a hurry. From what I could hear they were talking about a submarine. You're in the same business. You might be friends."

"Yes, we might," admitted Mr. Berg with a peculiar smile; "but, unless I'm very much mistaken, we're going to be rivals."

"Rivals? What do you mean?"

"I can't tell you now. Perhaps I may later. But if you don't mind, walk a little faster, please. I want to get to a long-distance telephone."

"What for?"

"I have just overheard something that I wish to communicate to my employers, Bentley & Eagert."

"Overheard something? I don't see what it could be, unless that lad—"

"You'll learn in good time," went on the submarine agent. "But I must telephone at once."

A little later the two men had reached a trolley line that ran into Atlantis, and they arrived at the city before Mr. Damon and Tom got there, as the latter had to go by a circuitous route. Mr. Berg lost no time in calling up his firm by telephone.

"I have had another talk with Mr. Swift," he reported to Mr. Bentley, who came to the instrument in Philadelphia.

"Well, what does he say?" was the impatient question. "I can't understand his not wanting to try for the Government prize. It is astonishing. You said you were going to discover the reason, Mn Berg, but you haven't done so."

"I have."

"What is it?"

"Well, the reason Mr. Swift and his son don't care to try for the fifty thousand dollar prize is that they are after one of three hundred thousand dollars."

"Three hundred thousand dollars!" cried Mr, Bentley. "What government is going to offer such a prize as that for submarines, when they are getting almost as common as airships? We ought to have a try for that ourselves. What government is it?"

"No government at all. But I think we ought to have a try for it, Mr. Bentley."

"Explain."

"Well, I have just learned, most accidentally, that the Swifts are going after sunken treasure—three hundred thousand dollars in gold bullion."

"Sunken treasure? Where?

"I don't know exactly, but off the coast of Uruguay," and Mr. Berg rapidly related what he had overheard Tom tell Mr. Damon. Mr. Bentley was much excited and impatient for more details, but his agent could not give them to him.

"Well," concluded the senior member of the firm of submarine boat builders, "if the Swifts are going after treasure, so can we. Come to Philadelphia at once, Mr. Berg, and we'll talk this matter over. There is no time to lose. We can afford to forego the Government prize for the chance of getting a much larger one. We have as much right to search for the sunken gold as the Swifts have. Come here at once, and we will make our plans."

"All right," agreed the agent with a smile as he hung up the receiver. "I guess," he murmured to himself, "that you won't be so high and mighty with me after this, Tom Swift. We'll see who has the best boat, after all. We'll have a contest and a competition, but not for a government prize. It will be for the sunken gold."

It was easy to see that Mr. Berg was much pleased with himself.

Meanwhile, Tom and Mr. Damon had reached Atlantis, and had purchased the oil. They started back, but Tom took a street leading toward the center of the place, instead of striking for the beach path, along which they had come.

"Where are you going?" asked Mr. Damon.

"I want to see if that Andy Foger has come back here," replied the lad, and he told of having been shut in the tank by the bully.

"I've never properly punished him for that trick," he went on, "though we did manage to burst his auto tires. I'm curious to know how he knew enough to turn that gear and shut the tank door. He must have been loitering near the shop, seen me go in the submarine alone, watched his chance and sneaked in after me. But I'd like to get a complete explanation, and if I once got hold of Andy I could make him talk," and Tom clenched his fist in a manner that augured no good for the squint-eyed lad. "He was stopping at the same hotel with Mr. Berg, and be hurried away after the trick he played on me. I next saw him in Shopton, but I thought perhaps he might have come back here. I'm going to inquire at the hotel," he added.

Andy's name was not on the register since his hasty flight, however, and Tom, after inquiring from the clerk and learning that Mr. Berg was still a guest at the hostelry, rejoined Mr. Damon.

"Bless my hat!" exclaimed that eccentric individual as they started back to the lonely beach where the submarine was awaiting her advent into the water. "The more I think of the trip I'm going to take, the more I like it."

"I hope you will," remarked Tom. "It will be a new experience for all of us. There's only one thing worrying me, and that is about Mr. Berg having overheard what I said."

"Oh, don't worry about that. Can't we slip away and leave no trace in the water?"

"I hope so, but I must tell dad and Mr. Sharp about what happened."

The aged inventor was not a little alarmed at what his son related, but he agreed with Mr. Damon, whom he heartily welcomed, that little was to be apprehended from Berg and his employers.

"They know we're after a sunken wreck, but that's all they do know," said Tom's father. "We are only waiting for the arrival of Captain Alden Weston, and then we will go. Even if Bentley & Eagert make a try for the treasure we'll have the start of them, and this will be a case of first come, first served. Don't worry, Tom. I'm glad you're going, Mn Damon. Come, I will show you our submarine."

As father and son, with their guest, were going to the machine shop, Mr. Sharp met them. He had a letter in his hand.

"Good news!" the balloonist cried. "Captain Weston will be with us to-morrow. He will arrive at the Beach Hotel in Atlantis, and wants one of us to meet him there. He has considerable information about the wreck."

"The Beach Hotel," murmured Tom. "That is where Mr. Berg is stopping. I hope he doesn't worm any of our secret from Captain Weston," and it was with a feeling of uneasiness that the young inventor continued after his father and Mr. Damon to where the submarine was.

Captain Weston's Advent

"Bless my water ballast, but that certainly is a fine boat!" cried Mr. Damon, when he had been shown over the new craft. "I think I shall feel even safer in that than in the Red Cloud."

"Oh, don't go back on the airship!" exclaimed Mn Sharp. "I was counting on taking you on another trip."

"Well, maybe after we get back from under the ocean," agreed Mr. Damon. "I particularly like the cabin arrangements of the Advance. I think I shall enjoy myself."

He would be hard to please who could not take pleasure from a trip in the submarine. The cabin was particularly fine, and the sleeping arrangements were good.

More supplies could be carried than was possible on the airship, and there was more room in which to cook and serve food. Mr. Damon was fond of good living, and the kitchen pleased him as much as anything else.

Early the next morning Tom set out for Atlantis, to meet Captain Weston at the hotel. The young inventor inquired of the clerk whether the seafaring man had arrived, and was told that he had come the previous evening.

"Is he in his room?" asked Tom.

"No," answered the clerk with a peculiar grin. "He's an odd character. Wouldn't go to bed last night until we had every window in his room open, though it was blowing quite hard, and likely to storm. The captain said he was used to plenty of fresh air. Well, I guess he got it, all right."

"Where is he now?" asked the youth, wondering what sort of an individual he was to meet.

"Oh, he was up before sunrise, so some of the scrubwomen told me. They met him coming from his room, and he went right down to the beach with a big telescope he always carries with him. He hasn't come back yet. Probably he's down on the sand."

"Hasn't he had breakfast?"

"No. He left word he didn't want to eat until about four bells, whatever time that is."

"It's ten o'clock," replied Tom, who had been studying up on sea terms lately. "Eight bells is eight o'clock in the morning, or four in the afternoon or eight at night, according to the time of day. Then there's one bell for every half hour, so four bells this morning would be ten o'clock in this watch, I suppose."

"Oh, that's the way it goes, eh?" asked the clerk. "I never could get it through my head. What is twelve o'clock noon?"

"That's eight bells, too; so is twelve o'clock midnight. Eight bells is as high as they go on a ship. But I guess I'll go down and see if I can meet the captain.

It will soon be ten o'clock, or four bells, and he must be hungry for breakfast. By the way, is that Mr. Berg still here?"

"No; he went away early this morning. He and Captain Weston seemed to strike up quite an acquaintance, the night clerk told me. They sat and smoked together until long after midnight, or eight bells," and the clerk smiled as he glanced down at the big diamond ring on his little finger.

"They did?" fairly exploded Tom, for he had visions of what the wily Mr. Berg might worm out of the simple captain.

"Yes. Why, isn't the captain a proper man to make friends with?" and the clerk looked at Tom curiously.

"Oh, yes, of course," was the hasty answer. "I guess I'll go and see if I can find him—the captain, I mean."

Tom hardly knew what to think. He wished his father, or Mr. Sharp, had thought to warn Captain Weston against talking of the wreck. It might be too late now.

The young inventor hurried to the beach, which was not far from the hotel. He saw a solitary figure pacing up and down, and from the fact that the man stopped, every now and then, and gazed seaward through a large telescope, the lad concluded it was the captain for whom he was in search. He approached, his footsteps making no sound on the sand. The man was still gazing through the glass.

"Captain Weston?" spoke Tom.

Without a show of haste, though the voice must have startled him, the captain turned. Slowly he lowered the telescope, and then he replied softly:

"That's my name. Who are you, if I may ask?"

Tom was struck, more than by anything else, by the gentle voice of the seaman. He had prepared himself, from the description of Mr. Sharp, to meet a gruff, bewhiskered individual, with a voice like a crosscut saw, and a rolling gait. Instead he saw a man of medium size, with a smooth face, merry blue eyes, and the softest voice and gentlest manner imaginable. Tom was very much disappointed. He had looked for a regular sea-dog, and he met a landsman, as he said afterward. But it was not long before our hero changed his mind regarding Captain Weston.

"I'm Tom Swift," the owner of that name said, "and I have been sent to show you the way to where our ship is ready to launch." The young inventor refrained from mentioning submarine, as it was the wish of Mn Sharp to disclose this feature of the voyage to the sailor himself.

"Ha, I thought as much," resumed the captain quietly. "It's a fine day, if I may be permitted to say so," and he seemed to hesitate, as if there was some doubt whether or not he might make that observation.

"It certainly is," agreed the lad. Then, with a smile he added: "It is nearly eight bells."

"Ha!" exclaimed the captain, also smiling, but even his manner of saying "Ha!" was less demonstrative than that of most persons. "I believe I am getting hungry, if I may be allowed the remark," and again he seemed asking Tom's pardon for mentioning the fact.

"Perhaps you will come back to the cabin and have a little breakfast with me," he went on. "I don't know what sort of a galley or cook they have aboard the Beach Hotel, but it can't be much worse than some I've tackled."

"No, thank you," answered the youth. "I've had my breakfast. But I'll wait for you, and then I'd like to get back. Dad and Mr. Sharp are anxious to meet you."

"And I am anxious to meet them, if you don't mind me mentioning it," was the reply, as the captain once more put the spyglass to his eye and took an observation. "Not many sails in sight this morning," he added. "But the weather is fine, and we ought to get off in good shape to hunt for the treasure about which Mr. Sharp wrote me. I believe we are going after treasure, he said; "that is, if you don't mind talking about it."

"Not in the least," replied Tom quickly, thinking this a good opportunity for broaching a subject that was worrying him. "Did you meet a Mr. Berg here last night, Captain Weston?" he went on.

"Yes. Mr. Berg and I had quite a talk. He is a well- informed man."

"Did he mention the sunken treasure?" asked the lad, eager to find out if his suspicions were true.

"Yes, he did, if you'll excuse me putting it so plainly," answered the seaman, as if Tom might be offended at so direct a reply. But the young inventor was soon to learn that this was only an odd habit with the seaman.

"Did he want to know where the wreck of the Boldero was located?" continued the lad. "That is, did he try to discover if you knew anything about it?"

"Yes," said Mr. Weston, "he did. He pumped me, if you are acquainted with that term, and are not offended by it. You see, when I arrived here I made inquiries as to where your father's place was located. Mr. Berg overheard me, and introduced himself as agent for a shipbuilding concern. He was very friendly, and when he said he knew you and your parent, I thought he was all right."

Tom's heart sank. His worst fears were to be realized, he thought.

"Yes, he and I talked considerable, if I may be permitted to say so," went on the captain. "He seemed to know about the wreck of the Boldero, and that she had three hundred thousand dollars in gold aboard. The only thing he didn't know was where the wreck was located. He knew it was off Uruguay somewhere, but just where he couldn't say. So he asked me if I knew, since he must have concluded that I was going with you on the gold-hunting expedition."

"And you do know, don't you?" asked Tom eagerly.

"Well, I have it pretty accurately charted out, if you will allow me that expression," was the calm answer. "I took pains to look it up at the request of Mr. Sharp."

"And he wanted to worm that information out of you?" inquired the youth excitedly.

"Yes, I'm afraid he did."

"Did you give him the location?"

"Well," remarked the captain, as he took another observation before closing up the telescope, "you see, while we were talking, I happened to drop a copy of a map I'd made, showing the location of the wreck. Mr. Berg picked it up to hand to me, and he looked at it."

"Oh!" cried Tom. "Then he knows just where the treasure is, and he may get to it ahead of us. It's too bad."

"Yes," continued the seaman calmly, "Mr. Berg picked up that map, and he looked very closely at the latitude and longitude I had marked as the location of the wreck."

"Then he won't have any trouble finding it," murmured our hero.

"Eh? What's that?" asked the captain, "if I may be permitted to request you to repeat what you said."

"I say he won't have any trouble locating the sunken Boldero," repeated Tom.

"Oh, but I think he will, if he depends on that map," was the unexpected reply. "You see," explained Mr. Weston, "I'm not so simple as I look. I sensed what Mr. Berg was after, the minute he began to talk to me. So I fixed up a little game on him. The map which I dropped on purpose, not accidentally, where he would see it, did have the location of the wreck marked. Only it didn't happen to be the right location. It was about five hundred miles out of the way, and I rather guess if Mr. Berg and his friends go there for treasure they'll find considerable depth of water and quite a lonesome spot. Oh, no, I'm not as easy as I look, if you don't mind me mentioning that fact; and when a scoundrel sets out to get the best of me, I generally try to turn the tables on him. I've seen such men as Mr. Berg before. I'm afraid, I'm very much afraid, the sight he had of the fake map I made won't do him much good. Well, I declare, it's past four bells. Let's go to breakfast, if you don't mind me asking you," and with that the captain started off up the beach, Tom following, his ideas all a whirl at the unlooked- for outcome of the interview.

TRIAL OF THE SUBMARINE

Tom felt such a relief at hearing of Captain Weston's ruse that his appetite, sharpened by an early breakfast and the sea air, came to him with a rush, and he had a second morning meal with the odd sea captain, who chuckled heartily when he thought of how Mn Berg had been deceived.

"Yes," resumed Captain Weston, over his bacon and eggs, "I sized him up for a slick article as soon as I laid eyes on him. But he evidently misjudged me, if I may be permitted that term. Oh, well, we may meet again, after we secure the treasure, and then I can show him the real map of the location of the wreck."

"Then you have it?" inquired the lad eagerly.

Captain Weston nodded, before hiding his face behind a large cup of coffee; his third, by the way.

"Let me see it?" asked Tom quickly. The captain set down his cup. He looked carefully about the hotel dining-room. There were several guests, who, like himself, were having a late breakfast.

"It's a good plan," the sailor said slowly, "when you're going into unknown waters, and don't want to leave a wake for the other fellow to follow, to keep your charts locked up. If it's all the same to you," he added diffidently, "I'd rather wait until we get to where your father and Mr. Sharp are before displaying the real map. I've no objection to showing you the one Mr. Berg saw," and again he chuckled.

The young inventor blushed at his indiscretion. He felt that the news of the search for the treasure had leaked out through him, though he was the one to get on the trail of it by seeing the article in the paper. Now he had nearly been guilty of another break. He realized that he must be more cautious. The captain saw his confusion, and said:

"I know how it is. You're eager to get under way. I don't blame you. I was the same myself when I was your age. But we'll soon be at your place, and then I'll tell you all I know. Sufficient now, to say that I believe I have located the wreck within a few miles. I got on the track of a sailor who had met one of the shipwrecked crew of the Boldero, and he gave me valuable information. Now tell me about the craft we are going in. A good deal depends on that."

Tom hardly knew what to answer. He recalled what Mr. Sharp had said about not wanting to tell Captain Weston, until the last moment, that they were going in a submarine, for fear the old seaman (for he was old in point of service though not in years) might not care to risk an under-water trip. Therefore Tom hesitated. Seeing it, Captain Weston remarked quietly:

"I mean, what type is your submarine? Does it go by compressed air, or water power?"

"How do you know it's a submarine?" asked the young inventor quickly, and in some confusion.

"Easy enough. When Mr. Berg thought he was pumping me, I was getting a lot of information from him. He told me about the submarine his firm was building, and, naturally, he mentioned yours. One thing led to another until I got a pretty good idea of your craft. What do you call it?"

"The Advance."

"Good name. I like it, if you don't mind speaking of it."

"We were afraid you wouldn't like it," commented Tom.

"What, the name?,'

"No, the idea of going in a submarine."

"Oh," and Captain Weston laughed. "Well, it takes more than that to frighten me, if you'll excuse the expression. I've always had a hankering to go under the surface, after so many years spent on top. Once or twice I came near going under, whether I wanted to or not, in wrecks, but I think I prefer your way. Now, if you're all done, and don't mind me speaking of it, I think we'll start for your place. We must hustle, for Berg may yet get on our trail, even if he has got the wrong route," and he laughed again.

It was no small relief to Mn Swift and Mr. Sharp to learn that Captain Weston had no objections to a submarine, as they feared he might have. The captain, in his diffident manner, made friends at once with the treasure-hunters, and he and Mr. Damon struck up quite an acquaintance. Tom told of his meeting with the seaman, and the latter related, with much gusto, the story of how he had fooled Mr. Berg.

"Well, perhaps you'd like to come and take a look at the craft that is to be our home while we're beneath the water," suggested Mr. Swift and the sailor assenting, the aged inventor, with much pride, assisted by Tom, pointed out on the Advance the features of interest. Captain Weston gave hearty approval, making one or two minor suggestions, which were carried out.

"And so you launch her to-morrow," he concluded, when he had completed the inspection "Well, I hope it's a success, if I may be permitted to say so."

There were busy times around the machine shop next day. So much secrecy had been maintained that none of the residents, or visitors to the coast resort, were aware that in their midst was such a wonderful craft as the submarine. The last touches were put on the under-water ship; the ways, leading from the shop to the creek, were well greased, and all was in readiness for the launching. The tide would soon be at flood, and then the boat would slide down the timbers (at least, that was the hope of all), and would float in the element meant to receive her. It was decided that no one should be aboard when the launching took place, as there was an element of risk attached, since it was not known just how buoyant the craft was. It was expected she would float, until the filled tanks took her to the bottom, but there was no telling.

"It will be flood tide now in ten minutes," remarked Captain Weston quietly, looking at his watch. Then he took an observation through the telescope. "No hostile ships hanging in the offing," he reported. "All is favorable, if you don't mind me saying so," and he seemed afraid lest his remark might give offense.

"Get ready," ordered Mr. Swift. "Tom, see that the ropes are all clear," for it had been decided to ease the Advance down into the water by means of strong cables and windlasses, as the creek was so narrow that the submarine, if launched in the usual way, would poke her nose into the opposite mud bank and stick there.

"All clear," reported the young inventor.

"High tide!" exclaimed the captain a moment later, snapping shut his watch.

"Let go!" ordered Mr. Swift, and the various windlasses manned by the inventor, Tom and the others began to unwind their ropes. Slowly the ship slid along the greased ways. Slowly she approached the water. How anxiously they all watched her! Nearer and nearer her blunt nose, with the electric propulsion plate and the auxiliary propeller, came to the creek, the waters of which were quiet now, awaiting the turn of the tide.

Now little waves lapped the steel sides. It was the first contact of the Advance with her native element.

"Pay out the rope faster!" cried Mr. Swift.

The windlasses were turned more quickly Foot by foot the craft slid along until, with a final rush, the stern left the ways and the submarine was afloat. Now would come the test. Would she ride on an even keel, or sink out of sight, or turn turtle? They all ran to the water's edge, Tom in the lead.

"Hurrah!" suddenly yelled the lad, trying to stand on his head. "She floats! She's a success! Come on! Let's get aboard!"

For, true enough, the Advance was riding like a duck on the water. She had been proportioned just right, and her lines were perfect. She rode as majestically as did any ship destined to sail on the surface, and not intended to do double duty.

"Come on, we must moor her to the pier," directed Mr. Sharp. "The tide will turn in a few minutes and take her out to sea."

He and Tom entered a small boat, and soon the submarine was tied to a small dock that had been built for the purpose.

"Now to try the engine," suggested Mr. Swift, who was almost trembling with eagerness; for the completion of the ship meant much to him.

"One moment," begged Captain Weston. "If you don't mind, I'll take an observation," he went on, and he swept the horizon with his telescope. "All clear," he reported. "I think we may go aboard and make a trial trip."

Little time was lost in entering the cabin and engine- room, Garret Jackson accompanying the party to aid with the machinery. It did not take long to start the motors, dynamos and the big gasolene engine that was the vital part of the craft. A little water was admitted to the tanks for ballast, since the food and other supplies were not yet on board. The Advance now floated with the deck aft of the conning tower showing about two feet above the surface of the creek. Mr. Swift and Tom entered the pilot house.

"Start the engines," ordered the aged inventor, "and we'll try my new system of positive and negative electrical propulsion."

There was a hum and whir in the body of the ship beneath the feet of Tom and his father. Captain Weston stood on the little deck near the conning tower.

"All ready?" asked the youth through the speaking tube to Mr. Sharp and Mr. Jackson in the engine-room.

"All ready," came the answer.

Tom threw over the connecting lever, while his father grasped the steering wheel. The Advance shot forward, moving swiftly along, about half submerged.

"She goes! She goes!" cried Tom

"She certainly does, if I may be permitted to say so," was the calm contribution of Captain Weston. "I congratulate you."

Faster and faster went the new craft. Mr. Swift headed her toward the open sea, but stopped just before passing out of the creek, as he was not yet ready to venture into deep water.

"I want to test the auxiliary propellers," he said. After a little longer trial of the electric propulsion plates, which were found to work satisfactorily, sending the submarine up and down the creek at a fast rate, the screws, such as are used on most submarines, were put into gear. They did well, but were not equal to the plates, nor was so much expected of them.

"I am perfectly satisfied," announced Mr. Swift as he once more headed the boat to sea. "I think, Captain Weston, you had better go below now."

"Why so?"

"Because I am going to completely submerge the craft. Tom, close the conning tower door. Perhaps you will come in here with us, Captain Weston, though it will be rather a tight fit."

"Thank you, I will. I want to see how it feels to be in a pilot house under water."

Tom closed the water-tight door of the conning tower. Word was sent through the tube to the engine-room that a more severe test of the ship was about to be made. The craft was now outside the line of breakers and in the open sea.

"Is everything ready, Tom?" asked his father in a quiet voice.

"Everything," replied the lad nervously, for the anticipation of being about to sink below the surface was telling on them all, even on the calm, old sea captain.

"Then open the tanks and admit the water," ordered Mr. Swift.

His son turned a valve and adjusted some levers. There was a hissing sound, and the Advance began sinking. She was about to dive beneath the surface of the ocean, and those aboard her were destined to go through a terrible experience before she rose again.

ON THE OCEAN BED

Lower and lower sank the submarine. There was a swirling and foaming of the water as she went down, caused by the air bubbles which the craft carried with her in her descent. Only the top of the conning tower was out of water now, the ocean having closed over the deck and the rounded back of the boat. Had any one been watching they would have imagined that an accident was taking place.

In the pilot house, with its thick glass windows, Tom, his father and Captain Weston looked over the surface of the ocean, which every minute was coming nearer and nearer to them.

"We'll be all under in a few seconds," spoke Tom in a solemn voice, as he listened to the water hissing into the tanks.

"Yes, and then we can see what sort of progress we will make," added Mr. Swift. "Everything is going fine, though," he went on cheerfully. "I believe I have a good boat."

"There is no doubt of it in my mind," remarked Captain Weston, and Tom felt a little disappointed that the sailor did not shout out some such expression as "Shiver my timbers!" or "Keel-haul the main braces, there, you lubber!" But Captain Weston was not that kind of a sailor, though his usually quiet demeanor could be quickly dropped on necessity, as Tom learned later.

A few minutes more and the waters closed over the top of the conning tower. The Advance was completely submerged. Through the thick glass windows of the pilot house the occupants looked out into the greenish water that swirled about them; but it could not enter. Then, as the boat went lower, the light from above gradually died out, and the semi-darkness gave place to gloom.

"Turn on the electrics and the searchlight, Tom," directed his father.

There was the click of a switch, and the conning tower was flooded with light. But as this had the effect of preventing the three from peering out into the water, just as one in a lighted room cannot look out into the night, Tom shut them off and switched on the great searchlight. This projected its powerful beams straight ahead and there, under the ocean, was a pathway of illumination for the treasure- seekers.

"Fine!" cried Captain Weston, with more enthusiasm than he had yet manifested. "That's great, if you don't mind me mentioning it. How deep are we?"

Tom glanced at a gage on the side of the pilot tower.

"Only about sixty feet," he answered.

"Then don't go any deeper!" cried the captain hastily. "I know these waters around here, and that's about all the depth you've got. You'll be on the bottom in a minute."

"I intend to get on the bottom after a while," said Mr. Swift, "but not here. I want to try for a greater distance under water before I come to rest on the ocean's bed. But I think we are deep enough for a test. Tom, close the tank intake pipes and we'll see how the Advance will progress when fully submerged."

The hissing stopped, and then, wishing to see how the motors and other machinery would work, the aged inventor and his son, accompanied by Captain Weston, descended from the conning tower, by means of an inner stairway, to the interior of the ship. The submarine could be steered and managed from below or above. She was now floating about sixty-five feet below the surface of the bay.

"Well, how do you like it?" asked Tom of Mr. Damon, as he saw his friend in an easy chair in the living-room or main cabin of the craft, looking out of one of the plate-glass windows on the side.

"Bless my spectacles, it's the most wonderful thing I ever dreamed of!" cried the queer character, as he peered at the mass of water before him. "To think that I'm away down under the surface, and yet as dry as a bone. Bless my necktie, but it's great! What are we going to do now?"

"Go forward," replied the young inventor.

"Perhaps I had better make an observation," suggested Captain Weston, taking his telescope from under his arm, where he had carried it since entering the craft, and opening it. "We may run afoul of something, if you don't mind me mentioning such a disagreeable subject." Then, as he thought of the impossibility of using his glass under water, he closed it.

"I shall have little use for this here, I'm afraid," he remarked with a smile. "Well, there's some consolation. We're not likely to meet many ships in this part of the ocean. Other vessels are fond enough of remaining on the surface. I fancy we shall have the depths to ourselves, unless we meet a Government submarine, and they are hardly able to go as deep as we can. No, I guess we won't run into anything and I can put this glass away."

"Unless we run into Berg and his crowd," suggested Tom in a low voice.

"Ha! ha!" laughed Captain Weston, for he did not want Mr. Swift to worry over the unscrupulous agent. "No, I don't believe we'll meet them, Tom. I guess Berg is trying to work out the longitude and latitude I gave him. I wish I could see his face when he realizes that he's been deceived by that fake map."

"Well, I hope he doesn't discover it too soon and trail us," went on the lad. "But they're going to start the machinery now. I suppose you and I had better take charge of the steering of the craft. Dad will want to be in the engine-room."

"All right," replied the captain, and he moved forward with the lad to a small compartment, shut off from the living-room, that served as a pilot house when the conning tower was not used. The same levers, wheels and valves were there as up above, and the submarine could be managed as well from there as from the other place.

"Is everything all right?" asked Mn Swift as he went into the engine-room, where Garret Jackson and Mr. Sharp were busy with oil cans.

"Everything," replied the balloonist. "Are you going to start now?"

"Yes, we're deep enough for a speed trial. We'll go out to sea, however, and try for a lower depth record, as soon as there's enough water. Start the engine."

A moment later the powerful electric currents were flowing into the forward and aft plates, and the Advance began to gather way, forging through the water.

"Straight ahead, out to sea, Tom," called his father to him.

"Aye, aye, sir," responded the youth.

"Ha! Quite seaman-like, if you don't mind a reference to it," commented Captain Weston with a smile. "Mind your helm, boy, for you don't want to poke her nose into a mud bank, or run up on a shoal."

"Suppose you steer?" suggested the lad. "I'd rather take lessons for a while."

"All right. Perhaps it will be safer. I know these waters from the top, though I can't say as much for the bottom. However, I know where the shoals are."

The powerful searchlight was turned, so as to send its beams along the path which the submarine was to follow, and then, as she gathered speed, she shot ahead, gliding through the waters like a fish.

Mr. Damon divided his time between the forward pilot-room, the living-apartment, and the place where Mr. Swift, Garret Jackson and Mr. Sharp were working over the engines. Every few minutes he would bless some part of himself, his clothing, or the ship. Finally the old man settled down to look through the plate-glass windows in the main apartment.

On and on went the submarine. She behaved perfectly, and was under excellent control. Some times Tom, at the request of his father, would send her toward the surface by means of the deflecting rudder. Then she would dive to the bottom again. Once, as a test, she was sent obliquely to the surface, her tower just emerging, and then she darted downward again, like a porpoise that had come up to roll over, and suddenly concluded to seek the depths. In fact, had any one seen the maneuver they would have imagined the craft was a big fish disporting itself.

Captain Weston remained at Tom's side, giving him instructions, and watching the compass in order to direct the steering so as to avoid collisions. For an hour or more the craft was sent almost straight ahead at medium speed. Then Mr. Swift, joining his son and the captain, remarked:

"How about depth of water here, Captain Weston?"

"You've got more than a mile."

"Good! Then I'm going down to the bottom of the sea! Tom, fill the tanks still more.

"Aye, aye, sir," answered the lad gaily. "Now for a new experience!"

"And use the deflecting rudder, also," advised his father. "That will hasten matters."

Five minutes later there was a slight jar noticeable.

"Bless my soul! What's that?" cried Mr. Damon. "Have we hit something?"

"Yes," answered Tom with a smile.

"What, for gracious sake?"

"The bottom of the sea. We're on the bed of the ocean."

FOR A BREATH OF AIR

They could hardly realize it, yet the depth-gage told the story. It registered a distance below the surface of the ocean of five thousand seven hundred feet—a little over a mile. The Advance had actually come to rest on the bottom of the Atlantic.

"Hurrah!" cried Tom. "Let's get on the diving suits, dad, and walk about on land under water for a change."

"No," said Mr. Swift soberly. "We will hardly have time for that now. Besides, the suits are not yet fitted with the automatic air-tanks, and we can't use them. There are still some things to do before we start on our treasure cruise. But I want to see how the plates are standing this pressure."

The Advance was made with a triple hull, the spaces between the layers of plates being filled with a secret material, capable of withstanding enormous pressure, as were also the plates themselves. Mr. Swift, aided by Mr. Jackson and Captain Weston, made a thorough examination, and found that not a drop of water had leaked in, nor was there the least sign that any of the plates had given way under the terrific strain.

"She's as tight as a drum, if you will allow me to make that comparison," remarked Captain Weston modestly. "I couldn't ask for a dryer ship."

"Well, let's take a look around by means the searchlight and the observation windows, and then we'll go back," suggested Mr. Swift. "It will take about two days to get the stores and provisions aboard and rig up the diving suits; then we will start for the sunken treasure.

There were several powerful searchlights on the Advance, so arranged that the bow, stern or either side could be illuminated independently. There were also observation windows near each light.

In turn the powerful rays were cast first at the bow and then aft. In the gleams could be seen the sandy bed of the ocean, covered with shells of various kinds. Great crabs walked around on their long, jointed legs, and Tom saw some lobsters that would have brought joy to the heart of a fisherman.

"Look at the big fish!" cried Mr. Damon suddenly, and he pointed to some dark, shadowy forms that swam up to the glass windows, evidently puzzled by the light.

"Porpoises," declared Captain Weston briefly. a whole school of them."

The fish seemed suddenly to multiply, and soon those in the submarine felt curious tremors running through the whole craft.

"The fish are rubbing up against it," cried Tom. "They must think we came down here to allow them to scratch their backs on the steel plates."

For some time they remained on the bottom, watching the wonderful sight of the fishes that swam all about them.

"Well, I think we may as well rise," announced Mr. Swift, after they had been on the bottom about an hour, moving here and there. "We didn't bring any provisions, and I'm getting hungry, though I don't know how the others of you feel about it."

"Bless my dinner-plate, I could eat, too!" cried Mr. Damon. "Go up, by all means. We'll get enough of under-water travel once we start for the treasure."

"Send her up, Tom," called his father. "I Want to make a few notes on some needed changes and improvements."

Tom entered the lower pilot house, and turned the valve that opened the tanks. He also pulled the lever that started the pumps, so that the water ballast would be more quickly emptied, as that would render the submarine buoyant, and she would quickly shoot to the surface. To the surprise of the lad, however, there followed no outrushing of the water. The Advance remained stationary on the ocean bed. Mr. Swift looked up from his notes.

"Didn't you hear me ask you to send her up, Tom?" he inquired mildly.

"I did, dad, but something seems to be the matter," was the reply.

"Matter? What do you mean?" and the aged inventor hastened to where his son and Captain Weston were at the wheels, valves and levers.

"Why, the tanks won't empty, and the pumps don't seem to work."

"Let me try," suggested Mr. Swift, and he pulled the various handles. There was no corresponding action of the machinery.

"That's odd," he remarked in a curious voice "Perhaps something has gone wrong with the connections. Go look in the engine-room, and ask Mr. Sharp if everything is all right there."

Tom made a quick trip, returning to report that the dynamos, motors and gas engine were running perfectly.

"Try to work the tank levers and pumps from the conning tower," suggested Captain Weston. "Sometimes I've known the steam steering gear to play tricks like that."

Tom hurried up the circular stairway into the tower. He pulled the levers and shifted the valves and wheels there. But there was no emptying of the water tanks. The weight and pressure of water in them still held the submarine on the bottom of the sea, more than a mile from the surface. The pumps in the engine-room were working at top speed, but there was evidently something wrong in the connections. Mr. Swift quickly came to this conclusion.

"We must repair it at once," he said. "Tom, come to the engine-room. You and I, with Mr. Jackson and Mr. Sharp, will soon have it in shape again."

"Is there any danger?" asked Mr. Damon in a perturbed voice. "Bless my soul, it's unlucky to have an accident on our trial trip."

"Oh, we must expect accidents," declared Mr. Swift with a smile. "This is nothing."

But it proved to be more difficult than he had imagined to re-establish the connection between the pumps and the tanks. The valves, too, had clogged or jammed, and as the pressure outside the ship was so great, the water would not run out of itself. It must be forced.

For an hour or more the inventor, his son and the others, worked away. They could accomplish nothing. Tom looked anxiously at his parent when the latter paused in his efforts.

"Don't worry," advised the aged inventor. "It's got to come right sooner or later."

Just then Mr. Damon, who had been wandering about the ship, entered the engine-room.

"Do you know," he said, "you ought to open a window, or something."

"Why, what's the matter?" asked Tom quickly, looking to see if the odd man was joking.

"Well, of course I don't exactly mean a window," explained Mr. Damon, "but we need fresh air."

"Fresh air!" There was a startled note in Mr. Swift's voice as he repeated the words.

"Yes, I can hardly breathe in the living-room, and it's not much better here."

"Why, there ought to be plenty of fresh air," went on the inventor. "It is renewed automatically."

Tom jumped up and looked at an indicator. He uttered a startled cry.

"The air hasn't been changed in the last hour!" he exclaimed. "It is bad. There's not enough oxygen in it. I notice it, now that I've stopped working. The gage indicates it, too. The automatic air-changer must have stopped working. I'll fix it."

He hurried to the machine which was depended on to supply fresh air to the submarine.

"Why, the air tanks are empty!" the young inventor cried. "We haven't any more air except what is in the ship now!"

"And we're rapidly breathing that up," added Captain Weston solemnly.

"Can't you make more?" cried Mr. Damon. "I thought you said you could make oxygen aboard the ship."

"We can," answered Mr. Swift, "but I did not bring along a supply of the necessary chemicals. I did not think we would be submerged long enough for that. But there should have been enough in the reserve tank to last several days. How about it, Tom?"

"It's all leaked out, or else it wasn't filled," was the despairing answer. "All the air we have is what's in the ship, and we can't make more."

The treasure-seekers looked at each other. It was an awful situation.

"Then the only thing to do is to fix the machinery and rise to the surface," said Mr. Sharp simply. "We can have all the air we want, then."

"Yes, but the machinery doesn't seem possible of being fixed," spoke Tom in a low voice.

"We must do it!" cried his father.

They set to work again with fierce energy, laboring for their very lives. They all knew that they could not long remain in the ship without oxygen. Nor could they desert it to go to the surface, for the moment they left the protection of the thick steel sides the terrible pressure of the water would kill them. Nor were the diving suits available. They must stay in the craft and die a miserable death-unless the machinery could be repaired and the Advance sent to the surface. The emergency expanding lifting tank was not yet in working order.

More frantically they toiled, trying every device that was suggested to the mechanical minds of Tom, his father, Mr. Sharp or Mr. Jackson, to make the pumps work. But something was wrong. More and more foul grew the air. They were fairly gasping now. It was difficult to breathe, to say nothing of working, in that atmosphere. The thought of their terrible position was in the minds of all.

"Oh, for one breath of fresh air!" cried Mr. Damon, who seemed to suffer more than any of the others. Grim death was hovering around them, imprisoned as they were on the ocean's bed, over a mile from the surface.

OFF FOR THE TREASURE

Suddenly Tom, after a moment's pause, seized a wrench and began loosening some nuts.

"What are you doing?" asked his father faintly, for he was being weakened by the vitiated atmosphere.

"I'm going to take this valve apart," replied his son. "We haven't looked there for the trouble. Maybe it's out of order."

He attacked the valve with energy, but his hands soon lagged. The lack of oxygen was telling on him. He could no longer work quickly.

"I'll help," murmured Mr. Sharp thickly. He took a wrench, but no sooner had he loosened one nut than he toppled over. "I'm all in," he murmured feebly.

"Is he dead?" cried Mr. Damon, himself gasping.

"No, only fainted. But he soon will be dead, and so will all of us, if we don't get fresh air," remarked Captain Weston. "Lie down on the floor, every one. There is a little fairly good air there. It's heavier than the air we've breathed, and we can exist on it for a little longer. Poor Sharp was so used to breathing the rarified air of high altitudes that he can't stand this heavy atmosphere."

Mr. Damon was gasping worse than ever, and so was Mr. Swift. The balloonist lay an inert heap on the floor, with Captain Weston trying to force a few drops of stimulant down his throat

With a fierce determination in his heart, but with fingers that almost refused to do his bidding, Tom once more sought to open the big valve. He felt sure the trouble was located there, as they had tried to locate it in every other place without avail.

"I'll help," said Mr. Jackson in a whisper. He, too, was hardly able to move.

More and more devoid of oxygen grew the air. It gave Tom a sense as if his head was filled, and ready to burst with every breath he drew. Still he struggled to loosen the nuts. There were but four more now, and he took off three while Mr. Jackson removed one. The young inventor lifted off the valve cover, though it felt like a ton weight to him. He gave a glance inside.

"Here's the trouble!" he murmured. "The valve's clogged. No wonder it wouldn't work. The pumps couldn't force the water out."

It was the work of only a minute to adjust the valve. Then Tom and the engineer managed to get the cover back on.

How they inserted the bolts and screwed the nuts in place they never could remember clearly afterward, but they managed it somehow, with shaking, trembling hands and eyes that grew more and more dim.

"Now start the pumps!" cried Tom faintly. "The tanks will be emptied, and we can get to the surface."

Mr. Sharp was still unconscious, nor was Mr. Swift able to help. He lay with his eyes closed. Garret Jackson, however, managed to crawl to the engine-room, and soon the clank of machinery told Tom that the pumps were in motion. The lad staggered to the pilot house and threw the levers over. An instant later there was the hissing of water as it rushed from the ballast tanks. The submarine shivered, as though disliking to leave the bottom of the sea, and then slowly rose. As the pumps worked more rapidly, and the sea was sent from the tank in great volumes, the boat fairly shot to the surface. Tom was ready to open the conning tower and let in fresh air as soon as the top was above the surface.

With a bound the Advance reached the top. Tom frantically worked the worm gear that opened the tower. In rushed the fresh, life-giving air, and the treasure-hunters filled their lungs with it.

And it was only just in time, for Mr. Sharp was almost gone. He quickly revived, as did the others, when they could breathe as much as they wished of the glorious oxygen.

"That was a close call," commented Mr. Swift. "We'll not go below again until I have provided for all emergencies. I should have seen to the air tanks and the expanding one before going below. We'll sail home on the surface now."

The submarine was put about and headed for her dock. On the way she passed a small steamer, and the passengers looked down in wonder at the strange craft.

When the Advance reached the secluded creek where she had been launched, her passengers had fully recovered from their terrible experience, though the nerves of Mr. Swift and Mr. Damon were not at ease for some days thereafter.

"I should never have made a submerged test without making sure that we had a reserve supply of air," remarked the aged inventor. "I will not be caught that way again. But I can't understand how the pump valve got out of order."

"Maybe some one tampered with it," suggested Mr. Damon. "Could Andy Foger, any of the Happy Harry gang, or the rival gold-seekers have done it?"

"I hardly think so," answered Tom. "The place has been too carefully guarded since Berg and Andy once sneaked in. I think it was just an accident, but I have thought of a plan whereby such accidents can be avoided in the future. It needs a simple device."

"Better patent it," suggested Mr. Sharp with a smile.

"Maybe I will," replied the young inventor. "But not now. We haven't time, if we intend to get fitted out for our trip."

"No; I should say the sooner we started the better," remarked Captain Weston. "That is, if you don't mind me speaking about it," he added gently, and the others smiled, for his diffident comments were only a matter of habit

The first act of the adventurers, after tying the submarine at the dock, was to proceed with the loading of the food and supplies. Tom and Mr. Damon looked to this, while Mr. Swift and Mr. Sharp made some necessary changes to the machinery. The next day the young inventor attached his device to the pump valve, and the loading of the craft was continued.

All was in readiness for the gold-seeking expedition a week later. Captain Weston had carefully charted the route they were to follow, and it was decided to move along on the surface for the first day, so as to get well out to sea before submerging the craft. Then it would sink below the surface, and run along under the water until the wreck was reached, rising at times, as needed, to renew the air supply.

With sufficient stores and provisions aboard to last several months, if necessary, though they did not expect to be gone more than sixty days at most, the adventurers arose early one morning and went down to the dock. Mr. Jackson was not to accompany them. He did not care about a submarine trip, he said, and Mr. Swift desired him to remain at the seaside cottage and guard the shops, which contained much valuable machinery. The airship was also left there.

"Well, are we all ready?" asked Mr. Swift of the little party of gold-seekers, as they were about to enter the conning tower hatchway of the submarine.

"All ready, dad," responded his son.

"Then let's get aboard," proposed Captain Weston. "But first let me take an observation."

He swept the horizon with his telescope, and Tom noticed that the sailor kept it fixed on one particular spot for some time.

"Did you see anything?" asked the lad.

"Well, there is a boat lying off there," was the answer. "And some one is observing us through a glass. But I don't believe it matters. Probably they're only trying to see what sort of an odd fish we are."

"All aboard, then," ordered Mr. Swift, and they went into the submarine. Tom and his father, with Captain Weston, remained in the conning tower. The signal was given, the electricity flowed into the forward and aft plates, and the Advance shot ahead on the surface.

The sailor raised his telescope once more and peered through a window in the tower. He uttered an exclamation.

"What's the matter?" asked Tom.

"That other ship—a small steamer—is weighing anchor and seems to be heading this way," was the reply.

"Maybe it's some one hired by Berg to follow us and trace our movements," suggested Tom.

"If it is we'll fool them," added his father. "Just keep an eye on them, captain, and I think we can show them a trick or two in a few minutes."

Faster shot the Advance through the water. She had started on her way to get the gold from the sunken wreck, but already enemies were on the trail of the adventurers, for the ship the sailor had noticed was steaming after them.

In the Diving Suits

There was no doubt that the steamer was coming after the submarine. Several observations Captain Weston made confirmed this, and he reported the fact to Mr. Swift.

"Well, we'll change our plans, then," said the inventor. "Instead of sailing on the surface we'll go below. But first let them get near so they may have the benefit of seeing what we do. Tom, go below, please, and tell Mr. Sharp to get every thing in readiness for a quick descent. We'll slow up a bit now, and let them get nearer to us."

The speed of the submarine was reduced, and in a short time the strange steamer had overhauled her, coming to within hailing distance.

Mr. Swift signaled for the machinery to stop and the submarine came to a halt on the surface, bobbing about like a half-submerged bottle. The inventor opened a bull's-eye in the tower, and called to a man on the bridge of the steamer:

"What are you following us for?"

"Following you?" repeated the man, for the strange vessel had also come to a stop. "We're not following you."

"It looks like it," replied Mr. Swift. "You'd better give it up."

"I guess the waters are free," was the quick retort. "We'll follow you if we like."

"Will you? Then come on!" cried the inventor as he quickly closed the heavy glass window and pulled a lever. An instant later the submarine began to sink, and Mr. Swift could not help laughing as, just before the tower went under water, he had a glimpse of the astonished face of the man on the bridge. The latter had evidently not expected such a move as that.

Lower and lower in the water went the craft, until it was about two hundred feet below the surface. Then Mr. Swift left the conning tower, descended to the main part of the ship, and asked Tom and Captain Weston to take charge of the pilot house.

"Send her ahead, Tom," his father said. "That fellow up above is rubbing his eyes yet, wondering where we are, I suppose."

Forward shot the Advance under water, the powerful electrical plates pulling and pushing her on the way to secure the sunken gold.

All that morning a fairly moderate rate of speed was maintained, as it was thought best not to run the new machinery too fast.

Dinner was eaten about a quarter of a mile below the surface, but no one inside the submarine would ever have known it. Electric lights made the place as brilliant as could be desired, and the food, which Tom and Mr. Damon prepared, was equal to any that could have been served on land. After the meal they opened the shutters over the windows in the sides of the craft, and looked at the myriads of fishes swimming past, as the creatures were disclosed in the glare of the searchlight.

That night they were several hundred miles on their journey, for the craft was speedy, and leaving Tom and Captain Weston to take the first watch, the others went to bed.

"Bless my soul, but it does seem odd, though, to go to bed under water, like a fish," remarked Mr. Damon. "If my wife knew this she would worry to death. She thinks I'm off automobiling. But this isn't half as dangerous as riding in a car that's always getting out of order. A submarine for mine, every time."

"Wait until we get to the end of this trip," advised Tom. "I guess you'll find almost as many things can happen in a submarine as can in an auto," and future events were to prove the young inventor to be right.

Everything worked well that night, and the ship made good progress. They rose to the surface the next morning to make sure of their position, and to get fresh air, though they did not really need the latter, as the reserve supply had not been drawn on, and was sufficient for several days, now that the oxygen machine had been put in running order.

On the second day the ship was sent to the bottom and halted there, as Mr. Swift wished to try the new diving suits. These were made of a new, light, but very strong metal to withstand the pressure of a great depth.

Tom, Mr. Sharp and Captain Weston donned the suits, the others agreeing to wait until they saw how the first trial resulted. Then, too, it was necessary for some one acquainted with the machinery to remain in the ship to operate the door and water chamber through which the divers had to pass to get out.

The usual plan, with some changes, was followed in letting the three out of the boat, and on to the bottom of the sea. They entered a chamber in the side of the submarine, water was gradually admitted until it equaled in pressure that outside, then an outer door was opened by means of levers, and they could step out

It was a curious sensation to Tom and the others to feel that they were actually walking along the bed of the ocean. All around them was the water, and as they turned on the small electric lights in their helmets, which lights were fed by storage batteries fastened to the diving suits, they saw the fish, big and little, swarm up to them, doubtless astonished at the odd creatures which had entered their domain. On the sand of the bottom, and in and out among the shells and rocks, crawled great spider crabs, big eels and other odd creatures seldom seen on the surface of the water. The three divers found no difficulty in breathing, as there were air tanks fastened to their shoulders, and a constant supply of oxygen was fed through pipes into the helmets. The pressure of water did not bother them, and after the first sensation Tom began to enjoy the novelty of it. At first the inability to speak to his companions seemed odd, but he soon got so he could make signs and motions, and be understood.

They walked about for some time, and once the lad came upon a part of a wrecked vessel buried deep in the sand. There was no telling what ship it was, nor how long it had been there, and after silently viewing it. they continued on

"It was great!" were the first words Tom uttered when he and the others were once more inside the submarine and had removed the suits. "If we can only walk around the wreck of the Boldero that way, we'll have all the gold out of her in no time. There are no life-lines nor air-hose to bother with in these diving suits."

"They certainly are a success," conceded Mr. Sharp.

"Bless my topknot!" cried Mr. Damon. "I'll try it next time. I've always wanted to be a diver, and now I have the chance."

The trip was resumed after the diving chamber had been closed, and on the third day Captain Weston announced, after a look at his chart, that they were nearing the Bahama Islands.

"We'll have to be careful not to run into any of the small keys," he said, that being the name for the many little points of land, hardly large enough to be dignified by the name of island. "We must keep a constant lookout."

Fortune favored them, though once, when Tom was steering, he narrowly avoided ramming a coral reef with the submarine. The searchlight showed it to him just in time, and he sheered off with a thumping in his heart.

The course was changed from south to east, so as to get ready to swing out of the way of the big shoulder of South America where Brazil takes up so much room, and as they went farther and farther toward the equator, they noticed that the waters teemed more and more with fish, some beautiful, some ugly and fear-inspiring, and some such monsters that it made one shudder to look at them, even through the thick glass of the bulls-eye windows.

AT THE TROPICAL ISLAND

It was on the evening of the fourth day later that Captain Weston, who was steering the craft, suddenly called out:

"Land ho!"

"Where away?" inquired Tom quickly, for he had read that this was the proper response to make.

"Dead ahead," answered the sailor with a smile. "Shall we make for it, if I may be allowed the question?"

"What land is it likely to be?" Mr. Swift wanted to know.

"Oh, some small tropical island," replied the seafaring man. "It isn't down on the charts. Probably it's too small to note. I should say it was a coral island, but we may be able to find a Spring of fresh water there, and some fruit."

"Then we'll land there," decided the inventor. "We can use some fresh water, though our distilling and ice apparatus does very well."

They made the island just at dusk, and anchored in a little lagoon, where there was a good depth of water.

"Now for shore!" cried Tom, as the submarine swung around on the chain. "It looks like a fine place. I hope there are cocoanuts and oranges here. Shall I get out the electric launch, dad?"

"Yes, you may, and we'll all go ashore. It will do us good to stretch our legs a bit."

Carried in a sort of pocket on the deck of the submarine was a small electric boat, capable of holding six. It could be slid from the pocket, or depression, into the water without the use of davits, and, with Mr. Sharp to aid him, Tom soon had the little craft afloat. The batteries were already charged, and just as the sun was going down the gold-seekers entered the launch and were soon on shore.

They found a good spring of water close at hand, and Tom's wish regarding the cocoanuts was realized, though there were no oranges. The lad took several of the delicious nuts, and breaking them open poured the milk into a collapsible cup he carried, drinking it eagerly. The others followed his example, and pronounced it the best beverage they had tasted in a long time.

The island was a typical tropical one, not very large, and it did not appear to have been often visited by man. There were no animals to be seen, but myriads of birds flew here and there amid the trees, the trailing vines and streamers of moss.

"Let's spend a day here to-morrow and explore it," proposed Tom, and his father nodded an assent. They went back to the submarine as night was beginning to gather, and in the cabin, after supper, talked over the happenings of their trip so far.

"Do you think we'll have any trouble getting the gold out of the wrecked vessel?" asked Tom of Captain Weston, after a pause.

"Well, it's hard to say. I couldn't learn just how the wreck lays, whether it's on a sandy or a rocky bottom. If the latter, it won't be so hard, but if the sand has worked in and partly covered it, we'll have some difficulties, if I may be permitted to say so. However, don't borrow trouble. We're not there yet, though at the rate we're traveling it won't be long before we arrive."

No watch was set that night, as it was not considered necessary. Tom was the first to arise in the morning, and he went out on the deck for a breath of fresh air before breakfast.

He looked off at the beautiful little island, and as his eye took in all of the little lagoon where the submarine was anchored he uttered a startled cry.

And well he might, for, not a hundred yards away, and nearer to the island than was the Advance, floated another craft—another craft, almost similar in shape and size to the one built by the Swifts. Tom rubbed his eyes to make sure he was not seeing double. No, there could be no mistake about it. There was another submarine at the tropical island.

As he looked, some one emerged from the conning tower of the second craft. The figure seemed strangely familiar. Tom knew in a moment who it was—Addison Berg. The agent saw the lad, too, and taking off his cap and making a mocking bow, he called out:

"Good morning! Have you got the gold yet?"

Tom did not know what to answer. Seeing the other submarine, at an island where he had supposed they would not be disturbed, was disconcerting enough, but to be greeted by Berg was altogether too much, Tom thought. His fears that the rival boat builders would follow had not been without foundation.

"Rather surprised to see us, aren't you?" went on Mr. Berg, smiling.

"Rather," admitted Tom, choking over the word.

"Thought you'd be," continued Berg. "We didn't expect to meet you so soon, but we're glad we did. I don't altogether like hunting for sunken treasure, with such indefinite directions as I have."

"You—are going to—" stammered Tom, and then he concluded it would be best not to say anything. But his talk had been heard inside the submarine. His father came to the foot of the conning tower stairway.

"To whom are you speaking, Tom?" he asked.

"They're here, dad," was the youth's answer.

"Here? Who are here?"

"Berg and his employers. They've followed us, dad."

"WE'LL RACE YOU FOR IT"

Mr. Swift hurried up on deck. He was accompanied by Captain Weston. At the sight of Tom's father, Mr. Berg, who had been joined by' two other men, called out:

"You see we also concluded to give up the trial for the Government prize, Mr. Swift. We decided there was more money in something else. But we still will have a good chance to try the merits of our respective boats. We hurried and got ours fitted up almost as soon as you did yours, and I think we have the better craft."

"I don't care to enter into any competition with you," said Mr. Swift coldly.

"Ah, but I'm afraid you'll have to, whether you want to or not," was the insolent reply.

"What's that? Do you mean to force this matter upon me?"

"I'm afraid I'll have to—my employers and I, that is. You see, we managed to pick up your trail after you left the Jersey coast, having an idea where you were bound, and we don't intend to lose you now."

"Do you mean to follow us?" asked Captain Weston softly.

"Well, you can put it that way if you like," answered one of the two men with Mr. Berg.

"I forbid it!" cried Mr. Swift hotly. "You have no right to sneak after us."

"I guess the ocean is free," continued the rascally agent.

"Why do you persist in keeping after us?" inquired the aged inventor, thinking it well to ascertain, if possible, just how much the men knew.

"Because we're after that treasure as well as you," was the bold reply. "You have no exclusive right to it. The sunken ship is awaiting the first comer, and whoever gets there first can take the gold from the wreck. We intend to be there first, but we'll be fair with you."

"Fair? What do you mean?" demanded Tom.

"This: We'll race you for it. The first one to arrive will have the right to search the wreck for the gold bullion. Is that fair? Do you agree to it?"

"We agree to nothing with you," interrupted Captain Weston, his usual diffident manner all gone. "I happen to be in partial command of this craft, and I warn you that if I find you interfering with us it won't be healthy for you. I'm not fond of fighting, but when I begin I don't like to stop," and he smiled grimly. "You'd better not follow us."

"We'll do as we please," shouted the third member of the trio on the deck of the other boat, which, as Tom could see, was named the Wonder. "We intend to get that gold if we can,"

"All right. I've warned you," went on the sailor, and then, motioning to Tom and his father to follow, he went below.

"Well, what's to be done?" asked Mr. Swift when they were seated in the living-room, and had informed the others of the presence of the rival submarine.

"The only thing I see to do is to sneak away unobserved, go as deep as possible, and make all haste for the wreck," advised the captain. "They will depend on us, for they have evidently no chart of the wreck, though of course the general location of it may be known to them from reading the papers. I hoped I had thrown them off the track by the false chart I dropped, but it seems they were too smart for us."

"Have they a right to follow us?" asked Tom.

"Legally, but not morally. We can't prevent them, I'm afraid. The only thing to do is to get there ahead of them. It will be a race for the sunken treasure, and we must get there first."

"What do you propose doing, captain?" asked Mr. Damon. "Bless my shirt-studs, but can't we pull their ship up on the island and leave it there?"

"I'm afraid such high-handed proceedings would hardly answer," replied Mr. Swift. "No, as Captain Weston says, we must get there ahead of them. What do you think will be the best scheme, captain?"

"Well, there's no need for us to forego our plan to get fresh water. Suppose we go to the island, that is, some of us, leaving a guard on board here. We'll fill our tanks with fresh water, and at night we'll quietly sink below the surface and speed away."

They all voted that an excellent idea, and little time was lost putting it into operation.

All the remainder of that day not a sign of life was visible about the Wonder. She lay inert on the surface of the lagoon, not far away from the Advance; but, though no one showed himself on the deck, Tom and his friends had no doubt but that their enemies were closely watching them.

As dusk settled down over The tropical sea, and as the shadows of the trees on the little island lengthened, those on board the Advance closed the Conning tower. No lights were turned on, as they did not want their movements to be seen, but Tom, his father and Mr. Sharp took their positions near the various machines and apparatus, ready to open the tanks and let the submarine sink to the bottom, as soon as it was possible to do this unobserved.

"Luckily there's no moon," remarked Captain Weston, as he took his place beside Tom. "Once below the surface and we can defy them to find us. It is odd how they traced us, but I suppose that steamer gave them the clue."

It rapidly grew dark, as it always does in the tropics, and when a cautious observation from the conning tower did not disclose the outlines of the other boat, those aboard the Advance rightly concluded that their rivals were unable to see them.

"Send her down, Tom," called his father, and with a hiss the water entered the tanks. The submarine quickly sank below the surface, aided by the deflecting rudder.

But alas for the hopes of the gold-seekers. No sooner was she completely submerged, with the engine started so as to send her out of the lagoon and to the open sea, than the waters all about were made brilliant by the phosphorescent phenomenon. In southern waters this frequently occurs. Millions of tiny creatures, which, it is said, swarm in the warm currents, give an appearance of fire to the ocean, and any object moving through it can plainly be seen. It was so with the Advance. The motion she made in shooting forward, and the undulations caused by her submersion, seemed to start into activity the dormant phosphorus, and the submarine was afloat in a sea of fire.

"Quick!" cried Tom. "Speed her up! Maybe we can get out of this patch of water before they see us."

But it was too late. Above them they could hear the electric siren of the Wonder as it was blown to let them know that their escape had been noticed. A moment later the water, which acted as a sort of sounding-board, or telephone, brought to the ears of Tom Swift and his friends the noise of the engines of the other craft in operation. She was coming after them. The race for the possession of three hundred thousand dollars in gold was already under way. Fate seemed against those on board the Advance.

THE RACE

Directed by Captain Weston, who glanced at the compass and told him which way to steer to clear the outer coral reef, Tom sent the submarine ahead, signaling for full speed to the engine-room, where his father and Mr. Sharp were. The big dynamos purred like great cats, as they sent the electrical energy into the forward and aft plates, pulling and pushing the Advance forward. On and on she rushed under water, but ever as she shot ahead the disturbance in the phosphorescent water showed her position plainly. She would be easy to follow.

"Can't you get any more speed out of her?" asked the captain of the lad.

"Yes," was the quick reply; "by using the auxiliary screws I think we can. I'll try it."

He signaled for the propellers, forward and aft, to be put in operation, and the motor moving the twin screws was turned on. At once there was a perceptible increase to the speed of the Advance.

"Are we leaving them behind?" asked Tom anxiously, as he glanced at the speed gage, and noted that the submarine was now about five hundred feet below the surface.

"Hard to tell," replied the Captain. "You'd have to take an observation to make sure."

"I'll do it," cried the youth. "You steer, please, and I'll go in the conning tower. I can look forward and aft there, as well as straight up. Maybe I can see the Wonder."

Springing up the circular ladder leading into the tower, Tom glanced through the windows all about the small pilot house. He saw a curious sight. It was as if the submarine was in a sea of yellowish liquid fire. She was immersed in water which glowed with the flames that contained no heat. So light was it, in fact, that there was no need of the incandescents in the tower. The young inventor could have seen to read a paper by the illumination of the phosphorus. But he had something else to do than observe this phenomenon. He wanted to see if he could catch sight of the rival submarine.

At first he could make out nothing save the swirl and boiling of the sea, caused by the progress of the Advance through it. But suddenly, as he looked up, he was aware of some great, black body a little to the rear and about ten feet above his craft.

"A shark!" he exclaimed aloud. "An immense one, too."

But the closer he looked the less it seemed like a shark. The position of the black object changed. It appeared to settle down, to be approaching the top of the conning tower. Then, with a suddenness that unnerved him for the time being, Tom recognized what it was; it was the underside of a ship. He could see the plates riveted together, and then, as be noted the rounded, cylindrical shape, he knew that it was a submarine. It was the Wonder. She was close at hand and was creeping up on the Advance. But, what was more dangerous, she seemed to be slowly settling in the water. Another moment and her great screws might crash into the Conning tower of the Swifts' boat and shave it off. Then the water would rush in, drowning the treasure-seekers like rats in a trap.

With a quick motion Tom yanked over the lever that allowed more water to flow into the ballast tanks. The effect was at once apparent. The Advance shot down toward the bottom of the sea. At the same time the young inventor signaled to Captain Weston to notify those in the engine-room to put on a little more speed. The Advance fairly leaped ahead, and the lad, looking up through the bull's-eye in the roof of the conning tower, had the satisfaction of seeing the rival submarine left behind.

The youth hurried down into the interior of the ship to tell what he had seen, and explain the reason for opening the ballast tanks. He found his father and Mr. Sharp somewhat excited over the unexpected maneuver of the craft.

"So they're still following us," murmured Mr. Swift. "I don't see why we can't shake them off."

"It's on account of this luminous water," explained Captain Weston. "Once we are clear of that it will be easy, I think, to give them the slip. That is, if we can get out of their sight long enough. Of course, if they keep close after us, they can pick us up with their searchlight, for I suppose they carry one."

"Yes," admitted the aged inventor, "they have as strong a one as we have. In fact, their ship is second only to this one in speed and power. I know, for Bentley & Eagert showed me some of the plans before they started it, and asked my opinion. This was before I had the notion of building a submarine. Yes, I am afraid we'll have trouble getting away from them."

"I can't understand this phosphorescent glow keeping up so long," remarked Captain Weston. "I've seen it in this locality several times, but it never covered such an extent of the ocean in my time. There must be changed conditions here now."

For an hour or more the race was kept up, and the two submarines forged ahead through the glowing sea. The Wonder remained slightly above and to the rear of the other, the better to keep sight of her, and though the Advance was run to her limit of speed, her rival could not be shaken off. Clearly the Wonder was a speedy craft.

"It's too bad that we've got to fight them, as well as run the risk of lots of other troubles which are always present when sailing under water," observed Mn Damon, who wandered about the submarine like the nervous person he was. "Bless my shirt-studs! Can't we blow them up, or cripple them in some way? They have no right to go after our treasure."

"Well, I guess they've got as much right as we have," declared Tom. "It goes to whoever reaches the wreck first. But what I don't like is their mean, sneaking way of doing it. If they went off on their own hook and looked for it

I wouldn't say a word. But they expect us to lead them to the wreck, and then they'll rob us if they can. That's not fair."

"Indeed, it isn't," agreed Captain Weston, "if I may be allowed the expression. We ought to find some way of stopping them. But, if I'm not mistaken," he added quickly, looking from one of the port bull's-eyes, "the phosphorescent glow is lessening. I believe we are running beyond that part of the ocean."

There was no doubt of it, the glow was growing less and less, and ten minutes later the Advance was speeding along through a sea as black as night. Then, to avoid running into some wreck, it was necessary to turn on the searchlight.

"Are they still after us?" asked Mr. Swift of his son, as he emerged from the engine-room, where he had gone to make some adjustments to the machinery, with the hope of increasing the speed.

"I'll go look," volunteered the lad. He climbed up into the conning tower again, and for a moment, as he gazed back into the black waters swirling all about, he hoped that they had lost the Wonder. But a moment later his heart sank as he caught sight, through the liquid element, of the flickering gleams of another searchlight, the rays undulating through the sea.

"Still following," murmured the young inventor. "They're not going to give up. But we must make 'em—that's all."

He went down to report what he had seen, and a consultation was held. Captain Weston carefully studied the charts of that part of the ocean, and finding that there was a great depth of water at hand, proposed a series of evolutions.

"We can go up and down, shoot first to one side and then to the other," he explained. "We can even drop down to the bottom and rest there for a while. Perhaps, in that way, we can shake them off."

They tried it. The Advance was sent up until her conning tower was out of the water, and then she was suddenly forced down until she was but a few feet from the bottom. She darted to the left, to the right, and even doubled and went back over the course she had taken. But all to no purpose. The Wonder proved fully as speedy, and those in her seemed to know just how to handle the submarine, so that every evolution of the Advance was duplicated. Her rival could not be shaken off.

All night this was kept up, and when morning came, though only the clocks told it, for eternal night was below the surface, the rival gold-seekers were still on the trail.

"They won't give up," declared Mr. Swift hopelessly.

"No, we've got to race them for it, just as Berg proposed," admitted Tom. "But if they want a straightaway race we'll give it to 'em Let's run her to the limit, dad."

"That's what we've been doing, Tom."

"No, not exactly, for we've been submerged a little too much to get the best speed out of our craft. Let's go a little nearer the surface, and give them the best race they'll ever have."

Then the race began; and such a contest of speed as it was! With her propellers working to the limit, and every volt of electricity that was available forced into the forward and aft plates, the Advance surged through the water, about ten feet below the surface. But the Wonder kept after her, giving her knot for knot. The course of the leading submarine was easy to trace now, in the morning light which penetrated ten feet down.

"No use," remarked Tom again, when, after two hours, the Wonder was still close behind them. "Our only chance is that they may have a breakdown."

"Or run out of air, or something like that," added Captain Weston. "They are crowding us pretty close. I had no idea they could keep up this speed. If they don't look out," he went on as he looked from one of the aft observation windows, "they'll foul us, and—"

His remarks were interrupted by a jar to the Advance. She seemed to shiver and careened to one side. Then came another bump.

"Slow down!" cried the captain, rushing toward the pilot house.

"What's the matter?" asked Tom, as he threw the engines and electrical machines out of gear. Have we hit anything?"

"No. Something has hit us," cried the captain. "Their submarine has rammed us."

"Rammed us!" repeated Mr. Swift. "Tom, run out the electric cannon! They're trying to sink us! We'll have to fight them. Run out the stern electric gnu and we'll make them wish they'd not followed us.

The Electric Gun

There was much excitement aboard the Advance. The submarine came to a stop in the water, while the treasure-seekers waited anxiously for what was to follow. Would they be rammed again? This time, stationary as they were, and with the other boat coming swiftly on, a hole might be stove through the Advance, in spite of her powerful sides.

They had not long to wait. Again there came a jar, and once more the Swifts' boat careened. But the blow was a glancing one and, fortunately, did little damage.

"They certainly must be trying to sink us," agreed Captain Weston. "Come, Tom, we'll take a look from the stern and see what they're up to."

"And get the stern electric gun ready to fire," repeated Mr. Swift. "We must protect ourselves. Mr. Sharp and I will go to the bow. There is no telling what they may do. They're desperate, and may ram us from in front"

Tom and the captain hurried aft. Through the thick plate-glass windows they could see the blunt nose of the Wonder not far away, the rival submarine having come to a halt. There she lay, black and silent, like some monster fish waiting to devour its victim.

"There doesn't appear to be much damage done back here," observed Tom. "No leaks. Guess they didn't puncture us."

"Perhaps it was due to an accident that they rammed us," suggested the captain.

"Well, they wouldn't have done it if they hadn't followed us so close," was the opinion of the young inventor. "They're taking too many chances. We've got to stop 'em."

"What is this electric gun your father speaks of?"

"Why, it's a regular electric cannon. It fires a solid ball, weighing about twenty-five pounds, but instead of powder, which would hardly do under water, and instead of compressed air, which is used in the torpedo tubes of the Government submarines, we use a current of electricity. It forces the cannon ball out with great energy."

"I wonder what they will do next?" observed the captain, peering through a bull'seye.

"We can soon tell," replied the youth. "We'll go ahead, and if they try to follow I'm going to fire on them."

"Suppose you sink them?"

"I won't fire to do that; only to disable them. They brought it on themselves. We can't risk having them damage us. Help me with the cannon, will you please, captain?"

The electric cannon was a long, steel tube in the after part of the submarine. It projected a slight distance from the sides of the ship, and by an ingenious arrangement could he swung around in a ball and socket joint, thus enabling it to shoot in almost any direction.

It was the work of but a few minutes to get it ready and, with the muzzle pointing toward the Wonder, Tom adjusted the electric wires and inserted the solid shot.

"Now we're prepared for them!" he cried. "I think a good plan will be to start ahead, and if they try to follow to fire on them. They've brought it on themselves."

"Correct," spoke Captain Weston.

Tom hurried forward to tell his father of this plan.

"We'll do it!" cried Mr. Swift. "Go ahead, Mr. Sharp, and we'll see if those scoundrels will follow."

The young inventor returned on the run to the electric cannon. There was a whir of machinery, and the Advance moved forward. She increased her speed, and the two watchers in the stern looked anxiously out of the windows to see what their rivals would do.

For a moment no movement was noticeable on the part of the Wonder. Then, as those aboard her appeared to realize that the craft on which they depended to pilot them to the sunken treasure was slipping away, word was given to follow. The ship of Berg and his employers shot after the Advance.

"Here they come!" cried Captain Weston. "They're going to ram us again!"

"Then I'm going to fire on them!" declared Tom savagely.

On came the Wonder, nearer and nearer. Her speed was rapidly increasing. Suddenly she bumped the Advance, and then, as if it was an unavoidable accident, the rear submarine sheered off to one side.

"They're certainly at it again!" cried Tom, and peering from the bull's-eye he saw the Wonder shoot past the mouth of the electric cannon. "Here it goes!" he added.

He shoved over the lever, making the proper connection. There was no corresponding report, for the cannon was noiseless, but there was a slight jar as the projectile left the muzzle. The Wonder could be seen to heel over.

"You hit her! You hit her!" cried Captain Weston. "A good shot!"

"I was afraid she was past me when I pulled the lever," explained Tom. "She went like a flash."

"No, you caught her on the rudder," declared the captain. "I think you've put her out of business. Yes, they're rising to the surface."

The lad rapidly inserted another ball, and recharged the cannon. Then he peered out into the water, illuminated by the light of day overhead, as they were not far down. He could see the Wonder rising to the surface. Clearly something had happened.

"Maybe they're going to drop down on us from above, and try to sink us," suggested the youth, while he stood ready to fire again. "If they do—"

His words were interrupted by a slight jar throughout the submarine.

"What was that?" cried the captain.

"Dad fired the bow gun at them, but I don't believe he hit them," answered the young inventor.

"I wonder what damage I did? Guess we'll go to the surface to find out."

Clearly the Wonder had given up the fight for the time being. In fact, she had no weapon with which to respond to a fusillade from her rival. Tom hastened forward and informed his father of what had happened.

"If her steering gear is out of order, we may have a chance to slip away," said Mr. Swift "We'll go up and see what we can learn."

A few minutes later Tom, his father and Captain Weston stepped from the conning tower, which was out of water, on to the little flat deck a short distance away lay the Wonder, and on her deck was Berg and a number of men, evidently members of the crew.

"Why did you fire on us?" shouted the agent angrily.

"Why did you follow us?" retorted Torn.

"Well, you've broken our rudder and disabled us," went on Berg, not answering the question. "You'll suffer for this! I'll have you arrested."

"You only got what you deserved," added Mr. Swift. "You were acting illegally, following us, and you tried to sink us by ramming my craft before we retaliated by firing on you."

"It was an accident, ramming you," said Berg. "We couldn't help it. I now demand that you help us make repairs."

"Well, you've got nerve!" cried Captain Weston, his eyes flashing. "I'd like to have a personal interview with you for about ten minutes. Maybe something besides your ship would need repairs then."

Berg turned away, scowling, but did not reply. He began directing the crew what to do about the broken rudder.

"Come on," proposed Tom in a low voice, for sounds carry very easily over water. "Let's go below and skip out while we have a chance. They can't follow now, and we can get to the sunken treasure ahead of them."

"Good advice," commented his father. "Come, Captain Weston, we'll go below and close the conning tower."

Five minutes later the Advance sank from sight, the last glimpse Tom had of Berg and his men being a sight of them standing on the deck of their floating boat, gazing in the direction of their successful rival. The Wonder was left behind, while Tom and his friends were soon once more speeding toward the treasure wreck.

CAPTURED

"Down deep," advised Captain Weston, as he stood beside Tom and Mr. Swift in the pilot house. "As far as you can manage her, and then forward. We'll take no more chances with these fellows."

"The only trouble is," replied the young inventor, "that the deeper we go the slower we have to travel. The water is so dense that it holds us back."

"Well, there is no special need of hurrying now," went on the sailor. "No one is following you, and two or three days difference in reaching the wreck will not amount to anything."

"Unless they repair their rudder, and take after us again," suggested Mr. Swift.

"They're not very likely to do that," was the captain's opinion. "It was more by luck than good management that they picked us up before. Now, having to delay, as they will, to repair their steering gear, while we can go as deep as we please and speed ahead, it is practically impossible for them to catch up to us. No, I think we have nothing to fear from them."

But though danger from Berg and his crowd was somewhat remote, perils of another sort were hovering around the treasure-seekers, and they were soon to experience them.

It was much different from sailing along in the airship, Tom thought, for there was no blue sky and fleecy clouds to see, and they could not look down and observe, far below them, cities and villages. Nor could they breathe the bracing atmosphere of the upper regions.

But if there was lack of the rarefied air of the clouds, there was no lack of fresh atmosphere. The big tanks carried a large supply, and whenever more was needed the oxygen machine would supply it.

As there was no need, however, of remaining under water for any great stretch of time, it was their practice to rise every day and renew the air supply, also to float along on the surface for a while, or speed along, with only the conning tower out, in order to afford a view, and to enable Captain Weston to take observations. But care was always exercised to make sure no ships were in sight when emerging on the surface, for the gold-seekers did not want to be hailed and questioned by inquisitive persons.

It was about four days after the disabling of the rival submarine, and the Advance was speeding along about a mile and a half under water. Tom was in the pilot house with Captain Weston, Mr. Damon was at his favorite pastime of looking out of the glass side windows into the ocean and its wonders, and Mr. Swift and the balloonists were, as usual, in the engine-room.

"How near do you calculate we are to the sunken wreck?" asked Tom of his companion.

"Well, at the calculation we made yesterday, we are within about a thousand miles of it now. We ought to reach it in about four more days, if we don't have any accidents."

"And how deep do you think it is?" went on the lad.

"Well, I'm afraid it's pretty close to two miles, if not more. It's quite a depth, and of course impossible for ordinary divers to reach. But it will be possible in this submarine and in the strong diving suits your father has invented for us to get to it. Yes, I don't anticipate much trouble in getting out the gold, once we reach the wreck of course—"

The captain's remark was not finished. From the engine- room there came a startled shout:

"Tom! Tom! Your father is hurt! Come here, quick!"

"Take the wheel!" cried the lad to the captain. "I must go to my father." It was Mr. Sharp's voice he had heard.

Racing to the engine-room, Tom saw his parent doubled up over a dynamo, while to one side, his hand on a copper switch, stood Mr. Sharp.

"What's the matter?" shouted the lad.

"He's held there by a current of electricity," replied the balloonist. "The wires are crossed."

"Why don't you shut off the current?" demanded the youth, as he prepared to pull his parent from the whirring machine. Then he hesitated, for he feared he, too, would be glued fast by the terrible current, and so be unable to help Mr. Swift.

"I'm held fast here, too," replied the balloonist. "I started to cut out the current at this switch, but there's a short circuit somewhere, and I can't let go, either. Quick, shut off all power at the main switchboard forward."

Tom realized that this was the only thing to do. He ran forward and with a yank cut out all the electric wires. With a sigh of relief Mr. Sharp pulled his hands from the copper where he had been held fast as if by some powerful magnet, his muscles cramped by the current. Fortunately the electricity was of low voltage, and he was not burned. The body of Mr. Swift toppled backward from the dynamo, as Tom sprang to reach his father.

"He's dead!" he cried, as he saw the pale face and the closed eyes.

"No, only badly shocked, I hope," spoke Mr. Sharp. "But we must get him to the fresh air at once. Start the tank pumps. We'll rise to the surface."

The youth needed no second bidding. Once more turning on the electric current, he set the powerful pumps in motion and the submarine began to rise. Then, aided by Captain Weston and Mr. Damon, the young inventor carried his father to a couch in the main cabin. Mr. Sharp took charge of the machinery.

Restoratives were applied, and there was a flutter of the eyelids of the aged inventor.

"I think he'll come around all right," said the sailor kindly, as he saw Tom's grief. "Fresh air will be the thing for him. We'll be on the surface in a minute."

Up shot the Advance, while Mr. Sharp stood ready to open the conning tower as soon as it should be out of water. Mr. Swift seemed to be rapidly reviving. With a bound the submarine, forced upward from the great depth, fairly shot out of the water. There was a clanking sound as the aeronaut opened the airtight door of the tower, and a breath of fresh air came in.

"Can you walk, dad, or shall we carry you?" asked Tom solitiously.

"Oh, I—I'm feeling better now," was the inventor's reply. "I'll soon be all right when I get out on deck. My foot slipped as I was adjusting a wire that had gotten out of order, and I fell so that I received a large part of the current. I'm glad I was not burned. Was Mr. Sharp hurt? I saw him run to the switch, just before I lost consciousness."

"No, I'm all right," answered the balloonist. "But allow us to get you out to the fresh air. You'll feel much better then."

Mr. Swift managed to walk slowly to the ladder leading to the conning tower, and thence to the deck. The others followed him. As all emerged from the submarine they uttered a cry of astonishment.

There, not one hundred yards away, was a great warship, flying a flag which, in a moment. Tom recognized as that of Brazil. The cruiser was lying off a small island, and all about were small boats, filled with natives, who seemed to be bringing supplies from land to the ship. At the unexpected sight of the submarine, bobbing up from the bottom of the ocean, the natives uttered cries of fright. The attention of those on the warship was attracted, and the bridge and rails were lined with curious officers and men.

"It's a good thing we didn't come up under that ship," observed Tom. "They would have thought we were trying to torpedo her. Do you feel better, dad?" he asked, his wonder over the sight of the big vessel temporarily eclipsed in his anxiety for his parent.

"Oh, yes, much better. I'm all right now. But I wish we hadn't disclosed ourselves to these people. They may demand to know where we are going, and Brazil is too near Uruguay to make it safe to tell our errand. They may guess it, however, from having read of the wreck, and our departure."

"Oh, I guess it will be all right," replied Captain Weston. "We can tell them we are on a pleasure trip. That's true enough. It would give us great pleasure to find that gold."

"There's a boat, with some officers in it, to judge by the amount of gold lace on them, putting off from the ship," remarked Mr. Sharp.

"Ha! Yes! Evidently they intend to pay us a formal visit," observed Mr. Damon. "Bless my gaiters, though. I'm not dressed to receive company. I think I'll put on my dress suit."

"It's too late," advised Tom. "They'll be here in a minute."

Urged on by the lusty arms of the Brazilian sailors, the boat, containing several officers, neared the floating submarine rapidly.

"Ahoy there!" called an officer in the bow, his accent betraying his unfamiliarity with the English language. "What craft are you?"

"Submarine, Advance, from New Jersey," replied Tom. "Who are you?"

"Brazilian cruiser San Paulo," was the reply. "Where are you bound?" went on the officer.

"On pleasure," answered Captain Weston quickly. "But why do you ask? We are an American ship, sailing under American colors. Is this Brazilian territory?"

"This island is—yes," came back the answer, and by this time the small boat was at the side of the submarine. Before the adventurers could have protested, had they a desire to do so, there were a number of officers and the crew of the San Paulo on the small deck.

With a flourish, the officer who had done the questioning drew his sword. Waving it in the air with a dramatic gesture, he exclaimed:

"You're our prisoners! Resist and my men shall cut you down like dogs! Seize them, men!"

The sailors sprang forward, each one stationing himself at the side of one of our friends, and grasping an arm.

"What does this mean?" cried Captain Weston indignantly. "If this is a joke, you're carrying it too far. If you're in earnest, let me warn you against interfering with Americans!"

"We know what we are doing," was the answer from the officer.

The sailor who had hold of Captain Weston endeavored to secure a tighter grip. The captain turned suddenly, and seizing the man about the waist, with an exercise of tremendous strength hurled him over his head and into the sea, the man making a great splash.

"That's the way I'll treat any one else who dares lay a hand on me!" shouted the captain, who was transformed from a mild-mannered individual into an angry, modern giant. There was a gasp of astonishment at his feat, as the ducked sailor crawled back into the small boat. And he did not again venture on the deck of the submarine.

"Seize them, men!" cried the gold-laced officer again, and this time he and his fellows, including the crew, crowded so closely around Tom and his friends that they could do nothing. Even Captain Weston found it impossible to offer any resistance, for three men grabbed hold of him but his spirit was still a fighting one, and he struggled desperately but uselessly.

"How dare you do this?" he cried.

"Yes," added Tom, "what right have you to interfere with us?"

"Every right," declared the gold-laced officer.

"You are in Brazilian territory, and I arrest you."

"What for?" demanded Mr. Sharp.

"Because your ship is an American submarine, and we have received word that you intend to damage our shipping, and may try to torpedo our warships. I believe you tried to disable us a little while ago, but failed. We consider that an act of war and you will be treated accordingly. Take them on board the San Paulo," the officer Went on, turning to his aides. "We'll try them by court-marital here. Some of you remain and guard this submarine. We will teach these filibustering Americans a lesson."

DOOMED TO DEATH

There was no room on the small deck of the submarine to make a stand against the officers and crew of the Brazilian warship. In fact, the capture of the gold-seekers had been effected so suddenly that their astonishment almost deprived them of the power to think clearly.

At another command from the officer, who was addressed as Admiral Fanchetti, several of the sailors began to lead Tom and his friends toward the small boat.

"Do you feel all right, father?" inquired the lad anxiously, as he looked at his parent. "These scoundrels have no right to treat us so."

"Yes, Tom, I'm all right as far as the electric shock is concerned, but I don't like to be handled in this fashion."

"We ought not to submit!" burst out Mr. Damon. "Bless the stars and stripes! We ought to fight."

"There's no chance," said Mr. Sharp. "We are right under the guns of the ship. They could sink us with one shot. I guess we'll have to give in for the time being."

"It is most unpleasant, if I may be allowed the expression," commented Captain Weston mildly. He seemed to have lost his sudden anger, hut there was a steely glint in his eyes, and a grim, set look around his month that showed his temper was kept under control only by an effort. It boded no good to the sailors who had hold of the doughty captain if he should once get loose, and it was noticed that they were on their guard.

As for Tom, he submitted quietly to the two Brazilians who had hold of either arm, and Mr. Swift was held by only one, for it was seen that he was feeble.

"Into the boat with them!" cried Admiral Fanchetti. "And guard them well, Lieutenant Drascalo, for I heard them plotting to escape," and the admiral signaled to a younger officer, who was in charge of the men guarding the prisoners.

"Lieutenant Drascalo, eh?" murmured Mr. Damon. "I think they made a mistake naming him. It ought to be Rascalo. He looks like a rascal."

"Silenceo!" exclaimed the lieutenant, scowling at the odd character'.

"Bless my spark plug! He's a regular fire-eater!" went on Mr. Damon, who appeared to have fully recovered his spirits.

"Silenceo!" cried the lieutenant, scowling again, but Mr. Damon did not appear to mind.

Admiral Fanchetti and several others of the gold-laced officers remained aboard the submarine, while Tom and his friends were hustled into the small boat and rowed toward the warship.

"I hope they don't damage our craft," murmured the young inventor, as he saw the admiral enter the conning tower.

"If they do, we'll complain to the United States consul and demand damages," said Mr. Swift

"I'm afraid we won't have a chance to communicate with the consul," remarked Captain Weston.

"What do you mean?" asked Mr. Damon. "Bless my shoelaces, but will these scoundrels—"

"Silenceo!" cried Lieutenant Drascalo quickly. "Dogs of Americans, do you wish to insult us?"

"Impossible; you wouldn't appreciate a good, genuine United States insult," murmured Tom under his breath.

"What I mean," went on the captain, "is that these people may carry the proceedings off with a high hand. You heard the admiral speak of a court-martial."

"Would they dare do that?" inquired Mr. Sharp.

"They would dare anything in this part of the world, I'm afraid," resumed Captain Weston. "I think I see their plan, though. This admiral is newly in command; his uniform shows that He wants to make a name for himself, and he seizes on our submarine as an excuse. He can send word to his government that he destroyed a torpedo craft that sought to wreck his ship. Thus he will acquire a reputation."

"But would his government support him in such a hostile act against the United States, a friendly nation?" asked Tom.

"Oh, he would not claim to have acted against the United States as a power. He would say that it was a private submarine, and, as a matter of fact, it is. While we are under the protection of the stars and stripes, our vessel is not a Government one," and Captain Weston spoke the last in a low voice, so the scowling lieutenant could not hear.

"What will they do with us?" inquired Mr. Swift.

"Have some sort of a court-martial, perhaps," went on the captain, "and confiscate our craft Then they will send us back home, I expect for they would not dare harm us."

"But take our submarine!" cried Tom. "The villains—"

"Silenceo!" shouted Lieutenant Drascalo and he drew his sword.

By this time the small boat was under the big guns of the San Paulo, and the prisoners were ordered, in broken English, to mount a companion ladder that hung over the side. In a short time they were on deck, amid a crowd of sailors, and they could see the boat going back to bring off the admiral, who signaled from the submarine. Tom and his friends were taken below to a room that looked like a prison, and there, a little later, they were visited by Admiral Fanchetti and several officers.

"You will be tried at once," said the admiral. "I have examined your submarine and I find she carries two torpedo tubes. It is a wonder you did not sink me at once."

"Those are not torpedo tubes!" cried Tom, unable to keep silent, though Captain Weston motioned him to do so.

"I know torpedo tubes when I see them," declared the admiral. "I consider I had a very narrow escape. Your country is fortunate that mine does not declare war against it for this act. But I take it you are acting privately, for you fly no flag, though you claim to be from the United States."

"There's no place for a flag on the submarine," went on Tom. "What good would it be under water?"

"Silenceo!" cried Lieutenant Drascalo, the admonition to silence seeming to be the only command of which he was capable.

"I shall confiscate your craft for my government," went on the admiral, "and shall punish you as the court-martial may direct. You will be tried at once."

It was in vain for the prisoners to protest. Matters were carried with a high hand. They were allowed a spokesman, and Captain Weston, who understood Spanish, was selected, that language being used. But the defense was a farce, for he was scarcely listened to. Several officers testified before the admiral, who was judge, that they had seen the submarine rise out of the water, almost under the prow of the San Paulo. It was assumed that the Advance had tried to wreck the warship, but had failed. It was in vain that Captain Weston and the others told of the reason for their rapid ascent from the ocean depths—that Mr. Swift had been shocked, and needed fresh air. Their story was not believed.

"We have heard enough!" suddenly exclaimed the admiral. "The evidence against you is over-whelming—er—what you Americans call conclusive," and be was speaking then in broken English. "I find you guilty, and the sentence of this court-martial is that you be shot at sunrise, three days hence!"

"Shot!" cried Captain Weston, staggering back at this unexpected sentence. His companions turned white, and Mr. Swift leaned against his son for support.

"Bless my stars! Of all the scoundrelly!" began Mr. Damon.

"Silenceo!" shouted the lieutenant, waving his sword.

"You will be shot," proceeded the admiral. "Is not that the verdict of the honorable court?" he asked, looking at his fellow officers. They all nodded gravely.

"But look here!" objected Captain Weston. "You don't dare do that! We are citizens of the United States, and—"

"I consider you no better than pirates," interrupted the admiral. "You have an armed submarine—a submarine with torpedo tubes. You invade our harbor with it, and come up almost under my ship. You have forfeited your right to the protection of your country, and I have no fear on that score. You will be shot within three days. That is all. Remove the prisoners."

Protests were in vain, and it was equally useless to struggle. The prisoners were taken out on deck, for which they were thankful, for the interior of the ship was close and hot, the weather being intensely disagreeable. They were told to keep within a certain space on deck, and a guard of sailors, all armed, was placed near them. From where they were they could see their submarine floating on the surface of the little bay, with several Brazilians on the small deck. The Advance had been anchored, and was surrounded by a flotilla of the native boats, the brown-skinned paddlers gazing curiously at the odd craft.

"Well, this is tough luck!" murmured Tom. "How do you feel, dad?"

"As well as can be expected under the circumstances," was the reply. "What do you think about this, Captain Weston?"

"Not very much, if I may be allowed the expression," was the answer.

"Do you think they will dare carry out that threat?" asked Mr. Sharp.

The captain shrugged his shoulders. "I hope it is only a bluff," he replied, "made to scare us so we will consent to giving up the submarine, which they have no right to confiscate. But these fellows look ugly enough for anything," he went on.

"Then if there's any chance of them attempting to carry it out," spoke Tom, "we've got to do something."

"Bless my gizzard, of course!" exclaimed Mr. Damon. "But what? That's the question. To be shot! Why, that's a terrible threat! The villains—"

"Silenceo!" shouted Lieutenant Drascalo, coming up at that moment.

THE ESCAPE

Events had happened so quickly that day that the gold-hunters could scarcely comprehend them. It seemed only a short time since Mr. Swift had been discovered lying disabled on the dynamo, and what had transpired since seemed to have taken place in a few minutes, though it was, in reality, several hours. This was made manifest by the feeling of hunger on the part of Tom and his friends.

"I wonder if they're going to starve us, the scoundrels?" asked Mr. Sharp, when the irate lieutenant was beyond hearing. "It's not fair to make us go hungry and shoot us in the bargain."

"That's so, they ought to feed us," put in Tom. As yet neither he nor the others fully realized the meaning of the sentence passed on them.

From where they were on deck they could look off to the little island. From it boats manned by natives were constantly putting off, bringing supplies to the ship. The place appeared to be a sort of calling station for Brazilian warships, where they could get fresh water and fruit and other food.

From the island the gaze of the adventurers wandered to the submarine, which lay not far away. They were chagrined to see several of the bolder natives clambering over the deck.

"I hope they keep out of the interior," commented Tom. "If they get to pulling or hauling on the levers and wheels they may open the tanks and sink her, with the Conning tower open."

"Better that, perhaps, than to have her fall into the hands of a foreign power," commented Captain Weston. "Besides, I don't see that it's going to matter much to us what becomes of her after we're—"

He did not finish, but every one knew what he meant, and a grim silence fell upon the little group.

There came a welcome diversion, however, in the shape of three sailors, bearing trays of food, which were placed on the deck in front of the prisoners, who were sitting or lying in the shade of an awning, for the sun was very hot

"Ha! Bless my napkin-ring!" cried Mr. Damon with something of his former gaiety. "Here's a meal, at all events. They don't intend to starve us. Eat hearty, every one."

"Yes, we need to keep up our strength," observed Captain Weston.

"Why?" inquired Mr. Sharp.

"Because we're going to try to escape!" exclaimed Tom in a low voice, when the sailors who had brought the food had gone. "Isn't that what you mean, captain?"

"Exactly. We'll try to give these villains the slip, and we'll need all our strength and wits to do it. We'll wait until night, and see what we can do."

"But where will we escape to?" asked Mr. Swift. "The island will afford no shelter, and—"

"No, but our submarine will," went on the sailor.

"It's in the possession of the Brazilians," objected Tom.

"Once I get aboard the Advance twenty of those brown- skinned villains won't keep me prisoner," declared Captain Weston fiercely. "If we can only slip away from here, get into the small boat, or even swim to the submarine, I'll make those chaps on board her think a hurricane has broken loose."

"Yes, and I'll help," said Mr. Damon.

"And I," added Tom and the balloonist

"That's the way to talk," commented the captain. "Now let's eat, for I see that rascally lieutenant coming this way, and we mustn't appear to be plotting, or he'll be suspicious."

The day passed slowly, and though the prisoners seemed to be allowed considerable liberty, they soon found that it was only apparent. Once Tom walked some distance from that portion of the deck where he and the others had been told to remain. A sailor with a gun at once ordered him back. Nor could they approach the rails without being directed, harshly enough at times, to move back amidships.

As night approached the gold-seekers were on the alert for any chance that might offer to slip away, or even attack their guard, but the number of Brazilians around them was doubled in the evening, and after supper, which was served to them on deck by the light of swinging lanterns, they were taken below and locked in a stuffy cabin. They looked helplessly at each other.

"Don't give up," advised Captain Weston. "It's a long night. We may be able to get out of here."

But this hope was in vain. Several times he and Tom, thinking the guards outside the cabin were asleep, tried to force the lock of the door with their pocket-knives, which had not been taken from them. But one of the sailors was aroused each time by the noise, and looked in through a barred window, so they had to give it up. Slowly the night passed, and morning found the prisoners pale, tired and discouraged. They were brought up on deck again, for which they were thankful, as in that tropical climate it was stifling below.

During the day they saw Admiral Fanchetti and several of his officers pay a visit to the submarine. They went below through the opened conning tower, and were gone some time.

"I hope they don't disturb any of the machinery," remarked Mr. Swift. "That could easily do great damage."

Admiral Fanchetti seemed much pleased with himself when he returned from his visit to the submarine.

"You have a fine craft," he said to the prisoners. "Or, rather, you had one. My government now owns it. It seems a pity to shoot such good boat builders, but you are too dangerous to be allowed to go."

If there had been any doubt in the minds of Tom and his friends that the sentence of the court-martial was only for effect, it was dispelled that day. A firing squad was told off in plain view of them, and the men were put through their evolutions by Lieutenant Drascalo, who had them load, aim and fire blank cartridges at an imaginary line of prisoners. Tom could not repress a shudder as he noted the leveled rifles, and saw the fire and smoke spurt from the muzzles.

"Thus we shall do to you at sunrise to-morrow," said the lieutenant, grinning, as he once more had his men practice their grim work.

It seemed hotter than ever that day. The sun was fairly broiling, and there was a curious haziness and stillness to the air. It was noticed that the sailors on the San Paula were busy making fast all loose articles on deck with extra lashings, and hatch coverings were doubly secured.

"What do you suppose they are up to?" asked Tom of Captain Weston.

"I think it is coming on to blow," he replied, "and they don't want to be caught napping. They have fearful storms down in this region at this season of the year, and I think one is about due."

"I hope it doesn't wreck the submarine," spoke Mr. Swift. "They ought to close the hatch of the conning tower, for it won't take much of a sea to make her ship considerable water."

Admiral Fanchetti had thought of this, however, and as the afternoon wore away and the storm signs multiplied, he sent word to close the submarine. He left a few sailors aboard inside on guard.

"It's too hot to eat," observed Tom, when their supper had been brought to them, and the others felt the same way about it. They managed to drink some cocoanut milk, prepared in a palatable fashion by the natives of the island, and then, much to their disgust, they were taken below again and locked in the cabin.

"Whew! But it certainly is hot!" exclaimed Mr. Damon as he sat down on a couch and fanned himself. "This is awful!"

"Yes, something is going to happen pretty soon," observed Captain Weston. "The storm will break shortly, I think."

They sat languidly about the cabin. It was so oppressive that even the thought of the doom that awaited them in the morning could hardly seem worse than the terrible heat. They could hear movements going on about the ship, movements which indicated that preparations were being made for something unusual. There was a rattling of a chain through a hawse hole, and Captain Weston remarked:

"They're putting down another anchor. Admiral Fanchetti had better get away from the island, though, unless he wants to be wrecked. He'll be blown ashore in less than no time. No cable or chain will hold in such storms as they have here."

There came a period of silence, which was suddenly broken by a howl as of some wild beast.

"What's that?" cried Tom, springing up from where he was stretched out on the cabin floor.

"Only the wind," replied the captain. "The storm has arrived."

The howling kept up, and soon the ship began to rock. The wind increased, and a little later there could be heard, through an opened port in the prisoners' cabin, the dash of rain.

"It's a regular hurricane!" exclaimed the captain. "I wonder if the cables will hold?"

"What about the submarine?" asked Mr. Swift anxiously.

"I haven't much fear for her. She lies so low in the water that the wind can't get much hold on her. I don't believe she'll drag her anchor."

Once more came a fierce burst of wind, and a dash of rain, and then, suddenly above the outburst of the elements, there sounded a crash on deck. It was followed by excited cries.

"Something's happened!" yelled Tom. The prisoners gathered in a frightened group in the middle of the cabin. The cries were repeated, and then came a rush of feet just outside the cabin door.

"Our guards! They're leaving!" shouted Tom.

"Right!" exclaimed Captain Weston. "Now's our chance! Come on! If we're going to escape we must do it while the storm is at its height, and all is in confusion. Come on!"

Tom tried the door. It was locked.

"One side!" shouted the captain, and this time he did not pause to say "by your leave." He came at the portal on the run, and his shoulder struck it squarely. There was a splintering and crashing of wood, and the door was burst open.

"Follow me!" cried the valiant sailor, and Tom and the others rushed after him. They could hear the wind howling more loudly than ever, and as they reached the deck the rain dashed into their faces with such violence that they could hardly see. But they were aware that something had occurred. By the light of several lanterns swaying in the terrific blast they saw that one of the auxiliary masts had broken off near the deck.

It had fallen against the chart house, smashing it, and a number of sailors were laboring to clear away the wreckage.

"Fortune favors us!" cried Captain Weston. "Come on! Make for the small boat. It's near the side ladder. We'll lower the boat and pull to the submarine."

There came a flash of lightning, and in its glare Tom saw something that caused him to cry out.

"Look!" he shouted. "The submarine. She's dragged her anchors!"

The Advance was much closer to the warship than she had been that afternoon. Captain Weston looked over the side.

"It's the San Paula that's dragging her anchors, not the submarine!" he shouted. "We're bearing down on her! We must act quickly. Come on, we'll lower the boat!"

In the rush of wind and the dash of rain the prisoners crowded to the accommodation companion ladder, which was still over the side of the big ship. No one seemed to be noticing them, for Admiral Fanchetti was on the bridge, yelling orders for the clearing away of the wreckage. But Lieutenant

Drascalo, coming up from below at that moment, caught sight of the fleeing ones. Drawing his sword, he rushed at them, shouting:

"The prisoners! The prisoners! They are escaping!"

Captain Weston leaped toward the lieutenant

"Look out for his sword!" cried Tom. But the doughty sailor did not fear the weapon. Catching up a coil of rope, he cast it at the lieutenant. It struck him in the chest, and he staggered back, lowering his sword.

Captain Weston leaped forward, and with a terrific blow sent Lieutenant Drascalo to the deck.

"There!" cried the sailor. "I guess you won't yell 'Silenceo!' for a while now."

There was a rush of Brazilians toward the group of prisoners. Tom caught one with a blow on the chin, and felled him, while Captain Weston disposed of two more, and Mr. Sharp and Mr. Damon one each. The savage fighting of the Americans was too much for the foreigners, and they drew back.

"Come on!" cried Captain Weston again. "The storm is getting worse. The warship will crash into the submarine in a few minutes. Her anchors aren't holding. I didn't think they would."

He made a dash for the ladder, and a glance showed him that the small boat was in the water at the foot of it. The craft had not been hoisted on the davits.

"Luck's with us at last!" cried Tom, Seeing it also. "Shall I help you, dad?"

"No; I think I'm all right. Go ahead."

There came such a gust of wind that the San Paula was heeled over, and the wreck of the mast, rolling about, crashed into the side of a deck house, splintering it. A crowd of sailors, led by Admiral Fanchetti, who were again rushing on the escaping prisoners, had to leap back out of the way of the rolling mast.

"Catch them! Don't let them get away!" begged the commander, but the sailors evidently had no desire to close in with the Americans.

Through the rush of wind and rain Tom and his friends staggered down the ladder. It was hard work to maintain one's footing, but they managed it. On account of the high side of the ship the water was comparatively calm under her lee, and, though the small boat was bobbing about, they got aboard. The oars were in place, and in another moment they had shoved off from the landing stage which formed the foot of the accommodation ladder.

"Now for the Advance!" murmured Captain Weston.

"Come back! Come back, dogs of Americans!" cried a voice at the rail over their heads, and looking up, Tom saw Lieutenant Drascalo. He had snatched a carbine from a marine, and was pointing it at the recent prisoners. He fired, the flash of the gun and a dazzling chain of lightning coming together. The thunder swallowed up the report of the carbine, but the bullet whistled uncomfortable close to Tom's head. The blackness that followed the lightning shut out the view of everything for a few seconds, and when the next flash came the adventurers saw that they were close to their submarine.

A fusillade of shots sounded from the deck of the warship, but as the marines were poor marksmen at best, and as the swaying of the ship disconcerted them, our friends were in little danger.

There was quite a sea once they were beyond the protection of the side of the warship, but Captain Weston, who was rowing, knew how to manage a boat skillfully, and he soon had the craft alongside the bobbing submarine.

"Get aboard, now, quick!" he cried.

They leaped to the small deck, casting the rowboat adrift. It was the work of but a moment to open the conning tower. As they started to descend they were met by several Brazilians coming up.

"Overboard with 'em!" yelled the captain. "Let them swim ashore or to their ship!"

With almost superhuman strength he tossed one big sailor from the small deck. Another showed fight, but he went to join his companion in the swirling water. A man rushed at Tom, seeking the while to draw his sword, but the young inventor, with a neat left-hander, sent him to join the other two, and the remainder did not wait to try conclusions. They leaped for their lives, and soon all could be seen, in the frequent lightning flashes, swimming toward the warship which was now closer than ever to the submarine

"Get inside and we'll sink below the surface!" called Tom. "Then we don't care what happens."

They closed the steel door of the conning tower. As they did so they heard the patter of bullets from carbines fired from the San Paulo. Then came a violent tossing of the Advance; the waves were becoming higher as they caught the full force of the hurricane. It took but an instant to sever, from within, the cable attached to the anchor, which was one belonging to the warship. The Advance began drifting.

"Open the tanks, Mr. Sharp!" cried Tom. "Captain Weston and I will steer. Once below we'll start the engines."

Amid a crash of thunder and dazzling flashes of lightning, the submarine began to sink. Tom, in the conning tower had a sight of the San Paulo as it drifted nearer and nearer under the influence of the mighty wind. As one bright flash came he saw Admiral Fanchetti and Lieutenant Drascalo leaning over the rail and gazing at the Advance.

A moment later the view faded from sight as the submarine sank below the surface of the troubled sea. She was tossed about for some time until deep enough to escape the surface motion. Waiting until she was far enough down so that her lights would not offer a mark for the guns of the warship, the electrics were switched on.

"We're safe now!" cried Tom, helping his father to his cabin. "They've got too much to attend to themselves to follow us now, even if they could. Shall we go ahead, Captain Weston?"

"I think so, yes, if I may be allowed to express my opinion," was the mild reply, in strange contrast to the strenuous work in which the captain had just been engaged.

Tom signaled to Mr. Sharp in the engine-room, and in a few seconds the Advance was speeding away from the island and the hostile vessel. Nor, deep as she was now, was there any sign of the hurricane. In the peaceful depths she was once more speeding toward the sunken treasure.

At the Wreck

"Well," remarked Mr. Damon, as the submarine hurled herself forward through the ocean, "I guess that firing party will have something else to do to-morrow morning besides aiming those rifles at us."

"Yes, indeed," agreed Tom. "They'll be lucky if they save their ship. My, how that wind did blow!"

"You're right," put in Captain Weston. "When they get a hurricane down in this region it's no cat's paw. But they were a mighty careless lot of sailors. The idea of leaving the ladder over the side, and the boat in the water."

"It was a good thing for us, though," was Tom's opinion.

"Indeed it was," came from the captain. "But as long as we are safe now I think we'd better take a look about the craft to see if those chaps did any damage. They can't have done much, though, or she wouldn't be running so smoothly. Suppose you go take a look, Tom, and ask your father and Mr. Sharp what they think. I'll steer for a while, until we get well away from the island."

The young inventor found his father and the balloonist busy in the engine-room. Mr. Swift had already begun an inspection of the machinery, and so far found that it had not been injured. A further inspection showed that no damage had been done by the foreign guard that had been in temporary possession of the Advance, though the sailors had made free in the cabins, and had broken into the food lockers, helping themselves plentifully. But there was still enough for the gold-seekers.

"You'd never know there was a storm raging up above," observed Tom as he rejoined Captain Weston in the lower pilot house, where he was managing the craft. "It's as still and peaceful here as one could wish."

"Yes, the extreme depths are seldom disturbed by a surface storm. But we are over a mile deep now. I sent her down a little while you were gone, as I think she rides a little more steadily."

All that night they speeded forward, and the next day, rising to the surface to take an observation, they found no traces of the storm, which had blown itself out. They were several hundred miles away from the hostile warship, and there was not a vessel in sight on the broad expanse of blue ocean.

The air tanks were refilled, and after sailing along on the surface for an hour or two, the submarine was again sent below, as Captain Weston sighted through his telescope the smoke of a distant steamer.

"As long as it isn't the Wonder, we're all right," said Tom. "Still, we don't want to answer a lot of questions about ourselves and our object."

"No. I fancy the Wonder will give up the search," remarked the captain, as the Advance was sinking to the depths.

"We must be getting pretty near to the end of our search ourselves," ventured the young inventor.

"We are within five hundred miles of the intersection of the forty-fifth parallel and the twenty-seventh meridian, east from Washington," said the captain. "That's as near as I could locate the wreck. Once we reach that point we will have to search about under water, for I don't fancy the other divers left any buoys to mark the spot."

It was two days later, after uneventful sailing, partly on the surface, and partly submerged, that Captain Weston, taking a noon observation, announced:

"Well, we're here!"

"Do you mean at the wreck?" asked Mr. Swift eagerly.

"We're at the place where she is supposed to lie, in about two miles of water," replied the captain. "We are quite a distance off the coast of Uruguay, about opposite the harbor of Rio de La Plata. From now on we shall have to nose about under water, and trust to luck."

With her air tanks filled to their capacity, and Tom having seen that the oxygen machine and other apparatus was in perfect working order, the submarine was sent below on her search. Though they were in the neighborhood of the wreck, the adventurers might still have to do considerable searching before locating it. Lower and lower they sank into the depths of the sea, down and down, until they were deeper than they had ever gone before. The pressure was tremendous, but the steel sides of the Advance withstood it

Then began a search that lasted nearly a week. Back and forth they cruised, around in great circles, with the powerful searchlight focused to disclose the sunken treasure ship. Once Tom, who was observing the path of light in the depths from the conning tower, thought he had seen the remains of the Boldero, for a misty shape loomed up in front of the submarine, and he signaled for a quick stop. It was a wreck, but it had been on the ocean bed for a score of years, and only a few timbers remained of what had been a great ship. Much disappointed, Tom rang for full speed ahead again, and the current was sent into the great electric plates that pulled and pushed the submarine forward.

For two days more nothing happened. They searched around under the green waters, on the alert for the first sign, but they saw nothing. Great fish swam about them, sometimes racing with the Advance. The adventurers beheld great ocean caverns, and skirted immense rocks, where dwelt monsters of the deep. Once a great octopus tried to do battle with the submarine and crush it in its snaky arms, but Tom saw the great white body, with saucer-shaped eyes, in the path of light and rammed him with the steel point. The creature died after a struggle.

They were beginning to despair when a full week had passed and they were seemingly as far from the wreck as ever. They went to the surface to enable Captain Weston to take another observation. It only confirmed the other, and showed that they were in the right vicinity. But it was like looking for a needle in a haystack, almost, to and the sunken ship in that depth of water.

"Well, we'll try again," said Mr. Swift, as they sank once more beneath the surface.

It was toward evening, on the second day after this, that Tom, who was on duty in the conning tower, saw a black shape looming up in front of the submarine, the searchlight revealing it to him far enough away so that he could steer to avoid it. He thought at first that it was a great rock, for they were moving along near the bottom, but the peculiar shape of it soon convinced him that this could not be. It came more plainly into view as the submarine approached it more slowly, then suddenly, out of the depths in the illumination from the searchlight, the young inventor saw the steel sides of a steamer. His heart gave a great thump, but he would not call out yet, fearing that it might be some other vessel than the one containing the treasure.

He steered the Advance so as to circle it. As he swept past the bows he saw in big letters near the sharp prow the word, Boldero.

"The wreck! The wreck!" he cried, his voice ringing through the craft from end to end. "We've found the wreck at last!"

"Are you sure?" cried his father, hurrying to his son, Captain Weston following.

"Positive," answered the lad. The submarine was slowing up now, and Tom sent her around on the other side. They had a good view of the sunken ship. It seemed to be intact, no gaping holes in her sides, for only her plates had started, allowing her to sink gradually.

"At last," murmured Mr. Swift. "Can it be possible we are about to get the treasure?"

"That's the Boldero, all right," affirmed Captain Weston. "I recognize her, even if the name wasn't on her bow. Go right down on the bottom, Tom, and we'll get out the diving suits and make an examination."

The submarine settled to the ocean bed. Tom glanced at the depth gage. It showed over two miles and a half. Would they be able to venture out into water of such enormous pressure in the comparatively frail diving suits, and wrest the gold from the wreck? It was a serious question.

The Advance came to a stop. In front of her loomed the great bulk of the Boldero, vague and shadowy in the flickering gleam of the searchlight As the gold-seekers looked at her through the bull's-eyes of the conning tower, several great forms emerged from beneath the wreck's bows.

"Deep-water sharks!" exclaimed Captain Weston, "and monsters, too. But they can't bother us. Now to get out the gold!"

ATTACKED BY SHARKS

For a few minutes after reaching the wreck, which had so occupied their thoughts for the past weeks, the adventurers did nothing but gaze at it from the ports of the submarine. The appearance of the deep-water sharks gave them no concern, for they did not imagine the ugly creatures would attack them. The treasure-seekers were more engrossed with the problem of getting out the gold.

"How are we going to get at it?" asked Tom, as he looked at the high sides of the sunken ship, which towered well above the comparatively small Advance.

"Why, just go in and get it," suggested Mr. Damon. "Where is gold in a cargo usually kept, Captain Weston? You ought to know, I should think. Bless my pocketbook!"

"Well, I should say that in this case the bullion would be kept in a safe in the captain's cabin," replied the sailor. "Or, if not there, in some after part of the vessel, away from where the crew is quartered. But it is going to be quite a problem to get at it. We can't climb the sides of the wreck, and it will be impossible to lower her ladder over the side. However, I think we had better get into the diving suits and take a closer look. We can walk around her."

"That's my idea," put in Mr. Sharp. "But who will go, and who will stay with the ship?"

"I think Tom and Captain Weston had better go, suggested Mr. Swift. "Then, in case anything happens, Mr. Sharp, you and I will be on board to manage matters."

"You don't think anything will happen, do you, dad?" asked his son with a laugh, but it was not an easy one, for the lad was thinking of the shadowy forms of the ugly sharks.

"Oh, no, but it's best to be prepared," answered his father.

The captain and the young inventor lost no time in donning the diving suits. They each took a heavy metal bar, pointed at one end, to use in assisting them to walk on the bed of the ocean, and as a protection in case the sharks might attack them. Entering the diving chamber, they were shut in, and then water was admitted until the pressure was seen, by gages, to be the same as that outside the submarine. Then the sliding steel door was opened. At first Tom and the captain could barely move, so great was the pressure of water on their bodies. They would have been crushed but for the protection afforded by the strong diving suits.

In a few minutes they became used to it, and stepped out on the floor of the ocean. They could not, of course, speak to each other, but Tom looked through the glass eyes of his helmet at the captain, and the latter motioned for the lad to follow. The two divers could breathe perfectly, and by means of small, but powerful lights on the helmets, the way was lighted for them as they advanced.

Slowly they approached the wreck, and began a circuit of her. They could see several places where the pressure of the water, and the strain of the storm in which she had foundered, had 'opened the plates of the ship, but in no case were the openings large enough to admit a person. Captain Weston put his steel bar in one crack, and tried to pry it farther open, but his strength was not equal to the task. He made some peculiar motions, but Tom could not understand them.

They looked for some means by which they could mount to the decks of the Boldero, but none was visible. It was like trying to scale a fifty-foot smooth steel wall. There was no place for a foothold. Again the sailor made some peculiar motions, and the lad puzzled over them. They had gone nearly around the wreck now, and as yet had seen no way in which to get at the gold. As they passed around the bow, which was in a deep shadow from a great rock, they caught sight of the submarine lying a short distance away. Light streamed from many hull's-eyes, and Tom felt a sense of security as he looked at her, for it was lonesome enough in that great depth of water, unable to speak to his companion, who was a few feet in advance.

Suddenly there was a swirling of the water, and Tom was nearly thrown off his feet by the rush of some great body. A long, black shadow passed over his head, and an instant later he saw the form of a great shark launched at Captain Weston. The lad involuntarily cried in alarm, but the result was surprising. He was nearly deafened by his own voice, confined as the sound was in the helmet he wore. But the sailor, too, had felt the movement of the water, and turned just in time. He thrust upward with his pointed bar. But he missed the stroke, and Tom, a moment later, saw the great fish turn over so that its mouth, which is far underneath its snout, could take in the queer shape which the shark evidently thought was a choice morsel. The big fish did actually get the helmet of Captain Weston inside its jaws, but probably it would have found it impossible to crush the strong steel. Still it might have sprung the joints, and water would have entered, which would have been as fatal as though the sailor had been swallowed by the shark. Tom realized this and, moving as fast as he could through the water, he came up behind the monster and drove his steel bar deep into it.

The sea was crimsoned with blood, and the savage creature, opening its mouth, let go of the captain. It turned on Tom, who again harpooned it. Then the fish darted off and began a wild flurry, for it was dying. The rush of water nearly threw Tom off his feet, but he managed to make his way over to his friend, and assist him to rise. A confident look from the sailor showed the lad that Captain Weston was uninjured, though he must have been frightened. As the two turned to make their way back to the submarine, the waters about them seemed alive with the horrible monsters.

It needed but a glance to show what they were, Sharks! Scores of them, long, black ones, with their ugly, undershot mouths. They had been attracted by the blood of the one Tom had killed, but there was not a meal for all of them off the dying creature, and the great fish might turn on the young inventor and his companion.

The two shrank closer toward the wreck. They might get under the prow of that and be safe. But even as they started to move, several of the sea wolves darted quickly at them. Tom glanced at the captain. What could they do? Strong as were the diving suits, a combined attack by the sharks, with their powerful jaws, would do untold damage.

At that moment there seemed some movement on board the submarine. Tom could see his father looking from the conning tower, and the aged inventor seemed to be making some motions. Then Tom understood. Mr. Swift was directing his son and Captain Weston to crouch down. The lad did so, pulling the sailor after him. Then Tom saw the bow electric gun run out, and aimed at the mass of sharks, most of whom were congregated about the dead one. Into the midst of the monsters was fired a number of small projectiles, which could be used in the electric cannon in place of the solid shot. Once more the waters were red with blood, and those sharks which were not killed swirled off. Tom and Captain Weston were saved. They were soon inside the submarine again. telling their thrilling story.

"It's lucky you saw us, dad," remarked the lad, blushing at the praise Mr. Damon bestowed on him for killing the monster which had attacked the captain.

"Oh, I was on the lookout," said the inventor. "But what about getting into the wreck?"

"I think the only way we can do it will be to ram a hole in her side," said Captain Weston. "That was what I tried to tell Tom by motions, but he didn't seem to understand me."

"No," replied the lad, who was still a little nervous from his recent experience. "I thought you meant for us to turn it over, bottom side up," and he laughed.

"Bless my gizzard! Just like a shark," commented Mr. Damon.

"Please don't mention them," begged Tom. "I hope we don't see any more of them."

"Oh, I fancy they have been driven far enough away from this neighborhood now," commented the captain. "But now about the wreck. We may be able to approach it from above. Suppose we try to lower the submarine on it? That will save ripping it open."

This was tried a little later, but would not work. There were strong currents sweeping over the top of the Boldero, caused by a submerged reef near which she had settled. It was a delicate task to sink the submarine on her decks, and with the deep waters swirling about was found to be impossible, even with the use of the electric plates and the auxiliary screws. Once more the Advance settled to the ocean bed, near the wreck.

"Well, what's to be done?" asked Tom, as he looked at the high steel sides.

"Ram her, tear a hole, and then use dynamite," decided Captain Weston promptly. "You have some explosive, haven't you, Mr. Swift?"

"Oh, yes. I came prepared for emergencies."

"Then we'll blow up the wreck and get at the gold."

Ramming the Wreck

Fitted with a long, sharp steel ram in front, the Advance was peculiarly adapted for this sort of work. In designing the ship this ram was calculated to be used against hostile vessels in war time, for the submarine was at first, as we know, destined for a Government boat. Now the ram was to serve a good turn.

To make sure that the attempt would be a success, the machinery of the craft was carefully gone over. It was found to be in perfect order, save for a few adjustments which were needed. Then, as it was night, though there was no difference in the appearance of things below the surface, it was decided to turn in, and begin work in the morning. Nor did the gold-seekers go to the surface, for they feared they might encounter a storm.

"We had trouble enough locating the wreck, said Captain Weston, "and if we go up we may be blown off our course. We have air enough to stay below, haven't we, Tom?"

"Plenty," answered the lad, looking at the gages.

After a hearty breakfast the next morning, the submarine crew got ready for their hard task. The craft was backed away as far as was practical, and then, running at full speed, she rammed the wreck. The shock was terrific, and at first it was feared some damage had been done to the Advance, but she stood the strain.

"Did we open up much of a hole?" anxiously asked Mr. Swift.

"Pretty good," replied Tom, observing it through the conning tower bull's-eyes, when the submarine had backed off again. "Let's give her another."

Once more the great steel ram hit into the side of the Boldero, and again the submarine shivered from the shock. But there was a bigger hole in the wreck now, and after Captain Weston had viewed it he decided it was large enough to allow a person to enter and place a charge of dynamite so that the treasure ship would be broken up.

Tom and the captain placed the explosive. Then the Advance was withdrawn to a safe distance. There was a dull rumble, a great swirling of the water, which was made murky; but when it cleared, and the submarine went back, it was seen that the wreck was effectively broken up. It was in two parts, each one easy of access.

"That's the stuff!" cried Tom. "Now to get at the gold!"

"Yes, get out the diving suits," added Mr. Damon. "Bless my watch-charm, I think I'll chance it in one myself! Do you think the sharks are all gone, Captain Weston?"

"I think so."

In a short time Tom, the captain, Mr. Sharp and Mr. Damon were attired in the diving suits, Mr. Swift not caring to venture into such a great depth of water. Besides, it was necessary for at least one person to remain in the submarine to operate the diving chamber.

Walking slowly along the bottom of the sea the four gold- seekers approached the wreck. They looked on all sides for a sight of the sharks, but the monster fish seemed to have deserted that part of the ocean. Tom was the first to reach the now disrupted steamer. He found he could easily climb up, for boxes and barrels from the cargo holds were scattered all about by the explosion. Captain Weston soon joined the lad. The sailor motioned Tom to follow him, and being more familiar with ocean craft the captain was permitted to take the lead. He headed aft, seeking to locate the captain's cabin. Nor was he long in finding it. He motioned for the others to enter, that the combined illumination of the lamps in their helmets would make the place bright enough so a search could be made for the gold. Tom suddenly seized the arm of the captain, and pointed to one corner of the cabin. There stood a small safe, and at the sight of it Captain Weston moved toward it. The door was not locked, probably having been left open when the ship was deserted. Swinging it back the interior was revealed.

It was empty. There was no gold bullion in it.

There was no mistaking the dejected air of Captain Weston. The others shared his feelings, but though they all felt like voicing their disappointment, not a word could be spoken. Mr. Sharp, by vigorous motions, indicated to his companions to seek further.

They did so, spending all the rest of the day in the wreck, save for a short interval for dinner. But no gold rewarded their search.

Tom, late that afternoon, wandered away from the others, and found himself in the captain's cabin again, with the empty safe showing dimly in the water that was all about.

"Hang it all!" thought the lad, "we've had all our trouble for nothing! They must have taken the gold with them."

Idly he raised his steel bar, and struck it against the partition back of the safe. To his astonishment the partition seemed to fall inward, revealing a secret compartment. The lad leaned forward to bring the light for his helmet to play on the recess. He saw a number of boxes, piled one upon the other. He had accidentally touched a hidden spring and opened a secret receptacle. But what did it contain?

Tom reached in and tried to lift one of the boxes. He found it beyond his strength. Trembling from excitement, he went in search of the others. He found them delving in the after part of the wreck, but by motions our hero caused them to follow him. Captain Weston showed the excitement he felt as soon as he caught sight of the boxes. He and Mr. Sharp lifted one out, and placed it on the cabin floor. They pried off the top with their bars.

There, packed in layers, were small yellow bars; dull, gleaming, yellow bars! It needed but a glance to show that they were gold bullion. Tom had found the treasure. The lad tried to dance around there in the cabin of the wreck, nearly three miles below the surface of the ocean, but the pressure of water was too much for him. Their trip had been successful.

HOME WITH THE GOLD

There was no time to be lost. They were in a treacherous part of the ocean, and strong currents might at any time further break up the wreck, so that they could not come at the gold. It was decided, by means of motions, to at once transfer the treasure to the submarine. As the boxes were too heavy to carry easily, especially as two men, who were required to lift one, could not walk together in the uncertain footing afforded by the wreck, another plan was adopted. The boxes were opened and the bars, a few at a time, were dropped on a firm, sandy place at the side of the wreck. Tom and Captain Weston did this work, while Mr. Sharp and Mr. Damon carried the bullion to the diving chamber of the Advance. They put the yellow bars inside, and when quite a number had been thus shifted, Mr. Swift, closing the chamber, pumped the water out and removed the gold. Then he opened the chamber to the divers again, and the process was repeated, until all the bullion had been secured.

Tom would have been glad to make a further examination of the wreck, for he thought he could get some of the rifles the ship carried, but Captain Weston signed to him not to attempt this.

The lad went to the pilot house, while his father and Mr. Sharp took their places in the engine-room. The gold had been safely stowed in Mr. Swift's cabin.

Tom took a last look at the wreck before he gave the starting signal. As he gazed at the bent and twisted mass of steel that had once been a great ship, he saw something long, black and shadowy moving around from the other side, coming across the bows.

"There's another big shark," he observed to Captain Weston. "They're coming back after us."

The captain did not speak. He was staring at the dark form. Suddenly, from what seemed the pointed nose of it, there gleamed a light, as from some great eye.

"Look at that!" cried Tom. "That's no shark!"

"If you want my opinion," remarked the sailor, "I should say it was the other submarine—that of Berg and his friends—the Wonder. They've managed to fix up their craft and are after the gold."

"But they're too late!" cried Tom excitedly. "Let's tell them so."

"No, advised the captain. "We don't want any trouble with them."

Mr. Swift came forward to see why his son had not given the signal to start. He was shown the other submarine, for now that the Wonder had turned on several searchlights, there was no doubt as to the identity of the craft.

"Let's get away unobserved if we can," he suggested. "We have had trouble enough."

It was easy to do this, as the Advance was hidden behind the wreck, and her lights were glowing but dimly. Then, too, those in the other submarine were so excited over the finding of what they supposed was the wreck containing the treasure, that they paid little attention to anything else.

"I wonder how they'll feel when they find the gold gone?" asked Tom as he pulled the lever starting the pumps.

"Well, we may have a chance to learn, when we get back to civilization," remarked the captain.

The surface was soon reached, and then, under fair skies, and on a calm sea, the voyage home was begun. Part of the time the Advance sailed on the top, and part of the time submerged.

They met with but a single accident, and that was when the forward electrical plate broke. But with the aft one still in commission, and the auxiliary screws, they made good time. Just before reaching home they settled down to the bottom and donned the diving suits again, even Mr. Swift taking his turn. Mr. Damon caught some large lobsters, of which he was very fond, or, rather, to be more correct, the lobsters caught him. When he entered the diving chamber there were four fine ones clinging to different parts of his diving suit. Some of them were served for dinner.

The adventurers safely reached the New Jersey coast, and the submarine was docked. Mr. Swift at once communicated with the proper authorities concerning the recovery of the gold. He offered to divide with the actual owners, after he and his friends had been paid for their services, but as the revolutionary party to whom the bullion was intended had gone out of existence, there was no one to officially claim the treasure, so it all went to Tom and his friends, who made an equitable distribution of it. The young inventor did not forget to buy Mrs. Baggert a fine diamond ring, as he had promised.

As for Berg and his employers, they were, it was learned later, greatly chagrined at finding the wreck valueless. They tried to make trouble for Tom and his father, but were not successful.

A few days after arriving at the seacoast cottage, Tom, his father and Mr. Damon went to Shopton in the airship. Captain Weston, Garret Jackson and Mn Sharp remained behind in charge of the submarine. It was decided that the Swifts would keep the craft and not sell it to the Government, as Tom said they might want to go after more treasure some day.

"I must first deposit this gold," said Mr. Swift as the airship landed in front of the shed at his home. "It won't do to keep it in the house over night, even if the Happy Harry gang is in jail."

Tom helped him take it to the bank. As they were making perhaps the largest single deposit ever put in the institution, Ned Newton came out.

"Well, Tom," he cried to his chum, "it seems that you are never going to stop doing things. You've conquered the air, the earth and the water."

"What have you been doing while I've been under water, Ned?" asked the young inventor.

"Oh, the same old thing. Running errands and doing all sorts of work in the bank."

Tom had a sudden idea. He whispered to his father and Mr. Swift nodded. A little later he was closeted with Mr. Prendergast, the bank president. It was not long before Ned and Tom were called in.

"I have some good news for you, Ned," said Mr. Prendergast, while Tom smiled. "Mr. Swift er—ahem—one of our largest depositors, has spoken to me about you, Ned. I find that you have been very faithful. You are hereby appointed assistant cashier, and of course you will get a much larger salary."

Ned could hardly believe it, but he knew then what Tom had whispered to Mr. Swift. The wishes of a depositor who brings much gold bullion to a bank can hardly be ignored.

"Come on out and have some soda," invited Tom, and when Ned looked inquiringly at the president, the latter nodded an assent.

As the two lads were crossing the street to a drug store, something whizzed past them, nearly running them down.

"What sort of an auto was that?" cried Tom.

"That? Oh, that was Andy Foger's new car," answered Ned. "He's been breaking the speed laws every day lately, but no one seems to bother him. It's because his father is rich, I suppose. Andy says he has the fastest car ever built."

"He has, eh?" remarked Tom, while a curious look came into his eyes. "Well, maybe I can build one that will beat his."

And whether the young inventor did or not you can learn by reading the fifth volume of this series, to be called "Tom Swift and His Electric Runabout; Or, The Speediest Car on the Road."

"Well, Tom, I certainly appreciate what you did for me in getting me a better position," remarked Ned as they left the drug store. "I was beginning to think I'd never get promoted. Say, have you anything to do this evening? If you haven't, I wish you'd come over to my house. I've got a lot of pictures I took while you were away."

"Sorry, but I can't," replied Tom.

"Why, are you going to build another airship or submarine?"

"No, but I'm going to see— Oh, what do you want to know for, anyhow?" demanded the young inventor with a blush. "Can't a fellow go see a girl without being cross-questioned?"

"Oh, of course," replied Ned with a laugh. "Give Miss Nestor my regards," and at this Tom blushed still more. But, as he said, that was his own affair.

Tom Swift and His Electric Runabout
(Or The Speediest Car on the Road)

TABLE OF CONTENTS :

Tom Hopes for a Prize

"Father," exclaimed Tom Swift, looking up from a paper he was reading, "I think I can win that prize!"

"What prize is that?" inquired the aged inventor, gazing away from a drawing of a complicated machine, and pausing in his task of making some intricate calculations. "You don't mean to say, Tom, that you're going to have a try for a government prize for a submarine, after all."

"No," not a submarine prize, dad," and the youth laughed. "Though our Advance would take the prize away from almost any other under-water boat, I imagine. No, it's another prize I'm thinking about."

"What do you mean?"

"Well, I see by this paper that the Touring Club of America has offered three thousand dollars for the speediest electric car. The tests are to come off this fall, on a new and specially built track on Long Island, and it's to be an endurance contest for twenty-four hours, or a race for distance, they haven't yet decided. But I'm going to have a try for it, dad, and, besides winning the prize, I think I'll take Andy Foger down a peg."

"What's Andy been doing now?"

"Oh, nothing more than usual. He's always mean, and looking for a chance to make trouble for me, but I didn't refer to anything special He has a new auto, you know, and he boasts that it's the fastest one in this country. I'll show him that it isn't, for I'm going to win this prize with the speediest car on the road."

"But, Tom, you haven't any automobile, you know," and Mr. Swift looked anxiously at his son, who was smiling confidently. "You can't be going to make your motor-cycle into an auto; are you?"

"No, dad."

"Then how are you going to take part in the prize contest? Besides, electric cars, as far as I know, aren't specially speedy."

"I know it, and one reason why this club has arranged the contest is to improve the quality of electric automobiles. I'm going to build an electric runabout, dad."

"An electric runabout? But it will have to be operated with a storage battery, Tom, and you haven't—"

"I guess you're going to say I haven't any storage battery, dad," interrupted Mr. Swift's son. "Well, I haven't yet, but I'm going to have one. I've been working on—"

"Oh, ho!" exclaimed the aged inventor with a laugh. "So that's what you've been tinkering over these last few weeks, eh, Tom? I suspected it was some new invention, but I didn't suppose it was that. Well, how are you coming on with it?"

"Pretty good, I think. I've got a new idea for a battery, and I made an experimental one. I gave it some pretty severe tests, and it worked fine."

"But you haven't tried it out in a car yet, over rough roads, and under severe conditions have you?"

"No, I haven't had a chance. In fact, when I invented the battery I had no idea of using it on a car I thought it might answer for commercial purposes, or for storing a current generated by windmills. But when I read that account in the papers of the Touring Club, offering a prize for the best electric car, it occurred to me that I might put my battery into an auto, and win."

"Hum," remarked Mr. Swift musingly. "I don't take much stock in electric autos, Tom. Gasolene seems to be the best, or perhaps steam, generated by gasolene. I'm afraid you'll be disappointed. All the electric runabouts I ever saw, while they were very nice cars, didn't seem able to go so very fast, or very far."

"That's true, but it's because they didn't have the right kind of a battery. You know an electric locomotive can make pretty good speed, Dad. Over a hundred miles an hour in tests."

"Yes, but they don't run by storage batteries. They have a third rail, and powerful motors," and Mr. Swift looked quizzically at his son. He loved to argue with him, for he said it made Tom think, and often the two would thus thresh out some knotty point of an invention, to the interests of both.

"Of course, Dad, there is a good deal of theory in what I'm thinking of," the lad admitted. "But it does seem to me that if you put the right kind of a battery into an automobile, it could scoot along pretty lively. Look what speed a trolley car can make."

"Yes, Tom, but there again they get their power from an overhead wire."

"Some of them don't. There's a new storage battery been invented by a New Jersey man, which does as well as the third rail or the overhead wire. It was after reading about his battery that I thought of a plan for mine. It isn't anything like his; perhaps not as good in some ways, but, for what I want, it is better in some respects, I think. For one thing it can be recharged very quickly."

"Now Tom, look here," said Mr. Swift earnestly, laying aside his papers, and coming over to where his son sat. "You know I never interfere with your inventions. In fact, the more you think of the better I like it. The airship you helped build certainly did all that could be desired, and—"

"That reminds me. Mr. Sharp and Mr. Damon are out in it now," interrupted Tom. "They ought to be back soon. Yes, Dad, the airship Red Cloud certainly scooted along."

"And the submarine, too," continued the aged inventor. "Your ideas regarding that were of service to me, and helped in our task of recovering the treasure, but I'm afraid you're going to be disappointed in the storage battery. You may get it to work, but I don't believe you can make it powerful enough to attain any great speed. Why don't you confine yourself to making a battery for stationary work?"

"Because, Dad, I believe I can build a speedy car, and I'm going to try it. Besides I want to race Andy Foger, and beat him, even if I don't win the prize. I'm going to build that car, and it will make fast time."

"Well, go ahead, Tom," responded his father, after a pause. "Of course you can use the shops here as much as you want, and Mr. Sharp, Mr. Jackson, and I will help you all we can. Only don't be disappointed, that's all."

"I won't, Dad. Suppose you come out to my shop and I'll show you a sample battery I've been testing for the last week. I have it geared to a small motor, and it's been running steadily for some time. I want to see what sort of a record it's made."

Father and son crossed the yard, and entered a shop which the lad considered exclusively his own. There he had made many machines, and pieces of apparatus, and had invented a number of articles which had been patented, and yielded him considerable of an income.

"There's the battery, Dad," he said, pointing to a complicated mechanism in one corner

"What's that buzzing noise?" asked Mr. Swift. "That's the little motor I run from the new cells. Look here," and Tom switched on an electric light above the experimental battery, from which he hoped so much. It consisted of a steel can, about the size of the square gallon tin in which maple syrup comes, and from it ran two wires which were attached to a small motor that was industriously whirring away.

Tom looked at a registering gauge connected with it.

"That's pretty good," remarked the young inventor.

"What is it, Tom?" and his father peered about the shop.

"Why this motor has run an equivalent of two hundred miles on one charging of the battery! That's much better than I expected. I thought if I got a hundred out of it I'd be doing well. Dad, I believe, after I improve my battery a bit, that I'll have the very thing I want! I'll install a set of them in a car, and it will go like the wind. I'll —" Tom's enthusiastic remarks were suddenly interrupted by a low, rumbling sound.

"Thunder!" exclaimed Mr. Swift. "The storm is coming, and Mr. Sharp and Mr. Damon in the airship—"

Hardly had he spoken than there sounded a crash on the roof of the Swift house, not far away. At the same time there came cries of distress, and the crash was repeated.

"Come on, Dad! Something has happened!" yelled Tom, dashing from the shop, followed by his parent. They found themselves in the midst of a rain storm, as they raced toward the house, on the roof of which the smashing noise was again heard.

Mr. Damon's Steering

Tom Swift was a lad of action, and his quickness in hurrying out to investigate what had happened when he was explaining about his new battery, was characteristic of him. Those of my readers who know him, through having read the previous books of this series, need not be told this, but you who, perhaps, are just making his acquaintance, may care to know a little more about him.

As told in my first book, "Tom Swift and His Motor-Cycle" the young inventor lived with his father, Barton Swift, a widower, in the town of Shopton, New York. Mr. Swift was also an inventor of note.

In my initial volume of this series, Tom became possessed of a motor-cycle in a peculiar way. It was sold to him by a Mr. Wakefield Damon, a wealthy gentleman who was unfortunate in riding it. On his speedy machine, which Tom improved by several inventions, he had a number of adventures. The principal one was being attacked by a number of bad men, known as the "Happy Harry Gang," who wished to obtain possession of a valuable turbine patent model belonging to Mr. Swift. Tom was taking it to a lawyer, when he was waylaid, and chloroformed. Later he traced the gang, and, with the assistance of Mr. Damon and Eradicate Sampson, an aged colored man who made a living for himself and his mule, Boomerang, by doing odd jobs, the lad found the thieves and recovered a motor-boat which had been stolen. But the men got away.

In the second volume, called "Tom Swift and His Motor-Boat," Tom bought at auction the boat stolen by, and recovered from, the thieves, and proceeded to improve it. While he was taking his father out on a cruise for Mr Swift's health, the Happy Harry Gang made a successful attempt to steal some valuable inventions from the Swift house. Tom started to trace them, and incidentally he raced and beat Andy Foger, a rich bully. On their way down the lake, after the robbery, Tom, his father and Ned Newton, Tom's chum, saw a man hanging from the trapeze of a blazing balloon over Lake Carlopa. The balloonist was Mr. John Sharp and he was rescued by Tom in a thrilling fashion. In his motor-boat, Tom had much pleasure, not the least of which was taking out a young lady named Miss Mary Nestor, whose acquaintance he had made after stopping her runaway horse, which his bicycle had frightened. Tom's association with Miss Nestor soon ripened into something deeper than mere friendship.

It developed that Mr Sharp, whom Tom had saved from the burning balloon, was an aeronaut of note, and had once planned to build an airship. After his recovery from his thrilling experience, he mentioned the matter to Mr. Swift and his son, with whom he took up his residence. This fitted right in with Tom's ideas, and soon father, son and the balloonist were constructing the Red Cloud, as they named their airship. It was finally completed, as

related in "Tom Swift and His Airship," made a successful trial trip, and won
a prize. It was planned to make a longer journey, and Tom, Mr. Sharp and
Mr. Damon agreed to go together. Mr. Damon was an odd individual, who was
continuously blessing some part of his anatomy, his clothing or some
inanimate object but, for all that, he was a fine man.

The night before Tom and his friends started off in their airship, the
Shopton Bank vault was blown open and seventy-five thousand dollars was
taken. Tom and his friends did not know of this, but, no sooner had the young
inventor, Mr. Sharp and Mr. Damon sailed away, than the police arrived at
Mr. Swift's house to arrest them. They were charged with the robbery, and
with having sailed away with the booty.

It appeared that Andy Foger said he had seen Tom hanging around the
bank the night of the robbery, with a bag of burglar tools in his possession.
Search was immediately begun for the airship, the occupants of which were,
meanwhile, speeding on.

Tom and his two friends had trouble. They were nearly burned up in a
forest fire, and were fired upon by a crowd of people with rifles, who, reading
of the bank robbery and the reward offered for the capture of the thieves,
hoped to bring down the airship. The fact that they were fired upon caused
Tom and the two aeronauts to descend to make an investigation, and for the
first time they learned of the bank theft. How they got track of the real
robbers, took the sheriff with them in the airship, and raided the gang will be
found set down at length in the book. Also how Tom administered
well-deserved thrashing to Andy Foger.

Mr. Swift did not accompany his son in the airship, and when asked why
he did not care to make the trip, said he was working on a new type of
submarine boat, which he hoped to enter in the government trials, to win a
prize. In the fourth volume of the series, called "Tom Swift and his
Submarine," you may read how successful Mr. Swift was.

When the submarine, called the Advance, was finished, the party made a
trip to recover three hundred thousand dollars in gold from a sunken treasure
ship, off the coast of Uruguay, South America. They sailed beneath the seas
for many miles, and were in great peril at times. One reason for this was that
a rival firm of submarine builders got wind of the treasure, and tried to get
ahead of the Swifts in recovering it. How Tom and his friends succeeded in
their quest, how they nearly perished at the bottom of the sea, how they were
captured by a foreign war vessel, and sentenced to death, how they fought
with a school of giant sharks and how they blew up the wreck to recover the
money is all told of in the book.

On their return to civilization with the gold, Mr. Swift, Tom, and their
friends deposited the money in the Shopton Bank, where Ned Newton
worked. Ned was a bright lad, but had not been advanced as rapidly as he
deserved, and Tom knew this. He asked his father to speak to the president,
Mr. Pendergast, in Ned's behalf, and, as a result the lad was made assistant

cashier, for the request of a man who controlled a three hundred thousand dollar deposit was not to be despised.

In building the submarine Tom and his father rented a large cottage on the New Jersey seacoast, but, on returning from their treasure-quest they went back to Shopton, leaving the submarine at the boathouse of the shore cottage, which was near the city of Atlantis. That was in the fall of the year, and all that winter the young inventor had been busy on many things, not the least of which was his storage battery. It was now spring, and seeing the item in the paper, about the touring club prize for an electric auto, had given him a new idea.

But all thoughts of electric cars, and everything else, were driven from the mind of the young man, when, with his father, he rushed out to see the cause of the crash on the roof of the Swift homestead.

"There's something up there, Tom," called his father, as he splashed on through the rain.

"That's right," added his son. "And somebody, too, to judge by the fuss they're making."

"Maybe the house has been struck by lightning!" suggested the aged inventor.

"No, the storm isn't severe enough for that; and, besides, if the house had been struck you'd hear Mrs. Baggert yelling, Dad. She—"

At that moment a woman's voice cried out:

"Mr. Swift! Tom! Where are you? Something dreadful has happened!"

"There she goes!" remarked Mr. Swift, as he splashed into a mud puddle.

"Bless my deflection rudder!" suddenly cried a voice from the flat roof of the Swift house. "Hello! I say, is anyone down there?"

"Yes, we are," answered Tom. "Is that you, Mr. Damon?"

"Bless my collar button! It certainly is."

"Where's Mr. Sharp? I don't hear him."

"Oh, I'm here all right," answered the balloonist. "I'm trying to get the airship clear of the chimney. Mr. Damon—"

"Yes, I steered wrong!" interrupted the odd man. "Bless my liver pin, but it was so dark I couldn't see, and when that clap of thunder came I shifted the deflection rudder instead of the lateral one, and tried to knock over your chimney."

"Are either of you hurt?" asked Mr. Swift anxiously.

"No, not at all," replied Mr. Sharp. "We were moving slowly, ready for a landing."

"Is the airship damaged?" inquired Tom.

"I don't know. Not much, I guess," was the answer of the aeronaut. "I've stopped the engine, and I don't like to start it again until I can see what shape we're in."

"I'll come up, with Mr. Jackson," called Tom, and he hastily summoned Garret Jackson, an engineer, who had been in the service of Mr. Swift for many years. Together they proceeded to the roof by a stairway that led to a scuttle.

"Is anyone killed?" asked Mrs. Baggert, as Tom hurried up the stairs. "Don't tell me there is, Tom!"

"Well, I don't have to tell you, for no one is," replied the young inventor with a laugh. "It's all right. The airship tried to collide with the chimney, that's all."

He was soon on the large, flat roof of the dwelling, and, with the aid of lanterns he, the engineer, and Mr. Sharp made a hasty examination.

"Anything wrong?" inquired Mr. Damon, looking out from the cabin of the Red Cloud where he had taken refuge after the crash, and to get out of the wet.

"Not much," answered Tom. "One of the forward planes is smashed, but we can rise by means of the gas, and float down. Is all clear, Mr. Sharp?"

"All clear," replied the balloonist, for the airship had now been wheeled back from the entanglement with the chimney.

"Then here we go!" cried Tom, as he and the aeronaut entered the craft, while Mr. Jackson descended through the scuttle.

There came a fiercer burst to the storm, and, amid a series of dazzling lightning flashes and the muttering of thunder, the airship rose from the roof. Tom switched on the search-light, and, starting the big propellers, guided the craft skillfully toward the big shed where it was housed when not in use.

With the grace of a bird it turned about in the air, and settled to the ground. It was the work of but a few minutes to run it into the shed. Then they all started for the house.

"Bless my umbrella! How it rains!" cried Mr. Damon, as he splashed on through numerous puddles. "We got back just in time, Mr. Sharp."

"Where did you go?" asked the lad.

"Why we took a flight of about fifty miles and stopped at my house in Waterfield for supper. Were you anxious about us?"

"A little when it began to storm," replied Tom.

"Anything new since we left?" asked Mr. Sharp, for it was the custom of himself, or some of his friends, to take little trips in the airship. They thought no more of it than many do of going for a short spin in an automobile.

"Yes, there is something new," said Mr. Swift, as the party, all drenched now, reached the broad veranda.

"Bless my gaiters!" cried Mr. Damon. "What is it? I hope the Happy Harry gang hasn't robbed you again; nor Berg and his men tried to take that treasure away from us, after we worked so hard to get it from the wreck."

"No, it isn't that," replied Mr. Swift. "The truth is that Tom thinks he has invented a storage battery that will revolutionize matters. He's going to build an electric automobile, he says."

"I am," declared the lad, as the others looked at him, "and it will be the speediest one you ever saw, too!"

THE MOTOR-CYCLE WINS

"Well, Tom," remarked Mr. Sharp, after a pause following the lad's announcement. "I didn't know you had any ambitions in that line. Tell us more about the battery. What system do you use; lead plates and sulphuric acid?"

"Oh, that's out of date long ago," declared the lad.

"Well, I don't know much about electricity," admitted the aeronaut. "I'll take my chances in an airship or a balloon, but when it comes to electricity I'm down and out."

"So am I," admitted Mr. Damon. "Bless my gizzard, it's all I can do to put a new spark plug in my automobile. Where is your new battery, Tom?"

"Out in my shop, running yet if it hasn't been frightened by the airship smash," replied the lad, somewhat proudly. "It's an oxide of nickel battery, with steel and oxide of iron negative electrodes."

"What solution do you use, Tom?" asked Mr. Swift. "I didn't get that far in questioning you before the crash came," he added.

"Well I have, in the experimental battery, a solution of potassium hydrate," replied the lad, "but I think I'm going to change it, and add some lithium hydrate to it. I think that will make it stronger."

"Bless my watch chain!" exclaimed Mr. Damon. "It's all Greek to me. Suppose you let us see it, Tom? I like to see wheels go 'round, but I'm not much of a hand for chemical terms."

"If you're sure you're not hurt by the airship smash, I will," declared the lad.

"Oh, we're not hurt a bit," insisted Mr. Sharp. "As I said we were moving slow, for I knew it was about time to land. Mr. Damon was steering—"

"Yes I thought I'd try my hand at it, as it seemed so easy," interrupted the eccentric man. "But never again—not for mine! I couldn't see the house, and, before I knew it we were right over the roof. Then the chimney seemed to stick itself up suddenly in front of us, and—well, you know the rest. I'm willing to pay for any damage I caused."

"Oh, not at all!" replied Tom. "It's easy enough to put on a new plane, or, for that matter, we can operate the Red Cloud without it. But come on, I'll show you my sample battery."

"Here, take umbrellas!" Mrs. Baggert called after them as they started toward the shop, for it was still raining.

"We don't mind getting wet," replied the young inventor. "It's in the interests of science."

"Maybe it is. You don't mind a wetting, but I mind you coming in and dripping water all over the carpets!" retorted the housekeeper.

"Bless my overshoes, I'm afraid we have wet the carpets a trifle now," admitted Mr. Damon ruefully, as he looked down at a puddle, which had formed where he had been standing.

"That's the reason I want you to take umbrellas this trip," insisted Mrs. Baggert.

They complied, and were soon in the shop, where Tom explained his battery. The small motor was still running and had, as the lad had said, gone the equivalent of over two hundred miles.

"If a small battery does as well as that, what will a larger one do?" asked Mr. Damon.

"Much better, I hope," replied the youth. "But Dad doesn't seem to have much faith in them."

"Well," admitted Mr. Swift, "I must say I am skeptical. Still, I acknowledge Tom has done some pretty good work along electrical lines. He helped me with the positive and negative plates on the submarine, and, maybe—well, we'll wait and see," he concluded.

"If you build a car I hope you give me a ride in it," said Mr. Damon. "I've ridden fast in the air, and swiftly on top of, and under, the water. Now I'd like to ride rapidly on top of the earth. The gasolene auto doesn't go very fast."

"I'll give you a ride that will make your hair stand up!" prophesied Tom, and the time was to come when he would make good that prediction.

The little party in the machine shop talked at some length about Tom's battery. He showed them how it was constructed, and gave them some of his ideas regarding the new type of auto he planned to build.

"Well," remarked Mr. Swift at length, "if you want to keep your brain fresh, Tom, you must get to bed earlier than this. It's nearly twelve o'clock."

"And I want to get up early!" exclaimed the lad. "I'm going to start to build a larger battery to-morrow."

"And I'm going to repair the airship," added Mr. Sharp.

"Bless my night cap, I promised my wife I'd be home early to- night, too!" suddenly exclaimed Mr. Damon. "I don't fancy making the trip back to Waterfield in my auto, though. Something will be sure to happen. I'll blow out a tire, or a spark plug will get sooty on me and—"

"It's raining harder than ever," interrupted Tom. "Better stay here to-night. You can telephone home." Which Mr. Damon did.

Tom was up early the next morning, in spite of the fact that he did not go to bed in good season, and before breakfast he was working at his new storage battery. After the meal he hurried back to the shop, but it was not long before he came out, wheeling his motor-cycle.

"Where are you going, Tom?" asked Mrs. Baggert.

"Oh, I've got to go to Mansburg to get some steel tubes for my new battery," he replied. "I thought I had some large enough, but I haven't." Mansburg was a good-sized town, near Shopton.

"Then I wish you'd bring me a bottle of stove polish," requested the housekeeper. "The liquid kind. I'm out of it, and the stove is as red as a cow."

"All right," agreed the lad, as he leaped into the saddle and pedaled off down the road. A moment later he had turned on the power, and was speeding along the highway, which was in good condition on account of the shower of the night before.

Tom was thinking so deeply of his new invention, and planning what he would do when he had his electric runabout built, that, almost before he knew it, he had reached Mansburg, purchased the steel tubes, and the stove polish, and was on his way back again.

As he was speeding along on a level road, he heard, coming behind him, an automobile. The lad turned to one side, but, in spite of this the party in the car began a serenade of the electric siren, and kept it up, making a wild discord.

"What's the matter with those fellows!" inquired Tom of himself. "Haven't I given them enough of the road, or has their steering gear broken?"

He looked back over his shoulder, and it needed but a glance to show that the car was all right, as regarded the steering apparatus. And it needed only another glance to disclose the reason for the shrill sound of the siren.

"Andy Foger!" exclaimed Tom. "I might have known. And Sam and Pete are with him. Well, if he wants to make me get off the road, he'll find that I've got as much right as he has!"

He kept on a straight course, wondering if the red-haired, and squint-eyed bully would dare try to damage the motor-cycle.

A little later Andy's car was beside Tom.

"Why don't you get out of the way," demanded Sam, who could usually be depended on to aid Andy in all his mean tricks.

"Because I'm entitled to half the road," retorted our hero.

"Humph! A slow-moving machine like yours hasn't any right on the road," sneered Andy, who had slowed down his car somewhat.

"I haven't, eh?" demanded Tom. "Well, if you'll get down out of that car for a few minutes I'll soon show you what my rights are!"

Now Andy, more than once, had come to personal encounters with Tom, much to the anguish of the bully. He did not relish another chastisement, but his mean spirit could not brook interference.

"Don't you want a race?" he inquired of Tom, in a sneering tone. "I'll give you a mile start, and beat you! I've got the fastest car built!"

"You have, eh?" asked Tom, while a grim look came over his face. "Maybe you'll think differently some day."

"Aw, he's afraid to race; come on," suggested Pete. "Don't bother with him, Andy."

"No, I guess it wouldn't be worth my while," was the reply of the bully, and he threw the second gear into place, and began to move away from the young inventor.

Tom was just as much pleased to be left alone, but he did not want Andy Foger to think that he could have matters all his own way. Tom's motor-cycle, since he had made some adjustments to it, was very swift. In fact there were few autos that could beat it. He had never tried it against Andy's new car, and he was anxious to do so.

"I wonder if I would stand any chance, racing him?" thought the young inventor, as he saw the car slowly pulling away from him. "I think I'll wait until he gets some distance ahead, and then I'll see how near I can come to him. If I get anywhere near him I'm pretty sure I can pass him. I'll try it."

When Andy and his cronies looked back, Tom did not appear to be doing anything save moving along at moderate speed on his machine.

"You don't dare race!" Pete Bailey shouted to him.

"Wait," was what Tom whispered to himself.

Andy's car was now some distance ahead. The young inventor waited a little longer, and then turned more power into his machine. It leaped forward and began to "eat up the road," as Tom expressed it. He had seen Andy throw in the third gear, but knew that there was a fourth speed on the bully's car.

"I don't know whether I can beat him on that or not," thought the lad dubiously. "If I try, and fail, they'll laugh at me. But I don't think I'm going to fail."

Faster and faster he rode. He was rapidly overhauling Andy's car now, and, as they heard him approach, the three cronies turned around.

"He's going to race you, after all, Andy!" cried Sam.

"You mean he's going to try," sneered Andy. "I'll give him all the racing he wants!"

In another few seconds Tom was beside the auto, and would have passed it, only Andy opened his throttle a little more. For a moment the auto jumped ahead, and then, as our hero turned on still more power, he easily held his own.

"Aw, you can never beat us!" yelled Pete.

"Of course not!" added Sam.

"I'll leave him behind in a second," prophesied Andy. "Wait until I throw in the other gear," he added to his cronies in a low voice. "He thinks he's going to beat me. I'll let him think so, and then I'll spurt ahead."

The two machines were now racing along side by side. Andy's car was going the limit on third gear, but he still had the fourth gear in reserve. Tom, too, still had a little margin of speed.

Suddenly Andy reached forward and yanked on a lever. There was a grinding of cogs as the fourth gear slipped into place, for Andy did not handle his car skillfully. The effect, however, was at once apparent. The automobile shot forward.

"Now where are you, Tom Swift?" cried Sam.

Tom said nothing. He merely shifted a lever, and got a better spark. He also turned on a little more gasolene and opened the muffler The quickness with which his motor-cycle shot forward almost threw him from the saddle, but he had a tight grip on the handle bars. He whizzed past the auto, but, as the latter gathered speed, it crept up to him, and, once more was on even terms.

Much chagrined at seeing Tom hold pace with him, even for an instant, Andy shouted;

"Get over on your own side there! You're crowding me!"

"I am not!" yelled back Tom, above the explosions of his machine.

The two were now racing furiously, and Andy, with a savage look, tried to get more speed out of his car. In spite of all the bully did, Tom was gradually forging ahead. A little hill was now in view.

"Here's where I make him take my dust!" cried Andy, but, to his surprise Tom still kept ahead. The auto began to lose ground, for it was not made to take hills on high gear.

"Change to third gear quick!" cried Sam.

Andy tried to do it. There was a hesitancy on the part of his car. It seemed to balk. Tom, looking back, slowed up a trifle. He could afford to, as Andy was being beaten.

"Go on! Go on!" begged Pete. "You'll have to keep on fourth gear to beat him, Andy."

"That's what!" murmured the bully. Once more he shifted the gears. There was a grinding, smashing sound, and the car lost speed. Then it slowed up still more, and finally stopped. Then it began to back down hill.

"I've stripped those blamed gears!" exclaimed Andy ruefully.

"Can't you beat him?" asked Pete.

"I could have, easily, if my gears hadn't broken," declared the bully, but, as a matter of fact, he could not have done so. "I oughtn't to have changed, going up hill," he added, as he jammed on the brakes, to stop the car from sliding down the slope.

Tom saw and heard.

"I thought you were so anxious to race," he said, exultantly, as well he might. "I don't want to try a contest down hill, though, Andy," and he laughed at the red-haired lad, who was furious.

"Aw, go on!" was all the retort the squint-eyed one could think of to make.

"I am going on," replied our hero. "Just to show you that I can go down hill, watch me."

He turned his motor-cycle, and approached Andy's stalled car, for Tom was some distance in advance of it, up the slope by this time. As he approached the auto, containing the three disconcerted cronies, something bounded out of Tom's pocket. It was the bottle of stove blacking he had purchased for Mrs. Baggert. The bottle fell in the soft dirt in front of his forward wheel, and a curious thing happened. Perhaps you have seen a bicycle or auto tire strike a stone at an angle, and throw it into the air with great force. That was what happened to the bottle. Tom's front wheel struck the cork, which fitted tightly, and, just as when you hit one end of the wooden "catty" and it bounds up, the bottle described a curve through the air, and flew straight toward Andy's car. It struck the brass frame of the wind shield with a crash.

The bottle broke, and in an instant the black liquid was spattered all over Andy, Sam and Pete. It could not have been done more effectively if Tom had thrown it by hand. All over their clothes, their hands and faces, and the front of the car went the dreary black. Tom looked on, hardly able to believe what he saw.

"Wow! Wup! Ug! Blug! Mug!" spluttered Sam, who had some of the stuff in his mouth.

"Oh! Oh!" yelled Pete.

"You did that on purpose, Tom Swift!" shouted Andy, wiping some of the blacking from his left eye. "I'll have you arrested for that! You've ruined my car, and look at my suit!"

"Mine's worse!" murmured Sam, glancing down at his light trousers, which were of the polka-dot pattern now.

"No, mine is," insisted Pete, whose white shirt was of the hue of a stove pipe.

Andy wiped some of the black stuff from his nose, whence it was dropping on the steering wheel.

"You just wait!" the bully called to Tom. "I'll get even with you for this!"

"It was an accident! I didn't mean to do that," explained Tom, trying not to laugh, as he dismounted from his motorcycle, ready to render what assistance he could.

TALK OF A NEW BANK

The three cronies were in a sorrowful plight. The black fluid dripped from them, and formed little puddles in the car. Andy had used his handkerchief to wipe some of the stuff from his face, but the linen was soon useless, for it quickly absorbed the blacking.

"There's a little brook over here," volunteered Tom. "You might wash in that. The stuff comes off easily. It isn't like ink," and he had to laugh, as he thought of the happening.

"Here! You quit that!" ordered Andy. "You've gone too far, Tom Swift!"

"Didn't I tell you it was an accident?" inquired the young inventor.

"It wasn't!" cried Sam. "You threw the bottle at us! I saw you!"

"It slipped from my pocket," declared the youth, and he described how the accident occurred. "I'll help you clean your car, Andy," he added.

"I don't want your help! If you come near me I'll—I'll punch your nose!" cried Andy, now almost beside himself with rage.

"All right, if you don't want my help I don't care," answered Tom, glad enough not to have to soil his hands and clothes. He felt that it was partly his fault, and he would have done all he could to remedy matters, but his good offers being declined, he felt that it was useless to insist further.

He remounted his motor-cycle, and rode off, the last view he had of the trio being one where they were at the edge of the brook, trying to remove the worst traces of the black fluid. As Tom turned around for a final glimpse, Andy shook his fist at him, and called out something.

"I guess Andy'll have it in for me," mused Tom. "Well, I can't help it. I owed him something on account, but I didn't figure on paying it in just this way," and he thought of the time the bully had locked him in the ballast tanks of the submarine, thereby nearly smothering him to death.

That night Andy Foger told his father what had happened, for Mr. Foger inquired the reason for the black stains on his son's face and hands. But Andy did not give the true version. He said Tom had purposely thrown the bottle of blacking at him.

"So that's the kind of a lad Tom Swift is, eh?" remarked Andy's father. "Well, Andy, I think you will soon have a chance to get even with him."

"How, pop?"

"I can't tell you now, but I have a plan for making Tom sorry he ever did anything to you, and I will also pay back some old scores to Mr. Swift and Mr. Damon. I'll ruin their bank for them, that's what I'll do."

"Ruin their bank, pop? How?"

"You wait and see. The Swift crowd will get off their high horse soon, or I'm mistaken. My plans are nearly completed, but I can't tell you about them. I'll ruin Mr. Swift, though, that's what I'll do," and Mr. Foger shook his head determinedly.

Tom was soon at his home, and Mrs. Baggert, hearing the noise of his machine, as it entered the front yard, came to the side door.

"Where's my blacking?" she asked, as our hero dismounted and untied the bundle of steel tubes he had purchased.

"I—I used it," he answered, laughing.

"Tom Swift! You don't mean to say you took my stove polish to use in your battery, do you?"

"No, I used it to polish off Andy Foger and some of his cronies," and the young inventor told, with much gusto, what had happened. Mrs. Baggert could not help joining in the laugh, and when Tom offered to ride back and purchase some more of the polish for her, she said it did not matter, as she could wait until the next day.

The lad was soon busy in his machine shop, making several larger cells for the new storage battery. He wanted to give it a more severe test. He worked for several days on this, and when he had one unit of cells complete, he attached the motor for an efficiency trial.

"We'll see how many miles that will make," he remarked to his father.

"Have you thought anything of the type of car you are going to build?" asked the aged inventor of his son.

"Yes, somewhat. It will be almost of the regulation style, but with two removable seats at the rear, with curtains for protection, and a place in front for two persons. This can also be protected with curtains when desired."

"But what about the motors and the battery?"

They will be located under the middle of the car. There will be one set of batteries there, together with the motor, and another set of batteries will be placed under the removable seats in what I call the tonneau, though, of course, it isn't really that. A smaller set will also be placed forward, and there will be ample room for carrying tools and such things."

"About how far do you expect your car will go with one charging of the battery?"

"Well, if I can make it do three hundred miles I'll be satisfied, but I'm going to try for four hundred."

"What will you do when your battery runs out?"

"Recharge it."

"Suppose you're not near a charging station?" "Well, Dad, of course those are some of the details I've got to work out. I'm planning a register gauge now, that will give warning about fifty miles before the battery is run down. That will leave me a margin to work on. And I'm going to have it fixed so I can take current from any trolley line, as well as from a regular charging station. My battery will be capable of being recharged very quickly, or, in case of need, I can take out the old cells and put in new ones.

"That's a very good idea. Well, I hope you succeed."

A few evenings after this, when Tom was busy in his machine shop, he heard some one enter. He looked up from the gauge of the motor, which he was studying, and, for a moment, he could make out nothing in the dark interior of the shop, for he was working in a brilliant light.

"Who's there?" he called sharply, for, more than once unscrupulous men had endeavored to sneak into the Swift shops to steal ideas of inventions; if not the actual apparatus itself.

"It's me—Ned Newton," was the cheerful reply.

"Oh, hello, Ned! I was wondering what had become of you," responded Tom. "Where have you been lately?"

"Oh, working overtime."

"What's the occasion?"

"We're trying out a new system to increase the bank business."

"What's the matter? Aren't you folks getting business enough, after the big deposits we made of the bullion from the wreck?"

"Oh, it's not that. But haven't you heard the news? There is talk of starting a rival bank in Shopton, and that may make us hustle to hold what business we have, to say nothing of getting new customers."

"A new bank, eh? Who's going to start it?" "Andy Foger's father, I hear. You know he was a director in our bank, but he got out last week."

"What for?"

"Well, he had some difficulty with Mr. Pendergast, the president. I fancy you had something to do with it, too."

"I?" Tom was plainly surprised.

"Yes, you know you and Mr. Damon and Mr. Sharp captured the bank robbers, and got back most of the money."

"I guess I do remember it! I wish you could have seen the gang when we raided them from the clouds, in our airship!"

"Well, you know Andy Foger hoped to collect the five thousand dollars reward for telling the police that you were the thief, and of course he got fooled, for you got the reward. Mr. Foger expected his son would collect the money, and when Andy got left, it made him sore. He's had a grudge against Mr. Pendergast, and all the other bank officials ever since, and now he's going to start a rival bank. So that's why I said it was partly due to you."

"Oh, I see. I thought at first you meant that it was on account of something that happened the other day."

"What was that?"

"Andy, Sam and Pete got the contents of a bottle of stove blacking," and Tom related the occurrence, at which Ned laughed heartily.

"I wouldn't be surprised though," added Ned, "to learn that Mr. Foger started the new bank more for revenge than anything else."

"So that's the reason you've been working late, eh?" went on Tom. "Getting ready for competition. Do you think a new bank will hurt the one you're with?"

"Well, it might," admitted Ned. "It's bound to make a change, anyhow, and now that I have a good position I don't want to lose it. I take more of an interest in the institution now that I'm assistant cashier, than I did when I was a clerk. So, naturally, I'm a little worried."

"Say, don't let it worry you," begged Tom, earnestly.

"Why not?"

"Because I know my father and Mr. Damon will stick to the old bank. They won't have anything to do with the one Andy Foger's father starts. Don't you worry."

"Well, that will help some," declared Ned. "They are both heavy depositors, and if they stick to the old bank we can stand it even if some of our smaller customers desert us."

"That's the way to talk," went on the young inventor. "Let Foger start his bank. It won't hurt yours."

"What are you making now?" asked Ned, a little later, looking with interest at the machinery over which Tom was bending, and to which he was making adjustments.

"New electric automobile. I want to beat Andy Foger's car worse than I did on my motorcycle, and I also want to win a prize," and the lad proceeded to relate the incidents leading up to his construction of the storage battery.

Tom and Ned were in the shop until long past midnight, and then the bank employee, with a look at his watch, exclaimed:

"Great Scott! I ought to be home."

"I'll run you over in Mr. Damon's car," proposed Tom. "He left it here the other day, while he and his wife went off on a trip, and he said I could use it whenever I wanted to."

"Good!" cried Ned.

The two lads came from Tom's particular workshop. As the young inventor closed the door he started suddenly, as he snapped shut the lock.

"What's the matter?" asked Ned quickly.

"I thought I heard a noise," replied Tom.

They both listened. There was a slight rustling in some bushes near the shop.

"It's a dog or a cat," declared Ned.

Tom took several cautious steps forward. Then he gave a spring, and made a grab for some one or something.

"Here! You let me be!" yelled a protesting voice.

"I will when I find out what you mean by sneaking around here," retorted Tom, as he came back toward Ned, dragging with him a lad. "It wasn't a dog or a cat, Ned," spoke the young inventor. "It's Sam Snedecker," and so it proved.

"You let me alone!" demanded Andy Foger's crony. "I ain't done nothin' to you," he whined.

"Here, Ned, you hold him a minute, while I make an investigation," called Tom, handing his prisoner over to his chum. "Maybe Pete or Andy are around."

"No, they ain't. I came alone," said Sam quickly, but Tom, not heeding, opened the shop, and, after turning on the electric lights, procured a lantern. He began a search of the shrubbery around the shop, while Ned held to the struggling Sam.

A Midnight Encounter

The moment Tom disappeared behind his machine shop, Sam Snedecker began a desperate struggle to escape from Ned Newton. Now Ned was a muscular lad, but his work in the bank was confining, and he did not have the chance to get out doors and exercise, as Sam had. Consequently Ned had his hands full in holding to the squirming crony of Andy Foger.

"You let me go!" demanded Sam, as he tried to twist loose.

"Not if I know it!" panted Ned.

Sam gave a sudden twist. Ned's foot slipped in the grass, and in a moment he went down, with Sam on top of him. Still he did not let go, and, finding he was still a prisoner Sam adopted new tactics.

Using his fists Sam began to pound Ned, but the bank employee, though suffering, would not call for help, to summon back Tom, who was, by this time, at the rear of the shop, looking about. Silently in the dark the two fought, and Ned found that Sam was getting away. Then Ned's hand came in contact with Sam's ear. It was the misfortune of the bully to have rather a large hearing apparatus, and once Ned got his fingers on an ear there was room enough to afford a good grip. He closed his hold tightly, and began to twist. This was too much for Sam. He set up a lusty howl.

"Wow! Ouch! Let go!" he pleaded, and he ceased to pound Ned, and no longer tried to escape. Tom came back on the run.

"What's the matter?" he cried. Then his light flashed on the two prostrate lads, and he understood without asking any further questions.

"Get up!" he cried, seizing Sam by the back of his neck, and yanking him to his feet. Ned arose, and secured a better grip on the sneaking lad.

"What's up?" demanded Tom, and Ned explained, following it by the question:

"See any more of 'em?"

"No, I guess he was here all alone," replied the young inventor. "What do you mean by sneaking around here this time of night?" he demanded of the captive.

"Don't you wish you knew?" was Sam's answer, with a leer. He realized that he had a certain advantage.

"You'd better tell before I turn you over to the police!" said Tom, sternly.

"You—you wouldn't do that; would you?" and Sam's voice that had been bold, became shaky.

"You were trespassing on our property, and that's against the law," declared Tom. "We have signs posted, warning people to keep off."

"I didn't mean any harm," whined Sam.

"Then what were you doing here, at this hour?"

"I was just taking a short cut home. I was out riding with Andy in his auto, and it broke down. I had to walk home, and I came this way. I didn't know you didn't allow people to cross your back lot. I wasn't doin' anything."

Tom hesitated. Sam might be telling the truth, but it was doubtful.

"What happened to Andy's auto?" the young inventor asked.

"He broke a wheel, going over a big stone on Berk's hill. He went to tell some one in the repair shop to go after the car, and I came on home. You've got no right to arrest me."

"I ought to, on general principles," commented Tom. "Well, skip out, and don't you come around here again. I'm going to get a savage bull dog, and the first one who comes sneaking around here after dark will be sorry. Move along now!"

Tom and Ned released their holds of Sam, and the latter lost no time in obeying the injunction to make himself scarce. He was soon lost to sight in the darkness.

"Think he was up to some mischief?" asked Ned.

"I'm almost sure of it," replied Tom, "but I can't see anything wrong. I guess we were too quick for him. I believe he, Andy and Pete Bailey tried to put up some job on me."

"Maybe they wanted to damage your new battery or car," suggested Ned.

"Hardly that. The car hasn't been started yet, and as for the battery, no one knows of it outside of you and my friends here. I'm keeping it secret. Well, if I'm going to take you home I'd better get a move on. Wait here and I'll run out Mr. Damon's car."

In a short time Tom was guiding the machine over the road to Shopton, Ned on the seat beside him. The young assistant cashier lived about a mile the other side of the village, and the two chums were soon at his house. Asking his friend to come and see him when he had a chance. Ned bid his chum good night, and the young inventor started back home.

He was driving slowly along, thinking more of his new invention than anything else, even more than of the mysterious visit of Sam Snedecker, when the lights on Mr. Damon's car flashed upon something big, black and bulky on the road just ahead of him. Tom, brought suddenly out of his fit of musing, jammed on the brakes, and steered to one side. Then he saw that the object was a stalled auto. He had only time to note this when a voice hailed him:

"Have you a tire pump you could lend us? Ours doesn't work, and we have had a blowout."

There was something about the voice that was strangely familiar, and Tom was wondering where he had heard it before, when into the glare of the lamps on his machine stepped Mr. Foger—Andy's father!

"Why, Mr. Foger!" exclaimed Tom. "I didn't know it was you."

"Oh, it's Tom Swift," remarked the man, and he did not seem especially pleased.

"Hey! What's that?" cried another voice, which Tom had no difficulty in recognizing as belonging to Andy. "What's the matter, Dad?"

"Why it happens to be your—ahem! It's Tom Swift in this other auto," went on Mr. Foger. "I didn't know you had a car," he added.

"I haven't," answered the lad. "This belongs to Mr. Damon. But can you see to fix your tire in the dark?" for Mr. Foger and his son had no lamps lighted.

"Oh, we have it all fixed," declared the man, "and, just as we were going to pump it up out lamps went out. Then we found that our pump wouldn't work. If you have one I would be obliged for the use of it," and he spoke somewhat stiffly.

"Certainly," agreed Tom, cheerfully, for he had no special grudge against Mr. Foger, though had he known Andy's father's plans, perhaps our hero would not have so readily aided him. The young inventor got down, removed one of his oil lamps in order that there might be some light on the operation, and then brought over his pump.

"I heard you had an accident," said Tom, a chain of thoughts being rapidly forged in his mind, as he thought of what Sam had told him.

"You heard of it?" repeated Mr. Foger, while Andy was busy pumping up the tire.

"Yes, a friend who was out riding with you said you had broken a wheel on Berk's hill. But I see he was slightly wrong. You're a good way from Berk's hill, and it's a tire that is broken, not a wheel."

"But I don't understand," said Mr. Foger. "No friend has been out riding with us. My son and I were out on a business trip, and—"

"Come on, pop. I've got it all pumped up. Jump in. There's your pump, Tom Swift. Much obliged," muttered Andy hastily. It was very evident that he wanted to prevent any further conversation between his parent and Tom.

"But I don't understand," went on the banker, clearly puzzled. "What friend gave you such information, Mr.—er—Tom Swift?"

"Sam Snedecker," replied the lad quickly. "I caught him sneaking around my machine shop about an hour ago, and when I asked him what he was doing he said he'd been out riding with Andy, and that they broke a wheel. I'm glad it was only a blown- out tire," and Tom's voice had a curious note in it.

"But there must be some mistake," insisted Mr. Foger. "Sam Snedecker was not riding with us this evening. We have been over to Waterfield—my son and I, and—"

"Come on, pop!" cried Andy desperately. "We must hurry home. Mom will be worried."

"Yes, I think she will. But I can't understand why Sam should say such a thing. However, we are much obliged for the use of your pump, Swift, and—"

But Andy prevented any further talk by starting the car with the muffler open, making a great racket, and he hurriedly drove off, almost before his father was seated, leaving Tom standing there in the road, beside his pump and lantern.

"So," mused the young inventor, "there's some game on. Sam wasn't with Andy, yet Andy evidently knew where Sam was, or he wouldn't have been so anxious to choke off talk. Mr. Foger knew nothing of Sam, naturally. But why have Andy and his father been on a midnight trip to Waterfield?"

That last question caused Tom to adopt a new line of thought.

"Waterfield," he mused. "That's where Mr. Damon lives. Mr. Damon is a heavy depositor in the old bank. Mr. Foger is going to start a new bank. I wonder if there's any connection there? This is getting mysterious. I must keep my eyes open. I never expected to meet Andy and his father tonight, any more than I expected to find Sam Snedecker sneaking around my shop, but it's a good thing I discovered both parties. I guess Andy must have had nervous prostration when I was talking to his father," and Tom grinned at the thought. Then, picking up the pump, and fastening the lantern in place, he drove Mr. Damon's auto slowly back home.

Tom said nothing to his father or Mr. Sharp, the next morning, about the incidents of the previous night. In the first place he could not exactly understand them, and he wanted to devote more time to thinking of them, before he mentioned the matter to his parent. Another reason was that Mr. Swift was a very nervous person, and the least thing out of the ordinary worried him. So the young inventor concluded to keep quiet.

His first act, after going to look at the small motor, which was being run with the larger, experimental storage battery, was to get out pencil and paper.

"I've got to plan the electric auto now that my battery is in a fair way to success," he said, for he noted that the one cell he had constructed had done over twice as much mileage in proportion, as had the small battery. "I'll soon start building the car," mused Tom, "and then I'll enter it in the race. I must write to that touring club and find how much time I have."

All that morning the young inventor drew plan after plan for an electric runabout, and rejected them. Finally he threw aside paper and pencil and exclaimed:

"It's no use. I can't think to-day. I'm dwelling too much on what happened last night. I must clear my brain.

"I know what I'll do. I'll get in my motor-boat and take a run over to Waterfield to see Mr. Damon. Maybe he's home by this time. Then I can ask him what Mr. Foger wanted to see him about, if he did call."

It was a fine May morning, and Tom was soon in his boat, the Arrow, gliding over Lake Carlopa, the waters of which sparkled in the sun. As he speeded up his craft, the lad looked about, thinking he might catch sight of Andy Foger, for the bully also owned a boat, called the Red Streak and, more than once, in spite of the fact that Andy's craft was the more powerful, Tom had beaten him in impromptu races. But there was no sign of his rival this morning, and Tom kept on to Waterfield. He found that Mr. Damon had not yet returned home.

"So far I've had my run for nothing," mused the youth. "Well, I might as well spend the rest of the morning in the boat."

He swung his craft out into the lake, and headed back toward Mansburg, intending to run up to the head of the body of water, which offered so many attractions that beautiful morning.

As Tom passed a small dock he saw a girl just putting out in a rowboat. The figure looked familiar and, having nothing special to do, the lad steered over closer. His first view was confirmed, and he called out cheerfully:

"Good morning, Miss Nestor. Going for a row?"

"Oh! Mr. Swift!" exclaimed the girl with a blush. "I didn't hear you coming. You startled me."

"Yes, the engine runs quite silently since I fixed it," resumed Tom. "But where are you going?"

"I was going for a row," answered the girl, "but I have just discovered that one of the oar locks is broken, so I am not going for a row," and she laughed, showing her white, even teeth.

"That's too bad!" remarked the lad. "I don't suppose," he added doubtfully, "that I could induce you to accept a motor-boat as a substitute for a rowing craft, could I?" and he looked quizzically at her.

"Are you asking me that as a hypothetical question?" she inquired.

"Yes," said Tom, trying not to smile.

"Well, if you are asking for information, merely, I will say that I could he induced to make such a change," and her face was nearly as grave as that of the young inventor's.

"What inducement would have to be used?" he asked.

"Suppose you just ask me in plain English to come and have a ride?" she suggested.

"All right, I will!" exclaimed the youth.

"All right, then I'll come!" she retorted with a laugh, and a few minutes later the two were in the Arrow, making a pretty picture as they speeded up the lake.

BUILDING THE CAR

"Well," remarked Tom to himself, about two hours later, when he had left Mary Nestor at her dock, and was on his way home, "I feel better than I did, and now I must do some hard thinking about my runabout. I want to get it the right shape to make the least resistance." He began to make some sketches when he got home, and at dinner he showed them to his father and Mr. Sharp. He said he had gotten an idea from looking at the airship.

"I'm going to make the front part, or what corresponds to the engine-hood in a gasolene car, pointed," he explained. "It will be just like the front of the aluminum gas container of the airship, only built of steel. In it will be a compartment for a set of batteries, and there will be a searchlight there. From the top of some supporters in front of the two rear seats, a slanting sheet of steel will come right down to meet the sloping nose of the car. First I was going to have curtains close over the top of the driver's seat, but I think a steel covering, with a celluloid opening will be better and make less wind resistance. I'll use leather side curtains when it rains. Under the front seats will be a compartment for more batteries, and there will be a third place under the rear seats, where I will also carry spare wheels and a repair kit. The motors will be slung under the body of the car, amidships, and there will also be room for some batteries there."

"How are you going to drive the car?" asked Mr. Sharp. "By a shaft?"

"Chain drive," explained Tom. "I can get more power that way, and it will be more flexible under heavy loads. Of course it will be steered in the usual way, and near the wheel will be the starting and reversing levers, and the gear handle."

"Gears!" exclaimed the aged inventor. "Are you going to gear an electric auto? I never heard of that. Usually the motor directly connected is all they use."

"I'm going to have two gears on mine," decided Tom.

"That's a new idea," commented the aeronaut.

"It is," admitted the lad, "and that's why my car is going to be so speedy. I'll make her go a hundred miles an hour, if necessary!"

"Nonsense!" exclaimed his father.

"I will!" cried the young inventor, enthusiastically. "You just wait and see. I couldn't do it but for the gears, but by using them I'll secure more speed, especially with the big reserve battery power I'll have. I know I've got the right idea, and I'm going to get right to work."

His father and Mr. Sharp were much interested, and closely examined his sketches. In a few days Tom had made detailed drawings, and the aged inventor looked at them critically. He had to admit that his son's theory was right, though how it would work out in practice was yet to be demonstrated. Mr. Swift offered some suggestions for minor changes, as did Mr. Sharp, and the lad adopted some of them. Then, with Mr. Jackson to help him, work was started on constructing the car.

Certain parts of it could be better purchased in the open market instead of being manufactured in Mr. Swift's shop, and thus Tom was able to get his new invention into some sort of shape sooner than would otherwise have been the case. He also started making the batteries, many of which would be needed.

Gradually the car began to take form on the floor of Tom's shop. It was rather a curious looking affair, the sharp forward part making it appear like some engine of war, or a projectile for some monster gun. But Tom cared little for looks. Speed, strength and ease of control were the chief features the lad aimed at, and he incorporated many new ideas into his electric car.

He was busy in the shop, one morning, when, above the noise caused by filing a piece of steel he heard some one exclaim:

"Bless my gizzard! If you aren't as busy as ever!"

"Mr. Damon!" cried Tom in delight. "When did you get back?"

"Last night," replied the eccentric man. "My wife and I stayed longer than we meant to. And whom do you think we met when we were off on our little trip?"

"Some of the Happy Harry gang?"

"Oh no. You'd never guess, so I'll tell you. It was Captain Weston."

"Indeed! And how has he been since he went in the submarine with us, and helped recover the gold from the wreck?"

"Very well. The first thing he said to me was: 'How is Tom Swift and his father, if I may be permitted to ask?'"

"Ha! Ha!" laughed the lad, at the recollection of the odd sea captain, who generally tagged on an apologetic expression to most of his remarks.

"He was getting ready to take part in some South American revolution," went on Mr. Damon. "He used most of his money that he got from the wreck to help finance their cause."

"I must tell Mr. Sharp," went on the lad. "He'll be interested."

"Anything new since I've been away?" asked the odd man. "Bless my shoe laces, but I'm glad to get back!"

Tom told of the prospect of a new bank being started, and of Sam's midnight visit, as well as the encounter with Mr. Foger and Andy.

"I went over to see what Mr. Foger wanted of you," went on the young inventor, "but you weren't home. Did he call?"

"The servant said he had been there, not once, but several times," remarked Mr. Damon. "That reminds me. He left a note for me, and I haven't read it yet. I'll do so now."

He tore open the letter, and hastily perused the contents.

"Ha!" he exclaimed. "So that's what he wanted to see me about!"

"What?" inquired Tom, with the privilege of and old friend.

"Mr. Foger says he's going to start a new bank, and he wants me to withdraw my deposit from the old one, and put it in his institution. Says he'll pay me bigger interest. And he adds that some of the old employees have gone with him."

"I hope you're not going to change," spoke Tom, thinking of his chum, Ned.

"Indeed I'm not. The old bank is good enough for me. By the way, doesn't a friend of yours work there?"

"Yes, Ned Newton. I'm wondering how he'll be affected?"

"Don't you worry!" exclaimed Mr. Damon. "Bless my check book! I'll speak to Pendergast about your friend. Maybe there'll be a chance to advance him further. I've got some mortgages falling due pretty soon, and I'll deposit the money from them in the old bank. Then we'll see what we can do about Ned."

"They'll make you a bank director, if you keep on putting in money," remarked our hero, with a smile.

"Not much they won't!" was the quick answer

"Bless my stocks and bonds! I've got trouble enough without becoming a bank director.

My doctor says my liver is out of order again, and I've got to eat a lemon every morning before breakfast."

"Eat a lemon?"

"Well, drink the juice! It's the same thing. But how is the electric runabout coming on?"

"Pretty good."

"Have you entered it in the races yet?"

"No, but I've written for information. I have until September to finish it. The races take place then."

"Let's see; they're on Long Island; aren't they? How do you calculate to do; run from here to there?"

"No, Dad still has the cottage he rented when we built the submarine and I think I'll make that my headquarters during the race. It's easy to run from there over to the Long Island track. They're building a new one, especially for the occasion.

"Well, I hope you win the prize. I must go to town now, as I have to attend to some business. I don't s'pose you want to come in my auto. I'm pretty sure something will break before I get there, and I'd like to have you along to fix it."

"Sorry, but I'm afraid I can't go," replied the lad. "I must get this car done, and then I've got to start on the batteries."

Mr. Damon rather reluctantly went off alone, looking anxiously at his car, for the machine got out of order on every trip he took.

It was a few days after this that Tom received a call from Ned one evening. The bank employee's face wore a happy smile.

"What's the matter; some one left you a fortune?" asked Tom.

"Pretty nearly as good. I've got a better position."

"What? Have you left the old bank, and gone to the new one?"

"No, I'm still in the same bank, but I'm one of the two cashiers now. Mr. Foger took several of the old employees when he opened his new bank, and that left vacancies. I was promoted, and so were one or two others. Mr. Damon spoke a good word for me."

"That's fine! He's a friend worth having."

"That's right. Your father also recommended me. But how are things with you? Has Andy made any more trouble?"

"No, and I don't believe he will. I guess he'll steer clear of me."

But Tom was soon to learn he was mistaken.

Tom Is Captured

Meanwhile the young inventor, aided by his father, Mr. Sharp and Garret Jackson, the engineer, worked hard over his new car, and the powerful batteries. A month passed, and such was the progress made that Tom felt justified in making formal entry of his vehicle for the races to be held by the Touring Club of America.

He paid a contingent fee and was listed as one of the competitors. As is usual in an affair of this kind, the promoters of it desired publicity, and they sought it through the papers.

Consequently each new entrant's name was published. In addition something was said about his previous achievements in the speed line.

No sooner was the name of Tom Swift received by the officials of the club, than it was at once recalled that young Swift had had a prominent part in the airship Red Cloud, and the submarine Advance. This gave an enterprising reporter a chance for a "special" for the Sunday supplement of a New York newspaper.

Tom, it was stated, was building a car which would practically annihilate distance and time, and there were many weird pictures, showing him flying along without touching the ground, in a car, the pictorial construction of which was at once fearful and wonderful.

Tom and his friends laughed at the yarn, at first, but it soon had undesirable results. The young inventor had desired to keep secret the fact that he was building a new electric vehicle, and a novel storage battery, but the article in the paper aroused considerable interest. Many persons came a long distance, hoping for a sight of the wonderful car, as pictured in the Sunday supplement, but they had to be denied. The news, thus leaking out, kept the Swift shops almost constantly besieged by many curious ones, who sought, by various means, to gain admission. Finally Tom and his father, after posting large signs, warning persons to keep away, added others to the effect that undesirable visitors might find themselves unexpectedly shocked by electricity, if they ventured too close. This had the desired effect, though the wires which were strung about carried such a mild charge that it would not have harmed a child. Then the only bothersome characters were the boys of the town, and, fearless and careless lads, they persisted in hanging around the Swift homestead, in the hope of seeing Tom dash away at the rate of five hundred miles an hour, which one enthusiastic writer predicted he would do.

"I've got a plan!" exclaimed Tom one day when the boys had been particularly troublesome.

"What is it?" asked his father.

"We'll hire Eradicate Sampson to stand guard with a bucket of whitewash. He'll keep the boys away."

The plan was put into operation, and Eradicate and his mule, Boomerang, were installed on the premises.

"Deed an' Ah'll keep dem lads away," promised the colored man. "Ah'll splash white stuff all ober 'em, if dey comes traipsin' around me."

He was as good as his word, and, when one or two lads had received a dose of the stuff, which punishment was followed by more severe from home, for having gotten their clothes soiled, the nuisance ceased, to a certain extent. Sam Snedecker and Pete Bailey were two who received a liberal sprinkling of the lime, and they vowed vengeance on Tom.

"And Andy Foger will help us, too," added Sam, as he withdrew, after an encounter with Eradicate.

"Doan't let dat worry yo', Mistah Swift!" exclaimed the darkey. "Jest let dat low-down-good-fo-nuffin' Andy Foger come 'round me, an' Ah'll make him t'ink he's de inside ob a chicken coop, dat's what Ah will."

Perhaps Andy heard of this, and kept away. In the meanwhile Tom kept on perfecting his car and battery. From the club secretary he learned that a number of inventors were working on electric cars, and there promised to be many of the speedy vehicles in the race.

After considerable labor Tom had succeeded in getting together one set of the batteries. He had them completed one afternoon, and wanted to give them a test that night. But, when he went to his father's chemical laboratory for a certain powder, which he needed to use in the battery solution, he found there was none.

"I'll have to ride in to Mansburg for some," he decided. "I'll go after supper, on my motorcycle, and test the battery to- night."

The young inventor left his house immediately after the evening meal. Along the road toward Mansburg he speeded, and, as he came to the foot of a hill, where once Andy Foger had put a big tree, hoping Tom would run into it and be injured, the youth recalled that circumstance.

"Andy has been keeping out of my way lately," mused Tom. "I wonder if he's up to any mischief? I don't like the way Sam Snedecker is hanging around the shop, either. It looks as if they were plotting something. But I guess Eradicate and his pail of whitewash will scare them off."

Tom got the powdered chemical he wanted in the drug store, and, after refreshing himself with some ice cream soda, he started back. As he rode along through the streets of the town he kept a lookout, and those of you who know how fond the lad was of a certain young lady, do not need to be told for whom he was looking. But he did not see her, and soon turned into the main highway leading to Shopton.

It was dark when he reached the hill, where once he had been so near an accident, and he slowed up as he coasted down it, using the brake at intervals.

Tom got safely to the bottom of the declivity, and was about to turn on the power of his machine, when, from the bushes that lined either side of the roadway, several figures sprang suddenly. They ranged themselves across the road, and one cried: "Halt!" in tones that were meant to be stern, but which seemed to Tom, to tremble somewhat. The young inventor was so surprised that he did not open the gasolene throttle, nor switch on his spark. As a consequence his motor-cycle lost momentum, and he had to take one foot from the pedal and touch the ground, to prevent himself from toppling over.

"Hold on there!" cried another voice. "We've got you where we want you, now! Hold on! Don't go!"

"I wasn't going to go," responded Tom calmly, trying to recognize the voice, which seemed to be unnatural. "What do you want, and who are you?"

"Never mind who we are. We want you and we've got you! Get off that wheel!"

"I don't see why I should!" exclaimed Tom, and he suddenly shifted his handle bars, so as to flash the bright headlight he carried, upon the circle of dark figures that opposed his progress. As the light flashed on them he was surprised to see that all the figures wore masks over their faces.

Tom started. Was this the Happy Harry gang after him again? He hoped not, yet the fact that the persons had on masks made the hold-up have an ugly look. Once more Tom flashed the light on the throng. There were exclamations of dismay.

"Douse that glim, somebody!" called a sharp voice, which Tom could not recognize.

A stone came whizzing through the air, from some one in the crowd. There was a smashing of glass as it hit the lantern, and the road was plunged in darkness. Tom tried to throw one leg over the saddle, and let down the supporting stand from the rear wheel, so the motorcycle would remain upright without him holding it. He determined to have revenge for that act of vandalism in breaking his lamp.

But, just as he was free of the seat, he was surrounded by a dozen persons, and several hands were laid on him.

"We've got you now!" some one fairly hissed in his ear. "Come along, and get what's coming to you!"

Tom tried to fight, but he was overpowered by numbers and, a little later, was dragged off into the woods in the darkness by the masked figures. His arms were securely bound with ropes, and a handkerchief was tied over his eyes. Tom Swift was a prisoner.

A Blinding Flash

Stumbling on through the dark woods, led by his captors, Tom tried to pierce the gloom and identify the persons who had firm grips on either side of him. But it was useless. A little light sifted down from the starlit sky above, but it was not sufficient. The young inventor was beginning to think, after all, that he had fallen into the hands of the Happy Harry gang, and he knew that if this was so he need expect no mercy.

But two things were against this belief. One was that the principal members of the gang were still in jail, or at least they were supposed to be, and another was that there were too many of the captors. Happy Harry's crowd never numbered so many.

"Maybe they're highwaymen," thought our hero, as he was dragged along "But that can't be," he reasoned further. "If they wanted to rob me they'd have done it back there in the road, and not brought me off here in the woods. Besides, I haven't anything for them to steal."

Suddenly Tom stumbled over a projecting root, and nearly fell, dragging along with him the person who had hold of his left arm.

"Look out there! What's the matter with you?" exclaimed one of the throng quickly, and at the sound of the voice Tom started.

"Andy Foger!" cried the young inventor, as he recovered himself, for he had recognized the voice of the red-haired bully. "What do you mean by holding me up in this way?" he demanded.

"Quiet!" urged a voice in his ear, and the tones were unfamiliar. "Mention no names!"

"I'm on to your game!" retorted Tom. "I know you're here, Andy, and Sam and Pete; and Jack Reynolds and Sid Holton," and he named two rather loose-charactered lads, who were often in the company of Andy and his cronies. "You'd better quit this nonsense," Tom went on. "I'll cause the arrest of all of you if you make trouble for me. I know who you are now!"

"You think you do," answered the voice in his ear, and the young inventor concluded that it must be some lad whom he did not know. "Nor is this nonsense," the other went on. "You are about to receive the punishment due you."

Our hero did not answer, but he was doing some hard thinking. He wondered why Andy and his crowd had captured him.

Suddenly the blackness of the woods was illuminated by the fitful gleam of a distant fire. Tom could see more plainly now, and he managed to count about ten dusky figures hurrying along, four being close to him, to prevent his escape, and the others running on ahead. The light became stronger, and, a moment later the prisoner and his captors emerged into a little clearing, where a fire was burning. Two figures, masked with black cloth, as were all in the crowd, stood about the blaze, putting on sticks of wood.

"Did you get him?" asked one of these figures eagerly.

"Yes, they got me, Sam Snedecker," answered Tom quickly, recognizing Sam's tones. "And they'll wish they hadn't before I'm done with them."

"Quiet!" ordered an unknown voice. "Members of the Deep Forest Throng, the prisoner is here!" the lad went on.

"'Tis well, bind the captive to the sacrificial tree," was the response from some one in the crowd.

Tom laughed. He was at ease now, for he recognized that those who had taken him prisoner were all lads of Andy's character. Most of them were Shopton youths, but some, evidently, were strangers in town. Tom felt he had little to fear.

"Bring him over here," ordered one, and Tom cried out:

"You wouldn't be giving those orders, Andy Foger, if my arms weren't tied. And if you'll untie me, I'll fight any two of you at once," offered the young inventor fiercely, for he hated the humiliation to which he was being subjected.

"Don't do it! Don't untie him!" begged some one.

"No danger, they won't. They're afraid to, Pete Bailey," replied Tom quickly, for he had recognized the voice of the other one of Andy's particular cronies.

"Aw, he knows who we are," whispered Sam, but not so low but that our hero heard him.

"No matter," was Andy's retort. "Let's go ahead with it. Tie him to that tree."

It was useless for Tom to struggle. He was bound too tightly by the rope, and the crowd was too many for him. In a few minutes he was securely fastened to a tree, not far from the camp-fire, which was replenished from time to time.

"Now for the judgment!" called one of the masked lads, in what he meant to be a sepulchral tone. "What is the charge against the prisoner? Brother Number One of the Deep Forest Throng, what is your accusation?"

"He's a regular snob, that's what's the trouble," answered Andy Foger, though whether he was "Brother Number One," did not appear. "He's too fresh and—and—"

"I'll make you wish you felt fresh when I get hold of you, Andy," murmured Tom.

"Quiet!" cried a tall lad. "What's the next charge?"

"He keeps an old colored man on guard at his place," was the answer, and Tom had no difficulty in recognizing the voice of Sid Holton. "The coon throws whitewash all over us. I got some of it."

"You wouldn't have, if you'd minded your own business," retorted Tom. "It served you right!"

"What is the verdict on the prisoner?" asked one who seemed to be the leader.

"I say let's tar and feather him!" cried Andy suddenly. "There's a barrel of tar back in the woods here, and we can get some feathers from a chicken coop. That would make him so he wouldn't be so uppish, I guess!"

"That's right! Tar and feathers!" exclaimed several.

Our hero's heart sank. He was not afraid, but he did not relish the indignity that was proposed. He resolved to fight to the last ounce of his strength against the masked lads.

"Can we get a kettle to heat the tar in?" asked some one.

"We'll find one," answered Sam Snedecker. "Come on, let's do it. You'll look pretty, Tom Swift, when we're through with you," he exulted.

Tom did not answer, but there was fierce anger in his heart. The tar and feather proposal seemed to meet with general favor.

"Members of the Deep Forest Throng, we will hold a consultation," proposed the leader, in his assumed deep voice. "Come over here, to one side. Brother Number Six, guard the prisoner well."

"There ain't no need to," answered a lad who had been instructed to mount guard over Tom. "He's tied so tight he can't move. I want to hear what you say."

"Very well then," assented the leader, "But look to his bonds."

The lad made a hasty examination of the ropes binding the young inventor to the tree, and Tom was glad that the examination was a hasty one. For he feared the guard might discover that one hand had been worked nearly free. The young inventor had done this while he leered at his captors.

Tom was not going to submit tamely to the nonsense, and from the moment he had been tied, he had been trying to get loose. He had nearly succeeded in freeing one hand when the crowd of masked boys moved off to one side, where they presently began to talk in excited whispers.

"I wonder how they came to catch me," thought the prisoner, as he worked feverishly to further loosen the ropes. "This looks as if it was a put-up job, with the masks, and everything." Later he learned that the idea was the outcome of a proposal of one of the new arrivals in town. He had organized the "Deep Forest Throng," as a sort of secret society, and Andy and his cronies had been induced to join. It was Andy's proposal to capture Tom, though, and, having seen him depart for Mansburg on his motor- cycle, and knowing that he would return along a road that ran near the woods where the Throng met, suggested that they take Tom captive. The idea was enthusiastically received, and Andy and his cronies thought they saw a chance to be revenged.

Tom, while he picked at the ropes, listened to what the boys were saying. He heard frequent mention of tar and feathers, and began to believe, that unless he could get free, while they were off there consulting, he might be forced to submit to the humiliating ordeal.

He managed to get one hand comparatively free, so that he could move it about, but then he struck several hard knots, and could make no further progress. The conference seemed on the point of breaking up.

"One of you go for a big kettle to boil the tar in," ordered the leader, "and the rest of you dig up some feathers."

"I must get loose!" thought Tom desperately. "If they try to tar and feather me it will be a risky business. I've got to get loose! They may burn me severely!"

But, though he tried with all his strength, the ropes would not loosen another bit. He had one hand free, and that was all. The crowd was moving back toward him.

"My knife!" thought the captive quickly. "If I can reach that in my pocket I can cut the ropes! Once I get loose I'll fight the whole crowd!"

He managed to get his free hand into his pocket. His fingers touched something. It was not his knife, and, for a moment he felt a pang of disappointment. Then, as he realized what it was that he had grasped, a new idea came to him.

"This will be better than the knife!" he thought exultantly. The crowd of lads was now surrounding him, some distance from the fire, which burned in front of the captive.

"Sentence has been passed upon you," remarked the leader. "Prepare to meet thy doom! Get the materials, brothers!"

"One moment!" called Tom, for he wanted the crowd all present to witness what he was about to do. "I'll give you one chance to let me go peaceably. If you don't—"

"Well, what will you do?" demanded Andy sneeringly, as he pulled his mask further over his face. "I guess you won't do anything, Tom Swift."

"I'll give you one chance to let me go, and I'll agree to say nothing about this joke," went on Tom. "If you don't I'll blow this place up!"

For a moment there was a silence.

"Ha! Ha! Ho! Ho!" laughed Sam Snedecker. "Listen to him! He'll blow the place up! I'd like to see you do it! You can't get loose in the first place, and you haven't anything to blow it up with in the second. I'd like to see you do it; hey, fellers?"

"Sure," came the answering chorus.

"Would you?" asked Tom quickly. "Then watch. Stand back if you don't want to get hurt, and remember that I gave you a chance to let me go!"

Tom made a rapid motion with the hand he had gotten loose. He threw something toward the blazing fire, which was now burning well. Something white sailed through the air, and fell amid the hot embers.

There was a moment's pause, and then a blinding flash of blue fire lighted up the woods, and a dull rumble, as when gun-powder is lighted in the open followed. A great cloud of white smoke arose, as the vivid blue glare died away, and it seemed as if a great wind swept over the place. Several of the masked lads were knocked down by the explosion, and when the rumble died away, and deep blackness succeeded the intense blue light, there came cries of pain and terror. The fire had been scattered, and extinguished by the explosion which Tom, though still bound to the tree had caused to happen in the midst of the Deep Forest Throng. Then, as the smoke rolled away, Andy Foger cried:

"Come on, fellows! Something's happened. I guess a volcano blew up!"

Tom Is Rescued

The Deep Forest Throng needed no urging to flee from the place of the mysterious explosion. Their prisoner, helpless as he had seemed, had proved too much for them. Slipping and stumbling along in the darkness, the masked lads had but one thought—to get away before they saw more of that blue fire, and the force of the concussion.

"Gee! My eyebrows are all singed off!" cried Sam Snedecker, as he tore loose his mask which had been rent in the explosion, and felt of his face.

"And my hands are burned," added Pete Bailey. "I stood closer to the fire than any of you."

"You did not! I got the worst of it!" cried Andy. "I was knocked down by the explosion, and I'll bet I'm hurt somewhere. I guess—Oh! Help! I'm falling in a mud hole!"

There was a splash, and the bully disappeared from the sight of his companions who, now that the moon had risen, could better see to flee from their prisoner.

"Help me out, somebody!" pleaded Andy. "I'm in a mud hole!"

They pulled him out, a sorry looking sight, and the red-haired lad, whose locks were now black with muck, began to lament his lot.

"Dry up!" commanded Sid Holton. "It's all your fault, for proposing such a fool trick as capturing Tom Swift. We might have known he would get the best of us."

"What was that stuff he used, anyhow?" asked Cecil Hedden, the lad responsible for the organization of the Deep Forest Throng. "He must be a wonder. Does he do sleight-of-hand tricks?"

"He does all sorts of tricks," replied Pete Bailey, feeling of a big lump on his head, caused by falling on a stone in the mad rush. "I guess we were chumps to tackle him. He must have put some kind of chemical in the fire, to make it blow up."

"Or else he summoned his airship by wireless, and had that balloonist, Mr. Sharp, drop a bomb in the blaze," suggested another lad.

"But how could he do anything? Wasn't he tied fast to that tree?" asked Cecil, the leader.

"You never know when you've got Tom Swift tied," declared Jack Reynolds. "You think you've got him, and you haven't. He's too slick for us. It's Andy's fault, for proposing to capture him."

"That's right! Blame it all on me," whined the squint-eyed bully. "You was just as anxious as I was to tar and feather him."

"Well, we didn't do it," commented Pete Bailey, dryly. "I s'pose he's loose now, laughin' at us. Gee, but that was an explosion though! It's a wonder some of us weren't killed! I guess I've had enough of this Deep Forest Throng business. No more for mine."

"Aw, don't be afraid," urged Cecil. "The next time we get him we'll be on our guard."

"You'll never catch Tom Swift again," predicted Pete.

"I'll go back now to where he is, if you will," agreed Cecil, who was older than the others.

"Not much!" cried Pete. "I've had enough."

This seemed to be the sentiment of all. Away they stumbled through the woods, and, emerging on the road, scattered to their several homes, not one but who suffered from slight burns, contusions, torn and muddy clothes or injured feelings as the outcome of the "joke" on the young inventor.

But our hero was not yet free from the bonds of his enemies. When they scattered and ran, after the vivid blue light, and the dull explosion, which, being unconfined, did no real damage, Tom was still fast to the tree. As his eyes became accustomed to the semi-darkness that followed the glare, he remarked:

"Well, I don't know that I'm much better off. I gave those fellows a good scare, but I'm not loose. But I can work to better advantage now."

Once more he resumed the effort to free himself, but in spite of the crude manner in which the knots had been made, the lad could not get loose. The more he pulled and tugged the tighter they seemed to become.

"This is getting serious," Tom mused. "If I could only reach my knife I could cut them, but it's in my pocket on the other side, and that bond's fast. Guess I'll have to stay here all night. Maybe I'd better call for help, but—"

His words, spoken half aloud, were suddenly interrupted by a crash in the underbrush. Somebody was approaching. At first Tom thought it was Andy and his cronies coming back, but a voice that called a moment later proved that this was not so.

"Is any one here?" shouted a man. "Any one hurt? What was that fire and explosion?"

"I'm here," replied Tom. "I'm not hurt exactly, but I'm tied to a tree. I'll be much obliged if you'll loosen me."

"Who are you?"

"Tom Swift. Is that you, Mr. Mason?"

"Yes. By jinks! I never expected to find you here, Tom. Over this way, men," he added calling aloud. "I've found him; it's Tom Swift."

There was the flicker of several lanterns amid the trees, and soon a number of men had joined Mr. Mason, and surrounded Tom. They were farmers living in the neighborhood.

"What in the name o' Tunket happened?" asked one. "Did you get hit by a meteor or a comet? Who tied you up; highwaymen?"

"Cut him loose first, and ask questions afterward," suggested Mr. Mason.

"Yes," added Tom, with a laugh, "I wish you would. I'm beginning to feel cramped."

With their knives, the farmers quickly cut the ropes, and some of them rubbed the arms of the lad to restore the circulation.

"What was it—highwaymen?" asked a man, unable to longer restrain his curiosity. "Did they rob you?"

"No, it wasn't highwaymen," replied the youth. "It was a trick of some boys I know," and to Tom's credit be it said that he did not mention their names. "They did it for a joke," he added.

"Boys' trick? Joke?" queried Mr. Mason. "Pretty queer sort of a joke, I think. They ought to be arrested."

"Oh, I fancy I gave them what was coming to them," went on the young inventor.

"Did they try to blow ye up, too?" asked Mr. Hertford. "What in th' name of Tunket was that blue light, and that explosion? I heard it an' saw it way over to my house."

"So did I," remarked Mr. Mason, and several others said the same thing. "We thought a meteor had fallen," he continued, "and we got together to make an investigation."

"It's a good thing for me you did," admitted Tom, "or I might have had to stay here all night."

"But was it a meteor?" insisted Mr. Hertford.

"No," replied the lad, "I did it."

"You?"

"Yes. You see after they tied me I found I could get one hand free. I reached in my pocket for my knife, but instead of it I managed to get hold of a package of powder I had."

"Gunpowder?" asked Mr. Mason.

"No, a chemical powder I use in an electrical battery. The powder explodes in fire, and makes quite a blue flash, and a lot of smoke, but it isn't very dangerous, otherwise I wouldn't have used it. When the boys were some distance away from the fire, I threw the powder in the blaze. It went off in a moment, and—"

"I guess they run some; didn't they?" asked Mr. Mason with a laugh.

"They certainly did," agreed Tom.

TOM HAS A FALL

The young inventor told more details of his adventure in the woods, but, though the farmers questioned him closely, he would not give a single name of his assailants.

"But I should think you'd want to have them punished," remarked Mr. Mason.

"I'll attend to that part later," answered Tom. "Besides, most of them didn't know what they were doing. They were led on by one or two. No, I'll fight my own battles. But I wish you'd lend me a lantern long enough to find my motor-cycle. The moon doesn't give much light in the woods, and those fellows may have hidden my machine."

Mr. Mason and his companions readily agreed to accompany Tom on a search for his wheel. It was found just where he had dismounted from it in the road. Andy and his cronies had evidently had enough of their encounter with our hero, and did not dare to annoy him further.

"Do you think you can ride home?" asked one of the farmers of the lad, when he had ascertained that his machine was in running order.

"Well, it's risky without my lantern," answered Tom. "They smashed that for me. But I guess I can manage."

"No, you can't!" insisted Mr. Mason. "You're stiff from being tied up; and you can't ride. Now you just wheel that contraption over to my place, and I'll hitch up and take you home. It isn't far."

"Oh, I couldn't think of troubling you," declared Tom. At the same time he felt that he was in no condition to ride.

"It's no trouble at all," insisted Mr. Mason. "I guess your father and I are good enough friends to allow me to have my way. You can come over and get your choo-choo bicycle in the morning."

A little later Tom was being rapidly driven toward his home, where he found his father and Mrs. Baggert, to say nothing of Mr. Sharp, somewhat alarmed over his absence, as it was getting late. The youth told as much of his adventure as he thought would not alarm his father, making a sort of joke of it, and, later, related all the details to the balloonist.

"We'll have to get after Andy again," declared the aeronaut. "He needs another toning down."

"Yes, similar to the one he got when we nearly ran away with his automobile, by catching the airship anchor on it," added Tom with a laugh. "But I fancy Andy will steer clear of me for a while. I'm sorry I had to use up that chemical powder, though. Now I can't start my battery until to-morrow."

But the next day Tom made up for lost time, by working from early until late. He went over to Mr. Mason's, got his motor-cycle, procured some more of the chemical, and soon had his storage battery in running order. Then he arranged for a more severe test, and while that was going on he worked at completing the body of the electric runabout. The vehicle was beginning to look like a car, though it was not of the regulation pattern.

For the next week Tom was very busy, so occupied, in fact, that he scarcely took time for his meals, which caused Mrs. Baggert no little worriment, for she was a housekeeper who liked to see others enjoy her cooking.

"Well, Tom, how are you coming on?" asked his father one night, as they sat on the porch, Mr. Sharp with them.

"Pretty well, Dad," was the answer of the young inventor. "I'll put the wheels on tomorrow, and then set the batteries. I've got the motor all finished; and all I'll have to do will be to connect it up, and then I'll be ready for a trial on the road."

"And you still think you'll beat all records?"

"I'm pretty sure of it, Dad. You see the amperage will be exceptionally high, and my batteries will have a large amount of reserve, with little internal resistance. But do you know I'm so tired I can hardly think. It's more of a job than I thought it would be."

Tom, a little later, strolled down the road. As he turned back toward the house and walked up the shrubbery lined path he heard a noise.

"Some one's hiding in there!" thought the lad, and he darted to an opening in the hedge to reach the other side. As he did so he saw a figure running away. Whether it was a man or a boy he could not tell in the darkness.

"Hold on there!" cried the young inventor, but, naturally, the fleeing one did not stop. Tom began to sprint, and as it was slightly down hill, he made good time. The figure ahead of him was running well, too, but Tom who could see better, now that he was out from under the trees, noticed that he was gaining. The fleeing one came to a little brook, and hesitated a moment before leaping across. This enabled Tom to catch up, and he made a grab for the figure, just as the man or boy sprang across the little stream.

Tom missed his grip, but he was not going to give up. He scarcely slackened his speed, but, with the momentum he had acquired in racing down the hill, he, too, leaped across the brook. As he landed on the other side he made another grab for the figure, a man, as Tom could now see, but he could make out no features, as the person's hat was pulled down over his face.

"I've got you now!" cried Tom exultantly, reaching out his hand. His fingers clutched something, but the next instant the young inventor went sprawling. The other had put out his foot, and tripped him neatly and, Tom throwing out his hands to save himself in the fall that was inevitable, went splashing into the brook at full length. The unknown, pausing a moment to view what he had done, turned quickly and raced off in the darkness.

CROSSED WIRES

More surprised than hurt, and with a feeling of chagrin and anger at the trick which had been played on him, Tom managed to scramble out of the brook. The water was not deep, but he had splashed in with such force that he was wet all over. And, as he got up, the water drip-ping from his clothes, the lad was conscious of a pain in his head. He put up his hand, and found that contact with a stone had raised a large lump on his forehead. It was as big as a hen's egg.

"Humph! I'll be a pretty sight to-morrow," murmured Tom. "I wonder who that fellow was, anyhow, and what he wanted? He tripped me neatly enough, whoever he was. I've a good notion to keep on after him."

Then, as he realized what a start the fleeing one had, the young inventor knew that it would be fruitless to renew the chase. Slowly he ascended the sloping bank, and started for home. As he did so he realized that he had, clasped in his fingers, something he had grabbed from the person he was pursuing just before his unlucky tumble.

"It's part of his watch chain!" exclaimed Tom, as he felt of the article. "I must have ripped it loose when I fell. Wonder what it is? Evidently some sort of a charm. Maybe it will be a clue." He tried to discern of what style it was, but in the dark woods this was impossible. Then the lad tried to strike a match, but those in his pocket had become wet from his unexpected bath. "I'll have to wait until I get home," he went on, and he hastened his steps, for he was anxious to see what he had torn loose from the person who appeared to be spying on him.

"Why Tom, what's the matter?" exclaimed Mrs. Baggert, when he entered the kitchen, dripping water at every step. "Is it raining outside? I didn't hear any storm."

"It was raining where I was," replied Tom angrily. "I fell in the brook. It was so hot I thought I'd cool off."

"With your best suit on!" ejaculated the housekeeper.

"It isn't my best," retorted the lad. "But I went in before I thought. It was an accident; I fell," he added, lest Mrs. Baggert take his joking remarks seriously. He did not want to tell her of the chase.

The chief concern of the lad now was to look at the charm and, as soon as Mrs. Baggert's attention was attracted elsewhere, Tom glanced at the object he still held tightly clenched in his hand. As the light from the kitchen fell upon it he could hardly repress an exclamation of astonishment.

For the charm that he held in his hand was one he had seen before dangling from the watch chain of Addison Berg, the agent for Bentley & Eagert, submarine boat builders, which firm had, as told in "Tom Swift and His Submarine," tried unsuccessfully to secure the gold treasure from the sunken wreck. Berg and his associates had even gone so far as to try to disable the Advance, the boat of Tom and his father, by ramming her when deep down under the ocean, but Mr. Swift's use of an electric cannon had broken the steering gear of the Wonder, the rival craft, and from that time on Tom and his friends had a clear field to search for the bullion held fast in the hold of the Boldero. "Addison Berg," murmured Tom, as he looked at the watch charm. "What can he be doing in this neighborhood? Hiding, too, as if he wanted to overhear something. That's the way he did when we were building our submarine, and now he's up to the same trick when I'm constructing my electric car. I'm sure this charm is his. It is such a peculiar design that I'm positive I can't be mistaken. I thought, when I was chasing after him, that it would turn out to be Andy Foger, or some of the boys, but it was too big for them. Addison Berg, eh? What can he be doing around here? I must not tell Dad, or he'd worry himself sick. But I must be on my guard."

Tom examined the charm closely. It was a compass, but made in an odd form, and was much ornamented.

The young inventor had noticed it on several occasions when he had been in conversation with Mr. Berg previous to the attempt on the part of the owners of the rival submarine to wreck Tom's boat. He felt that he could not be mistaken in identifying the charm.

"Berg was afraid I'd catch him, and ask for an explanation that would have been awkward to make," thought the lad, as he turned the charm over in his hand. "That's why he tripped me up. But I'll get at the bottom of this yet. Maybe he wants to steal my ideas for an electric car."

Tom's musings were suddenly interrupted by Mrs. Baggert.

"I hope you're not going to stand there all night," she said, with a laugh. "You're in the middle of a puddle now, but when you get over dreaming I'd like to mop it up."

"All right," agreed the young inventor, coming to himself suddenly. "Guess I'd better go get some dry clothes on."

"You'd better go to bed," advised Mrs. Baggert. "That's where your father and Mr. Sharp are. It's late."

The more Tom thought over the strange occurrence the more it puzzled him. He mused over the presence of Berg as he went about his work the next day, for that it was the agent whom he had pursued he felt positive.

"But I can't figure out why he was hanging around here," mused Tom.

Then, as he found that his thoughts over the matter were interfering with his work, he resolutely put them from him, and threw himself energetically into the labor of completing his electric car. The new batteries, he found, were working well, and in the next two days he had constructed several more, joining them so as to get the combined effect.

It was the afternoon of the third day from Tom's unexpected fall into the brook that the young inventor decided on the first important test of his new device. He was going to try the motor, running it with his storage battery. Some of the connections were already in place, the wires being fastened to the side of the shop, where they were attached to switches. Tom did not go over these, taking it for granted that they were all right. He soon had the motor, which he was to install in his car, wired to the battery, and then he attached a gauge, to ascertain, by comparison, how many miles he could hope to travel on one charging of the storage battery.

"Guess I'll call Dad and Mr. Sharp in to see how it works, before I turn on the current," he said to himself. He was about to summon his parent and the aeronaut from an adjoining shop, where they were working over a new form of dynamo, when the lad caught sight of the watch charm he had left on his desk, in plain sight.

"Better put that away," he remarked. "Dad or Mr. Sharp might see it, and ask questions. Then I'd have to explain, and I don't want to, not until I get further toward the bottom of this thing."

He put the charm away, and then summoned his father and the balloonist.

"You're going to see a fine experiment," declared Tom. "I'm going to turn on the full strength of my battery."

"Are you sure it's all right, Tom?" asked his father. "You can't be too careful when you're dealing with electricity of high voltage, and great ampere strength.

"Oh, it's all right, Dad," his son assured him "Now watch my motor hum."

He walked over to a big copper switch, and grasped the black rubber handle to pull it over which would send the current from the storage battery into the combination of wheels and gears that he hoped, ultimately, would propel his electric automobile along the highways, or on a track, at the rate of a hundred miles an hour.

"Here she goes!" cried Tom. For an instant he hesitated and then pulled the switch. At the same time his hand rested on another wire, stretched across a bench.

No sooner had the switch closed than there was a blinding flash, a report as of a gun being fired, and Tom's body seemed to straighten out. Then a blue flame appeared to encircle him and he dropped to the floor of the shop, an inert mass.

"He's killed!" cried Mr. Swift, springing forward.

"Careful!" cautioned the balloonist. "He's been shocked! Don't touch him until I turn off the current!" As he pulled out the switch, the aeronaut gave a glance at the apparatus.

"There's something wrong here!" he cried. "The wires have been crossed! That's what shocked Tom, but he never made the wrong connections! He's too good an electrician! There's been some one in this shop, changing the wires!"

THE TRYOUT

Once the current was cut off it was safe to approach the body of the young inventor. Mr Sharp stooped over and lifted Tom's form from the floor, for Mr. Swift was too excited and trembled too much to be of any service. Our hero was as one dead. His body was limp, after that first rigid stretching out, as the current ran through him; his eyes were closed, and his face was very pale.

"Is—is there any hope?" faltered Mr. Swift.

"I think so," replied the balloonist. "He is still breathing- faintly. We must summon a doctor at once. Will you telephone for one, while I carry him in the house?"

As Mr. Sharp emerged from the shop, bearing Tom's body, an automobile drew up in front of the place.

"Bless my soul!" exclaimed a voice. "Tom's hurt! How did it happen? Bless my very existence!"

"Oh, Mr. Damon, you're just in time!" exclaimed Mr. Sharp, "Tom's had a bad shock. Will you go for a doctor in your auto?"

"Better than that! Let me take Tom in the car to Dr. Whiteside's office," proposed the eccentric man. "It will be better that way."

"Yes, yes," agreed Mr. Swift eagerly. "Put Tom in the auto!"

"If only it doesn't break down," added Mr. Damon fervently. "Bless my spark plug, but it would be just my luck!"

But they started off all right, Mr. Swift riding in front with Mr. Damon, and Mr. Sharp supporting Tom in the tonneau. Only a little fluttering of the eyelids, and a slow, faint breathing told that Tom Swift still lived.

Mr. Damon never guided a car better than he did his auto that day. Several speed laws were broken, but no one appeared to stop them, and, in record time they had the young inventor at the physician's house. Fortunately Dr. Whiteside was at home, and, under his skillful treatment Tom was soon out of danger. His heart action was properly started, and then it was only a question of time. As the doctor had plenty of room it was decided to let the lad remain that night, and Tom was soon installed in a spare bedroom, with the doctor's pretty daughter to wait on him occasionally.

"Oh, I'm all right," the youth insisted, when Miss Whiteside told him it was time for his medicine. "I'm all right."

"You're not!" she declared. "I ought to know, for I'm going to be a nurse, some day, and help papa. Now take this or I'll have to hold your nose, as they do the baby's," and she held out a spoonful of unpleasant looking mixture, extending her dainty forefinger and thumb of her other hand, as if to administer dire punishment to Tom, if he did not obey.

"Well, I give in to superior strength," he said with a laugh, as he noted, with approval, the laughing face of his nurse.

Then he fell into a deep sleep, and was so much better the next morning that he could be taken home in Mr. Damon's auto.

"But mind, no hard work for three or four days," insisted the physician. "I want your heart to get in shape for that big race you were telling me about. The shock was a severe strain to it."

Tom promised, reluctantly, and, though he did no work, his first act, on reaching home, was to go out to the shop, to inspect the battery and motor. To his surprise the motor was running for the lad had established the connection, in spite of his shock and his father and Mr. Sharp had decided to let the machinery run until he came back.

"And look at the record it's made!" cried Tom delightedly as he glanced at the gauge "Better than I figured on. That battery is a wonder. I'll have the fastest electric runabout you ever saw."

"If the wires don't get crossed again," put in Mr. Sharp. "You'd better make an examination, Tom," and, for the first time, the young inventor learned how he had been shocked.

"Crossed wires! I should say they were crossed!" he exclaimed as he looked at the switches and copper conductors. "Somebody has been tampering with them. No wonder I was shocked!"

"Who did it?" asked Mr. Sharp.

Tom considered for a moment, before answering. Then he said:

"I believe it was Addison Berg. He must have wanted to do some damage, to get even with us for getting that treasure away from him."

"Berg?" questioned the balloonist, and Tom told of the night he had been tripped into the brook, and exhibited the watch charm he had secured. Mr. Sharp recognized it at once. A further examination confirmed the belief that the submarine agent had sneaked into Tom's workshop, and had altered the wires.

"They were all right when I came out of the shop that night," declared Tom. "I left the old connections just as I thought I had arranged them, and only added the new ones, when I went to try my battery. The old connections were crossed, but I didn't notice it. Then when I turned on the current I got the shock. I don't s'pose Berg thought I'd be so nearly killed. Probably he wanted to burn out my motor, and spoil it. If it was Andy Foger I could understand it, but a man like Berg—"

"He's probably wild with anger because his submarine got the worst of it in the race for the gold," interrupted the balloonist. "Well, we'll have to be on our guard, that's all. What was the matter with Eradicate, that he didn't see him enter the shop?"

"Rad went to a colored dance that night," said Tom. "I let him off. But after this I'll have the shop guarded night and day. My motor might have been ruined, if that first charge hadn't gone through my body instead of into the machinery." The improper connections were soon removed and others substituted.

It was agreed between Tom and Mr. Sharp that they would say nothing regarding Mr. Berg to Mr. Swift. The aeronaut caused cautious inquiries to be made, and learned that the agent had been discharged by the submarine firm, because of some wrong- doing in connection with the craft Wonder, and it was surmised that the agent believed Tom to be at the bottom of his troubles.

In a few days the young inventor was himself again, and as further trials of his battery showed it to be even better than its owner hoped, arrangements were made for testing it in the car on the road.

The runabout was nearly finished, but it lacked a coat of varnish, and some minor details, when Tom, assisted by his father, Mr Sharp and Mr. Jackson, one morning, about a week later, installed the motor and battery units. It did not take long to gear up the machinery, connect the battery and, though the car was rather a crude looking affair, Tom decided to give it a try-out

"Want to come along, Dad?" he asked, as he tightened up some binding posts, and looked to see that the steering wheel, starting and reverse levers worked properly, and that the side chains were well lubricated.

"Not the first time," replied his father. "Let's see how it runs with you, first."

"Oh, I want some sort of a load in it," went on the lad. "It won't be a good test unless I have a couple of others besides myself. How about you, Mr. Damon?" for the old gentleman was spending a few days at the Swift homestead.

"Bless my shoe buttons! I'll come!" was the ready answer. "After the experience I've been through in the airship and submarine, nothing can scare me. Lead on, I'll follow!"

"I don't suppose you'll hang back after that; will you, Mr. Sharp?" asked the lad, with a laugh.

"I don't dare to, for the sake of my reputation," was the reply, for the balloonist who had made many ascensions, and dropped thousands of feet in parachutes, was naturally a brave man.

So he and Mr. Damon climbed into the rear seats of the odd- looking electric car, while Tom took his place at the steering wheel.

"Are you all ready?" he asked.

"Let her go!" fired back Mr. Sharp.

"Bless my galvanometer, don't go too fast on the start," cautioned Mr. Damon, nervously.

"I'll not," agreed the young inventor. "I want to get it warmed up before I try any speeding."

He turned on the current. There was a low, humming purr, which gradually increased to a whine, and the car moved slowly forward. It rolled along the gravel driveway to the road, Tom listening to every sound of the machinery, as a mother listens to the breathing of a child.

"She's moving!" he cried.

"But not much faster than a wheelbarrow," said his father, who sometimes teased his son.

"Wait!" cried the youth.

Tom turned more current into the motor. The purring and humming increased, and the car seemed to leap forward. It was in the road now, and, once assured that the steering apparatus was working well, Tom suddenly turned on much more speed.

So quickly did the electric auto shoot forward that Mr. Damon and Mr. Sharp were jerked back against the cushions of the rear seats.

"Here! What are you doing?" inquired Mr. Sharp.

"I'm going to show you a little speed," answered Tom.

The car was now moving rapidly, and there was a smoothness and lightness to its progress that was absent from a gasolene auto. There was no vibration from the motor. Faster and faster it ran, until it was moving at a speed scarcely less than that of Mr. Damon's car, when it was doing its best. Of course that was not saying much, for the car owned by the odd gentleman was not a very powerful one, but it could make fast time occasionally.

"Is this the best you can do?" asked Mr. Damon. "Not that it isn't fast," he hastened to add, "and I was wondering if it was your limit."

"Not half!" cried Tom, as he turned on a little more power. "I'm not trying for a record to-day. I just want to see how the battery and motor behaves."

"Pretty well, I should say," commented Mr. Sharp.

"I'm satisfied—so far," agreed the lad.

They were now moving along the highway at a good speed—moving almost silently, too, for the motor, save for a low hum, made no noise. So quiet was the car, in fact, that it was nearly the cause of a disaster. Tom was so interested in the performance of his latest invention, that, before he knew it, he had come up behind a farmer, driving a team of skittish horses. As the big machine went past them, giving no warning of its approach, the steeds reared up, and would have bolted, but for the prompt action of the driver.

"Hey!" he cried, angrily, as Tom speeded past, "don't you know you got to give warnin' when you're comin' with one of them ther gol-swizzled things! By Jehossephat I'll have th' law on ye ef ye do thet ag'in!"

"I forgot to ring the bell," apologized Tom, as he sent out a peal from the gong, and then, he let out a few more amperes, and the speed increased.

"Hold on! I guess this is fast enough!" cried Mr. Damon, as his hat blew off.

"Fast?" answered Tom. "This is nothing to what I'll do when I use the full power. Then I'll—"

He was interrupted by a sharp report, and a vivid flash of fire on a switch board near the steering wheel. The motor gave a sort of groan, and stopped, the car rolling on a little way, and then becoming stationary.

"Bless my collar button!" ejaculated Mr. Damon.

"What's the matter?" inquired Mr. Sharp.

"Some sort of a blow-out," answered Tom ruefully, as he shoved the starting handle over, trying to move the car. But it would not budge. The new auto had "gone dead" on her first tryout. The young inventor was grievously disappointed.

Towed by a Mule

"Bless my gizzard! Is it anything serious?" asked Mr. Damon. "Will it blow up, or anything like that?"

"No," replied the lad, as he leaped out of the car, and began to make an examination. Mr. Sharp assisted him.

"The motor seems to be all right," remarked the balloonist, as he inspected it.

"Yes," agreed our hero, "and the batteries have plenty of power left in them yet. The gauge shows that. I can't understand what the trouble can be, unless—" He paused in his remark and uttered an exclamation. "I've found it!" he cried.

"What?" demanded the aeronaut.

"Some of the fuses blew out. I turned on too much current, and the fuses wouldn't carry it. I put them in to save the motor from being burned out, but I didn't use heavy enough ones. I see where my mistake was."

"But what does it mean?" inquired Mr. Damon.

"It means that we've got to walk back home," was Tom's sorrowful answer. "The car is stalled, for I haven't any extra fuses with me."

"Can't you connect up the battery by using some extra wire?" asked Mr. Sharp. "I have some," and he drew a coil of it from his pocket.

"I wouldn't dare to. It might be so heavy that it would carry more current than the motor could stand. I don't want to burn that out. No, I guess we'll have to walk home, or rather I will. You two can stay here until I come back with heavier fuses. I'm sorry."

Tom had hardly ceased speaking, when, from around the turn in the road proceeded a voice, and, at the sound of it all three started, for the voice was saying:

"Now it ain't no use fer yo' to act dat-a-way, Boomerang. Yo' all ain't got no call t' git contrary now, jest when I wants t' git home t' mah dinner. I should t'ink you'd want t' git t' de stable, too. But ef yo' all ain't mighty keerful I'll cut down yo' rations, dat's what I'se goin' to do. G'lang, now, dat's a good feller. Ho! Ho! I knowed dat'd fetch yo' all. When yo' all wiggles yo' ears dat-a-way, dat's a suah sign yo' all is gwine t' move."

Then followed the sound of a rattletrap of a wagon approaching.

"Eradicate! It's Eradicate!" exclaimed Tom.

"And his mule, Boomerang!" added Mr. Sharp. "He's just in time!" commented Mr. Damon with a sigh of relief, as the ancient outfit, in charge of the aged colored man, came along. Eradicate had been sent to Shopton to get a load of wood for Mr. Swift, and was now returning. At the sight of the stalled auto the mule pricked up his long ears, and threw them forward.

"Whoa dar, now, Boomerang!" cried Eradicate. "Doan't yo' all commence t' gittin' skittish. Dat machine ain't gwine t' hurt yo'. Why good land a' massy!

Ef 'tain't Mistah Swift!" cried the colored man, as he caught sight of Tom. "What's de trouble?" he asked.

"Broke down," answered the young inventor briefly. "You always seem to come along when I'm in trouble, Rad."

"Dat's right," assented the darkey, with a grin. "Me an' trouble am ole acquaintances. Sometimes she hits me a clip on de haid, den, ag'in Boomerang, mah mule, gits it. He jest had his trouble. Got a stone under his shoe, an' didn't want t' move. Den when I did git him started he balked on me. But I'se all right now. But I suah am sorry fo' you. Can't I help yo' all, Mistah Swift?"

"Yes, you can, Rad," answered Tom. "Drive home as fast as you can, and ask Dad to send back with you some of those fuses he'll find on my work bench. He knows what I want. Hurry there and hurry back."

Eradicate shook his head doubtfully.

"What's the matter? Don't you want to go?" asked Mr. Sharp, a trifle nettled. "We can't get the car started until we have some new fuses.."

"Oh, I wants t' go all right 'nuff, Mistah Sharp," was Eradicate's prompt answer. "Yo' all knows I'd do anyt'ing t' 'blige yo' or Mistah Swift. But hits dish yeah mule, Boomerang. I jest done promised him dat we were gwine home t' dinnah, an' he 'spects a manger full ob oats. Ef I got to Mistah Swift's house wid him, I couldn't no mo' git him t' come back widout his dinnah, dan yo' all kin git dat 'ar car t' move widout dem fusin' t'ings yo' all talked about."

"Bless my necktie!" exclaimed Mr. Damon. "That's all nonsense! You don't suppose that mule understands what you say to him, do you? How does he know you promised him his dinner?"

"I doan't know how he know, Mistah Damon," replied Eradicate, "but he do know, jest de same. I know hit would be laik pullin' teeth an' wuss too, t' git Boomerang t' start back wid dem foosd t'ings until after he's had his dinner. Wouldn't it, Boomerang?"

The mule waved his long ears as if in answer.

"Bless my soul, I believe he does understand!" cried Mr. Damon.

"Of course he do," put in the colored man. "I'se awful sorry. Now if it were afternoon I could bring back dem what-d'ye-call- 'ems in a jiffy, 'cause Boomerang allers feels good arter he has his dinnah, but befo' dat—" and Eradicate shook his head, as if there was no more to be said on the subject.

"Well," remarked Tom, sadly, "I guess there's no help for it. We'll have to walk home, unless you two want to wait until I can ride back with Eradicate, and come back on my motor cycle. Then I'll have to leave the cycle here, for I can't get it in the car."

"Bless my collar button!" cried Mr. Damon. "It's like the puzzle of the fox, the goose and the bag of corn on the banks of a stream. I guess we'd better all walk."

"Hold on!" exclaimed Mr. Sharp. "Is your mule good and strong, Eradicate?"

"Strong? Why dish yeah mule could pull a house ober—dat is when he's got a mind to. An' he'd do most anyt'ing now, 'ca'se he's anxious t' git home t' his dinnah; ain't yo' all, Boomerang?"

Once more the mule waved his ears, like signal flags.

"Then I have a proposition to make," went on the balloonist. "Unhitch the mule from the load of wood, and hitch him to the auto. We've got some rope along, I noticed. Then the mule can pull us and the runabout home."

"Good idea!" cried Mr. Damon.

"Dat's de racket!" ejaculated Eradicate. "I'll jest sequesterate dish year load ob wood side ob de road, an' hitch Boomerang to de auto."

Tom said nothing for a few seconds. He gazed sadly at his auto, which he hoped would win the touring club's prize. It was a bitter pill for him to swallow.

"Towed by a mule!" he exclaimed, shaking his head, and smiling ruefully. "The fastest car in this country towed by a mule! It's tough luck!"

"'Tain't half so bad as goin' widout yo' dinnah, Mistah Swift!" remarked Eradicate, as he began to harness the mule to the electric runabout.

Boomerang made no objection to the transfer. He looked around once or twice as he was being made fast to the auto and, when the word was given he stepped out as if pulling home stalled cars was his regular business. Tom sat beside Eradicate on the front seat, and steered, while the colored man drove the mule, and Mr. Sharp and Mr. Damon were in the "tonneau" seats as Tom called them.

"I hope no one sees us," thought Tom, but he was doomed to disappointment. When nearly home he heard an auto approaching, and in it were Andy Foger, Sam Snedecker and Pete Bailey. The three cronies stared at the odd sight of Boomerang ambling along, with his great ears flapping, drawing Tom's speedy new car.

"Ha! Ha!" laughed Andy. "So that's the motive power he's going to use! Look at him, fellows. I thought his new electric, that was going to beat my car, and win the prize, was to be two hundred horse power. Instead it's one mule power! That's rich!" and Andy's chums joined in the laugh at poor Tom.

The young imventor said nothing, for there was nothing he could say. In dignified silence he passed the car containing his enemies, they, meanwhile, jeering at him.

"Dat's all right," spoke Eradicate, sympathizing with his young employer. "Maybe dey'll 'want a tow derselves some day, an' when dey does, I'll make Boomerang pull 'em in a ditch."

But this was small comfort to Tom. He made up his mind, though, that he would demonstrate that his car could do all that he had claimed for it, and that very soon.

A Great Run

Boomerang did not belie the reputation Eradicate had given him as a beast of strength. Though the electric runabout was heavy, the mule managed to move it along the road at a fair speed, with the four occupants. Perhaps the animal knew that at the end of his journey a good feed awaited him. At any rate they were soon within sight of the Swift home.

Mr. Damon and Mr. Sharp refrained from making any comments that might hurt Tom's feelings, for they realized the chagrin felt by the young inventor in having his apparatus go back on him at the first trial. But our hero was not the kind of a lad who is disheartened by one failure, or even half a dozen.

The humor of the situation appealed to him, and, as he turned the auto into the driveway, and noticed Boomerang's long ears waving to and fro, he laughed.

The lad insisted on putting new fuses in the car before he ate his dinner, and then, satisfied that the motor was once more in running order, he partook of a hasty meal, and began making several changes which he had decided were desirable. He finished them in time to go for a little run in the car all alone on a secluded road late that afternoon.

Tom returned, with eyes shining, and cheeks flushed with elation.

"Well, how did it go? asked his father.

"Fine! Better than I expected," responded his son enthusiastically. "When it gets to running smoothly I'll pass anything on the road."

"Don't be too sure," cautioned Mr. Swift, but Tom only smiled.

There was still much to do on the electric runabout, and Tom spent the next few days in adjusting the light steel wind-shield, that was to come down over the driver's seat. He also put in a powerful electric search-light, which was run by current from the battery, and installed a new speedometer and an instrument to tell how much current he was using, and how much longer the battery would run without being exhausted. This was to enable him to know when to begin re-charging it. When the current was all consumed it was necessary to store more in the battery. This could be done by attaching wires from a dynamo, or, in an emergency by tapping an electric light wire in the street. But as the battery would enable the car to run many miles on one charging, Tom did not think he would ever have to resort to the emergency charging apparatus. He had a new system for this, one that enabled him to do the work in much less than the usual time.

With his new car still unpainted, and rather rough and crude in appearance, the lad started out alone one morning, his father and Mr. Sharp having declined to accompany him, on the plea of business to attend to, and Mr. Damon not being at the Swift house.

Tom rode about for several hours, giving his car several severe tests in the way of going up hills, and speeding on the level. He was proceeding along a quiet country road, in a small town about fifteen miles from Shopton, when, as he flashed past the small railroad station, he saw a familiar figure standing on the platform.

"Why, Ned!" called Tom, "what are you doing over here?"

"I might ask the same thing of you. Is that your new car? It doesn't look very new."

"Yes, this is it. I haven't had a chance to paint and varnish it yet. But you ought to see it go. What are doing here, though?"

"I came over on some bank business. A customer here had some bonds he wanted to dispose of and I came for them. You see we're enlarging our business since the new bank started."

"Has it hurt your bank any?"

"Not yet, but Foger and his associates are trying hard to make us lose money. Say, did you ever see such a place as this? I've got to wait two hours for a train back to Shopton."

"No you haven't."

"Why not? Have they changed the timetable since I came over this morning?"

"No, but you can ride back with me. I'm going, and I'll show you what my new electric car can do."

"Good!" cried the young bank cashier. "You're just in time. I was wondering how I could kill two hours, but now I'll get in your new car and—"

"And maybe we'll kill a few chickens, or a dog or two when we get her speeded up," put in Tom, with a laugh in which Ned joined.

The two lads, seated in the front part of the auto, were soon moving down the hard highway. Suddenly Tom pulled a lever and the steel wind-shield came sliding down from the top case, meeting the forward battery compartment, and forming a sort of slanting roof over the heads of the two occupants.

"Here! What's this?" cried Ned.

"We're going to hit it up in a few minutes," replied the young inventor, "and I want to reduce the wind resistance."

"Oh, I thought maybe we were going through a bombardment. It's all right, go ahead, don't mind me. I'm game."

There was a celluloid window in the steel wind-shield, and through this the lads could observe the road ahead of them.

As they swung along it, the speed increasing, Ned saw an auto ahead of them.

"Whose car is that?" he asked.

"Don't know," replied Tom. "We'll be up to it in about half a minute, though."

As the electric runabout, more dilapidated looking than ever from the layer of dust that covered it, passed the other auto, which was a powerful car, the solitary occupant of it, a middle-aged man, looked to one side, and, seeing the queer machine, remarked:

"You fellows are going the wrong way to the junk heap. Turn around."

"Is that so?" asked Tom, his eyes flashing at the cheap wit of the man. "Why we came out here to show you the way!"

"Do you want to race?" asked the man eagerly, too eagerly, Ned thought. "I'll give you a brush, if you do, and a handicap into the bargain."

"We don't need it," replied the young inventor quickly.

"I'll wager fifty dollars I can beat you bad on this three-mile stretch," went on the autoist. "How about it?"

"I'll race you, but I don't bet," answered Tom, a bit stiffly.

"Oh, be a sport," urged the man.

Tom shook his head. He had slowed down his machine, and was running even with the gasolene car now. He noticed that it was a new one, of six cylinders, and looked speedy. Perhaps he was foolish to pit his untried car against it. Yet he had confidence in his battery and motor.

"Well, we'll race for the fun of it then," went on the man. "Do you want a handicap?"

Tom shook his head again, and there came around his mouth a grim look.

"All right," assented the other. "Only you're going to be beat badly. I never saw an electric car yet that could do anything except to crawl along."

"You're going to see one now," was all the retort Tom permitted himself.

"Here we go then!" cried the man, and he gave his gear handle a yank, and shoved over the sparking and gasolene levers.

His car instantly shot ahead, and went "chug chugging" down the road in a cloud of dust. At the same moment Tom, in answer to a look from Ned, who feared his friend was going to be left behind, turned more power into the motor. The humming, purring sound increased and the electric car forged ahead.

"Can you catch him?" asked Ned.

"Watch," was all Tom said.

The hum of the motor became a sort of whine, and the electric rapidly acquired speed. It crept up on the gasolene car, as an express train overtakes a freight, and the man, looking back, and expecting to see his rival far behind was surprised to note the queer looking vehicle lapping his rear wheels.

"Well, you are coming on, aren't you?" he asked. "Maybe you'll keep up now!" He shifted the gears, using a little more gasolene. For a moment his car opened a wide gap between it and Tom's, but the young inventor had only begun to race. Still louder purred the motor, and in a few minutes Tom was running on even terms with his competitor. The man looked annoyed, and tried, by the skilful use of gasolene and sparking levers, to leave Tom behind. But the electric held her own.

"I've got to go the limit I see," remarked the man at last, glancing sideways at the other car. "I'll tell 'em you're coming," he added, "though I must say your electric does better than any of its kind I ever came across."

"I'm not done yet," was the comment of our hero. But the man did not hear him, for he was yanking into place the lever that enabled him to run on direct drive for fourth speed.

Forward shot his car, and, for perhaps a quarter of a mile it led. The racers were almost at the end of the three-mile level stretch of road, and if Tom was going to win the impromptu contest it seemed high time he began.

"Can you catch him?" asked Ned anxiously.

"Watch," was his chum's reply. "I haven't used my high speed gear yet. I'm afraid the fuses won't stand it, but here goes for a try, anyhow."

He threw over a switch, changed a lever and then, having pushed into place the last gear, he grasped the steering wheel more firmly.

There was need of it, for, in an instant, the electric runabout, with the motors fairly roaring, swept up the road, after the gasolene car that was almost hidden from sight in a cloud of dust. Faster and faster went Tom's car. The young inventor was listening with critical ear to the song of the machinery. He wanted to learn if it was running sweet and true, for that is how a careful mechanic tests his apparatus. Foot by foot the distance between the two cars lessened. Now the electric was lapping the rear wheels of the gasolene machine, but the driver did not know it. His whole attention was on the road ahead of him.

"Half a mile more!" cried Ned, naming the distance which yet remained of the straight stretch. "Can you do it, Tom?"

His chum nodded. He shoved the controller handle over to the last notch, and then waited an anxious second. Would the fuse carry the extra load? It seemed so, for there was a slight increase of power.

An instant later Tom gave a sudden twist to the steering wheel. It was well that he did, for he was passing the gasolene car dangerously close. Then he was ahead of it, and in a second he was three lengths in advance.

Desperately the man opened his muffler, and sought to gain by this advantage, but though his car gave off explosions like a battery of guns in action, he could not gain on Tom. The electric shot around a curve in the road, winner of the impromptu race by an eighth of a mile.

"Well," asked Tom of his chum, as he slowed down, for the road now was not so good, "did I do it?"

"You certainly did. Whew! But we did scoot along?"

"Eighty miles an hour there one spell," went on the young inventor, glancing at a gauge. "But I've got to do better than that to win the big race."

Andy Foger's Black Eye

Around the bend came the six-cylinder touring car. The driver, with a surprised look on his face, was slacking up. He ran his machine up alongside of Tom's.

"Say," he asked, in dazed tones, "did you take a short cut, or anything like that to get ahead of me?"

"No," answered the youth.

"And you didn't jump me in the air?"

"No," was Tom's answer, smilingly given.

"Well, all I've got to say is that you've got a wonderful car there, Mr.—er—er—" He paused suggestively.

"Swift is my name," our hero answered. "Thomas Swift, of Shopton."

"Ah, I've heard of you. My name is Layton —Paul Layton. I'm from Netherton. Let's see, you built an airship, didn't you?"

"I helped," Tom admitted modestly.

"Well, you beat me fair and square, and if I do say it myself I've got a fairly speedy car. Took two firsts at the Indianapolis meet last month. But you certainly scooted ahead of me. Where did you buy that electric, if I may ask?"

"I made it."

"I might have known," admitted the man. "But are you going to put them on the market? If you are I'd like to get one. I want the fastest car going, and you seem to have it."

"I hadn't thought of manufacturing them for sale," said the young inventor. "If I do, I'll let you know."

"I wish you would. My! I had no idea you could beat me, but you did—fair and square."

There was some more talk, and then Mr. Layton started on, after exacting from Tom a further promise to let him know if any electrics were to be made for sale.

"You certainly have a wonderful car," complimented Ned, as he and his chum took a short cut to Shopton.

"Well, I'm not quite satisfied with it," declared Tom.

"Why not?"

"Well, I've set a hundred miles an hour as my limit. I didn't make but eighty to-day. I've got to have more speed if I go up against the crowd that will race for the touring club's prize."

"Can you make a hundred miles?"

"I think so. I've got to change my gears, though, and use heavier fuses. I was afraid every second that one of the fuses would melt, and leave me stranded. But they stood pretty well. Of course, when the car, geared as it is now, has been run a little longer it will go faster, but it won't come up to a hundred miles an hour. That's what I want, and that's what I'm going to get," and the lad looked very determined.

Ned was taken to the bank, and, as Tom turned his machine around, to go home, he saw, standing on the steps of the new bank, which was almost across the street from the old one, Andy Foger, and the bully's father. The red-haired lad laughed at Tom's rough looking car, and said something to his parent, but Mr. Foger did not notice Tom. Not that this caused our hero any uneasiness, however.

But, as he swung away from the bank, he saw, coming up the street a figure that instantly attracted his attention. It was that of Mr. Berg, and Tom at once recalled the night he had pursued the submarine agent, and torn loose his watch charm. Mr. Berg was evidently going to enter the new bank, for, at the sight of the former agent, Mr. Foger descended the steps, and went to meet him.

Tom, however, had decided upon a plan of action. He steered his machine in toward the curb, ran up the steel wind-shield, and called:

"Mr. Berg!"

"Eh? What's that?" asked the agent, in some surprise. Then, as he caught sight of Tom, and recognized him, he added: "I'm very busy now, my young friend. You'll have to excuse me."

"I won't detain you a moment," went on Tom, casually. "I have something of yours that I wish to return to you."

"Something of mine?" Mr. Berg was evidently puzzled. He approached the electric car, in spite of the fact that Mr. Foger was calling him. "Something of mine? What is it?"

"This!" exclaimed Tom suddenly, extending the compass watch charm, which he always carried with him of late.

"That! Where did you get that. I lost it—"

Mr. Berg paused in some confusion.

"I grabbed it off your watch chain the night you were hiding in our shrubbery, and tripped me into the brook," answered the lad, looking the man squarely in the eye.

"Hiding? Tripped you? Grabbed that off my chain—" stammered Mr. Berg. He had taken the charm up in his fingers, but now he quickly dropped it back into Tom's hand. "I guess you're mistaken," he added quickly. "That's not mine. I never had one— I—er—that's not mine—at least—Oh, you'll have to excuse me, young man, I'm in a hurry, and I have an important engagement!" and with that Mr. Berg wheeled off, and joined Mr. Foger, who stood on the sidewalk, waiting for him.

"I thought sure it was yours," said Tom, easily. "Perhaps Mr. Foger will keep it in one of the safety-deposit boxes of his bank, until the owner claims it," and he looked at the banker.

"What's that?" asked Andy's father.

"This watch charm which I grabbed off Mr. Berg's chain the night he was sneaking around our house, and crossed the electric wires," went on the lad.

"Don't listen to him. He doesn't know what he is saying!" exclaimed the former submarine boat agent. "It's not my charm. He's crazy!"

"Oh, am I?" thought Tom, with a grim look on his face. "Well, we'll see about that, Mr. Berg," and, putting the charm back in his pocket, Tom swung his machine toward home, while the agent and the banker entered the new institution.

"So they're getting chummy," mused Tom. "Andy and Berg were friends when Andy shut me up in the submarine tank, and now Berg comes here to do business, and Foger and his associates are trying to put the old bank out of business. I wonder if there's any connection there? I must keep my eyes open. Berg is an unscrupulous man, and so is Andy's father, to say nothing of the red-haired bully himself. He had nerve to deny that was his charm. Well, maybe I'll catch him some day."

Tom spent a busy week making new adjustments to his electric car, changing the gear and providing for heavier fuses. He was planning for another trip on the road, as the time for the great race was drawing near, and he wanted the mechanism to be in perfect shape.

One evening, as he was preparing for a short night trip to Mansburg, where he had promised to call for Miss Nestor, Tom left his machine standing in the road in front of the house, while he went back to get a robe, as it threatened to be chilly.

As he came back to enter the car, he saw some one standing near it.

"Is that you, Ned?" he called. "Come, take a spin."

Hardly had he spoken than there sounded from the machine a whirr that told of the current being turned on.

"Don't do that!" cried Tom, knowing at once that it could not be Ned, who never meddled with the machinery.

A blinding flash and a loud report followed, and Tom saw some one leap from his car, and try to run away. But the figure stumbled, and, a moment later the young inventor was upon him, grappling with him.

"Here! Let me go!" cried a voice, and Tom uttered an exclamation of surprise.

"Andy Foger!" he cried. "I've caught you! You tried to damage my car!"

"Yes, and I'm hurt, too!" whined Andy. "My father will sue you for damages if I die."

"No danger of that; you're too mean," murmured Tom, as he maintained a tight grip on the bully.

"You let me go!" demanded Andy, squirming to get away.

"Wait until I see what damage you've done,'~ retorted the young inventor. "The worst, though, would be the blowing out of a fuse, for I had the gear disconnected. You wait a minute now. Maybe it's you who'll have to pay damages."

"You let me go!" fairly screamed Andy, and he aimed a blow at Tom. It caught our hero on the chest and Tom's fighting blood was up in an instant.

He drew back his left hand, and delivered a blow that landed fairly on Andy's right eye. The bully staggered and went down in the dust.

"There!" cried Tom, righteously angry. "That will teach you not to try to damage my car, and then hit me into the bargain! Now clear out, before I give you some more!"

Whining and blubbering Andy arose to his feet.

"You just wait. I'll get square with you for this," he threatened.

"You can accept part of that as pay for what you did in the tar and feathering game," added Tom. Then, as Andy moved in front of one of the electric side lamps on the car, Tom uttered a whistle of surprise. For both of Andy's eyes were bruised and swollen, though Tom had only hit him once.

"Look at me!" cried the bully, more squint-eyed than ever. "Look at me! You hit me in one eye, and that explosion hit me in the other! My father will sue you for this."

As he hurried off down the road Tom understood. Andy coming along, had seen Tom's car standing there, and, thinking to do some mischief, had climbed in, and turned on the power. Perhaps he hoped it would run into the roadside ditch and be smashed. But as the gear was out, turning on the electric current had a different effect. As the bully pulled the handle over too quickly, throwing almost the entire force of the battery into the wires at once, the load was too heavy for them. A safety fuse blew out, causing the flare and the explosion, and a piece of the soft lead-like metal had hit the red-haired lad in the eye. Tom's fist had completed the work on the other optic, and for several days thereafter Andy Foger remained in seclusion. When he did go out there were many embarrassing questions put to him, as to when he had had the fight. Andy didn't care to answer. As for Tom, it did not take long to put a new fuse in his car, and he greatly enjoyed his ride with Miss Nestor that night.

TROUBLE AT THE BANK

Coming in rather late from his trip to Mansburg, and thinking of some things he and Miss Nestor had talked about, Tom was rather surprised, on reaching the house, to see a light in his father's particular room, where the aged inventor did his reading and his planning of new devices.

"Dad's up rather late," said Tom to himself. "I wonder if he's studying over some new machine."

The lad ran his auto into the temporary garage he had built for it, and connected the wires of a burglar alarm he had arranged, to give warning in case any of his enemies should seek to damage the car.

Tom encountered Garret Jackson, the aged inventor who was going his rounds, seeing that everything was all right about the various shops.

"Anybody with my father, Garret?" asked the lad. "I see he's still up."

"Yes," was the rather unexpected reply. "Mr. Damon is with him. They've been in your father's room all the evening—ever since you went away in the car."

"Anything the matter?" inquired the young inventor, a bit anxious, as he thought of the Happy Harry gang.

"Well, I don't know," and the engineer seemed puzzled. "They called me in once to know if everything was all right outside, and to inquire if you were back. I saw, then, that they were busy figuring over something, but I didn't take much notice. Only I heard Mr. Damon say: 'There's going to be trouble if we can't realize on those bonds,' and then I came away."

"Is that all he said?" asked Tom.

"No, he said 'Bless my buttons,' or something like that; but he blesses so many things I didn't pay much attention."

"That's right," agreed the lad. "But I wonder what the trouble is about? I must go see."

As he passed along the hall, out of which his father's combined study and library opened, the aged inventor came to the door.

"Is that you, Tom?" he asked.

"Yes, Dad."

"Come in here, if you haven't anything else to do. Mr. Damon is here."

Tom needed but a single glance at the faces of his father and Mr. Damon to see that something was troubling the two. The table in front of them was littered with papers covered with rows of figures.

"What's the matter?" asked Tom.

"Well, I suppose I ought not to let it bother me, but it does," replied his father.

"Something wrong with your patents, Dad? Has the crowd of bad men been bothering you again?"

"No, it isn't that. It's trouble at the bank, Tom."

"Has it been robbed again?" asked the lad quickly. "If it has I can prove an alibi," and he smiled at the recollection of the time he and Mr. Damon had been accused of looting the vault, as told in "Tom Swift and His Airship."

"No, it hasn't been robbed in just that way," put in Mr. Damon. "But, bless my shoe laces, it's almost as bad! You see, Tom, since Mr. Foger started the new bank he's done his best to cripple the one in which your father and I are interested. I may say we are very vitally interested in it, for, since the withdrawal of Foger and his associates, your father and I have been elected directors."

"I didn't know that," remarked the lad.

"No, I didn't tell you, because you were so busy on your electric car," rejoined Mr. Swift. "But Mr. Damon and I, being both large depositors, were asked to assume office, and, as I was not very busy on patent affairs, I consented."

"But what is the trouble?" inquired Tom.

"I'm coming to it," resumed Mr. Damon. "Bless my check book, I'm coming to it! You see we have lost several good customers, by reason of Foger opening the new bank. That wouldn't have mattered so much, as between your father and myself, and one or two others, we have enough capital to carry on the business of the bank. But there is a more serious matter. We hold a number of very good securities, but they are of a class hard to realize cash for, on short notice. In other words they are not active bonds, though they are issued by reliable concerns. Then, too, the bank has lost considerable money by not doing as much business as it formerly did. In short we don't know just what to do, Tom, and your father and I were discussing it, when you came in."

"Do you need more money?" asked Tom. "I have some, that is my share from the submarine treasure, and some I have allowed to accumulate as royalties from my patents. It's about ten thousand dollars, and you're welcome to it."

"Thank you, Tom," spoke his father. "We may use your cash, but we'll need a great deal more than that."

"But why?" asked the lad. "I don't understand. If you have good bonds, can't you dispose of them, and get the money?"

"We could, Tom, yes, if we had time," replied Mr. Damon. "But to throw the bonds on the market at short notice would mean that we would not get a good price for them. We would lose considerable."

"But why do it in a hurry?"

"Because there is need of hurry," responded Mr. Swift.

"That's it," joined in Mr. Damon. "We have to have cash in a hurry, Tom, to meet pressing demands, and we don't just see our way clear to get it. I am trying to raise it on some private securities I own, but I can't get an answer within several days. Meanwhile the bank may fail, because of lack of funds. Of course no one would lose anything, ultimately, as we could go into the hands of a receiver, and, eventually, pay dollar for dollar. Your father and I, and some of the other directors, might lose a little, but the depositors would not. But your father and I don't like the idea of failing. It's something I've never done, and I'm too old to start in now, bless my cash ledger if I'm not!"

"And for the sake of my reputation in this community I don't want to see the bank close its doors," added Mr. Swift. "It would give Foger too good a chance to crow over us."

"And you need cash in a hurry," went on Tom. "How much?"

"Fifty thousand dollars at least," replied Mr. Damon.

"And if you don't get it?"

The eccentric man shrugged his shoulders.

"Well," remarked Mr. Swift musingly, "I don't see that we need worry you about it, Tom. Perhaps—"

Mr. Swift was interrupted by a ring at the front door. The three looked at each other. It was late for a caller, and Mrs. Baggert had gone to bed.

"I'll answer it," volunteered Tom. He switched on the electric light in the hall, and opened the door. He was confronted by Mr. Pendergast, the president of the bank.

"Is your father in?" asked Mr. Pendergast, and he seemed to be much agitated.

"Yes, he is," replied the lad. "Come this way, please."

"I want to see him on important business," went on the president, as he followed the young inventor. "I'm afraid I have bad news for him and Mr. Damon. Bad news, Tom, bad news," and the aged banker's voice trembled. Tom, with a chill of apprehension seeming to clutch his heart, threw open the library door.

A Run on the Bank

"Why, Mr. Pendergast!" exclaimed Mr. Damon, rising quickly as Tom ushered in the aged president. "Whatever is the matter? You here at this hour? Bless my trial balance! Is anything wrong?

"I'm afraid there is," answered the bank head. "I have just received word which made it necessary for me to see you both at once. I'm glad you're here, Mr. Damon."

He sank wearily into a chair which Tom placed for him, and Mr. Swift asked:

"Have you been able to raise any cash, Mr. Pendergast?"

"No, I am sorry to say I have not, but I did not come here to tell you that. I have bad news for you. As soon as we open our doors in the morning, there will be a run on the bank." "A run on the bank?" repeated Mr. Swift.

"The moment we begin business in the morning," went on Mr. Pendergast.

"Bless my soul, then don't begin business!" cried Mr. Damon.

"We must," insisted Mr. Pendergast. "To keep the doors closed would be a confession at once that we have failed. No, it is better to open them, and stand the run as long as we can. When we have exhausted our cash—" he paused.

"Well?" asked Mr. Damon.

"Then we'll fail—that's all."

"But we mustn't let the bank fail!" cried Mr. Swift. "I am willing to put some of my personal fortune into the bank capital in order to save it. So is my son here."

"That's right," chimed in Tom heartily. "All I've got. I'm not going to let Andy Foger get ahead of us; nor his father either."

"I'll help to the limit of my ability," added Mr. Damon.

"I appreciate all that," continued the president. "But the unfortunate part of it is that we need cash. You gentlemen, like myself, probably, have your money tied up in stocks and bonds. It is hard to get cash quickly, and we must have cash as soon as we open in the morning, to pay the depositors who will come flocking to the doors. We must prepare for a run on the bank."

"How do you know there will be a run?" asked the young inventor.

"I received word this evening, just before I came here," replied Mr. Pendergast. "A poor widow, who has a small amount in the bank, called on me and said she had been advised to withdraw all her cash. She said she preferred to see me about it first, as she did not like to lose her interest. She said a number of her acquaintances, some of whom are quite heavy depositors, had also been warned that the bank was unsound, and that they ought to take out their savings and deposits at once."

"Did she say who had thus warned her?" inquired Mr. Swift.

"She did," was the reply, "and that shows me that there is a conspiracy on foot to ruin our bank. She stated that Mr. Foger had told her our institution was unsound."

"Mr. Foger!" cried Mr. Damon. "So this is one of his tricks to bolster up his new bank! He hopes the people who withdraw their money from our bank will deposit with him. I see his game. He's a scoundrel, and if it's possible I'm going to sue him for damages after this thing is over."

"Did he warn the others?" inquired the aged inventor.

"Not all of them," answered the president. "Some received letters from a man signing himself Addison Berg, warning them that our bank, was likely to fail any day."

"Addison Berg!" exclaimed Tom. "That must have been the important business he had with Mr. Foger, the day I showed him the watch charm! They were plotting the ruin of our bank then," and he told his father about his disastrous pursuit of the submarine agent.

"Very likely Foger is working with Berg," admitted Mr. Damon. "We will attend to them later. The question is, what can we do to save the bank?"

"Get cash, and plenty of it," advised Mr. Pendergast. "Suppose we go over the whole situation again?" and they fell to talking stocks: bonds, securities, mortgages and interest, until the youth, interested as he was in the situation, could follow it no longer.

"Better go to bed, Tom," advised his father. "You can't help us any, and we have many details to go over."

The lad reluctantly consented, and he was soon dreaming that he was in his electric auto, trying to pull up a thousand pound lump of gold from the bottom of the sea. He awoke to find the bedclothes in a lump on his chest, and, removing them, fell into a deep slumber.

When the young inventor awoke the next morning, Mrs. Baggert told him that his father and Mr. Damon had risen nearly an hour before, had partaken of a hearty breakfast, and departed.

"They told me to tell you they were at the bank," said the housekeeper.

"Did Mr. Pendergast stay all night?" inquired Tom.

"I heard some one go away about two o'clock this morning," replied the housekeeper. "I don't know who it was."

"They must have had a long session," thought Tom, as he began on his bacon, eggs and coffee. "I'll take a run down to the bank in my electric in a little while."

The car was still in rather crude shape, outwardly, but the mechanism was now almost perfect. Tom charged the batteries well before starting put.

The youth had no sooner come in sight of the old Shopton bank, to distinguish it from the Second National, which Mr. Foger had started, than he was aware that something unusual had occurred. There was quite a crowd about it, and more persons were constantly arriving to swell the throng.

"What's the matter?" asked Tom, of one of the few police officers of which Shopton boasted, though the lad did not need to be told.

"Run on the bank," was the brief answer. "It's failed."

Tom felt a pang of disappointment. Somehow, he had hoped that his father and his friends might have been able to stave off ruin. As he approached nearer Tom was made aware that the crowd was in an ugly mood.

"Why don't they open the doors and give us our money?" cried one excited woman. "It's ours! I worked hard for mine, an' now they want to keep it from us. I wish I'd put it in the new bank."

"Yes, that's the best place," added another. "That Mr. Foger has lots of money."

"I can see the hand of Andy's father, and that of Mr. Berg, at work here," thought Tom, "They have spread rumors of the bank's trouble, and hope to profit by it. I wish I could find a way to beat them at their own game."

As the minutes passed, and the bank was not opened, the ugly temper of the crowd increased. The few police could do nothing with the mob, and several, bolder than the rest, advocated battering down the doors. Some went up the steps and began to pound on the portals. Tom looked for a sight of his father or Mr. Damon, but could not see either.

It was not the regular hour for opening the bank, but when the police reminded the people of this they only laughed.

"I guess they ain't going to open anyhow!" shouted a man. "They've got our money, and they're going to keep it. What difference is an hour, anyway?"

"Yes, if they have the money, why don't they open, and not wait until ten o'clock?" cried another. "I've got a hundred and five dollars in there, and I want it!"

More excited persons were arriving every minute. The crowd surged this way, and that. Many looked anxiously at the clock in the tower of the town hall. The gilded hands pointed to a few minutes of ten. Would the bank open its doors when the hour boomed out? Many were anxiously asking this question.

Tom sat in his electric car, near the front of the bank. The interest of the crowd, which under ordinary circumstances would have been centered in the queer vehicle, was not drawn toward it. The people were all thinking of their money.

Suddenly one of the two doors of the bank slowly opened. There was a yell from the crowd, and a rush to get in. But the police managed to hold the leaders back, and then Tom saw that it was Ned Newton, who stood in the partly-opened portal. He held up his hand to indicate silence, and a hush fell over the mob.

"The bank is open for business," Ned announced, "but there must be no rush. The building is not large enough to accommodate you all. If you form a line, you will be admitted in turn. The bank hopes to pay you all."

"Hopes!" cried a woman scornfully. "We can't eat hopes, young man, nor yet pay the rent with it. Hopes indeed!"

But Ned had said all he cared to, and, with rather a white face, he went back inside. The one door remained open and, with a policeman on either side, a line of anxious depositors was slowly formed. Tom watched them crowding and surging forward, all eager to be first to get their cash out, lest there be not enough for all. As he watched, the young inventor was aware that some was signaling to him from the big window of the bank. He looked more closely and saw Ned Newton beckoning to him, and the young cashier was motioning Tom to go around to the rear, where a door of the bank opened on a small alley. Wondering what was wanted, Tom slowly ran his machine down the side street, and up the alley. No one paid any attention to him.

A porter admitted the lad, and he made his way to the private offices, where he knew his father and Mr. Damon would be. In the corridors he could hear the murmur of the throng and the chink of money, as the tellers paid it out.

"Well, Tom, this is bad business," remarked Mr. Swift, as he saw his son. The lad noticed that Mr. Damon was in the telephone booth.

"Yes, Dad," admitted Tom. "It's a run, all right. What are you going to do?"

"The best we can. Pay out all the cash we have, and hope that before that time, the people will come to their senses. The bank is all right if they would only wait. But I'm afraid they won't and, after we pay out all the cash we have, we'll have to close the doors. Then there's sure to be an unpleasant scene, and maybe some of the more hot-headed ones will advocate violence. We have given orders to the tellers to pay out as slowly as possible, so as to enable us to gain some time."

"And all you need is money; is that it, Dad?"

"That's it, Tom, but we have exhausted every possibility. Mr. Damon is trying a forlorn hope now, but, even if he is successful—"

Before Mr. Swift had ceased speaking, Mr. Damon fairly burst from the telephone booth. He was much excited.

"I've got it! I've got it!" he cried.

"What?" asked Mr. Swift and Tom in the same breath.

"The cash, or, what's just as good, the promise of it. I called up Mr. Chase, of the Clayton National Bank, and he has agreed to take the railroad securities I offered him as collateral, and let me have sixty thousand dollars on them! That will give us cash enough to weather the storm. Hurrah! We're all right now. Bless my check book!"

"The Clayton National Bank," remarked Mr. Swift, and his voice was hopeless. "It's forty miles away, Mr. Damon, and no railroad around here runs anywhere near it. No one could get there and back with the cash to-day, in time to save us from ruin. It's impossible! Our last chance is gone."

"How far did you say it was, Dad?" asked Tom quickly.

"Forty miles there, over forty, I guess, and not very good roads. We would need to have the cash here before three o'clock to be of any service to us. No, it's out of the question. The bank will have to fail!"

"No!" cried the young inventor, and his voice rang out through the room. "I'll get the cash for you!"

"How?" gasped Mr. Damon. "You can't get there and back in time?"

"Yes, I can!" cried Tom. "In my electric runabout! I can make it go a hundred miles an hour, if necessary! Probably I'll have to run slow over the bad roads; but I can do it! I know I can. I'll get the sixty thousand dollars for you!"

For a moment there was silence. Then Mr. Damon cried:

"Good! And I'll go with you and deliver the securities to Mr. Chase. Come on, Tom Swift! Bless my collar button, but maybe we can yet save the old bank after all!"

AFTER THE CASH

Tom's proposal as a way out of the difficulty, and the prompt seconding of it by Mr. Damon, seemed to deprive the other bank officials, Mr. Swift included, of the power of speech for a few moments. Then, as there came to the room where the scene had taken place, the sound of the mob outside, clamoring for cash, Mr. Pendergast, the president, remarked in a low voice:

"It seems to be the only way. Do you think you can do it, Tom Swift?"

"I'm sure of it, as far as my electric car is concerned," replied the young inventor. "If we get the cash I'll have it back here on time. The runabout is all ready for a fast trip."

"Then don't lose any time, Tom," advised his father. "Every minute counts."

"Yes," added Mr. Damon. "Come on. I've got the securities in my valise, and we can bring the cash back in the same satchel. Come on, Tom."

The eccentric character caught up his valise, and started from the room. Tom followed.

"Now, my son, be careful," advised his father. "You know the need of haste, but don't take unnecessary risks. You'd better go out the back way, as the crowd is easily excited."

Little more was said. Mr. Swift clasped his son's hand in a firm pressure, and the bank president nervously bade the lad good-by. Then, slipping out of the bank, by the rear entrance, the porter closing the door after them, Tom and Mr. Damon took their places in the electric machine.

"Just imagine you're racing for that three-thousand-dollar prize, offered by the Touring Club of America, Tom," observed Mr. Damon, as he deposited the valise at his feet.

"I don't have to do that," replied the youth. "I'm trying for a bigger prize than that. I want to save the bank, and defeat the schemes of the Fogers—father and son."

Tom turned on the power, and the machine rolled out on the main street. As it turned the corner, leaving the impatient crowd of depositors, now larger than ever, behind, Mr. Damon glanced over at the new bank, and, as he did so, he called to Tom:

"There are the Fogers now."

The young inventor looked, and saw Andy and his father on the steps of the new institution.

At the sight of the electric car, speeding along, Andy turned and spoke to his parent. What he said seemed to impress Mr. Foger, for he started, and looked more intently at Tom and Mr. Damon. Then, as Tom watched, he saw the two excitedly conversing, and a moment later Andy ran off in the direction in which Sam Snedecker and Pete Bailey lived.

"I wonder if he's up to any tricks?" thought Tom, as he turned on more power. "Well, if he is, I'll soon be where he can't reach me."

The young inventor did not dare send his car at full speed through the streets of the town, and it was not until several minutes had passed that they could go at more than the ordinary rate. But once the open country was reached Tom "opened her up full," and the song the motor sung was one of power. The vehicle quickly gathered headway and was soon fairly whizzing along.

"If we keep this up we'll be there and back in good time," remarked Mr. Damon.

"Yes, but we can't do it," replied his companion. "The road to Clayton is a poor one, and we'll soon be on it. Then we'll have to go slow. But I'll make all the time I can until then."

So, for several miles more they crept along, at times having to reduce to almost a walking pace, because of bad roads. Mr. Damon looked at his watch almost every other minute.

"Eleven o'clock," he remarked, as they passed a milestone, "and we're not half way there. Bless my gizzard, but I'm afraid we won't make it, Tom. We left about ten, and we ought to be back by two o'clock to do any good. That's four hours, and it will take some time to transfer the securities, and get the cash. Every minute counts."

"I know it," answered Tom, "and I'm going to count every minute."

With eager eyes he watched every inch of the road, to steer to the best advantage. His hands gripped the wheel until his knuckles showed white with the strain, and, every now and then his right hand adjusted the speed lever or the controller handle, while his foot was on the emergency brake, ready to stop the car at the first sign of danger.

And there was danger, not infrequently, for the road was up and down hill, over frail bridges, and along steep cliffs. It was no pleasure tour they were on.

When a little over half the distance had been made they came to a better road, and Tom was able to use full speed ahead. Then the electric went so fast that, had it not been for the steel wind- shield in front, Mr. Damon, at any rate, would have been short of breath.

"This is going some!" he cried to Tom. The lad nodded grimly, and shoved the controller handle over to the last notch. Then came a bad stretch and they had to slow down again. As they were about out of it there came a little flash of fire and the motor stopped.

"Bless my overshoes!" cried Mr. Damon. "What's that; a fuse blown out?"

"No," replied Tom, with a puzzled air. "But something has gone wrong." Hastily he got out, and made an examination. He found it was only one of the unimportant wires which had short-circuited, and it was soon adjusted. But they had lost five precious minutes. Tom tried to make up for lost time, but came to a hill a little later, and this reduced their speed.

"Do you think we can make it before twelve?" asked Mr. Damon anxiously. "We've got to, if we're to get back before three, Tom."

"I'll try," was the calm answer, and Tom's jaw was shut still more tightly. Once again came more favorable roads and pushing the car to the limit the occupants were rejoiced, a little later, as they topped a hill, to come in sight of a fairly large city.

"There's Clayton!" cried Mr. Damon.

Ten minutes later they were rolling through the main street, and as they stopped in front of the bank, the noon whistles blew shrill and noisily.

"You did it, Tom!" cried Mr. Damon, springing out with the valise of securities. "Now be ready for the return trip. I'll be with you as soon as possible."

He went up the bank steps three at a time, like some boy instead of an elderly man. Tom looked after him for a second and then got down to oil up his car, and make some adjustments that had rattled loose from the rough road. Unmindful of the curious throng that gathered he crawled under the machine with his oil- can.

He had finished his work, and was back in his seat, ready to start, but Mr. Damon had not reappeared.

"It's taking him a good while to get that cash," thought Tom. "Maybe the securities were no good."

But, a few minutes later, Mr. Damon came hurrying from the bank. The valise he carried seemed much heavier than when he went in.

"It's all right, Tom," he said. "I've got it. Now for the trip home, and I hope we don't have any accidents. It took longer than I thought to check over the bonds and receipt for them. But I've got the cash. Now to save the bank!"

He took his place beside the young inventor, holding the valise between his knees, while Tom turned on the power and sent his car dashing down the street, and toward the road that led to Shopton.

Stopped on the Road

"Did Mr. Chase make any objection to giving you the cash?" asked Tom, as he shoved the controller over another notch, and caused the motor to make a higher note in its song of speed.

"Oh, no, he was very nice about it," replied Mr. Damon. "He said he hoped our bank would pull through. Said if we needed more cash we could have it."

It was nearly one o'clock, and they had the worst part of the journey yet to go. Thirty miles of stiff roads lay between them and Shopton, the last five and the first five being fairly good, with, here and there, soft spots.

Up hill and down went the electric auto. At every opportunity Tom let out all the speed he could draw from the motor, but there were many times when he had to slow down. He had just made the ascent of a steep hill, and was turning into a fairly good road, skirting the edge of a steep cliff, when there came a sharp report.

"Bless my soul! That's a fuse, I'm sure of it!" cried Mr. Damon.

"No," announced Tom, as he quickly shut off the power. "It's a puncture. One of the inner tubes of the tire has been pierced. I was afraid of that tube."

"What have you got to do; put on a new tire?" asked Mr. Damon.

"No, I'm going to put on a new wheel. I carry two spare ones with tires all ready inflated. It won't take long."

But the process of changing wheels consumed more time than Tom anticipated for the nut was stuck, and he and Mr. Damon had to exert all their strength before they could loosen it. When the new wheel was in place ten minutes had been lost.

"Hold on now, I'm going to speed her!" cried Tom, when they were once more in their seats, and speed the machine he did. The road was rough, but despite this the lad turned on almost full power. Over the bumps they went, around curves and into rain- washed ruts careening from side to side, and throwing Mr. Damon about, as he expressed it afterward, "like a bean inside of a football." As for the young inventor his grasp of the steering wheel, and the manner in which he could brace himself against the foot pedals, held him more firmly in place. On and on they rushed, covering mile after mile, and approaching Shopton where so much depended on their arrival.

Good and bad stretches of the road alternated, but now that Tom had seen of what mettle his car was made, he did not spare it as much as he had on the first trip. He saw that his machine would stand hard knocks, and the way the battery and motor was behaving was a joy to him. He knew that if he could make that eighty-mile run in safety he stood a good chance of winning the prize, for no harder test could have been devised.

But the race was still far from won. There was a particularly unsafe stretch of road yet to be covered, and then would come a smooth highway into Shopton.

"Ten miles more," observed Mr Damon, snapping shut his big gold watch. "Ten miles more, and it's a quarter of two now. We ought to be there at a quarter after, and that will be in good time, eh, Tom?"

"I think so, but I don't know about this piece of road we're coming to. It seems worse than when we passed over it this morning."

As he spoke the auto began to slow up, for the wheels had struck some heavy sand, and it was necessary to reduce the current. Tom turned back the controller handle, but watched with eager eyes for a sign that the roadbed was harder, so that he could increase speed.

As the car turned around a curve, passing through a lonely stretch of country, with woods on either side of the highway, Tom glancing up, uttered a cry of astonishment.

"What's the matter; something gone wrong?" asked his companion.

For answer Tom pointed. There, just ahead of them, was a big load of hay, and it was evident that the driver, was in no particular hurry.

"We can't pass that without getting in over. our hubs!" cried Tom. "If we turn out the side ditches are so soft that we'll need help to pull out, and the road is so narrow for several miles that we'll have to trail along behind that fellow."

"Bless my check book!" cried Mr. Damon. "Are we going to lose, after all, on account of a load of hay? No, I'll buy it from him first, at double the market price, tip it over, set fire to it, toss it in the ditch, and then we can go past!"

"Maybe that will answer," retorted Tom, smiling grimly.

He put on a little more speed, and was soon close up behind the load of hay, ringing his electric bell as a warning.

"I say!" called Mr. Damon to the unseen driver, "can't you turn out and let us pass?"

"Ha! Hum! Wa'al I guess not!" came the answer, in unmistakable farmer's accents. "You automobile fellers is too gol-hanged smart, racin' along th' roads. I've got just as good a right here as you fellers have, by heck!" The driver did not show himself.

"We know that," responded Tom, as quickly as he could, for he did not want to anger the man. "But our machine is so heavy that if we turn into the ditch I'm afraid we'll be mired."

"Huh! So'll I," was the retort from the unseen driver.. "Think I want t' spile my load of hay?"

"But you have wide tires on, and you wouldn't sink in far," answered the young inventor. "Besides, it's very necessary that we get past. A great deal depends on our speed."

"So it does on mine," was the reply. "Ef I git t' market late I'll have t' stay all night, an' spend money on a hotel bill."

"I'll pay it! I'll pay your bill if you'll only pull out!" cried Mr. Damon. "I'll give you a hundred dollars

He suddenly ceased speaking. From the bushes along the road sprang several ragged, masked figures. Each one, aiming his weapon at Tom, said in a low voice, that could not have been heard by the driver of the hay wagon:

"Slow up your machine, young feller! We want to speak with you, and don't you make a loud noise, or it won't be healthy for you!"

"Why of all the-!" began Mr. Damon, but another of the footpads leveling his weapon at the eccentric man growled:

"Dry up, if you don't want to get shot!"

Mr. Damon subsided. Discretion was very plainly the better part of valor. Tom had shut off the current. The load of hay continued on ahead. Tom thought perhaps the driver of it might have been in collusion with the thieves, to cause the auto to slow up.

"What do you want with us?" asked the young inventor, trying to speak calmly, but finding it a hard task, with a revolver pointed at him.

"You know what we want," exclaimed the leader, in a low voice. "We want that cash you got from the bank, and we're going to have it! Come, now, shell out!" and he advanced toward the automobile.

ON TIME

Close around the electric auto crowded the members of the hold-up gang. Their eyes seemed to glare through the holes in their black masks. Instantly Tom thought of the other occasion when he was halted by masked figures. Could these, by any possibility, be the same individuals? Was this a trick of Andy Foger and his cronies?

Tom tried to pierce through the disguises. Clearly the persons were men—not boys—and they wore the ragged clothes of tramps. Also, there was an air of dogged determination about them.

"Well, are you going to shell out?" asked the leader, taking a step nearer, "or will we have to take it?"

"Bless my very existence! You don't mean to say that you're going to take the money—I mean how do you know we have any money?" and Mr. Damon hastily corrected himself. "What right have you to stop us in this way? Don't you know that every minute counts? We are in a hurry."

"I know it," spoke the leading masked figure with a laugh. "I know you have considerable money in that shebang, and I know what you hope to do with it, prevent the run on the Shopton National Bank. But we need that money as much as some other people and, what's more, we're going to have it! Come on, shell out!"

"Oh, why didn't we bring a gun!" lamented Mr. Damon in a low voice to Tom. "Isn't there anything we can do? Can't you give them an electric shock, Tom?"

"I'm afraid not. If it wasn't for that hay wagon we could turn on the current and make a run for it. But we'd only go into the ditch if we tried to pass now."

The load of hay was down the road, but as Tom looked he noticed a curious thing. It seemed to be nearer than it was when the attack of the masked men came. The wagon actually seemed to have backed up. Once more the thought came to the lad that possibly the load of fodder might be one of the factors on which the thieves counted. They might have used it to make the auto halt, and the man, or men, on it were probably in collusion with the footpads. There was no doubt about it, the load of hay was coming nearer, backing up instead of moving away. Tom couldn't understand it. He gave a swift glance at the robbers. They had not appeared to notice this, or, if they had, they gave no sign.

"Then we can't do anything," murmured Mr. Damon.

"I don't see that we can," replied the young inventor in a low voice.

"And the money we worked so hard to get won't do the bank any good," and Mr. Damon sighed.

"It's tough luck," agreed Tom.

"Come now, fork over that cash!" called the leader, advancing still closer. "None of that talk between you there. If you think you can work some trick on us you're mistaken. We're desperate men, and we're well armed. The first show of resistance you make, and we shoot—get that, fellows?" he added to his followers, and they nodded grimly.

"Well," remarked Mr. Damon with an air of submission, "I only want to warn you that you are acting illegally, and that you are perpetrating a desperate crime."

"Oh, we know that all right," answered one of the men, and Tom gave a start. He was sure he had heard that voice before. He tried to remember it—tried to penetrate the disguise —but he could not.

"I'll give you ten seconds more to hand over that bag of money," went on the leader. "If you don't, we'll take it and some of you may get hurt in the process."

There seemed nothing else to do. With a white face, but with anger showing in his eyes Mr. Damon reached down to get the valise. Tom had retained his grip of the steering wheel, and the starting lever. He hoped, at the last minute, he might see a chance to dash away, and escape, but that load of hay was in the path. He noted that it was now quite near, but the thieves paid no attention to it.

Tom might have reversed the power, and sent his machine backward, but he could not see to steer it if he went in that direction, and he would soon have gone into the ditch. There was nothing to do save to hand over the cash, it seemed.

Mr. Damon had the bag raised from the car, and the leader of the thieves was reaching up for it, when there came a sudden interruption.

From the load of hay there sounded a fusillade of pistol shots, cracking out with viciousness. This was instantly followed by the appearance of three men who came running from around the load of hay, down the road toward the thieves. Each man carried a pitchfork, and as they ran, one of the trio shouted:

"Right at 'em, boys! Jab your hay forks clean through the scoundrels! By Heck, I guess we'll show 'em we know how t' tackle a hold-up gang as well as the next fellow! Right at 'em now! Charge 'em! Stick your forks right through 'em!" Again there sounded a fusillade of pistol shots.

The thieves turned as one man, and glanced at the relief so unexpectedly approaching. They gave one look at the three determined looking farmers, with their sharp, glittering pitchforks, and then, without a word, they turned and fled, leaping into the bushes that lined the roadway. The underbrush closed after them and they were hidden from sight.

On came the three farmers, waving their effective weapons, the pistol shots still ringing out from the load of hay. Tom could not understand it, and could see no one firing—could detect no smoke.

"Are they gone? Did they rob ye?" asked the foremost of the trio, a burly, grizzled farmer. Bust my buttons, but I guess we skeered 'em all right!"

"Bless my shoe buttons, but you certainly have!" cried Mr. Damon, descending from the automobile, and wringing the hand of the farmer, while

Tom, thrust the bag of money under his legs and waited further developments. The pistol shots rang out until one of the men called:

"That'll do, Bub! We've skeered 'em like Mrs. Zenoby's pet cat! You needn't crack that whip any more."

"Whip!" cried Tom. "Was that a whip?"

"That's what it was," explained the leading farmer. "Bub Armstrong, my nephew, can crack it to beat th' band," and as if in proof of this there emerged from behind the load of hay a small lad, carrying a large whip, to which he gave a few trial cracks, like pistol shots, as if to show his ability.

"It's all right, Bub," his uncle assured him. "We made 'em run."

"But I don't exactly understand," spoke Mr. Damon. "I thought you were in league with those thieves, stopping us as you did with your big load."

"So did I," admitted Tom.

"Ha! Ha!" laughed the farmer. "That's a pretty good joke. Excuse me for laughin'. My name's Lyon, Jethro Lyon, of Salina Township, an' these is my two sons, Ade and Burt. You see we're on our way to Shopton, an' my nephew, Bub, he went along. We thought you was some of them sassy automobile fellers at first when you hollered to us you wanted to pass. Then when we looked back, we seen them burglars goin' t' rob you, at least that's what we suspicioned," and he paused suggestively.

"That was it," Tom said.

"Wa'al, when we seen that, we held a sort of consultation on thet load of hay, where they couldn't see us. It was so big you know," he needlessly explained. "Wa'al, we calcalated we could help you, so I jest quietly backed up, until we was near enough. I told Bub to take the long whip, an' crack it for all he was wuth, so's it would sound like reinforcements approachin' with guns, an' he done it."

"He certainly done it," added Burt.

"Wa'al," resumed Mr. Lyon, "then me an my sons we jest slipped down off the front seat, an' come a runnin' with our pitchforks. I reckoned them burglars would run when they see us an' heard us, an' they done so."

"Yep, they done so," added Ade, like an echo.

"I can't tell you how much obliged we are to you," said Mr. Damon. "We have sixty thousand dollars in this valise, and they would have had it in another minute, and the bank would have failed."

"Sixty thousand dollars!" gasped Mr. Lyon, and his sons and nephew echoed the words. Mr. Damon briefly explained about the money, and he and the young inventor again thanked their rescuers, who had so unexpectedly, and in such a novel manner, put the thieves to flight.

"An' you've got t' git t' Shopton before three o'clock with thet cash?" asked Mr. Lyon.

"That's what we hoped to do," replied Tom "but I'm afraid we won't now. It's half past two, and

"Don't say another word," interrupted Mr. Lyon. "I know what ye mean. My hay's in the road. But don't let that worry ye none. I'll pull out of your road in a jiffy, an' if we do go down in th' ditch, why we can throw off part of th' load, lighten th' wagon, an' pull out again. You've got t' hustle if ye git t' Shopton by three o'clock."

"I can do it with a clear road," declared Tom, confidently.

"Then ye'll have th' clear road," Mr. Lyon assured him. "Come boys, let's git th' hay t' one side."

The farmers pulled into the ditch. As they had feared the wagon went in almost to the hubs, but they did not mind, and, even as Tom and Mr. Damon shot past them, they fell to work tossing off part of the fodder, to lighten the wagon. The young inventor and his companion waved a grateful farewell to them as they fairly tore past, for Tom had turned on almost the full current.

"Do you suppose that was the Happy Harry gang, or some members of it who were not captured and sent to jail?" asked Mr. Damon.

"I don't believe so," answered the lad, shaking his head. "Maybe they didn't really want to rob us. Perhaps they only wanted to delay us so we wouldn't get to the bank on time."

"Bless my top knot, you may be right!" cried Mr. Damon.

Further conversation became difficult, as they struck a rough part of the road, where the vehicle swayed and jolted to an alarming degree. But Tom never slackened pace. On and on they rushed, Mr. Damon frequently looking at his watch.

"We've got twenty minutes left," he remarked as they came out on the smooth stretch of road, that led directly into Shopton.

Then Tom turned all the reserve power into the motor. The machinery almost groaned as the current surged into the wires, but it took up the load, and the electric car, swaying more than ever, dashed ahead with its burden of wealth.

Now they were in the town, now speeding down the street leading to the bank. One or two policemen shouted after them, for they were violating the speed laws, but it was no time to stop for that. On and on they dashed.

They came in sight of the bank. A long line of persons was still in front. They seemed more excited than in the morning, for the hour of three was approaching, and they feared the bank would close its doors, never to open them again.

"The run is still on," observed Mr. Damon.

"But it will soon be over," predicted Tom.

Some news of the errand of the automobile must have penetrated the crowd, for as Tom swung past the front entrance to the bank, to go up the rear alley, he was greeted with a cheer.

"They're got the cash!" a man cried. "I'm satisfied now. I don't draw out my deposit."

"I want to see the cash before I'll believe it," said another.

Tom slowed up to make the turn into the alley. As he did so he glanced across the street to the new bank. In the window stood Andy Foger and his father. There was a look of surprise on their faces as they saw the arrival of the powerful car, and, Tom fancied, also a look of chagrin.

Up the alley went the car, police keeping the crowd from following. The porter was at the door. So, also, was Mr. Pendergast and Mr. Swift, while some of the other officers were grouped behind them.

"Did you get the money?" gasped the president.

"We did," answered Tom. "Are we on time, Dad?"

"Just on time, my boy! They're paying out the last of the cash now! You're on time, thank fortune!"

OFF TO THE BIG RACE

From their task of handing out money to eager depositors, the wearied tellers looked up as Tom and Mr. Damon entered with the big valise crammed full of money. It was opened, and the bundles of bills turned out on a table.

"Perhaps you'd better make an announcement to the crowd, Mr. Pendergast," suggested Mr. Swift. "Tell them we now have cash enough to meet all demands, and that the bank will be kept open until every one is paid."

"I will," agreed the aged president. His announcement was received with cheers, and had exactly the effect the inventor hoped it would.

Many, learning that the bank was safe, and that they could have their money whenever they wanted it, concluded not to withdraw it, thus saving the interest. Scores in the waiting crowd turned out of line and went home. Their example was contagious, and, though many still remained to get their deposits, the run was broken. Only part of the sixty thousand dollars Tom and Mr. Damon had brought through after a race with time, was needed. But had it not been for the moral effect of the cash arriving as it did, the bank would have failed.

"You have a great car, Tom Swift," complimented Mr. Pendergast, when the excitement had somewhat cooled down, and the story of the hold-up had been told.

"I think so myself," agreed the young inventor modestly. "I must get ready for the races now."

"And as for those farmers, I think I'll send them a reward," went on the president. "They deserve something for the trouble they had with the load of hay. I certainly shall send them a reward," which he did, and a substantial one, too.

Of course the hold-up was at once reported to the police after the run had quieted down, but Chief Simonson surprised Tom by saying that he had expected it.

"The gang that held you up," said the police officer, "was one that escaped from a jail, about twenty miles away. I got a tip after you left, that they were going to rob you, for, in some way, they learned about the money you and Mr. Damon were to bring from the bank. The unfortunate part of it was that the tip I got was to the effect that the hold-up would take place just outside of Clayton. I telephoned to the police there, just after you left, and they said they'd send out a posse. But the gang changed their plans; and held you up near here, where I wasn't expecting it. But I'll get 'em yet."

Chief Simonson did not arrest the gang, but some other police officers did, and they were taken back to jail. They were not prosecuted for the attempted robbery of Tom, as it was considered difficult to fix the guilt on them, but they received such a long additional sentence for breaking jail, that it will be many years before they are released.

When Tom reached home that night he found some mail from the officials of the Touring Club of America. It was to the effect that arrangements for the big contest had been completed, and that contesting cars must be on the ground by September first.

"That gives me two weeks yet," thought our hero.

He read further of the regulations covering the race. Each car must proceed from the home town or city of the owner, and go to the track under its own power. This was a new regulation, it was stated, and was adopted to better develop the industry of building electric autos. Two passengers, or one in addition to the driver, must be carried, it was stated, and this one would also be expected to be in the car during the entire race.

Regarding the race proper it was stated that at first it had been decided to make it a twenty-four hour endurance contest, but that for certain reasons this was changed, as it was found that few storage batteries could go this length of time without a number of rechargings. Therefore the race was to be one for distance—five hundred miles, on the new Long Island track, and the car first covering that distance would win. Cars were allowed to change their batteries as often as they needed to, but all time lost would count against them. There were other rules and regulations of minor importance.

"Well," remarked Tom, as he read through the circulars, "I must get my car in shape. It will be quite a tip to Long Island, and I think my best plan will be to go direct to the cottage we had when we were building the submarine, and from there proceed to the track. That will comply with the rules, I think. But who will I get to go with me? I suppose Mr. Damon or Mr. Sharp will be willing. I'll ask them."

He broached the matter to his two friends that night, and they both agreed to go to Long Island in the car, though only Mr. Sharp would accompany Tom in the race. The next two weeks were busy ones for Tom. He worked night and day over his car, getting it in shape for the big event.

The young inventor made some changes in his battery, and also adopted a new gear, which would give greater speed. He also completed the exterior of the auto, giving it several coats of purple paint and varnish, so that when it was finished, though it was different in shape from most autos, it was as fine an appearing car as one could wish. He arranged to carry two extra wheels, with tires inflated, and, under the rear seats, or tonneau, as he called it, Tom fitted up a complete tire-repairing outfit. Mr. Sharp agreed to ride there, and in case there was need to use more than two spare wheels during the race, the rubber shoes or inner tubes could be mended while the car was swinging around the track.

Mr. Damon would ride in front with Tom on the cross-country trip, and occasionally relieve him at steering, or would help to manage the electrical connections. Spare fuses, extra parts, wires and different things he thought he might need, the young inventor stored in his car. He also found means to install a small additional storage battery, to give added power in case of emergency.

Tom learned from the racing officials that if he made a trip from Shopton to the cottage on the coast, near the city of Atlantis, and later traveled from there to the track, it would fulfill the conditions of the contest.

Finally all was in readiness, and one morning, having spent the better part of the night going over his machine, to see that he had forgotten nothing, Tom invited Mr. Damon and Mr. Sharp to enter, and prepare for the trip to Long Island.

"Well, Tom, I certainly hope you win that race," remarked Mrs. Baggert, as she stood in the doorway, waving a farewell.

"If I do I'll buy you a pair of diamond earrings to match the diamond ring I gave you from the money I got from the wreck," promised the lad with a laugh.

"An' ef yo' sees dat Andy Foger," added Eradicate Sampson, while he rubbed the long ears of Boomerang, his mule, "ef yo' sees him, jest run ober him once or twice fer mah sake, Mistah Swift."

"I'll do it for my own, too," agreed Tom.

The youth shook hands with his father, who wished him good luck, and then, after a final look at his car, he climbed to his seat, and turned on the power. There was a low hum from the motor and the electric started off. Would it return a winner or loser of the big race?

IN A DITCH

Through the streets of Shopton went Tom Swift and his friends. News of the big contest the young inventor was about to take part in, had circulated around town, and there were not wanting many to wish him good luck. The lad responded smilingly to the farewells he received. As they passed the bank, Ned Newton came out on the steps.

"Wish I was going along," he called.

"So do I," replied Tom. "How's everything? Is the bank all right since the run?" for he had not had time to pay much attention to the institution since his memorable race against time, to get the money.

"Stronger and better than ever," was Ned's answer, as he came to the curb, where Tom slowed up. "I hear," he added in a whisper, "that the other fellows are going out of business—Foger and his crowd you know. They loaned money on unsecured notes to make a good showing, and now they can't get it back But we're all right. Hope you win the race."

"So do I."

"What will a certain person do while you're away?" went on Ned, with a wink.

"I don't know what you mean," replied Tom, trying not to blush. "Do you mean my dad or Mrs. Baggert?"

"Neither, you old hypocrite you! I meant Miss Mary Nestor."

"Oh, hadn't you heard?" inquired Tom innocently. "She is going to Long Island to visit some friends, and she'll be at the race."

"You lucky dog," murmured Ned with a laugh, as he went into the bank.

Once more the electric auto started off, and was soon on the quiet country road, where Tom speeded it up moderately. He hoped to be able to make the entire distance to the shore cottage on the single charge of current he had put into the battery at home, and, as there was no special need for haste, he wanted to save his power. The machine was running smoothly, and seemed able to make a long race against time

The travelers ate lunch that day at Pendleton, a town some distance from Shopton. They had covered a substantial part of their trip. After a brief rest they started on again. Tom had planned to spend two days and one night on the road, hoping to be able to reach the shore cottage on the evening of the second day. There, after recharging the battery, he would spend a night, or two, and proceed to the track, ready for the race.

They found the roads fairly good, with bad stretches here and there, which made it necessary for them to slow down. This delayed them, and they found the shadows lengthening, and darkness approaching, when they were still several miles from Burgfield, where they intended to sleep.

"Will it be all right to travel at night?" asked Mr. Damon, a bit nervously.

"Why, are you thinking of hold-up men?" inquired Mr. Sharp.

"No, but I was wondering about the condition of the roads," replied the eccentric man. "We don't want to run into a rock, or collide with something."

"I guess this will light up the road far enough in advance, so that we can see where we are going," suggested Tom, as he switched on the powerful electric search-light. Though it was not dark enough to illuminate the highway to the best advantage, the powerful gleam shone dazzlingly in front of the swiftly moving auto.

"I guess that will show up every pebble in the road," commented the balloonist. It's very powerful."

Tom turned off the light, as, until it was darker, he could see to better advantage unaided by it. He slowed down the speed somewhat, but was still going at a good rate.

"There's a bridge somewhere about here," remarked the lad, when they had gone on a mile further. I remember seeing it on my road map. It's not very strong, and we'll have to run slow over it."

"Bless my gizzard, I hope we don't go through it!" cried Mr. Damon. "Is your car very heavy, Tom?"

"Not heavy enough to break the bridge. Ah, there it is. Guess I'll turn on the light so we can see what we're doing."

Just ahead of them loomed up the super-structure of a bridge, and Tom turned the searchlight switch. At the instant he did so, whether he did not keep a steady hand on the steering wheel, or whether the auto went into a rut from which it could not be turned, did not immediately develop, but the car suddenly shot from the straight road, and swerved to one side. There was a lurch, and the front wheels sank down.

"Look out! We're going into the river!" yelled Mr. Damon.

Tom jammed on the brakes and shut off the current. The auto came to a sudden stop. The young inventor turned the searchlight downward, to illuminate the ground directly in front of the car.

"Are we in the river?" asked Mr. Sharp.

"No," replied Tom in great chagrin. "We're in a muddy ditch. One at the side of the road. Wheels in over the hubs! There should have been a guard rail here. We're stuck for fair!"

THE POWER GONE

"Bless my overshoes!" cried Mr. Damon. "Stuck in the mud, eh?"

"Hard and fast," added Tom, in disgust.

"What's to be done?" inquired Mr. Sharp.

"I should say we'll have to stay here until daylight, and wait for some other auto to come along and pull us out," was Mr. Damon's opinion. "It's might unpleasant, too, for there doesn't seem to be any place around here where we can spend the night in any kind of comfort. If we had the submarine or the airship, now, it wouldn't so much matter."

"No, and this won't matter a great deal," remarked the young inventor quickly. "We'll soon be out of this, but it will be hard work."

"What do you mean?" asked Mr. Sharp.

"I mean that we've got to pull ourselves out of this mud hole," explained the lad, as he prepared to descend. "I was afraid something like this would happen, so I came prepared for it. I've got ropes and pulleys with me, in the car. We'll fasten the rope to the machine, attach one pulley to the bridge, another to the car, and I guess we can get out of the mud. We'll try, anyhow."

"Well, I must say you looked pretty far ahead," complimented Mr. Damon.

From a box under the tonneau Tom took out a thin but strong rope and two compound pulleys, which would enable considerable force to be applied. Mr. Sharp detached one of the powerful oil lamps, and the three travelers took a look at the auto. It was indeed deep in the mud and it seemed like a hopeless task to try to get it out unaided. But Tom insisted that they could do it, and the rope was soon attached, the hook of one pulley being slipped around one of the braces of the bridge.

"Now, all together!" cried the lad, as he and his friends grasped the long rope. They gave a great heave. At first it seemed like pulling on a stone wall. The rope strained and the pulleys creaked.

"I—guess—we—will—pull—the—bridge—over!" gasped Mr. Sharp.

"Something's got to give way!" puffed Tom. "Now, once more! All together!"

Suddenly they felt the rope moving. The pulleys creaked still more and, by the light of the lamp, they could see that the auto was slowly being pulled backward, out of the mud, and onto the hard road. In a few minutes it was ready to proceed again.

The rope and pulleys were put away, and, after Tom had made an examination of the car to see that it had sustained no damage, they were off again, making good time to the hotel in Burgfield, where they spent the night. They had an early breakfast, and, as Tom went out to the barn to look at his car, he saw it surrounded by a curious throng of men and boys. One of the boys was turning some of the handles and levers.

"Here! Quit that!" yelled Tom, and the meddlesome lad leaped down in fright. "Do you want to start the car and have it smash into something?" demanded the young inventor.

"Aw, nothin' happened," retorted the lad. "I pulled every handle on it, an' it didn't move."

"Good reason," murmured Tom, for he had taken the precaution to remove a connecting plug, without which the machine could not be started.

The three were soon under way again, and covered many miles over the fine country roads, the weather conditions being delightful. On inquiry they found that by taking an infrequently used highway, they could save several miles. It was over an unoccupied part of country, rather wild and desolate, but they did not mind that.

They were whizzing along, talking of Tom's chances for winning the race when, after climbing a slight grade, the auto came to a sudden stop on the summit.

"What's the matter?" asked Mr. Sharp. "Why are you stopping here, Tom?"

"I didn't stop," was the surprising answer, and the lad shoved the starting lever back and forth.

But there was no response. There was no hum from the motor. The machine was "dead."

"That's queer," murmured the young inventor

"Maybe a fuse blew out," suggested Mr. Damon, that seeming to be his favorite form of trouble.

"If it had you'd have known it," remarked Mr. Sharp.

"There's plenty of current in the battery, according to the registering gauge," murmured the lad. "I can't understand it." He reversed the current, thinking the wires might have become crossed, but the machine would move neither backward nor forward, yet the dial indicated that there was enough power stored away to send it a hundred miles or more.

"Perhaps the dial hand has become caught," suggested Mr. Sharp. "That sometimes happens on a steam gauge, and indicates a high pressure when there isn't any. Hit it slightly, and see if the hand swings back."

Tom did so. At once the hand fell to zero, indicating that there was not an ampere of current left. The battery was exhausted, but this fact had not been indicated on the gauge.

"I see now!" cried Tom. "It was those fellows at the hotel barn! They monkeyed with the mechanism, short circuited the battery, and jammed the gauge so I couldn't tell when my power was gone. If I had known there wasn't enough to carry us I could have recharged the battery at the hotel. But I figured that I had enough current for the entire trip, and so there would have been, if it hadn't leaked away. Now we're in a pretty pickle."

"Bless my hat band!" cried Mr. Damon. "Does that mean we can't move?"

"Guess that's about it," answered Mr. Sharp, and Tom nodded.

"Well, why can't we go on to some place where they sell electricity, and get enough to take us where we want to go?" asked the odd character, whose ideas of machinery were somewhat hazy.

"The only trouble is we can't carry the heavy car with us," replied Tom. "It's too big to pick up and take to a charging station."

"Then we've got to wait until some one comes along with a team of horses, and tows us in," commented Mr. Sharp. "And that will be some time, on this lonely road."

Tom shook his head despondently. He went all over the car again, but was forced to the first conclusion, that the reserve current had leaked away, in consequence of the meddling prank of the youth at the hotel. The situation was far from pleasant, and the delay would seriously interfere with their plans.

Suddenly, as Tom was pacing up and down the road, he heard from afar, a peculiar humming sound. He paused to listen.

"Trolley car," observed Mr. Sharp. "Maybe one of us could go somewhere on the trolley and get help. There it is," and he pointed to the electric vehicle, moving along about half a mile away, at the foot of a gentle slope.

At the sight of the car Tom uttered a cry. "I have it!" he exclaimed. "None of us need go for help! It's right at hand!" His companions looked curiously, as the young inventor pointed triumphantly to the fast disappearing electric.

ON THE TRACK

"What do you mean?" asked Mr. Damon. "Will the electric trolley pull us to a charging station?"

"No, we'll not need to go to a station," answered the youth. "If we can get my car to the trolley tracks I can charge my battery from there. And I think we can push the auto near enough. It's down hill, and I've got a long wire so we won't have to go too close."

"Good!" cried Mr. Sharp. "But attach the rope to the front of the car, Tom. Mr. Damon and I will pull it. You'll have to ride in it to steer it."

"We can take turns at riding," was Tom's answer, for he did not want his companions to do all the work.

"Nonsense! You ride," said Mr. Damon. "You're lighter than we are, and can steer better. It won't be any trouble at all to pull this car down hill."

It proved to be an easy task, and in a short time the "dead" auto was near enough to the electric line to permit Tom to run his charging wire over to it.

"Why bless my soul!" exclaimed Mr. Damon, looking up. "There's no overhead trolley wire. The car must run on storage batteries."

"Third rail, more likely," was the opinion of Mr. Sharp and so it proved.

"I can charge from either the third rail or the trolley wire," declared Tom, who was insulating his hands in rubber gloves, and getting his wires ready. In a short time he had the proper connections made, and the much-needed current was soon flowing into the depleted battery, or batteries, for there were several sets, though the whole source of motive power was usually referred to as a "storage battery."

"How long will it take?" asked Mr. Damon.

"About two hours," answered the lad. "We'll probably have to disconnect our wires several times, whenever a trolley car comes past. By my system I can recharge the battery very quickly.

"Do you suppose the owners of the road will make any objection?" asked the balloonist.

"I'm going to pay for the current I use," explained the young inventor. "I have a meter which tells how much I take."

The hum of an approaching car was heard, and Tom took the wires from the third rail. The car came to a stop opposite the automobile, the passengers, as well as the crew, looking curiously at the queer racing machine. Tom explained to the conductor what was going on, and asked the fare-collector to notify those in charge of the power station that all current used would be paid for. The conductor said this would be satisfactory, he was sure, and the car proceeded, Tom resuming the charging of his battery.

Allowing plenty of reserve power to accumulate, and making sure that the gauge would not stick again, and deceive him, the owner of the speedy electric was soon ready to proceed again. They had been delayed a little over three hours, for they had to make several shifts, as the cars came past.

They reached their shore cottage late that night, and, after seeing that the runabout was safely locked in the big shed where the submarine had been built, they all went to bed, for they were very tired.

Tom sent word, the next day, to the managers of the race, that he would be on hand at the time stipulated, and announced that he had made part of the trip, as required, under the power of the auto itself.

The next day was spent in overhauling the machinery, tightening up some loose bearings, oiling different parts, and further charging the battery. Tires were looked to, and the ones on the spare wheels were gone over to prepare for any emergency that might arise when the race was started.

On the third day, Tom, Mr. Sharp and Mr. Damon, leaving the cottage completed the trip to Havenford, Long Island, where the new track had been constructed.

They reached the place shortly before noon, and, if they had been unaware of the location they could not have missed it, for there were many autos speeding along the road toward the scene of the race, which would take place the following day.

Several electric cars passed Tom and his friends, whizzing swiftly by, but the young inventor was not going to show off his speed until the time came. Besides, he did not want to run any risks of an accident. But some of the contestants seemed anxious for impromptu "brushes," and more than one called to our hero to "speed up and let's see what she can do." But Tom smiled, and shook his head.

There were many gasolene and some steam autos going out to the new track, which was considered a remarkable piece of engineering. It was in the shape of an octagon, and the turns were considered very safe. It was a five mile track, and to complete the race it would be necessary to make a hundred circuits.

Through scores of autos Tom and his friends threaded their way, the young inventor keeping a watchful eye on the various types of machine with which he would soon have to compete.

There were many kinds. Some were larger and some smaller than his. Many obviously carried very large batteries, but whether they had the speed or not was another question. Some, in spurts, seemed to Tom, to be fully as fast as his own, and he began to have some doubts whether he would win the race.

"But I'm not going to give up until the five hundredth mile is finished," he thought, grimly.

They were now in sight of the track, and noted many machines speeding around it.

"Go on in and try your car, Tom," urged Mr. Sharp.

"Yes, do," added Mr. Damon. "Let's see how it travels."

"I will, after I notify the proper officials that I have arrived," decided the lad.

The formalities were soon complied with. Tom received his entry card, after paying the fee, made affidavit that he had completed the entire trip from home under his own power, save for the little stretch when the car was pulled, which did not count against him, and was soon ready to go on the track. Only electric cars were allowed there.

As the young inventor guided his latest effort in the machine line onto the big track there were murmurs of surprise from the throngs.

"That's a queer machine," said one.

"Yes, but it looks speedy," was another's opinion.

"There's the car for my money," added a third, pointing to a big red electric which was certainly whizzing around the track. Tom noted the red car. Behind it was a green one, also moving at a fast rate of speed.

"Those will be my nearest rivals," thought the lad, as he guided his car onto the track. A moment later he was sending the auto ahead at moderate speed, while the other contestants looked at the new arrival, as if trying to discover whether in it they would have a dangerous competitor.

WINNING THE PRIZE

After making two circuits of the track at moderate speed, Tom turned on more power, deciding to see how the machine would behave on the turns, going at a fast speed. As it happened he forged ahead just as the big red car was coming up behind him. The driver of it took this for a challenge and threw his controller handle forward.

"Come on!" he cried to our hero, when even with him.

Tom did not want to decline the invitation, and the impromptu race was under way. Soon the green car came rushing up, and for two miles the three kept almost in line. It was evident that neither the green nor the red car drivers wanted to "open out," until they saw Tom do so.

He was willing to oblige them, and suddenly increased his speed. They did the same, and went ahead of him. Then Tom turned on a little more juice and got the lead, but the two men were right after him, and they see-sawed like this for two more miles. Then, with a cry the man in the red car, with a sudden burst of speed, left Tom and the green car behind. The green car was soon up to its rival, but Tom decided he would not spurt.

The lad and his friends spent the early part of the night in making a final inspection of the machinery, finding it in good order. Then, with his head filled with visions of the race on the morrow Tom went to bed. He had made inquiries, by telephone, of the friends of Miss Nestor, and learned that she had not arrived. Tom felt a distinct sense of disappointment.

The day of the race could not have been better. It was ideal weather, and conditions at the track were just right. Tom was up early, and went over every inch of his car with a nervous dread that he might find something the matter.

The final details of the race were completed, and the entrants given their numbers and places. Tom drew a good position, not the best, but he had no reason to complain. Half an hour before the start he again telephoned to see if Miss Nestor had arrived, but she had not, and it was with rather gloomy thoughts that the lad entered his car, in which Mr. Sharp had already taken his place. Mr. Damon went to the grandstand to watch the race.

"I wanted Mary to see me win," thought our hero, for he had grimly set his mind on coming in ahead.

There was a great crowd in the grandstand and scattered about the big track, which took in a large extent of territory. In spite of its size—five miles around—it seemed solidly packed for the entire length with autos, containing gay parties who had come to see the electric contest. There was a band playing gay airs, as Tom guided his machine through the entrance gate, and onto the track.

The judges made their final inspection. There were twenty cars entered, but it was obvious that some of them would not last long, as their battery capacity was not large enough. Their owners might have relied on recharging, but how they could do this under the usual slow system, and hope to win, Tom could not see. He hoped to run the entire distance on the single charge, but, if by some accident part of his current should leak away, his battery could be charged in a short time, by means of his new system, to run for a considerable distance, or he could install a new one already charged, for he had two sets on hand. Tom glanced over the cars of his competitors. They were to be sent away in batches, the affair being a handicap one, with time allowance for the smaller powered cars. Tom noted that his car and the red and the green ones were in the same bunch. Tom's car was purple.

"Are you all ready?" asked the starter of the first group of races.

"Ready," was the low-voiced response.

"Crack!" went the pistol, and there followed the hum of the motors as the current set the mechanism to work. Forward went the cars, amid the crash of the band and the cheers of the crowd. The big race was under way.

"Do you feel nervous, Tom?" asked Mr. Sharp.

"Not a bit," replied the lad.

Around and around the track flew the speedy electrics. It was evident that the holding of a meet solely for cars of this character had brought out many new ideas that would be to the benefit of the industry. Some cars were "freaks" and others, like Tom's, showed a distinct advance over previous styles of construction.

A five-hundred mile race around a track is rather a monotonous affair, except for what happens, and things very soon began to happen at this race.

As Tom had expected, several of the machines were forced to withdraw. Tire troubles beset some, and others found that they were hopelessly out of it because of low power, or lack of battery capacity.

Tom determined not to let the red or the green car gain any advantage over him, and so he watched those two vehicles narrowly. On the other hand, the red and the green electrics were evidently afraid of one another and of Tom.

They all three kept pretty much together for the first thirty miles. By this time the race had settled down into a steady grind. There was some excitement when the steering gear of one car broke, and it crashed Into the fence, injuring the driver, but the race went on.

The young inventor was holding his own with his two chief rivals, and was feeling rather proud of his car, when there came from it a report like a pistol shot.

"Blow out!" yelled Tom desperately, steering to one of the several repair stations on the inner side of the track. "Be ready with the extra wheel, Mr. Sharp!"

"Right you are!" cried the balloonist. The car was scarcely stopped when he had leaped out, and had the lifting jack under the left rear wheel, where the tire had gone to the bad. He and Tom labored like Trojans to take off the wheel, and put on the other. They lost five minutes, and when they got under way again the red and the green cars were three quarters of a lap ahead.

"You've got to catch them!" declared Sharp firmly.

But the red and the green car drivers saw their advantage, and were determined to hold it. Tom could not catch them without going his limit, and he did not want to do this just yet. However, he had his opportunity when about two hundred miles had been covered. Both the red and the green cars had tire troubles, but the red one was delayed scarcely two minutes as there was a corps of mechanics on hand to take off the defective wheel and put on another. Still Tom regained his lost ground, and once more the race between those three cars was even.

In the rear of Tom's car Mr. Sharp was mending the blown-out tire, though there was still one spare wheel on reserve. Tom, in front, peered eagerly at the track. Nearly side by side raced the red and the green cars, the latter somewhat to the rear.

It was at the three hundred and fiftieth mile that Tom had another blow-out. This time it took a little longer to change the wheel, and the red and green cars gained a full lap on him. The track was now so dusty that it was difficult to see the contesting cars. Many had dropped out, and more were on the verge of giving up.

With the odds against him, Tom started in to regain the lost ground. Narrowly he watched his electric power. Slowly he saw it dropping. Would he have enough left to finish out the race? He feared not. The hours were passing. Still there was a hundred miles yet to go twenty circuits of the track. Some of the spectators were getting weary and leaving. The band played spasmodically.

Suddenly Tom saw the red car shoot to one side of the track, toward a charging station; The green car followed.

"That's our cue!" cried the young inventor "We need a little more 'juice' and now is the time to get it."

The lad ran to the shed where his charging wires were, and they were connected in a trice. He allowed twenty-five minutes for the charging, as he knew with his improved battery he could get enough current in that time to finish the contest. Before the red and green car drivers had finished installing new batteries, for they could not recharge as quickly as could our hero, Tom was on the track again. But, in a little while, his two rivals were after him.

It was now a spectacular race. Around and around swept the three big cars. All the others were practically out of it. The crowd became lively airs. Mile after mile was reeled off. The day was passing. Tired and covered with dust from the track, Tom still sat at the steering wheel.

"Two laps more!" cried Mr. Sharp, as the starter's pistol gave this warning. "Can you get away from 'em, Tom?"

The red and the green cars were following closely. The young inventor looked back and nodded. He turned on more power, almost to the limit—that he was saving for the final spurt. But after him still came the two big cars. Suddenly the red car shot ahead, just as the last lap was beginning. The green tried to follow, but there was a flash of fire, a loud report, and Tom knew a fuse had blown out. There was no time for his rival to put in a new one. The race was now between Tom and the red car. Could the lad catch and pass it?

They were now only a mile from the finish. The red car was three lengths ahead. With a quick motion Tom turned on the last bit of power. There seemed to come a roar from his Motor and his car shot ahead. It was on even terms with the red car when what Tom had been fearing for the last five minutes happened. his fuse blew out.

"Too bad! It's all up with us!" cried Mr. Sharp.

"No!" cried Tom in a ringing voice. "I've got an emergency fuse ready!" He snapped a switch in place, putting into commission another fuse. The motor that had lost speed began to pick it up again. Tom had pulled back the controller handle, but he now shoved it forward again, notch by notch, until it was at the limit. He had fallen back from the red car, and the occupants of that, with a yell of triumph, prepared to cross the line a winner.

But, like a race horse that nerves himself for the last desperate spurt, Tom's machine fairly leaped ahead. With his hands gripping the rim of the steering wheel, until it seemed that the bones of his fingers would protrude, Tom sent his car straight for the finishing tape. There was a yell from the spectators. Men were standing up, waving their hats and shouting. Women were fairly screaming. Mr. Damon was blessing everything within sight. Mr. Sharp, in his excitement, was pushing on the back of the front seats as if to shove the car ahead.

Then, as the pistol announced the close of the race, Tom's car, with what seemed a mighty leap, like a hunter clearing a ditch, forged ahead, and crossed the line a length in advance of the red car. Tom Swift had Won.

Amid the cheers of the crowd the lad slowed up, and, at the direction of the judges, wheeled back to the stand, to receive the prize. A certified check for three thousand dollars was handed him, and he received the congratulations of the racing officials. The driver of the red car also generously praised him.

"You won fair and square," he said, shaking hands with Tom.

The young inventor and his friends drove their car to their shed. As Tom was descending, weary and begrimed with dust he heard a voice asking:

"Mayn't I congratulate you also?"

He wheeled around, to confront Mary Nestor, immaculate in a summer gown.

"Why—why," he stammered. "I—I thought you didn't come."

"Oh, yes I did," she answered, laughing. "I wouldn't have missed it for anything. I arrived late, but I saw the whole race. Wasn't it glorious. I'm so glad you won!" Tom was too, now, but he shrank back when Miss Nestor held out both daintily gloved hands to him. His hands were covered with oil and dirt.

"As if I cared for my gloves!" she cried, and she took possession of his hands, a proceeding to which Tom was nothing loath. "Are you going to race any more?" she asked, as he walked along by her side, away from the gathering crowd.

"I don't know," he replied. "My car is speedier than I thought it was. Perhaps I may enter it in other contests."

But what Tom Swift did later on will be told in another volume, to be called, "Tom Swift and His Wireless Message; or, The Castaways of Earthquake Island"—a strange tale of ship-wreck and mystery.

The run back home was made without incident, save for a broken chain, easily repaired, the day following the race, and Tom later received a number of invitations to give exhibitions of speed. Several automobile manufacturers wanted to secure the rights to his machine, but he said he desired to consider the matter before acting. He did not forget his promise to Mrs. Baggert, regarding the diamond earrings, and bought her the finest pair he could find.

"Come on, Mr. Sharp," proposed Tom, a week or so after the big race, "let's go for a spin in the airship. I want to see how it feels to be among the clouds once more," and they were soon soaring aloft.

The new bank, started by Mr. Foger, did not flourish long. It closed its doors in less than six months, but the old institution was stronger than ever. Mr. Berg disappeared, and Tom never learned whether the agent really was the man he had chased, and whose watch charm he tore loose, though he always had his suspicions. Nor did it ever develop who crossed the electric wires, so that Tom was so nearly fatally shocked. Andy Foger disliked our hero more than ever, and on several occasions caused him not a little trouble, but Tom was able to look after himself.

Tom Swift and His Wireless Message
(Or the Castaways of Earthquake Island)

TABLE OF CONTENTS:

AN APPEAL FOR AID

Tom Swift stepped from the door of the machine shop, where he was at work making some adjustments to the motor of his airship, and glanced down the road. He saw a cloud of dust, which effectually concealed whatever was causing it.

"Some one must be in a hurry this morning," the lad remarked, "Looks like a motor speeding along. *My!* but we certainly do need rain," he added, as he looked up toward the sky. "It's very dusty. Well, I may as well get back to work. I'll take the airship out for a flight this afternoon, if the wind dies down a bit."

The young inventor, for Tom Swift himself had built the airship, as well as several other crafts for swift locomotion, turned to re- enter the shop.

Something about the approaching cloud of dust, however, held his attention. He glanced more intently at it.

"If it's an automobile coming along," he murmured, "it's moving very slowly, to make so much fuss. And I never saw a motor-cycle that would kick up as much sand, and not speed along more. It ought to be here by now. I wonder what it can be?"

The cloud of highway dirt rolled along, making some progress toward Tom's house and the group of shops and other buildings surrounding it. But, as the lad had said, the dust did not move at all quickly in comparison to any of the speedy machines that might be causing it. And the cloud seemed momentarily to grow thicker and thicker.

"I wonder if it could be a miniature tornado, or a cyclone or whirlwind?" and Tom spoke aloud, a habit of his when he was thinking, and had no one to talk to. "Yet it can hardly be that." he went on. "Guess I'll watch and see what it is."

Nearer and nearer came the dust cloud. Tom peered anxiously ahead, a puzzled look on his face. A few seconds later there came from the midst of the obscuring cloud a voice, exclaiming:

"G'lang there now, Boomerang! Keep to' feet a-movin' an' we sho' will make a record. 'Tain't laik we was a autermobiler, er a electricity car, but we sho' hab been goin' sence we started. Yo' sho' done yo'se'f proud t'day, Boomerang, an' I'se gwine t' keep mah promise an' gib yo' de bestest oats I kin find. Ah reckon Massa Tom Swift will done say we brought dis yeah message t' him as quick as anybody could."

Then there followed the sound of hoofbeats on the dusty road, and the rattle of some many-jointed vehicle, with loose springs and looser wheels.

"Eradicate Sampson!" exclaimed Tom. "But who would ever think that the colored man's mule could get up such speed as that cloud of dust indicates. His mule's feet must be working overtime, but he goes backward about as often as he moves forward. That accounts for it. There's lots of dust, but not much motion."

Once more, from the midst of the ball-like cloud of dirt came the voice of the colored man:

"Now behave yo'se'f, Boomerang. We'm almost dere an' den yo' kin sit down an' rest if yo' laik. Jest keep it up a little longer, an' we'll gib Massa Tom his telephone. G'lang now, Boomerang."

The tattoo of hoofbeats was slowing up now, and the cloud of dust was not so heavy. It was gradually blowing away. Tom Swift walked down to the fence that separated the house, grounds and shops from the road. As he got there the sounds of the mule's progress, and the rattle of the wagon, suddenly ceased.

"G'lang! G'lang! Don't yo' dare t' stop now, when we am most dere!" cried Eradicate Sampson. "Keep a-movin', Boomerang!"

"It's all right, Eradicate. I'm here," called Tom, and when the last of the dust had blown away, the lad waved his hand to an aged colored man, who sat upon the seat of perhaps the most dilapidated wagon that was ever dignified by such a name. It was held together with bits of wire, rope and strings, and each of the four wheels leaned out at a different angle. It was drawn by a big mule, whose bones seemed protruding through his skin, but that fact evidently worried him but little, for now the animal was placidly sleeping, while standing up, his long ears moving slowly to and fro.

"Am dat yo', Massa Tom?" asked Eradicate, ceasing his task of jerking on the lines, to which operation the mule paid not the least attention.

"Yes, I'm here, Rad," replied Tom, smiling. "I came out of my shop to see what all the excitement was about. How did you ever get your mule to make so much dust?"

"I done promise him an extra helpin' ob oats ef he make good time," said the colored man. "An' he done it, too. Did yo' see de dust we made?"

"I sure did, but you didn't do much else. And you didn't make very good time. I watched you, and you came along like an ice wagon after a day's work on the Fourth of July. You were going fast, but moving slow."

"I 'spects we was, Massa Tom," was the colored man's answer. "But Boomerang done better dan I 'spected he would. I done tole him yo'd be in a hurry t' git yo' telephone, an' he sho' did trot along."

"My telephone?" repeated Tom, wonderingly. "What have you and your mule Boomerang to do with my telephone? That's up in the house."

"No, it ain't! it's right yeah in mah pocket," chuckled Eradicate, opening a ragged coat, and reaching for something. "I got yo' telephone right yeah." he went on. "De agent at de station see me dribin' ober dis way, an' he done ast he t' deliber it. He said as how he ain't got no messenger boy now, 'cause de one he done hab went on a strike fo' five cents mo' a day. So I done took de telephone," and with that the colored man pulled out a crumpled yellow envelope.

"Oh, you mean a telegram," said Tom, with a laugh, as he took the message from the odd colored man.

"Well, maybe it's telegraf, but I done understood de agent t' say telephone. Anyhow, dere it is. An' I s'pects we'd better git along, Boomerang."

The mule never moved, though Eradicate yanked on the reins, and used a splintered whip with energy.

"I said as how we'd better git along, Boomerang," went on the darkey, raising his voice, "Dinnah am mos' ready, an' I'm goin' t' giv yo' an extra helpin' ob oats."

The effect of these words seemed magical. The mule suddenly came to life, and was about to start off.

"I done thought dat would cotch yo', Boomerang," chuckled Eradicate.

"Wait a minute, Rad," called Tom, who was tearing open the envelope of the telegram. "I might want to send an answer back by you. I wonder who is wiring me now?"

He read the message slowly, and Eradicate remarked:

"Taint no kind ob use, Massa Tom, fo' t' send a message back wif me."

"Why not?" asked the young inventor, looking up from the sheet of yellow paper.

"'Case as how I done promised Boomerang his airman, an' he won't do nothin' till he has it. Ef I started him back t' town now he would jest lay down in de road. I'll take de answer back fo' you dis arternoon."

"All right, perhaps that will do," assented Tom. "I haven't quite got the hang of this yet. Drop around this afternoon, Rad," and as the colored man, who, with his mule Boomerang, did odd jobs around the village, started off down the highway, in another cloud of dust, Tom Swift resumed the reading of the message.

"Hum, this is rather queer," he mused, when having read it once, he began at it again. "It must have cost him something to send all this over the wire. He could just as well have written it. So he wants my help, eh? Well, I never heard of him, and he may be all right, but I had other plans, and I don't know whether I can spare the time to go to Philadelphia or not. I'll have to think it over. An electric airship, eh? He's sort of following along the lines of my inventions. Wants my aid—hum—well, I don't know—"

Tom's musings were suddenly cut short by the approach of an elderly gentleman, who was walking slowly down the path that led from the house to the country highway which ran in front of it.

"A telegram, Tom?" asked the newcomer.

"Yes, dad," was the reply. "I was just coming in to ask your advice about it. Eradicate brought it to me."

"What, with his mule, Boomerang?" and the gentleman seemed much amused. "How did he ever get up speed enough to deliver a telegram?"

"Oh, Eradicate has some special means he uses on his mule when he's in a hurry. But listen to this message, dad. It's from a Mr. Hosmer Fenwick, of Philadelphia. He says:"

"'Tom Swift—Can you come on to Philadelphia at once and aid me in perfecting my new electric airship? I want to get it ready for a flight before some government experts who have promised to purchase several if it works well. I am in trouble, and I can't get it to rise off the ground. I need help. I have heard about your airship, and the other inventions you and your father have perfected, and I am sure you can aid me. I am stuck. Can you hurry to the Quaker City? I will pay you well. Answer at once!'"

"Well?" remarked Mr. Swift, questioningly, as his son finished reading the telegram. "What are you going to do about it, Tom?"

"I don't exactly know, dad. I was going to ask your advice. What would you do? Who is this Mr. Fenwick?"

"Well, he is an inventor of some note, but he has had many failures. I have not heard of him in some years until now. He is a gentleman of wealth, and can he relied upon to do just as he says. We are slightly acquainted. Perhaps it would be well to aid him, if you can spare the time. Not that you need the money, but inventors should be mutually helpful. If you feel like going to Philadelphia, and aiding him in getting his electric airship in shape, you have my permission."

"I don't know," answered Tom, doubtfully. "I was just getting my monoplane in shape for a little flight. It was nothing particular, though. Dad, I think I WILL take a run to Philadelphia, and see if I can help Mr. Fenwick. I'll wire him that I am coming, to-morrow or next day."

"Very well," assented Mr. Swift, and then he and his son went into one of the shops, talking of a new invention which they were about to patent.

Tom little knew what a strange series of adventures were to follow his decision to go to the Quaker City, nor the danger involved in aiding Mr. Fenwick to operate his electric airship.

MISS NESTOR'S NEWS

"When do you think you will go to Philadelphia, Tom?" asked Mr. Swift, a little later, as the aged inventor and his son were looking over some blueprints which Garret Jackson, an engineer employed by them, had spread out on a table.

"I don't exactly know," was the answer. "It's quite a little run from Shopton, because I can't get a through train. But I think I'll start tomorrow."

"Why do you go by train?" asked Mr. Jackson.

"Why—er—because—" was Tom's rather hesitating reply. "How else would I go?"

"Your monoplane would be a good deal quicker, and you wouldn't have to change cars," said the engineer. "That is if you don't want to take out the big airship. Why don't you go in the monoplane?"

"By Jove! I believe I will!" exclaimed Tom. "I never thought of that, though it's a wonder I didn't. I'll not take the *Red Cloud*, as she's too hard to handle alone. But the *Butterfly* will be just the thing," and Tom looked over to where a new monoplane rested on the three bicycle wheels which formed part of its landing frame. "I haven't had it out since I mended the left wing tip," he went on, "and it will also be a good chance to test my new rudder. I believe *I Will* go to Philadelphia by the *Butterfly*."

"Well, as long as that's settled, suppose you give us your views on this new form of storage battery," suggested Mr. Swift, with a fond glance at his son, for Tom's opinion was considered valuable in matters electrical, as those of you, who have read the previous books in this series, well know.

The little group in the machine shop was soon deep in the discussion of ohms, amperes, volts and currents, and, for a time, Tom almost forgot the message calling him to Philadelphia.

Taking advantage of the momentary lull in the activities of the young inventor, I will tell my readers something about him, so that those who have no previous introduction to him may feel that he is a friend.

Tom Swift lived with his father, Barton Swift, a widower, in the village of Shopton, New York. There was also in the household Mrs. Baggert, the aged housekeeper, who looked after Tom almost like a mother. Garret Jackson, an engineer and general helper, also lived with the Swifts.

Eradicate Sampson might also be called a retainer of the family, for though the aged colored man and his mule Boomerang did odd work about the village, they were more often employed by Tom and his father than by any one else. Eradicate was so called because, as he said, he "eradicated" the dirt. He did whitewashing, made gardens, and did anything else that was needed. Boomerang was thus named by his owner, because, as Eradicate said, "yo' nebber know jest what dat mule am goin' t' do next. He may go forward or he may go backward, jest laik them Australian boomerangs."

There was another valued friend of the family, Wakeneld Damon by name, to whom the reader will be introduced in due course. And then there was Mary Nestor, about whom I prefer to let Tom tell you himself, for he might be jealous if I talked too much about her.

In the first book of this series, called "Tom Swift and His Motor- Cycle," there was told how he became possessed of the machine, after it had nearly killed Mr. Damon, who was learning to ride it. Mr. Damon, who had a habit of "blessing" everything from his collar button to his shoe laces, did not "bless" the motor-cycle after it tried to climb a tree with him; and he sold it to Tom very cheaply. Tom repaired it, invented some new attachments for it, and had a number of adventures on it. Not the least of these was trailing after a gang of scoundrels who tried to get possession of a valuable patent model belonging to Mr. Swift.

Our second book, called "Tom Swift and His Motor-Boat," related some exciting times following the acquisition by the young inventor of a speedy craft which the thieves of the patent model had stolen. In the boat Tom raced with Andy Foger, a town bully, and beat him. Tom also took out on pleasure trips his chum, Ned Newton, who worked in a Shopton bank, and the two had fine times together. Need I also say that Mary Nestor also had trips in the motor-boat? Besides some other stirring adventures in his speedy craft Tom rescued, from a burning balloon that fell into the lake, the aeronaut, John Sharp. Later Mr. Sharp and Tom built an airship, called the *Red Cloud*, in which they had some strenuous times.

Their adventures in this craft of the air form the basis for the third book of the series, entitled "Tom Swift and His Airship." In the *Red Cloud*, Tom and his friends, including Mr. Damon, started to make a record flight. They left Shopton the night when the bank vault was blown open, and seventy-five thousand dollars stolen.

Because of evidence given by Andy Foger, and his father, suspicion pointed to Tom and his friends as the robbers, and they were pursued. But they turned the tables by capturing the real burglars, and defeating the mean plans of the Fogers.

Not satisfied with having mastered the air Tom and his father turned their attention to the water. Mr. Swift perfected a new type of craft, and in the fourth book of the series, called "Tom Swift and His Submarine," you may read how he went after a sunken treasure. The party had many adventures, and were in no little danger from their enemies before they reached the wreck with its store of gold.

The fifth book of the series, named "Tom Swift and His Electrical Runabout," told how Tom built the speediest car on the road, and won a prize with it, and also saved a bank from ruin.

Tom had to struggle against odds, not only in his inventive work, but because of the meanness of jealous enemies, including Andy Foger, who seemed to bear our hero a grudge of long standing. Even though Tom had, more than once, thrashed Andy well, the bully was always seeking a chance to play some mean trick on the young inventor. Sometimes he succeeded, but more often the tables were effectually turned.

It was now some time since Tom had won the prize in his electric car and, in the meanwhile he had built himself a smaller airship, or, rather, monoplane, named the *Butterfly*. In it he made several successful trips about the country, and gave exhibitions at numerous aviation meets; once winning a valuable prize for an altitude flight. In one trip he had met with a slight accident, and the monoplane had only just been repaired after this when he received the message summoning him to Philadelphia.

"Well, Tom," remarked his father that afternoon, "if you are going to the Quaker City, to see Mr. Fenwick to-morrow, you'd, better be getting ready. Have you wired him that you will come?"

"No, I haven't, dad," was the reply. "I'll get a message ready at once, and when Eradicate comes back I'll have him take it to the telegraph office."

"I wouldn't do that, Tom."

"Do what?"

"Trust it to Eradicate. He means all right, but there's no telling when that mule of his may lie down in the road, and go to sleep. Then your message won't get off, and Mr. Fenwick may be anxiously waiting for it. I wouldn't like to offend him, for, though he and I have not met in some years, yet I would be glad if you could do him a favor. Why not take the message yourself?"

"Guess I will, dad. I'll run over to Mansburg in my electric car, and send the message from there. It will go quicker, and, besides, I want to get some piano wire to strengthen the wings of my monoplane."

"All right, Tom, and when you telegraph to Mr. Fenwick, give him my regards, and say that I hope his airship will be a success. So it's an electric one, eh? I wonder how it works? But you can tell me when you come back."

"I will, dad. Mr. Jackson, will you help me charge the batteries of my car? I think they need replenishing. Then I'll get right along to Mansburg."

Mansburg was a good-sized city some miles from the village of Shopton, and Tom and his father had frequent business there.

The young inventor and the engineer soon had the electric car in readiness for a swift run, for the charging of the batteries could be done in much less than the time usual for such an operation, owing to a new system perfected by Tom. The latter was soon speeding along the road, wondering what sort of an airship Mr. Fenwick would prove to have, and whether or not it could be made to fly.

"It's easy enough to build an airship," mused Tom, "but the difficulty is to get them off the ground, and keep them there." He knew, for there had been several failures with his monoplane before it rose like a bird and sailed over the tree-tops.

The lad was just entering the town, and had turned around a corner, twisting about to pass a milk wagon, when he suddenly saw, darting out directly in the path of his car, a young lady.

"Look out!" yelled Tom, ringing his electric gong, at the same time shutting off the current, and jamming on the powerful brakes.

There was a momentary scream of terror from the girl, and then, as she looked at Tom, she exclaimed:

"Why, Tom Swift! What are you trying to do? Run me down?"

"Mary—Miss Nestor!" ejaculated our hero, in some confusion.

He had brought his car to a stop, and had thrown open the door, alighting on the crossing, while a little knot of curious people gathered about.

"I didn't see you," went on the lad. "I came from behind the milk wagon, and—"

"It was my fault," Miss Nestor hastened to add. "I, too, was waiting for the milk wagon to pass, and when it got out of my way, I darted around the end of it, without looking to see if anything else was coming. I should have been more careful, but I'm so excited that I hardly know what I'm doing."

"Excited? What's the matter?" asked Tom, for he saw that his friend was not her usual calm self. "Has anything happened, Mary?"

"Oh, I've such news to tell you!" she exclaimed.

"Then get in here, and we'll go on." advised Tom. "We are collecting a crowd. Come and take a ride; that is if you have time."

"Of course I have," the girl said, with a little blush, which Tom thought made her look all the prettier. "Then we can talk. But where are you going?"

"To send a message to a gentleman in Philadelphia, saying that I will help him out of some difficulties with his new electric airship. I'm going to take a run down there in my monoplane, *Butterfly*, to-morrow, and—"

"My! to hear you tell it, one would think it wasn't any more to make an airship flight than it was to go shopping," interrupted Mary, as she entered the electric car, followed by Tom, who quickly sent the vehicle down the street.

"Oh, I'm getting used to the upper air," he said. "But what is the news you were to tell me?"

"Did you know mamma and papa had gone to the West Indies?" asked the girl.

"No! I should say that WAS news. When did they go? I didn't know they intended to make a trip."

"Neither did they; nor I, either. It was very sudden. They sailed from New York yesterday. Mr. George Hosbrook, a business friend of papa's, offered to take them on his steam yacht, *Resolute*. He is making a little pleasure trip, with a party of friends, and he thought papa and mamma might like to go."

"He wired to them, they got ready in a rush, caught the express to New York, and went off in such a hurry that I can hardly realize it yet. I'm left all alone, and I'm in such trouble!"

"Well, I should say that was news," spoke Tom.

"Oh, you haven't heard the worst yet," went on Mary. "I don't call the fact that papa and mamma went off so suddenly much news. But the cook just left unexpectedly, and I have invited a lot of girl friends to come and stay with me, while mamma and papa are away; and now what shall I do without a cook? I was on my way down to an intelligence office, to get another servant, when you nearly ran me down! Now, isn't that news?"

"I should say it was—two kinds," admitted Tom, with a smile. "Well, I'll help you all I can. I'll take you to the intelligence office, and if you can get a cook, by hook or by crook, I'll bundle her into this car, and get her to your house before she can change her mind. And so your people have gone to the West Indies?"

"Yes, and I wish I had the chance to go."

"So do I," spoke Tom, little realizing how soon his wish might be granted. "But is there any particular intelligence office you wish to visit?"

"There's not much choice," replied Mary Nestor, with a smile, "as there's only one in town. Oh. I do hope I can get a cook! It would be dreadful to have nothing to eat, after I'd asked the girls to spend a month with me; wouldn't it?"

Tom agreed that it certainly would, and they soon after arrived at the intelligence office.

TOM KNOCKS OUT ANDY

"Do you want me to come in and help you?" asked the young inventor, of Miss Nestor.

"Do you know anything about hiring a cook?" she inquired, with an arch smile.

"I'm afraid I don't," the lad was obliged to confess.

"Then I'm a little doubtful of your ability to help me. But I'm ever so much obliged to you. I'll see if I can engage one. The cook who just left went away because I asked her to make some apple turnovers. Some of the girls who are coming are very fond of them."

"So am I," spoke Tom, with a smile.

"Are you, indeed? Then, if the cook I hope to get now will make them, I'll invite you over to have some, and—also meet my friends."

"I'd rather come when just you, and the turnovers and the cook are there," declared Tom, boldly, and Mary, with a blush, made ready to leave the electric car.

"Thank you," she said, in a low voice.

"If I can't help you select a cook," went on Tom, "at least let me call and take you home when you have engaged one."

"Oh, it will be too much trouble," protested Miss Nestor.

"Not at all. I have only to send a message, and get some piano wire, and then I'll call back here for you. I'll take you and the new cook back home flying."

"All right, but don't fly so fast. The cook may get frightened, and leave before she has a chance to make an apple turnover."

"I'll go slower. I'll be back in fifteen minutes," called Tom, as he swung the car out away from the curb, while Mary Nestor went into the intelligence office.

Tom wrote and sent this message to Mr. Hostner Fenwick, of Philadelphia:

"Will come on to-morrow in my aeroplane, and aid you all I can. Will not promise to make your electric airship fly, though. Father sends regards."

"Just rush that, please," he said to the telegraph agent, and the latter, after reading it over, remarked:

"It'll rush itself, I reckon, being all about airships, and things like that," and he laughed as Tom paid him.

Selecting several sizes of piano wire of great strength, to use as extra guy-braces on the Butterflv, Tom re-entered his electric car, and hastened back to the intelligence office, where he had left his friend. He saw her standing at the front door, and before he could alight, and go to her, Miss Nestor came cut to meet him.

"Oh, Tom!" she exclaimed, with a little tragic gesture, "what do you think?"

"I don't know," he answered good-naturedly. "Does the new cook refuse to come unless you do away with apple turnovers?"

"No, it isn't that. I have engaged a real treasure, I'm sure, but as soon as I mentioned that you would take us home in the electric automobile, she flatly refused to come. She said walking was the only way she would go. She hasn't been in this country long. But the worst of it is that a rich woman has just telephoned in for a cook, and if I don't get this one away, the rich lady may induce her to come to her house, and I'll be without one! Oh, what shall I do?" and poor Mary looked quite distressed.

"Humph! So she's afraid of electric autos; eh?" mused Tom. "That's queer. Leave it to me, Mary, and perhaps I can fix it. You want to get her away from here in a hurry; don't you?"

"Yes, because servants are so scarce, that they are engaged almost as soon as they register at the intelligence office. I know the one I have hired is suspicious of me, since I have mentioned your car, and she'll surely go with Mrs. Duy Puyster when she comes. I'm sorry I spoke of the automobile."

"Well, don't worry. It's partly my fault, and perhaps I can make amends. I'll talk to the new cook," decided the young inventor.

"Oh, Tom, I don't believe it will do any good. She won't come, and all my girl friends will arrive shortly." Miss Nestor was quite distressed.

"Leave it to me," suggested the lad, with an assumed confidence he did not feel. He left the car, and walked toward the office. Entering it, with Miss Nestor in his wake, he saw a pleasant-faced Irish girl, sitting on a bench, with a bundle beside her.

"And so you don't want to ride in an auto?" began Tom.

"No, an' it's no use of the likes of you askin' me, either," answered the girl, but not impudently. "I am afeered of thim things, an' I won't work in a family that owns one."

"But we don't own one," said Mary.

The girl only sniffed.

"It is the very latest means of traveling," Tom went on, "and there is absolutely no danger. I will drive slowly."

"No!" snapped the new cook.

Tom was rather at his wits' ends. At that moment the telephone rang, and Tom and Mary, listening, could hear the proprietress of the intelligence office talking to Mrs. Duy Puyster over the wire.

"We must get her away soon," whispered Mary, with a nod at the Irish girl, "or we'll lose her."

Tom was thinking rapidly, but no plan seemed to come to him. A moment later one of the assistants of the office led out from a rear room another Irish girl,—who, it seems, had just engaged herself to work in the country.

"Good-by, Bridget," said this girl, to the one Mary Nestor had hired. "I'm off now. The carriage has just come for me. I'm goin' away in style."

"Good luck, Sarah," wished Bridget.

Tom looked out of the window. A dilapidated farm wagon, drawn by two rusty-looking horses, just drawing up at the curb.

"There is your employer, Sarah," said the proprietress of the office. "You will have a nice ride to the country and I hope you will like the place."

A typical country farmer alighted from the wagon, leaving a woman, evidently his wife, or the seat. He called out:

"I'll git th' servant-gal, 'Mandy, an' we'll drive right out hum. Then you won't have such hard work any more."

"An' so that's the style you was tellin' me of; eh, Sarah?" asked the cook whom Miss Nestor had engaged. "That's queer style, Sarah."

Sarah was blushing from shame and mortification. Tom was quick to seize the advantage thus offered.

"Bridget, if YOU appreciate style," he said, "you will come in the automobile. I have one of the very latest models, and it is very safe. But perhaps you prefer a farm wagon."

"Indade an' I don't!" was the ready response. "I'll go wid you now if only to show Sarah Malloy thot I have more style than her! She was boastin' of the fine place she had, an' th' illigant carriage that was comin' t' take her to the counthry. If that's it I want none of it! I'll go wid you an' th' young gintleman. Style indade!" and, gathering up her bundle she followed Tom and Mary to the waiting auto.

They entered it and started off, just as Mrs. Duy Puyster drove up in her elegantly appointed carriage, while Sarah, with tears of mortification in her eyes, climbed up beside the farmer and his wife.

"You saved the day for me, Tom," whispered Miss Nestor, as the young inventor increased the speed of his car. "It was only just in time."

"Don't forget the apple turnovers," he whispered back.

Once she had made the plunge, the new cook seemed to lose her fears of the auto, and enjoyed the ride. In a short time she had been safely delivered at Miss Nestor's home, while that young lady repeated her thanks to Tom, and renewed her invitation for him to come and sample the apple turnovers, which Tom promised faithfully to do, saying he would call on his return from Philadelphia.

Musing on the amusing feature of his trip, Tom was urging his auto along at moderate speed, when, as he turned down a country road, leading to his home, he saw, coming toward him, a carriage, drawn by a slow-moving, white horse, and containing a solitary figure.

"Why, that looks like Andy Foger," spoke Tom, half aloud. "I wonder what he's doing out driving? His auto must be out of commission. But that's not strange, considering the way he abuses the machine. It's in the repair shop half the time."

He slowed down still more, for he did not know but that Andy's horse might be skittish. He need have no fears, however, for the animal did not seem to have much more life than did Eradicate's mule, Boomerang.

As Tom came nearer the carriage, he was surprised to see Andy deliberately swing his horse across the road, blocking the highway by means of the carriage and steed.

"Well, Andy Foger, what does that mean?" cried Tom, indignantly, as he brought his car to a sudden stop. "Why do you block the road?"

"Because I want to," snarled the bully, taking out a notebook and pencil, and pretending to make some notes about the property in front of which he had halted. "I'm in the real estate business now," went on Andy, "and I'm getting descriptions of the property I'm going to sell. Guess I've got a right to stop in the road if I want to!"

"But not to block it up," retorted Tom. "That's against the law. Pull over and let me pass!"

"Suppose I don't do it?"

"Then I'll make you!"

"Huh! I'd like to see you try it!" snapped Andy. "If you make trouble for me, it will be the worse for you."

"If you pull to one side, so I can pass, there'll be no trouble," said Tom, seeing that Andy wished to pick a quarrel.

"Well, I'm not going to pull aside until I finish putting down this description," and the bully continued to write with tantalizing slowness.

"Look here!" exclaimed Tom Swift, with sudden energy. "I'm not going to stand for this! Either you pull to one side and let me pass, or—"

"Well, what will you do?" demanded the bully.

"I'll shove you to one side, and you can take the consequences!"

"You won't dare to!"

"I won't, eh? Just you watch."

Tom threw forward the lever of his car. There was a hum of the motor, and the electric moved ahead. Andy had continued to write in the book, but at this sound he glanced up.

"Don't you dare to bunk into me!" yelled Andy. "If you do I'll sue you for damages!"

"Get out of the way, or I'll shove you off the road!" threatened Tom, calmly.

"I'll not go until I get ready."

"Oh, yes you will," responded our hero quietly. He sent his car ahead slowly but surely. It was within a few feet of the carriage containing Andy. The bully had dropped his notebook, and was shaking his fist at Tom.

As for the young inventor he had his plans made. He saw that the horse was a quiet, sleepy one, that would not run away, no matter what happened, and Tom only intended to gently push the carriage to one side, and pass on.

The front of his auto came up against the other vehicle.

"Here, you stop!" cried Andy, savagely.

"It's too late now," answered Tom, grimly.

Andy reached for the horsewhip. Tom put on a little more power, and the carriage began to slide across the road, but the old horse never opened his eyes.

"Take that!" cried Andy, raising his whip, with the intention of slashing Tom across the face, for the front of the auto was open. But the blow never fell, for, the next instant, the carriage gave a lurch as one of the wheels slid against a stone, and, as Andy was standing up, and leaning forward, he was pitched head first out into the road.

"By Jove! I hope I haven't hurt him!" gasped Tom, as he leaped from his auto, which he had brought to a stop.

The young inventor bent over the bully. There was a little cut on Andy's forehead, and his face was white. He had been most effectually knocked out entirely by his own meanness and fault, but, none the less, Tom was frightened. He raised up Andy's head on his arm, and brushed back his hair. Andy was unconscious.

Mr. Damon Will Go Along

At first Tom was greatly frightened at the sight of Andy's pale face. He feared lest the bully might be seriously hurt. But when he realized that the fall from the carriage, which was a low one, was not hard, and that Andy had landed on his outstretched hands before his head came in contact with the earth, our hero was somewhat reassured.

"I wish I had some water, with which to bathe his head," Tom murmured, and he looked about in vain for some. But it was not needed, for, a moment later, Andy opened his eyes, and, when he saw Tom bending over, and holding him, the bully exclaimed:

"Here! You let me go! Don't you hit me again, Tom Swift, or I'll punch you!"

"I didn't hit you," declared Tom, while Andy tore himself away, and struggled to his feet.

"Yes, you did, too, hit me!"

"I did not! You tried to strike me with your whip, as I was shoving your carriage out of the way, which I had a perfect right to do, as you were blockading the highway. You lost your balance and fell. It was your own fault."

"Well, you'll suffer for it, just the same, snarled Andy, and then, putting his hand to his head, and bringing it away, with some drops of blood on it, he cried out:"

"Oh, I'm hurt! I'm injured! Get a doctor, or maybe I'll bleed to death!" He began blubbering, for Andy, like all bullies, was a coward.

"You're not hurt," asserted Tom, trying not to laugh. "It's only a scratch. Next time don't try to blockade the whole street, and you won't get into trouble. Are you able to drive home; or shall I take you in my car?"

"I wouldn't ride in your car!" snapped the ugly lad. "You go on, and mind your business now, and I'll pay you back for this, some day. I could have you arrested!"

"And so could I have you locked up for obstructing traffic. But I'll not. Your rig isn't damaged, and you'd better drive home."

The old white horse had not moved, and was evidently glad of the rest. A glance satisfied Tom that the carriage had not been damaged, and, getting into his car, while Andy was brushing the dust from his clothes, our hero started the motor.

There was now room enough to pass around the obstructing carriage, and soon Tom was humming down the road, leaving a much discomfited bully behind him.

"Tom Swift is too smart—thinking he can run everybody, and everything, to suit himself," growled Andy, as he finished dusting off his clothes, and wiping the blood from his face. As Tom had said, the wound was but a scratch, though the bully's head ached, and he felt a little dizzy. "I wish I'd hit him with the horsewhip," he went on, vindictively. "I'll get square with him some day."

Andy had said this many times, but he had never yet succeeded in permanently getting the best of Tom. Pondering on some scheme of revenge the rich lad—for Mr. Foger, his father, was quite wealthy— drove on.

Meanwhile Tom, rather wishing the little encounter had not taken place, but refusing to blame himself for what had occurred, was speeding toward home.

"Let's see," he murmured, as he drove along in his powerful car. "I've got quite a lot to do if I make an early start for Philadelphia, in my airship, to-morrow. I want to tighten the propeller on the shaft a trifle, and give the engine a good try-out. Then, too, I think I'd better make the landing springs a little stiffer. The last time I made a descent the frame was pretty well jarred up. Yes, if I make that air trip to-morrow I'll have to do some tall hustling when I get home."

The electric runabout swung into the yard of the Swift house, and Tom brought it to a stop opposite the side door. He looked about for a sight of his father, Mrs. Baggert or Garret Jackson. The only person visible was Eradicate Sampson, working in the garden.

"Hello, Rad," called Tom. "Anybody home?"

"Yais, Massa Tom," answered the colored man. "Yo' dad an' anodder gen'mans hab jest gone in de house."

"Who's the other gentleman, Rad?" asked Tom, and the negro, glad of an excuse to cease the weeding of the onion bed, came shuffling forward.

"It's de gen'mans what is allers saying his prayers," he answered.

"Saying his prayers?" repeated Tom.

"Yep. Yo' knows what I means, Massa Tom. He's allers askin' a blessin' on his shoes, or his rubbers, or his necktie."

"Oh, you mean Mr. Wakefield Damon."

"Yais, sah, dat's who I done means. Mr, Wakefull Lemon—dat's sho' him."

At that moment there sounded, within the house, the voices of Mr. Swift, and some one else in conversation.

"And so Tom has decided to make a run to the Quaker City in the *Butterfly*, to-morrow," Mr. Swift was saying, "and he's going to see if he can be of any service to this Mr. Fenwick."

"Bless my watch chain!" exclaimed the other voice. "You don't say so! Why I know Mr. Fenwick very well—he and I used to go to school together, but bless my multiplication tables—I never thought he'd amount to anything! And so he's built an airship; and Tom is going to help him with it? Why, bless my collar button, I've a good notion to go along and see what happens. Bless my very existence, but I think I will!"

"That's Mr. Damon all right," observed Tom, with a smile, as he advanced toward the dining-room, whence the voices proceeded.

"Dat's what I done tole you!" said Eradicate, and, with slow and lagging steps he went back to weed the onion bed.

"How are you, Mr. Damon," called our hero, as he mounted the steps of the porch.

"Why, it's Tom—he's back!" exclaimed the eccentric man. "Why, bless my shoe laces, Tom! how are you? I'm real glad to see you. Bless my eyeglasses, but I am! I just returned from a little western trip, and I thought I'd ran over and see how you are. I came in my car— had two blowouts on the way, too. Bless my spark plug, but the kind of tires one gets now-a-days are a disgrace! However, I'm here, and your father has just told me about you going to Philadelphia in your monoplane, to help a fellow-inventor with his airship. It's real kind of you. Bless my topknot if it isn't! Do you know what I was just saying?"

"I heard you mention that you knew Mr. Fenwick," replied Tom, with a smile, as he shook hands with Mr. Damon.

"So I do, and, what's more, I'd like to see his airship. Will your *Butterfly* carry two passengers?"

"Easily, Mr. Damon."

"Then I'll tell you what I'm going to do. If you'll let me I'll take that run to Philadelphia with you!"

"Glad to have you come along," responded Tom, heartily.

"Then I'll go, and, what's more, if Fenwick's ship will rise, I'll go with you in that—bless my deflection rudder if I don't, Tom!" and puffing top his cheeks, as he exploded these words, Mr. Damon fairly raised himself on his tiptoes, and shook Tom's hand again.

VOL-PLANING TO EARTH

For a moment after Mr. Damon's announcement Tom did not reply. Mr. Swift, too, seemed a little at a loss for something to say. They did not quite know how to take their eccentric friend at times.

"Of course I'll be glad of your company, Mr. Damon," said Tom: "but you must remember that my *Butterfly* is not like the *Red Cloud*. There is more danger riding in the monoplane than there is in the airship. In the latter, if the engine happens to stop, the sustaining gas will prevent us from falling. But it isn't so in an aeroplane. When your engine stops there—"

"Well, what happens?" asked Mr. Damon, impatiently, for Tom hesitated.

"You have to vol-plane back to earth."

"Vol-plane?" and there was a questioning note in Mr. Damon's voice.

"Yes, glide down from whatever height you are at when the engine stalls. Come down in a series of dips from the upper currents. Vol- planing, the French call it, and I guess it's as good a word as any."

"Have you ever done it?" asked the odd character.

"Oh, yes, several times."

"Then, bless my fur overcoat! I can do it, too, Tom. When will you be ready to start?"

"To-morrow morning. Now you are sure you won't get nervous and want to jump, if the engine happens to break down?"

"Not a bit of it. I'll vol-plane whenever you are ready," and Mr. Damon laughed.

"Well, we'll hope we won't have to," went on Tom. "And I'll be very glad of your company. Mr. Fenwick will, no doubt, be pleased to see you. I've never met him, and it will be nice to have some one to introduce me. Suppose you come out and see what sort of a craft you are doomed to travel in to-morrow, Mr. Damon. I believe you never saw my new monoplane."

"That's right, I haven't, but I'd be glad to. I declare, I'm getting to be quite an aviator," and Mr. Damon chuckled. A little later, Tom, having informed his father of the sending of the message. took his eccentric friend out to the shop, and exhibited the *Butterfly*.

As many of you have seen the ordinary monoplane, either on exhibition or in flight, I will not take much space to describe Tom's. Sufficient to say it was modeled after the one in which Bleriot made his first flight across the English channel.

The body was not unlike that of a butterfly or dragon fly, long and slender, consisting of a rectangular frame with canvas stretched over it, and a seat for two just aft of the engine and controlling levers. Back of the seat stretched out a long framework, and at the end was a curved plane, set at right angles to it. The ends of the plane terminated in flexible wings, to permit of their being bent up or down, so as to preserve the horizontal equilibrium of the craft.

At the extreme end was the vertical rudder, which sent the monoplane to left or right.

Forward, almost exactly like the front set of wings of the dragon fly, was the large, main plane, with the concave turn toward the ground. There was the usual propeller in front, operated by a four cylinder motor, the cylinders being air cooled, and set like the spokes of a wheel around the motor box. The big gasolene tank, and other mechanism was in front of the right-hand operator's seat, where Tom always rode. He had seldom taken a passenger up with him, though the machine would easily carry two, and he was a little nervous about the outcome of the trip with Mr. Damon.

"How do you like the looks of it?" asked the young inventor, as he wheeled the *Butterfly* out of the shed, and began pumping up the tires of the bicycle wheels on which it ran over the ground, to get impetus enough with which to rise.

"It looks a little frail, compared to the big *Red Cloud*, Tom," answered the eccentric man, "but I'm going up in her just the same; bless my buttons if I'm not."

Tom could not but admire the grit of his friend.

The rest of the day was busily spent making various adjustments to the monoplane, putting on new wire stays, changing the rudder cables, and tuning up the motor. The propeller was tightened on the shaft, and toward evening Tom announced that all was in readiness for a trial flight.

"Want to come, Mr. Damon?" he asked.

"I'll wait, and see how it acts with you aboard," was the answer. "Not that I'm afraid, for I'm going to make the trip in the morning, but perhaps it won't work just right now."

"Oh, I guess it will," ventured Tom, and in order to be able to know just how his *Butterfly* was going to behave, with a passenger of Mr. Damon's weight, the young inventor placed a bag of sand on the extra seat.

The monoplane was then wheeled to the end of the starting ground. Tom took his place in the seat, and Mr. Jackson started the propeller. At first the engine failed to respond, but suddenly with a burst of smoke, and a spluttering of fire the cylinders began exploding. The hat of Mr. Damon, who was standing back of the machine, was blown off by the wind created by the propeller.

"Bless my gaiters!" he exclaimed, "I never thought it was as strong as that!"

"Let go!" cried Tom to Mr. Jackson and Eradicate, who were holding back the monoplane from gliding over the ground.

"All right," answered the engineer.

An instant later the explosions almost doubled, for Tom turned on more gasolene. Then, like some live thing, the *Butterfly* rushed across the starting ground. Faster and faster it went, until the young inventor, knowing that he had motion enough, tilted his planes to catch the wind.

Up he went from earth, like some graceful bird, higher and higher, and then, in a big spiral, he began ascending until he was five hundred feet in the air. Up there he traveled back and forth, in circles, and in figure eights, desiring to test the machine in various capacities.

Suddenly the engine stopped, and to those below, anxiously watching, the silence became almost oppressive, for Tom had somewhat descended, and the explosions had been plainly heard by those observing him. But now they ceased!

"His engine's stalled!" cried Garret Jackson.

Mr. Swift heard the words, and looked anxiously up at his son.

"Is he in any danger?" gasped Mr. Damon.

No one answered him. Like some great bird, disabled in mid flight, the monoplane swooped downward. A moment later a hearty shout from Tom reassured them.

"He shut off the engine on purpose," said Mr. Jackson. "He is vol- planing back to earth!"

Nearer and nearer came the *Butterfly*. It would shoot downward, and then, as Tom tilted the planes, would rise a bit, losing some of the great momentum. In a series of maneuvers like this, the young inventor reached the earth, not far from where his father and the others stood. Down came the *Butterfly*, the springs of the wheel frame taking the shock wonderfully well.

"She's all right—regular bird!" cried Tom, in enthusiasm, when the machine had come to a stop after rolling over the ground, and he had leaped out. "We'll make a good flight to-morrow, Mr. Damon, if the weather holds out this way."

"Good!" cried the eccentric man. "I shall be delighted."

They made the start early the next morning, there being hardly a breath of wind. There was not a trace of nervousness noticeable about Mr. Damon, as he took his place in the seat beside Tom. The lad had gone carefully over the entire apparatus, and had seen to it that, as far as he could tell, it was in perfect running order.

"When will you be back, Tom?" asked his father.

"To-night, perhaps, or to-morrow morning. I don't know just what Mr. Fenwick wants me to do. But if it is anything that requires a long stay, I'll come back, and let you know, and then run down to Philadelphia again. I may need some of my special tools to work with. I'll be back to-night perhaps."

"Shall I keep supper for you?" asked Mrs. Baggert, the housekeeper.

"I don't know," answered Tom, with a laugh. "Perhaps I'll drop down at Miss Nestor's, and have some apple turnovers," for he had told them or the incident of hiring the new cook. "Well," he went on to Mr. Damon, "are you all ready?"

"As ready as I ever shall be. Do you think we'll have to do any vol- planing, Tom?"

"Hard to say, but it's not dangerous when there's no wind. All right, Garret. Start her off."

The engineer whirled the big wooden, built-up propeller, and with a rattle and roar of the motor, effectually drowning any but the loudest shouts, the

Butterfly was ready for her flight. Tom let the engine warm up a bit before calling to his friends to let go, and then, when he had thrown the gasolene lever forward, he shouted a good-by and cried:

"All right! Let go!"

Forward, like a hound from the leash, sprang the little monoplane. It ran perhaps for five hundred feet, and then, with a tilting of the wings, to set the air currents against them, it sprang into the air.

"We're off!" cried Mr. Damon, waving his hand to those on the ground below.

"Yes, we're off," murmured Tom. "Now for the Quaker City!"

He had mapped out a route for himself the night before, and now, picking out the land-marks, he laid as straight a course as possible for Philadelphia.

The sensation of flying along, two thousand feet high, in a machine almost as frail as a canoe, was not new to Tom. It was, in a degree, to Mr. Damon, for, though the latter had made frequent trips in the large airship, this mode of locomotion, as if he was on the back of some bird, was much different. Still, after the first surprise, he got used to it.

"Bless my finger ring!" he exclaimed, "I like it!"

"I thought you would," said Tom, in a shout, and he adjusted the oil feed to send more lubricant into the cylinders.

The earth stretched out below them, like some vari-colored relief map, but they could not stop to admire any particular spot long, for they were flying fast, and were beyond a scene almost as quickly as they had a glimpse of it.

"How long will it take us?" yelled Mr. Damon into Tom's ear.

"I hope to do it in three hours," shouted back the young inventor.

"What! Why it takes the train over five hours."

"Yes, I know, but we're going direct, and it's only about two hundred and fifty miles. That's only about eighty an hour. We're doing seventy-five now, and I haven't let her out yet."

"She goes faster than the *Red Cloud*," cried Mr. Damon.

Tom nodded. It was hard work to talk in that rush of air. For an hour they shot along, their speed gradually increasing. Tom called out the names of the larger places they passed over. He was now doing better than eighty an hour as the gage showed. The trip was a glorious one, and the eyes of the young inventor and his friend sparkled in delight as they rushed forward. Two hours passed.

"Going to make it?" fairly howled Mr. Damon.

Tom nodded again.

"Be there in time for dinner," he announced in a shout.

It lacked forty minutes of the three hours when Tom, pointing with one hand down below, while with the other he gripped the lever of the rudder, called:

"North Philadelphia!"

"So soon?" gasped Mr. Damon. "Well, we certainly made speed! Where are you going to land?"

"I don't know," answered the young inventor, "I'll have to pick out the best place I see. It's no fun landing in a city. No room to run along, after you're down."

"What's the matter with Franklin Field?" cried Mr. Damon. "Out where they play football."

"Good! The very thing!" shouted Tom.

"Mr. Fenwick lives near there," went on Mr. Damon, and Tom nodded comprehendingly.

They were now over North Philadelphia, and, in a few minutes more were above the Quaker City itself. They were flying rather low, and as the people in the streets became aware of their presence there was intense excitement. Tom steered for the big athletic field, and soon saw it in the distance.

With a suddenness that was startling the motor ceased its terrific racket. The monoplane gave a sickening dip, and Tom had to adjust the wing tips and rudder quickly to prevent it slewing around at a dangerous angle.

"What's the matter?" cried Mr. Damon, "Did you shut it off on purpose?"

"No!" shouted Tom, "Something's gone wrong!"

"Gone wrong! Bless my overshoes! Is there any danger?"

"We'll have to vol-plane to earth," answered Tom, and there was a grim look on his face. He had never executed this feat with a passenger aboard He was wondering how the *Butterfly* would behave. But he would know very soon, for already the tiny monoplane was shooting rapidly toward the big field, which was now swarming with a curious crowd.

The New Airship

For a brief instant after the stopping of the motor, and the consequent sudden dropping toward the earth of the monoplane, Tom glanced at Mr. Damon. The latter's face was rather pale, but he seemed calm and collected. His lips moved slightly, and Tom, even in those tense moments, wondered if the odd gentleman was blessing anything in particular, or everything in general.

Tom threw up the tilting plane, to catch more air beneath it, and bring the *Butterfly* in a more parallel position to the earth. This, in a manner, checked the downward flight, and they glided along horizontally for a hundred feet or more.

"Is—is there any great danger, Tom?" asked Mr. Damon.

"I think not," answered the young inventor, confidently. "I have done this same thing before, and from greater heights. The only thing that bothers me is that there are several cross-currents of air up here, which make it difficult to manage the planes and wing tips. But I think we'll make a good landing."

"Bless my overcoat!" exclaimed Mr. Damon "I certainly hope so."

Conversation was more easily carried on now, as the motor was not spitting fire and throbbing like a battery of Gatling guns. Tom thought perhaps it might start on the spark, as the propeller was slowly swinging from the force of air against it. He tried, but there was no explosion. He had scarcely hoped for it, as he realized that some part of the mechanism must have broken.

Down they glided, coming nearer and nearer to the earth. The crowd in the big athletic field grew larger. Shouts of wonder and fear could be heard, and people could be seen running excitedly about. To Tom and Mr. Damon they looked like dolls.

Reaching the limit of the parallel glide the monoplane once more shot down on an incline toward the earth with terrible speed. The ground seemed to rush up to meet Mr. Damon.

"Look out!" he cried to Tom. "We're going to hit something!"

"Not yet," was the calm answer "I'm going to try a new stunt. Hold fast!"

"What are you going to do?"

"Some spirals. I think that will let us down easier, but the craft is likely to tilt a bit, so hold on."

The young inventor shifted the movable planes and rudder, and, a moment later, the *Butterfly* swung violently around, like a polo pony taking a sudden turn after the ball. Mr. Damon slid to one side of his seat, and made a frantic grab for one of the upright supports.

"I made too short a turn!" cried Tom, easing off the craft, which righted itself in an instant. "The air currents fooled me."

Under his skillful guidance, the monoplane was soon slowly approaching the earth in a series of graceful curves. It was under perfect control, and a smile of relief came on the face of the young inventor. Seeing it Mr. Damon took courage, and his hands, which had grasped the uprights with such firmness that his knuckles showed white with the strain, were now removed. He sat easily in his seat.

"We're all right now," declared Tom. "I'll take a couple of forward glides now, and we'll land."

He sent the machine straight ahead. It gathered speed in an instant. Then, with an upward tilt it was slackened, almost as if brakes had been applied. Once more it shot toward the earth, and once more it was checked by an up-tilted plane.

Then with a thud which shook up the occupants of the two seats, the *Butterfly* came to the ground, and ran along on the three bicycle wheels. Swiftly it slid over the level ground. A more ideal landing place would have been hard to find. Scores of willing hands reached out, and checked the momentum of the little monoplane, and Tom and Mr. Damon climbed from their seats.

The crowd set up a cheer, and hundreds pressed around the aviators. Several sought to reach, and touch the machine, for they had probably never been so close to one before, though airship flights are getting more and more common.

"Where did you come from?"

"Are you trying for a record?"

"How high did you get?"

"Did you fall, or come down on purpose?"

"Can't you start your motor in mid-air?"

These, and scores of other questions were fairly volleyed at Tom and Mr. Damon. The young inventor good-naturedly answered them as best he could.

"We were coming down anyhow," he explained, "but we did not calculate on vol-planing. The motor was stalled, and I had to glide. Please keep away from the machine. You might damage it."

The arrival of several policemen, who were attracted by the crowd, served to keep the curious ones back away from the *Butterfly*, or the men, boys and women (for there were a number of the latter in the throng) might have caused serious trouble.

Tom made a hasty examination of the motor, and, having satisfied himself that only a minor difficulty had caused it to stop, he decided to put the monoplane in some safe place, and proceed to Mr. Fenwick's house.

The lad was just asking one of the officers if the air craft could not be put in one of the grandstands which surrounded the field, when a voice on the outskirts of the crowd excitedly exclaimed:

"Let me pass, please. I want to see that airship. I'm building one myself, and I need all the experience I can get. Let me in, please."

A man pushed his way into the crowd, and wormed his way to where Tom and Mr. Damon stood. At the sight of him, the eccentric individual cried out:

"Why bless my pocket-knife! If it isn't Mr. Fenwick!"

"Mr. Fenwick?" gasped Tom.

"Yes. The inventor we came to see!"

At the same moment the newcomer cried out:

"Wakefield Damon!"

"That's who I am," answered Tom's friend, "and let me introduce you to Mr. Swift, the inventor of more machines than I can count. He and I were coming to see you, when we had a slight accident, and we landed here. But that didn't matter, for we intended to land here anyhow, as I knew it was near your house. Only we had to vol-plane back to earth, and I can't say that I'd care for that, as a steady diet. Bless my radiator, but I'm glad we've arrived safely."

"Did you come all the way from your home in that?" asked Mr. Fenwick of Tom, as he shook hands with him, and nodded at the monoplane.

"Oh, yes. It's not much of a trip."

"Well, I hope my airship will do as well. But something seems to be wrong with it, and I have hopes that you can help me discover what it is, I know your father, and I have heard much of your ability. That is why I requested your aid."

"I'm afraid I've been much overrated," spoke Tom, modestly, "but I'll do all I can for you. I must now leave my monoplane in a safe place, however."

"I'll attend to that," Mr. Fenwick hastened to assure him. "Leave it to me."

By this time a lieutenant of police, in charge of several reserve officers, had arrived on the scene, for the crowd was now very large, and, as Mr. Fenwick knew this official, he requested that Tom's machine be protected from damage. It was arranged that it could be stored in a large, empty shed, and a policeman would be left on guard. Then, seeing that it was all right, Tom, Mr. Damon and Mr. Fenwick started for the latter's house.

"I am very anxious to show you the *Whizzer*," said Mr. Fenwick, as they walked along.

"The *Whizzer*?" repeated Tom, wonderingly.

"Yes, that's what I call my electric airship. It hasn't 'whizzed' any to speak of yet, but I have hopes that it will, now that you are here to help me. We will take one of these taxicabs, and soon be at my house. I was out for a stroll, when I saw your monoplane coming down, and I hastened to Franklin Field to see it."

The three entered an automobile, and were soon being driven to the inventor's home. A little later he led them out to a big shed which occupied nearly all of a large lot, in back of Mr. Fenwick's house.

"Does it take up all that room?" asked Tom.

"Oh, yes, the *Whizzer* is pretty good size. There she is!" cried Mr. Fenwick proudly, as he threw open the doors of the shed, and Tom and Mr. Damon, locking in, saw a large triplane, with a good-sized gas bag hovering over it, and a strange collection of rudders, wings and planes sticking out from either side. Amidships was an enclosed car, or cabin, and a glimpse into it served to disclose to the young inventor a mass of machinery.

"There she is! That's the *Whizzer!*" cried Mr. Fenwick, with pride in his voice. "What do you think of her, Tom Swift?"

Tom did not immediately answer. He looked dubiously at the electric airship and shrugged his shoulders. It seemed to him, at first glance, that, it would never sail.

MAKING SOME CHANGES

"Well, what do you think of it?" asked Mr. Fenwick again, as Tom walked all about the electric airship, still without speaking.

"It's big, certainly," remarked the lad.

"Bless my shoe horn! I should say it was!" burst out Mr. Damon. "It's larger than your *Red Cloud*, Tom."

"But will it go? That's what I want to know," insisted the inventor. "Do you think it will fly, Tom? I haven't dared to try it yet, though a small model which I made floated in the air for some time. But it wouldn't move, except as the wind blew·it."

"It would be hard to say, without a careful examination, whether this large one will fly or not," answered Tom.

"Then give it a careful examination," suggested Mr. Fenwick. "I'll pay you well for your time and trouble."

"Oh if I can help a fellow inventor, and assist in making a new model of airship fly, I'm only too glad to do it without pay," retorted Tom, quickly. "I didn't come here for that. Suppose we go in the cabin, and look at the motor. That's the most important point, if your airship is to navigate."

There was certainly plenty of machinery in the cabin of the *Whizzer*. Most of it was electrical, for on that power Mr. Fenwick intended to depend to sail through space. There was a new type of gasolene engine, small but very powerful, and this served to operate a dynamo. In turn, the dynamo operated an electrical motor, as Mr. Fenwick had an idea that better, and more uniform, power could be obtained in this way, than from a gasolene motor direct. One advantage which Tom noticed at once, was that the *Whizzer* had a large electric storage battery.

This was intended to operate the electric motor in case of a break to the main machinery, and it seemed a good idea. There were various other apparatuses, machines, and appliances, the nature of which Tom could not readily gather from a mere casual view.

"Well, what's your opinion, now that you have seen the motor?" asked Mr. Fenwick, anxiously.

"I'd have to see it in operation," said Tom.

"And you shall, right after dinner," declared the inventor. "I'd like to start it now, and hear what you have to say, but I'm not so selfish as that. I know you must be hungry after your trip from Shopton, as they say aeroplaning gives one an appetite."

"I don't know whether it's that or not," answered Tom with a laugh, "but I am certainly hungry."

"Then we'll postpone the trial until after dinner. It must be ready by this time, I think," said Mr. Fenwick, as he led the way back to the house. It was magnificently furnished, for the inventor was a man of wealth, and only took up aeroplaning as a "fad." An excellent dinner was served, and then the three returned once more to the shed where the *Whizzer* was kept.

"Shall I start the motor in here?" asked Mr. Fenwick, when he had summoned several of the machinists whom he employed, to aid himself and the young inventor.

"It would be better if we could take it outside," suggested Tom, "yet a crowd is sure to gather, and I don't like to work in a mob of people."

"Oh, we can easily get around that," said Mr. Fenwick. "I have two openings to my aeroplane shed. We can take the *Whizzer* out of the rear door, into a field enclosed by a high fence. That is where I made all my trials, and the crowd couldn't get in, though some boys did find knot-holes and use them. But I don't mind that. The only thing that bothers me is that I can't make the *Whizzer* go up, and if it won't go up, it certainly won't sail. That's my difficulty, and I hope you can remedy it, Tom Swift."

"I'll do the best I can. But let's get the airship outside."

This was soon accomplished, and in the open lot Tom made a thorough and careful examination of the mechanism. The motor was started, and the propellers, for there were two, whirled around at rapid speed.

Tom made some tests and calculations, at which he was an expert, and applied the brake test, to see how much horse power the motor would deliver.

"I think there is one trouble that we will have to get over," he finally said to Mr. Fenwick.

"What is that?"

"The motor is not quite powerful enough because of the way in which you have it geared up. I think by changing some of the cogs, and getting rid of the off-set shaft, also by increasing the number of revolutions, and perhaps by using a new style of carburetor, we can get more speed and power."

"Then we'll do it!" cried Mr. Fenwick, with enthusiasm. "I knew I hadn't got everything just right. Do you think it will work after that?"

"Well," remarked Tom, hesitatingly, "I think the arrangement of the planes will also have to be changed. It will take quite some work, but perhaps, after a bit, we can get the *Whizzer* up in the air."

"Can you begin work at once?" asked the inventor, eagerly.

Tom shook his head.

"I can't stay long enough on this trip," he said. "I promised father I would be back by to-morrow at the latest, but I will come over here again, and arrange to stay until I have done all I can. I need to get some of my special tools, and then, too, you will require some other supplies, of which I will give you a list. I hope you don't mind me speaking in this way, Mr. Fenwick, as though I knew more about it than you do," added Tom, modestly.

"Not a bit of it!" cried the inventor heartily. "I want the benefit of your advice and experience, and I'll do just as you say. I hope you can come back soon."

"I'll return the first of the week," promised Tom, "and then we'll see what can be done. Now I'll go over the whole ship once more, and see what I need. I also want to test the lifting capacity of your gas bag."

The rest of the day was a busy one for our hero. With the aid of Mr. Damon and the owner of the *Whizzer*, he went over every point carefully. Then, as it was too late to attempt the return flight to Shopton, he telegraphed his father, and he and Mr. Damon remained over night with Mr. Fenwick.

In the morning, having written out a list of the things that would be needed, Tom went out to Franklin Field, and repaired his own monoplane. It was found that one of the electric wires connected with the motor had broken, thus cutting off the spark. It was soon repaired, and, in the presence of a large crowd, Tom and Mr. Damon started on their return flight.

"Do you think you can make the *Whizzer* work, Tom?" asked Mr. Damon, as they were flying high over Philadelphia.

"I'm a little dubious about it," was the reply. "But after I make some changes I may have a different opinion. The whole affair is too big and clumsy, that's the trouble; though the electrical part of it is very good."

Shopton was reached without incident, in about three hours, and there was no necessity, this time, of vol-planing back to earth. After a short rest, Tom began getting together a number of special tools and appliances, which he proposed taking back to Philadelphia with him.

The young inventor made another trip to Mr. Fenwick's house the first of the following week. He went by train this time, as he had to ship his tools, and Mr. Damon did not accompany him. Then, with the assistance of the inventor of the *Whizzer*, and several of his mechanics, Tom began making the changes on the airship.

"Do you think you can make it fly?" asked Mr. Fenwick, anxiously, after several days of labor.

"I hope so," replied our hero, and there was more confidence in his tone than there had been before. As the work progressed, he began to be more hopeful. "I'll make a trial flight, anyhow, in a few days," he added.

"Then I must send word to Mr. Damon," decided Mr. Fenwick. "He wants to be on hand to see it, and, if possible, go up; so he told me."

"All right," assented Tom. "I only hope it does go up," he concluded, in a low tone.

Andy Foger's Revenge

During the following week, Tom was kept busy over the airship. He made many important changes, and one of these was to use a new kind of gas in the balloon bag. He wanted a gas with a greater lifting power than that of the ordinary illuminating vapor which Mr. Fenwick had used.

"Well," remarked Tom, as he came from the airship shed one afternoon, "I think we can give it a try-out, Mr. Fenwick, in a few days more. I shall have to go back to Shopton to get some articles I need, and when I come back I will bring Mr. Damon with me, and we will see what the *Whizzer* can do."

"Do you mean we will make a trial flight?"

"Yes."

"For how long a distance?"

"It all depends on how she behaves," answered Tom, with a smile. "If possible, we'll make a long flight."

"Then I'll tell you what I'm going to do," went on the inventor, "I'm going to put aboard a stock of provisions, and some other supplies and stores, in case we are two or three days in the air."

"It might not be a bad plan," agreed Tom, "though I hardly think we will be gone as long as that."

"Well, being out in the air always makes me hungry," proceeded Mr. Fenwick, "so I'm going to take plenty of food along."

The time was to come, and that very soon, when this decision of the inventor of the *Whizzer* stood the adventurers in good stead.

Tom returned to Shopton the next day, and sent word to have Mr. Damon join him in time to go back to the Quaker City two days later.

"But why don't you start right back to Philadelphia to-morrow," asked Mr. Swift of his son.

"Because," answered Tom, and that was all the reason he would give, though had any one seen him reading a certain note a few minutes before that, which note was awaiting him on his arrival from the Quaker City, they would not have wondered at his decision.

The note was brief. It merely said:

"Won't you come, and have some apple turnovers? The new cook is a treasure, and the girls are anxious to meet you."

It was signed: Mary Nestor.

"I think I could enjoy some apple turnovers," remarked Tom, with a smile.

Having gotten ready the few special appliances he wished to take back to Philadelphia with him, Tom went, that evening, to call on Miss Nestor. True to her promise, the girl had a big plate full of apple turnovers, which she gaily offered our hero on his arrival, and, on his laughing declination to partake of so many, she ushered him into a room full of pretty girls, saying:

"They'll help you eat them, Tom. Girls, here is Mr. Swift, who doesn't mind going up in the air or under the ocean, or even catching runaway horses," by which last she referred to the time Tom saved her life, and first made her acquaintance.

As for the young inventor, he gave a gasp, almost as if he had plunged into a bath of icy water, at the sight of so many pretty faces staring at him. He said afterward that he would rather have vol-planed back to earth from a seven-mile height, than again face such a battery of sparkling eyes.

But our hero soon recovered himself, and entered into the merriment of the evening, and, before he knew it he was telling Miss Nestor and her attractive guests something of his exploits.

"But I'm talking altogether too much about myself." he said, finally. "How is the new cook Miss Nestor; and have you heard from your father and mother since they sailed on the *Resolute* for the West Indies?"

"As to the new cook, she is a jewel of the first water," answered Miss Nestor. "We all like her, and she is anxious for another ride in a taxicab, as she calls your auto."

"She shall have it," declared Tom, "for those are the best apple turnovers I ever ate."

"I'll tell her so," declared Mary. "She'll appreciate it coming from an inventor of your ability."

"Have you heard from your parents?" asked Tom, anxious to change the subject.

"Oh, yes. I had a wire to-day. They stopped at St. Augustine to let me know they were having a glorious time aboard the yacht. Mr. Hosbrook, the owner, is an ideal host, mamma said. They are proceeding directly to the West Indies, now. I do hope they will arrive safely. They say there are bad storms down there at this time of year."

"Perhaps, if they are shipwrecked, Mr. Swift will go to their rescue in one of his airships, or a submarine," suggested Mabel Jackson, one of the several pretty girls.

"Oh, I hope he doesn't have to!" exclaimed Mary. "Don't speak of shipwrecks! It makes me shudder," and she seemed unduly alarmed.

"Of course they won't have any trouble," asserted Tom, confidently, more to reassure Miss Nestor, than from any knowledge he possessed; "but if they do get cast away on a desert island, I'll certainly go to their rescue," he added.

It was late when Tom started for home that night, for the society of Miss Nestor and her friends made the time pass quickly. He promised to call again, and try some more samples of the new cook's culinary art, as soon as he had gotten Mr. Fenwick's airship in shape for flying.

As, later that night, the young inventor came in sight of his home, and the various buildings and shops surrounding it, his first glance was toward the shed which contained his monoplane, *Butterfly*. That little craft was Tom's pet. It had not cost him anything like as much as had his other inventions, either in time or money, but he cared more for it than for his big airship, *Red*

Cloud. This was principally because the *Butterfly* was so light and airy, and could be gotten ready so quickly for a flight across country. It was capable of long endurance, too, for an extra large supply of gasolene and oil was carried aboard.

So it was with rather a start of surprise that Tom saw a light in the structure where the *Butterfly* was housed.

"I wonder if dad or Mr. Jackson can be out there?" he mused. "Yet, I don't see why they should be. They wouldn't be going for a flight at night. Or perhaps Mr. Damon arrived, and is out looking it over."

A moment's reflection, however, told Tom that this last surmise could not be true, since the eccentric man had telegraphed, saying he would not arrive until the next day.

"Somebody's out there, however," went on Tom, "and I'm going to see who it is. I hope it isn't Eradicate monkeying with the monoplane. He's very curious, and he might get it out of order."

Tom increased his pace, and moved swiftly but softly toward the shed. If there was an intruder inside he wanted to surprise him. There were large windows to the place, and they would give a good view of the interior. As Tom approached, the light within flickered, and moved to and fro.

Tom reached one of the casements, and peered in. He caught a glimpse of a moving figure, and he heard a peculiar ripping sound. Then, as he sprang toward the front door, the light suddenly went out, and the young inventor could hear some one running from the shop.

"They've seen me, and are trying to get away," thought the lad. "I must catch them!"

He fairly leaped toward the portal, and, just as he reached it, a figure sprang out. So close was Tom that the unknown collided with him, and our hero went over on his back. The other person was tossed back by the force of the impact, but quickly recovered himself, and dashed away.

Not before, however, Tom had had a chance to glance at his face, and, to the chagrin of the young inventor, he recognized, by the dim light of a crescent moon, the countenance of Andy Foger! If additional evidence was needed Tom fully recognized the form as that of the town bully.

"Hold on there, Andy Foger!" shouted the young inventor. "What are you doing in my shed? What right have you in there? What did you do?"

Back came the answer through the night:

"I told you I'd get square with you. and I've done it," and then Andy's footsteps died away, while a mocking laugh floated back to Tom. What was Andy's revenge?

The *Whizzer* Flies

For a moment, Tom gazed after the fleeting figure of the cowardly bully. He was half-minded to give pursuit, and then, realizing that he could find Andy later if he wanted him, the young inventor decided his best plan would be to see what damage had been done. For that damage would follow Andy's secret visit to the shop, Tom was certain.

Nor was his surmise wrong. Stepping into the building, the lad switched on the lights, and he could not repress an exclamation of chagrin as he looked toward his trim little monoplane, the *Butterfly*.

Now it was a *Butterfly* with broken wings, for Andy had slashed the canvas of the planes in a score of places.

"The scoundrel!" growled Tom. "I'll make him suffer for this! He's all but ruined my aeroplane."

Tom walked around his pet machine. As he came in front, and saw the propeller, he gave another exclamation. The fine wooden blades of several layers, gracefully curved, which had cost him so much in time and labor to build up, and then fashion to the right shape, had been hacked, and cut with an axe. The propeller was useless!

"More of Andy's work," murmured Tom. "This is about the worst yet!"

There came over him a feeling of great despondency, which was succeeded by a justifiable rage. He wanted to take after the bully, and give him a merciless beating. Then a calmer mood came over Tom.

"After all, what's the use?" he reasoned. "Whipping Andy wouldn't mend the *Butterfly*. She's in bad shape, but I can repair her, when I get time. Luckily, he didn't meddle with the engine. That's all right." A hasty examination had shown this. "I guess I won't do anything now," went on Tom. "I'll have my hands full getting Mr. Fenwick's airship to run. After that I can come back here and fix up my own. It's a good thing I don't have to depend on her for making the trip to Philadelphia. Poor *Butterfly*! you sure are in a bad way," and Tom felt almost as if he was talking to some living creature, so wrapped up was he in his trim little monoplane.

After another disheartening look at his air craft, the young inventor started to leave the shop. He looked at a door, the fastening of which Andy had broken to gain admittance.

"I should have had the burglar alarm working, and this would never have happened," reasoned Tom. All the buildings were arranged so that if any one entered them after a certain hour, an alarm would ring in the house. But of late, the alarm had not been set, as Tom and his father were not working on any special inventions that needed guarding. It was due to this oversight that Andy was able to get in undetected.

"But it won't happen again," declared Tom, and he at once began connecting the burglar-apparatus. He went into the house, and told his father and the engineer what had occurred. They were both indignant, and the engineer declared that he would sleep with one eye open all night, ready to respond to the first alarm.

"Oh, there's no danger of Andy coming back right away," said Tom. "He's too frightened. I wouldn't be surprised if he disappeared for a time. He'll be thinking that I'm after him."

This proved true, as Andy had left town next morning, and to all inquiries his mother said he had gone to visit relatives. She was not aware of her son's meanness, and Tom did not tell her.

Mr. Damon arrived from his home in Waterfield that day, and, with many "blessings," wanted to know if Tom was ready for the trial of the electrical airship.

"Yes, we'll leave for Philadelphia to-morrow," was the answer.

"Are we going in the *Butterfly*? Bless my watch chain, but I like that little machine!"

"It will be some time before you again have a flight in her," said Tom, sorrowfully, as he told of Andy's act of vandalism.

"Why, bless my individuality!" cried Mr. Damon, indignantly. "I never heard of such a thing! Never!"

It did little good to talk of it, however, and Tom wanted to forget about it. He wished he had time to repair the monoplane before he left home, but there was much to do to get ready for the trial of the *Whizzer*.

"When will you be back, Tom?" asked Mr. Swift, as his son and Mr. Damon departed for the Quaker City the following morning.

"Hard to say, dad. If I can make a long flight in the *Whizzer* I'll do so. I may even drop down here and pay you a visit. But if I find there are many more changes to make in her construction, which is more than likely, I can't say when I'll return. I'll keep you posted, however, by writing."

"Can't you arrange to send me some wireless messages?" asked the older inventor, with a smile.

"I could, if I had thought to rig up the apparatus on Mr. Fenwick's airship," was the reply. "I'll hardly have time to do it now, though."

"Send wireless messages from an aeroplane?" gasped Mr. Damon. "Bless my gizzard! I never heard of such a thing!"

"Oh, it can be done," Tom assured him. And this was a fact. Tom had installed a wireless apparatus on his *Red Cloud* recently, and it is well known that several of the modern biplanes can send wireless messages. The crossing and bracing wires of the frame are used for sending wires, and in place of ground conductors there are trailers which hang below the aeroplane. The current is derived directly from the engine, and the remaining things needed are a small step-up transformer, a key and a few other small parts. Tom had gone a step farther than this, and had also arranged to receive wireless messages, though few modern aeroplanes are thus equipped as yet.

But, of course, there was no time now to install a wireless apparatus on Mr. Fenwick's craft. Tom thought he would be lucky if he got the *Whizzer* to make even a short flight.

"Well, let me hear from you when you can," requested Mr. Swift, and Tom promised. It was some time after that, and many strange things happened before Tom Swift again communicated with his father, at any length.

The young inventor had bidden farewell to Miss Nestor the night previous. She stated that she had a message that day from her parents aboard the *Resolute*, which spoke a passing steamer. Mr. and Mrs. Nestor, and the other guests of Mr. Hosbrook were well, and anticipated a fine time on reaching the West Indies.

Tom now said good-by to his father, the housekeeper and Mr. Jackson, not forgetting, of course, Eradicate Sampson.

"Don't let Andy Foger come sneaking around here, Rad," cautioned the young inventor.

"'Deed an' I won't!" exclaimed the colored man. "Ef he do, I'll hab Boomerang kick him t' pieces, an' den I'll whitewash him so his own folks won't know him! Oh, don't you worry, Massa Tom. Dat Andy won't do no funny business when I'm around!"

Tom laughed, and started for the station with Mr. Damon. They arrived in Philadelphia that afternoon, the trip being very slow, as compared with the one made by the monoplane. They found Mr. Fenwick anxiously awaiting them, and Tom at once started work on the airship.

He kept at it until late that night, and resumed early the next morning. Many more changes and adjustments were made, and that afternoon, the young inventor said:

"I think we'll give it a try-out, Mr. Fenwick."

"Do you mean make a flight?"

"Yes, if she'll take it; but only a short one. I want to get her up in the air, and see how she behaves."

"Well, if you find out, after you're up, that she does well, you may want to take a long flight," suggested Mr. Fenwick. "If you do, why I have everything aboard necessary for a long voyage. The *Whizzer* is well stocked with provisions."

An hour later, the big electric machine was wheeled out into the yard, for, in spite of her size, four men could easily move the craft about, so well was she balanced. Aside from a few personal friends of the inventor, himself, his machinists, Tom and Mr. Damon, no one was present at the try-out.

Tom, Mr. Damon and Mr. Fenwick climbed into the car which was suspended below the gas bag, and between the wing-like planes on either side. The young inventor had decided to make the *Whizzer* rise by scudding her across the ground on the bicycle wheels, with which she was equipped, and then by using the tilting planes to endeavor to lift her off the earth. He wanted to see if she would go up that way, without the use of the gas bag.

All was in readiness. The motor was started and the machinery began to hum and throb. The propellers gained speed with every revolution. The airship had been made fast by a rope, to which was attached a strong spring balance, as it was desired to see how much pull the engine would give.

"Eight hundred pounds," announced one of the machinists.

"A thousand would be better, but we'll try it," Murmured Tom. "Cast off!"

The rope was loosened, and, increasing the speed of the engine, Tom signalled to the men to give a little momentum to the craft. She began running over the smooth ground. There was a cheer from the few spectators. Certainly the *Whizzer* made good time on the earth.

Tom was anxiously watching the gages and other instruments. He wanted a little more speed, but could not seem to get it. He ran the motor to the utmost, and then, seeing the necessity of making an attempt to get up into the air, before the end of the speeding ground was reached, he pulled the elevating plane lever.

The front of the *Whizzer* rose, and then settled down. Tom quickly shut off the power, and jammed on the brake, an arrangement of spikes that dug into the earth, for the high board fence loomed up before him.

"What's the matter?" cried Mr. Fenwick, anxiously.

"Couldn't get up speed enough," answered the young inventor. "We must have more momentum to make her rise."

"Can it be gotten?"

"I think so. I'll gear the motor higher."

It took an hour to do this. Once more the scale test was applied. It registered a pull of fifteen hundred pounds now.

"We'll go up," said Tom, grimly.

Once more the motors spit out fire, and the propellers whirled so that they looked like mere circles of light. Once more the *Whizzer* shot over the ground, but this time, as she neared the fence, she rose up like a bird, cleared it like a trick horse, and soared off into the air!

The *Whizzer* was flying!

Over the Ocean

"Hurrah!" cried Mr. Fenwick in delight. "My machine is really flying at last!"

"Yes," answered Tom, as he adjusted various levers and gears, "she is going. It's not as high as I'd like, but it is doing very well, considering the weight of the craft, and the fact that we have not used the gas bag. I'm going to let that fill now, and we'll go up. Don't you want to steer, Mr. Fenwick?"

"No, you manage it, Tom, until it's in good running shape. I don't want to 'hoodoo' it. I worked as hard as I could, and never got more than two feet off the ground. Now I'm really sailing. It's great!"

He was very enthusiastic, and Tom himself was not a little pleased at his own success, for certainly the airship had looked to be a very dubious proposition at first.

"Bless my gaiters! But we are doing pretty well," remarked Mr. Damon, looking down on the field where Mr. Fenwick's friends and the machinists were gathered, cheering and waving their hands.

"We'll do better," declared Tom.

He had already set the gas machine in operation, and was now looking over the electric apparatus, to see that it was working well. It needed some adjustments, which he made.

All this while the *Whizzer* was moving about in a big circle, for the rudder had been automatically set to so swing the craft. It was about two hundred feet high, but soon after the gas began to enter the bag it rose until it was nearly five thousand feet high. This satisfied Tom that the airship could do better than he expected, and he decided to return nearer earth.

In going down, he put the craft through a number of evolutions designed to test her ability to answer the rudders promptly. The lad saw opportunity for making a number of changes, and suggested them to Mr. Fenwick.

"Are you going any farther?" asked the owner of the *Whizzer*, as he saw that his craft was slowly settling.

"No, I think we've done enough for the first day," said Tom, "But I'd like you to handle her now, Mr. Fenwick. You can make the landing, while I watch the motor and other machines."

"Yes. I guess I can make a landing all right," assented the inventor. "I'm better at coming down than going up."

He did make a good descent, and received the congratulation of his friends as he stepped from the airship. Tom was also given much praise for his success in making the craft go at all, for Mr. Fenwick and his acquaintances had about given up hope that she ever would rise.

"Well, what do you think of her?" Mr. Fenwick wanted to know of the young inventor, who replied that, as soon as some further changes had been made, they would attempt a long flight.

This promise was kept two days later. They were busy days for Tom, Mr. Fenwick and the latter's assistants. Tom sent a short note to his father telling of the proposed long flight, and intimated that he might make a call in Shopton if all went well. He also sent a wire to Miss Nestor, hinting that she might have some apple turnovers ready for him.

But Tom never called for that particular pastry, though it was gotten ready for him when the girl received his message.

All was in readiness for the long flight, and a preliminary test had demonstrated that the *Whizzer* had been wonderfully improved by the changes Tom made. The young inventor looked over the supply of food Mr. Fenwick had placed aboard, glanced at the other stores, and asked:

"How long do you expect to be gone, Mr. Fenwick?"

"Why, don't you think we can stay out a week?"

"That's quite a while," responded Tom. "We may be glad to return in two days, or less. But I think we're all ready to start. Are any of your friends going?"

"I've tried to pursuade some of them to accompany me, but they are a bit timid," said the inventor. "I guess we three will make up the party this time, though if our trip is a successful one I'll be overwhelmed with requests for rides, I suppose."

As before, a little crowd gathered to see the start. The day was warm, but there was a slight haziness which Tom did not like. He hoped, though, that it would pass over before they had gone far.

"Do you wish to head for any particular spot, Mr. Fenwick?" asked Tom, as they were entering the cabin.

"Yes, I would like to go down and circle Cape May, New Jersey, if we could. I have a friend who has a summer cottage there, and he was always laughing at my airship. I'd just like to drop down in front of his place now, and pay him a call."

"We'll try it," assented Tom, with a smile.

An auspicious start was made, the *Whizzer* taking the air after a short flight across the ground, and then, with the lifting gas aiding in pulling the craft upward, the airship started to sail high over the city of Philadelphia.

So swiftly did it rise that the cheers of the little crowd of Mr. Fenwick's friends were scarcely heard. Up and up it went, and then a little later, to the astonishment of the crowds in the streets, Tom put the airship twice in a circle around the statue of William Penn, on the top of the City Hall.

"Now you steer," the lad invited Mr. Fenwick. "Take her straight across the Delaware River, and over Camden, New Jersey, and then head south, for Cape May. We ought to make it in an hour, for we are getting up good speed."

Leaving the owner in charge of his craft, to that gentleman's no small delight, Tom and Mr. Damon began an inspection of the electrical and other machinery. There was much that needed attention, but Tom soon had the automatic apparatus in working order, and then less attention need be given to it.

Several times the young investor looked out of the windows with which the cabin was fitted. Mr. Damon noticed this.

"Bless my shoe laces, Tom," he said. "What's the matter?"

"I don't like the looks of the weather," was the answer. "I think we're in for a storm."

"Then let's put back."

"No, it would be too bad to disappoint Mr. Fenwick, now that we have made such a good start. He wants to make a long flight, and I can't blame him," spoke Tom, in a low voice.

"But if there's danger—"

"Oh, well, we can soon be at Cape May, and start back. The wind is freshening rather suddenly, though," and Tom looked at the anemometer, which showed a speed of twenty miles an hour. However, it was in their favor, aiding them to make faster time.

The speed of the *Whizzer* was now about forty miles an hour, not fast for an air craft, but sufficiently speedy in trying out a new machine. Tom looked at the barograph, and noted that they had attained an altitude of seven thousand five hundred feet.

"That's better than millionaire Daxtel's distance of seven thousand one hundred and five feet," remarked the lad, with a smile, "and it breaks Jackson's climb of seven thousand three hundred and three feet, which is pretty good for your machine, Mr. Fenwick."

"Do you really think so?" asked the pleased inventor.

"Yes. And we'll do better than that in time. but it's best to go slow at first, until we see how she is standing the strain. This is high and fast enough for the present."

They kept on, and as Tom saw that the machinery was working well, he let it out a little, The *Whizzer* at once leaped forward, and, a little later they came within sight of Cape May, the Jersey coast resort.

"Now to drop down and visit my friend," said Mr. Fenwick, with a smile. "Won't he be surprised!"

"I don't think we'd better do it," said Tom.

"Why not?"

"Well, the wind is getting stronger every minute and it will be against us on the way back. If we descend, and try to make another ascension we may fail. We're up in the air now, and it may be easy to turn around and go back. Then, again, it may not, but it certainly will be easier to shift around up here than down on the ground. So I'd rather not descend—that is, not entirely to the ground."

"Well, just as you say, though I wanted my friend to know I could build a successful airship."

"Oh, we can get around that. I'll take her down as low as is safe, and fly over his house, if you'll point it out, and you can drop him a message in one of the pasteboard tubes we carry for that purpose."

"That's a good idea," assented Mr. Fenwick. "I'll do it."

Tom sent the *Whizzer* down until the hotels and cottages could be made out quite plainly. After looking with a pair of opera glasses, Mr. Fenwick picked out the residence of his friend, and Tom prepared to circle about the roof.

By this time the presence of the airship had become known to hundreds, and crowds were eagerly watching it.

"There he is! There's my friend who didn't believe I would ever succeed!" exclaimed Mr. Fenwick, pointing to a man who stood in the street in front of a large, white house. "I'll drop him a message!"

One was in readiness in a weighted pasteboard cylinder, and soon it was falling downward. The airship was moving slowly, as it was beating against the wind.

Leaning out of the cabin window, Mr. Fenwick shouted to his friend:

"Hey, Will! I thought you said my airship would never go! I'll come and give you a ride, some day!"

Whether the gentleman understood what Mr. Fenwick shouted at him is doubtful, but he saw the inventor waving his hand, and he saw the falling cylinder, and a look of astonishment spread over his face, as he ran to pick up the message.

"We're going up now, and will try to head for home," said Tom, a moment later, as he shifted the rudder.

"Bless my storage battery!" cried Mr. Damon. "But we have had a fine trip."

"A much better one than we'll have going back," observed Tom, in a low voice.

"Why; what's the matter?" asked the eccentric man.

"The wind has increased to a gale, and will be dead against us," answered Tom.

Mr. Fenwick was busy writing another message to drop, and he paid little attention to the young inventor. Tom sent the craft well up into the air, and then tried to turn it about, and head back for Philadelphia. No sooner had he done so than the airship was met by the full force of the wind, which was now almost a hurricane. It had steadily increased, but, as long as they were moving with it, they did not notice it so much. Once they attempted to stem its fury they found themselves almost helpless.

Tom quickly realized this, and, giving up his intention of beating up against the wind, he turned the craft around, and let it fly before the gale, the propellers aiding to get up a speed of seventy miles an hour.

Mr. Fenwick, who had dropped the last of his messages, came from his small private cabin, to where Mr. Damon and Tom were in a low-voiced conversation near the engines. The owner of the *Whizzer*, happened to look down through a plate-glass window in the floor of car. What he saw caused him to give a gasp of astonishment.

"Why—why!" he exclaimed. "We—we're over the ocean."

"Yes," answered Tom, quietly, as he gazed down on the tumbling billows below them. They had quickly passed over Cape May, across the sandy beach, and were now well out over the Atlantic.

"Why—why are we out here?" asked Mr. Fenwick. "Isn't it dangerous— in an airship that hasn't been thoroughly tried yet?"

"Dangerous? Yes, somewhat," replied Tom, slowly. "But we can't help ourselves, Mr. Fenwick. We can't turn around and go back in this gale, and we can't descend."

"Then what's to be done?"

"Nothing, except to keep on until the gale blows itself out."

"And how long will that be?"

"I don't know—a week, maybe."

"Bless my coffee pot, I'm glad we've got plenty on board to eat!" exclaimed Mr. Damon.

A NIGHT OF TERROR

After the first shock of Tom's announcement, the two men, who were traveling with him in the airship, showed no signs of fear. Yet it was alarming to know that one was speeding over the mighty ocean, before a terrific gale, with nothing more substantial under one that a comparatively frail airship.

Still Mr. Damon knew Tom of old, and had confidence in his ability, and, while Mr. Fenwick was not so well acquainted with our hero, he had heard much about him, and put faith in his skill to carry them out of their present difficulty.

"Are you sure you can't turn around and go back?" asked Mr. Fenwick. His knowledge of air-currents was rather limited.

"It is out of the question," replied Tom, simply. "We would surely rip this craft to pieces if we attempted to buffet this storm."

"Is it so bad, then?" asked Mr. Damon, forgetting to bless anything in the tense excitement of the moment.

"It might be worse," was the reply of the young inventor. "The wind is blowing about eighty miles an hour at times, and to try to turn now would mean that we would tear the planes loose from the ship. True, we could still keep up by means of the gas bag, but even that might be injured. Going as we are, in the same direction as that in which the wind is blowing, we do not feel the full effect of it."

"But, perhaps, if we went lower down, or higher up, we could get in a different current of air," suggested Mr. Fenwick, who had made some study of aeronautics.

"I'll try," assented Tom, simply. He shifted the elevating rudder, and the *Whizzer* began to go up, slowly, for there was great lateral pressure on her large surface. But Tom knew his business, and urged the craft steadily. The powerful electric engines, which were the invention of Mr. Fenwick, stood them in good stead, and the barograph soon showed that they were steadily mounting.

"Is the wind pressure any less?" inquired Mr. Damon, anxiously.

"On the contrary, it seems to be increasing," replied Tom, with a glance at the anemometer. "It's nearly ninety miles an hour now."

"Then, aided by the propellers, we must be making over a hundred miles an hour." said the inventor.

"We are,—a hundred and thirty," assented Tom.

"We'll be blown across the ocean at this rate," exclaimed Mr. Damon. "Bless my soul! I didn't count on that."

"Perhaps we had better go down," suggested Mr. Fenwick. "I don't believe we can get above the gale."

"I'm afraid not," came from Tom. "It may be a bit better down below."

Accordingly, the rudder was changed, and the *Whizzer* pointed her nose downward. None of the lifting gas was let out, as it was desired to save that for emergencies.

Down, down, down, went the great airship, until the adventurers within, by gazing through the plate glass window in the floor of the cabin, could see the heaving, white-capped billows, tossing and tumbling below them.

"Look out, or we'll be into them!" shouted Mr. Damon.

"I guess we may as well go back to the level where we were," declared Tom. "The wind, both above and below that particular strata is stronger, and we will be safer up above. Our only chance is to scud before it, until it has blown itself out. And I hope it will be soon."

"Why?" asked Mr. Damon, in a low voice.

"Because we may be blown so far that we can not get back while our power holds out, and then—" Tom did not finish, but Mr. Damon knew what he meant—death in the tossing ocean, far from land, when the *Whizzer*, unable to float in the air any longer, should drop into the storm-enraged Atlantic.

They were again on a level, where the gale blew less furiously than either above or below, but this was not much relief. It seemed as if the airship would go to pieces, so much was it swayed and tossed about. But Mr. Fenwick, if he had done nothing else, had made a staunch craft, which stood the travelers in good stead.

All the rest of that day they swept on, at about the same speed. There was nothing for them to do, save watch the machinery, occasionally replenishing the oil tanks, or making minor adjustments.

"Well," finally remarked Mr. Damon, when the afternoon was waning away, "if there's nothing else to do, suppose we eat. Bless my appetite, but I'm hungry! and I believe you said, Mr. Fenwick, that you had plenty of food aboard."

"So we have, but the excitement of being blown out to sea on our first real trip, made me forget all about it. I'll get dinner at once, if you can put up with an amateur's cooking."

"And I'll help," offered Mr. Damon. "Tom can attend to the airship, and we'll serve the meals. It will take our minds off our troubles."

There was a well equipped kitchen aboard the *Whizzer* and soon savory odors were coming from it. In spite of the terror of their situation, and it was not to be denied that they were in peril, they all made a good meal, though it was difficult to drink coffee and other liquids, owing to the sudden lurches which the airship gave from time to time as the gale tossed her to and fro.

Night came, and, as the blackness settled down, the gale seemed to increase in fury. It howled through the slender wire rigging of the *Whizzer*, and sent the craft careening from side to side, and sometimes thrust her down into a cavern of the air, only to lift her high again, almost like a ship on the heaving ocean below them.

As darkness settled in blacker and blacker, Tom had a glimpse below him, of tossing lights on the water.

"We just passed over some vessel," he announced. "I hope they are in no worse plight than we are." Then, there suddenly came to him a thought of the parents of Mary Nestor, who were somewhere on the ocean, in the yacht *Resolute* bound for the West Indies.

"I wonder if they're out in this storm, too?" mused Tom. "If they are, unless the vessel is a staunch one, they may be in danger."

The thought of the parents of the girl he cared so much for being in peril, was not reassuring to Tom, and he began to busy himself about the machinery of the airship, to take his mind from the presentiment that something might happen to the *Resolute*.

"We'll have our own troubles before morning," the lad mused, "if this wind doesn't die down."

There was no indication that this was going to be the case, for the gale increased rather than diminished. Tom looked at their speed gage. They were making a good ninety miles an hour, for it had been decided that it was best to keep the engine and propellers going, as they steadied the ship.

"Ninety miles an hour," murmured Tom. "And we've been going at that rate for ten hours now. That's nearly a thousand miles. We are quite a distance out to sea."

He looked at a compass, and noted that, instead of being headed directly across the Atlantic they were bearing in a southerly direction.

"At this rate, we won't come far from getting to the West Indies ourselves," reasoned the young inventor. "But I think the gale will die away before morning."

The storm did not, however. More fiercely it blew through the hours of darkness. It was a night of terror, for they dared not go to sleep, not knowing at what moment the ship might turn turtle, or even rend apart, and plunge with them into the depths of the sea.

So they sat up, occasionally attending to the machinery, and noting the various gages. Mr. Damon made hot coffee, which they drank from time to time, and it served to refresh them.

There came a sudden burst of fury from the storm, and the airship rocked as if she was going over.

"Bless my heart!" cried Mr. Damon, springing up. "That was a close call!"

Tom said nothing. Mr. Fenwick looked pale and alarmed.

The hours passed. They were swept ever onward, at about the same speed, sometimes being whirled downward, and again tossed upward at the will of the wind. The airship was well-nigh helpless, and Tom, as he realized their position, could not repress a fear in his heart as he thought of the parents of the girl he loved being tossed about on the swirling ocean, in a frail pleasure yacht.

A Downward Glide

They sat in the cabin of the airship, staring helplessly at each other. Occasionally Tom rose to attend to one of the machines, or Mr. Fenwick did the same. Occasionally, Mr. Damon uttered a remark. Then there was silence, broken only by the howl of the gale.

It seemed impossible for the *Whizzer* to travel any faster, yet when Tom glanced at the speed gage he noted, with a feeling of surprise, akin to horror, that they were making close to one hundred and fifty miles an hour. Only an aeroplane could have done it, and then only when urged on by a terrific wind which added to the speed produced by the propellers.

The whole craft swayed and trembled, partly from the vibration of the electrical machinery, and partly from the awful wind. Mr. Fenwick came close to Tom, and exclaimed:

"Do you think it would be any use to try once more to go above or below the path of the storm?"

Tom's first impulse was to say that it would be useless, but he recollected that the craft belonged to Fenwick, and surely that gentleman had a right to make a suggestion. The young inventor nodded.

"We'll try to go up," he said. "If that doesn't work, I'll see if I can force her down. It will be hard work, though. The wind is too stiff."

Tom shifted the levers and rudders. His eyes were on the barograph— that delicate instrument, the trembling hand of which registered their height. Tom had tilted the deflection rudder to send them up, but as he watched the needle he saw it stationary. They were not ascending, though the great airship was straining to mount to an upper current where there might be calm.

It was useless, however, and Tom, seeing the futility of it, shifted the rudder to send them downward. This was more easily accomplished, but it was a change for the worse, since, the nearer to the ocean they went, the fiercer blew the wind.

"Back! Go back up higher!" cried Mr. Damon,

"We can't!" yelled Tom. "We've got to stay here now!"

"Oh, but this is awful!" exclaimed Mr. Fenwick. "We can never stand this!"

The airship swaged more than ever, and the occupants were tossed about in the cabin, from side to side. Indeed, it did seem that human beings never could come alive cut of that fearful ordeal.

As Tom looked from one of the windows of the cabin, he noted a pale, grayish sort of light outside. At first he could not understand what it was, then, as he observed the sickly gleams of the incandescent electric lamps, he knew that the hour of dawn was at hand.

"See!" he exclaimed to his companions, pointing to the window. "Morning is coming."

"Morning!" gasped Mr. Damon. "Is the night over? Now, perhaps we shall get rid of the storm."

"I'm afraid not," answered Tom, as he noted the anemometer and felt the shudderings of the *Whizzer* as she careened on through the gale. "It hasn't blown out yet!"

The pale light increased. The electrics seemed to dim and fade. Tom looked to the engines. Some of the apparatus was in need of oil, and he supplied it. When he came back to the main cabin, where stood Mr. Damon and Mr. Fenwick, it was much lighter outside.

"Less than a day since we left Philadelphia," murmured the owner of the *Whizzer*, as he glanced at a distance indicator, "yet we have come nearly sixteen hundred miles. We certainly did travel top speed. I wonder where we are?"

"Still over the ocean," replied Mr. Damon, as he looked down at the heaving billows rolling amid crests of foam far below them. "Though what part of it would be hard to say. We'll have to reckon out our position when it gets calmer."

Tom came from the engine room. His face wore a troubled look, and he said, addressing the older inventor:

"Mr. Fenwick, I wish you'd come and look at the gas generating apparatus. It doesn't seem to be working properly."

"Anything wrong?" asked Mr. Damon, suspiciously.

"I hope not," replied Tom, with all the confidence he could muster. "It may need adjusting. I am not so familiar with it as I am with the one on the *Red Cloud*. The gas seems to be escaping from the bag, and we may have to descend, for some distance."

"But the aeroplanes will keep us up," said Mr. Daman.

"Yes—they will," and Tom hesitated. "That is, unless something happens to them. They are rather frail to stand alone the brunt of the gale, and I wish—"

Tom did not complete the sentence. Instead, he paused suddenly and seemed to be intently listening.

From without there came a rending, tearing, crashing sound. The airship quivered from end to end, and seemed to make a sudden dive downward. Then it appeared to recover, and once more glided forward.

Tom, followed by Mr. Fenwick, made a rush for the compartment where the machine was installed. They had no sooner reached it than there sounded an explosion, and the airship recoiled as if it had hit a stone wall.

"Bless my shaving brush! What's that?" cried Mr. Damon. "Has anything happened?"

"I'm rather afraid there has," answered Tom, solemnly. "It sounded as though the gas bag went up. And I'm worried over the strength of the planes. We must make an investigation!"

"We're falling!" almost screamed Mr. Fenwick, as he glanced at the barograph, the delicate needle of which was swinging to and fro, registering different altitudes.

"Bless my feather bed! So we are!" shouted Mr. Damon. "Let's jump, and avoid being caught under the airship!"

He darted for a large window, opening from the main cabin, and was endeavoring to raise it when Tom caught his hand.

"What are you trying to do," asked the lad, hoarsely.

"Save my life! I want to get out of this as soon as I can. I'm going to jump!"

"Don't think of it! You'd be instantly killed. We're too high for a jump, even into the ocean."

"The ocean! Oh, is that still below us? Is there any chance of being saved? What can be done?" Mr. Damon hesitated.

"We must first find out how badly we are damaged," said Tom, quietly. "We must keep our heads, and be calm, no matter what happens. I need your help, Mr. Damon."

This served to recall the rather excited man to his senses. He came back to the centre of the cabin, which was no easy task, for the floor of it was tilted at first one angle, and then another. He stood at Tom's side.

"What can I do to help you?" he asked. Mr. Fenwick was darting here and there, examining the different machines. None of them seemed to be damaged.

"If you will look and see what has happened to our main wing planes, I will see how much gas we have left in the bag," suggested Tom. "Then we can decide what is best to be done. We are still quite high, and it will take some time to complete our fall, as, even if everything is gone, the material of the bag will act as a sort of parachute."

Mr. Damon darted to a window in the rear of the cabin, where he could obtain a glimpse of the main wing planes. He gave a cry of terror and astonishment.

"Two of the planes are gone!" he reported. "They are torn and are hanging loose."

"I feared as much," retorted Tom, quietly, "The gale was too much for them."

"What of the lifting gas?" asked Mr. Fenwick, quickly.

"It has nearly all flowed out of the retaining bag."

"Then we must make more at once. I will start the generating machine." He darted toward it.

"It will be useless," spoke Tom, quietly.

"Why?"

"Because there is no bag left to hold it. The silk and rubber envelope has been torn to pieces by the gale. The wind is even stronger than it was last night."

"Then what's to be done?" demanded Mr. Damon, with a return of his alarmed and nervous manner. "Bless my fingernails! What's to be done?"

For an instant Tom did not answer. It was constantly getting lighter, though there was no sun, for it was obscured by scudding clouds. The young inventor looked critically at the various gages and indicators.

"Is—is there any chance for us?" asked Mr. Fenwick, quietly.

"I think so," answered Tom, with a hopeful smile. "We have about two thousand feet to descend, for we have fallen nearly that distance since the accident."

"Two thousand feet to fall!" gasped Mr. Damon. "We can never do it and live!"

"I think so," spoke Tom.

"Bless my gizzard! How?" fairly exploded Mr. Damon.

"By vol-planing down!"

"But, even if we do, we will fall into the ocean!" cried Mr. Fenwick. "We will be drowned!"

"No," and Tom spoke more quietly than before. "We are over a large island." he went on, "and I propose to let the disabled airship vol- plane down to it. That is our only chance."

"Over an island!" cried Mr. Damon. He looked down through the floor observation window. Tom had spoken truly. At that moment they were over a large island, which had suddenly loomed up in the wild and desolate waste of the ocean. They had reached its vicinity just in time.

Tom stepped to the steering and rudder levers, and took charge. He was going to attempt a most difficult feat—that of guiding a disabled airship back to earth in the midst of a hurricane, and landing her on an unknown island. Could he do it?

There was but one answer. He must try. It was the only chance of saving their lives, and a slim one at best

Down shot the damaged *Whizzer* like some giant bird with broken wings, but Tom Swift was in charge, and it seemed as if the craft knew it, as she began that earthward glide

ON EARTHQUAKE ISLAND

Mingled feelings possessed the three adventurers within the airship. Mr. Damon and Mr. Fenwick had crowded to the window, as Tom spoke, to get a glimpse of the unknown island toward which they were shooting. They could see it more plainly now, from the forward casement, as well as from the one in the bottom of the craft. A long, narrow, rugged piece of land it was, in the midst of the heaving ocean, for the storm still raged and lashed the waves to foam.

"Can you make it?" asked Mr. Damon, in a low voice.

"I think so," answered Tom, more cheerfully.

"Shall I shut down the motor?" inquired the older inventor.

"Yes, you might as well. We don't need the propellers now, and I may be better able to make the glide without them."

The buzzing and purring electrical apparatus was shut down. Silence reigned in the airship, but the wind still howled outside. As Tom had hoped, the ship became a little more steady with the stopping of the big curved blades, though had the craft been undamaged they would have served to keep her on an even keel.

With skillful hand he so tilted the elevating planes that, after a swift downward glide, the head of the *Whizzer* would be thrown up, so to speak, and she would sail along in a plane parallel to the island. This had the effect of checking her momentum, just as the aviator checks the downward rush of his monoplane or biplane when he is making a landing.

Tom repeated this maneuver several times, until a glance at his barograph showed that they had but a scant sixty feet to go. There was time but for one more upward throwing of the *Whizzer*'s nose, and Tom held to that position as long as possible. They could now make out the topography of the island plainly, for it was much lighter. Tom saw a stretch of sandy beach, and steered for that.

Downward shot the airship, inert and lifeless. It was not like gliding his little *Butterfly* to earth after a flight, but Tom hoped he could make it. They were now within ten feet of the earth, skimming forward. Tom tried another upward tilt, but the forward planes would not respond. They could get no grip on the air.

With a crash that could have been heard some distance the *Whizzer* settled to the sand. It ran along a slight distance, and then, as the bicycle wheels collapsed under the pressure, the airship seemed to go together in a shapeless mass.

At the first impact with the earth, Tom had leaped away from the steering wheel and levers, for he did not want to be crushed against them. Mr. Damon and Mr. Fenwick, in pursuance of a plan adopted when they found that they were falling, had piled a lot of seat cushions around them. They had also provided some as buffers for Tom, and our hero, at the instant of the crash, had thrown himself behind and upon them.

It seemed as if the whole ship went to pieces. The top of the main cabin crashed down, as the side supports gave way, but, fortunately, there were strong main braces, and the roof did not fall completely upon our friends.

The whole bottom of the craft was forced upward and had it not been for the protecting cushions, there might have been serious injuries for all concerned. As it was they were badly bruised and shaken up.

After the first crash, and succeeding it an instant later, there came a second smash, followed by a slight explosion, and a shower of sparks could be seen in the engine room.

"That's the electrical apparatus smashing through the floor!" called Tom. "Come, let's get out of here before the gasolene sets anything on fire. Are you all right, Mr. Damon, and you, Mr. Fenwick?"

"Yes, I guess so," answered the inventor. "Oh, what a terrible crash! My airship is ruined!"

"You may be glad we are alive," said Mr. Damon. "Bless my top knot, I feel—"

He did not finish the sentence. At that moment a piece of wood, broken from the ceiling, where it had hung by a strip of canvas came crashing down, and hit Mr. Damon on the head.

The eccentric man toppled over on his pile of cushions, from which he was arising when he was struck.

"Oh, is he killed?" gasped Mr. Fenwick.

"I hope not!" cried Tom. "We must get him out of here, at all events. There may be a fire."

They both sprang to Mr. Damon's aid, and succeeded in lifting him out. There was no difficulty in emerging from the airship as there were big, broken gaps, on all sides of what was left of the cabin. Once in the outer air Mr. Damon revived, and opened his eyes.

"Much hurt?" asked Tom, feeling of his friend's head.

"No—no, I—I guess not," was the slow answer. "I was stunned for a moment. I'm all right now. Nothing broken, I guess," and his hand went to his head.

"No, nothing broken," added Tom, cheerfully, "but you've got a lump there as big as an ostrich egg. Can you walk?"

"Oh, I'm all right. Bless my stars, what a wreck!"

Mr. Damon looked at the remains of the airship. It certainly was a wreck! The bent and twisted planes were wrapped about the afterpart, the gas bag was but a shred, the frame was splintered and twisted, and the under part, where the starting wheels were placed, resembled a lot of broken bicycles. The cabin looked like a shack that had sustained an explosion of dynamite.

"It's a wonder we came out alive," said Mr. Fenwick, in a low voice.

"Indeed it is," agreed Tom, as he came back with a tin can full of sea water, with which to bathe Mr. Damon's head. The lad had picked up the can from where it had rolled from the wreck, and they had landed right on the beach.

"It doesn't seem to blow so hard," observed Mr. Damon, as he was tenderly sopping his head with a handkerchief wet in the salt water.

"No, the wind is dying out, but it happened too late to do us any good," remarked Tom, sorrowfully. "Though if it hadn't blown us this far, we might have come to grief over the ocean, and be floundering in that, instead of on dry land."

"That's so," agreed Mr. Fenwick, who was carefully feeling of some bruises on his legs. "I wonder where we are, anyhow?"

"I haven't the least idea," responded Tom. "It's an island, but which one, or where it is I don't know. We were blown nearly two thousand miles, I judge."

He walked over and surveyed the wreck. Now that the excitement was over he was beginning to be aware of numerous bruises and contusions, His legs felt rather queer, and on rolling up his trousers he found there was a deep cut in the right shin, just below his knee. It was bleeding, but he bandaged it with a spare handkerchief, and walked on.

Peering about, he saw that nearly the whole of the machinery in the engine room, including most of the electrical apparatus, had fallen bodily through the floor, and now rested on the sand.

"That looks to be in pretty good shape." mused Tom, "but it's a question whether it will ever be any good to us. We can't rebuild the airship here, that's certain."

He walked about the wreck, and then returned to his friends. Mr. Damon was more like himself, and Mr. Fenwick had discovered that he had only minor bruises.

"Bless my coffee cup!" exclaimed Mr. Damon. "I declare, I feel hungry. I wonder if there's anything left to eat in the wreck?"

"Plenty," spoke Tom, cheerfully. "I'll get it out. I can eat a sandwich or too myself, and perhaps I can set up the gasolene stove, and cook something."

As the young inventor was returning to the wreck, he was halted halfway by a curious trembling feeling. At first he thought it was a weakness of his legs, caused by his cut, but a moment later he realized with a curious, sickening sensation that it was the ground- -the island itself—that was shaking and trembling.

The lad turned back. Mr. Damon and Mr. Fenwick were staring after him with fear showing on their faces.

"What was that?" cried the inventor.

"Bless my gizzard! Did you feel that, Tom?" cried Mr. Damon. "The whole place is shaking!"

Indeed, there was a stronger tremor now, and it was accompanied by a low, rumbling sound, like distant thunder. The adventurers were swaying to and fro.

Suddenly they were tossed to the ground by a swaying motion, and not far off a great crack opened in the earth. The roaring, rumbling sound increased in volume.

"An earthquake! It's an earthquake!" cried Tom. "We're in the midst of an earthquake!"

A Night in Camp

The rumbling and roaring continued for perhaps two minutes, during which time the castaways found it impossible to stand, for the island was shaking under their feet with a sickening motion. Off to one side there was a great fissure in the earth, and, frightened as he was, Tom looked to see if it was extending in their direction.

If it was, or if a crack opened near them, they might be precipitated into some bottomless abyss, or into the depths of the sea. But the fissure did not increase in length or breadth, and, presently the rumbling, roaring sound subsided. The island grew quiet and the airship travelers rose to their feet.

"Bless my very existence! What happened?" cried Mr. Damon.

"It was an earthquake; wasn't it, Tom?" asked Mr. Fenwick.

"It sure was," agreed the young inventor. "Rather a hard one, too. I hope we don't have any more."

"Do you think there is any likelihood of it?" demanded Mr. Damon. "Bless my pocketbook! If I thought so I'd leave at once."

"Where would you go?" inquired Tom, looking out across the tumbling ocean, which had hardly had a chance to subside from the gale, ere it was again set in a turmoil by the earth-tremor.

"That's so—there isn't a place to escape to," went on the eccentric man, with something like a groan. "We are in a bad place—do you think there'll be more quakes, Tom?"

"It's hard to say. I don't know where we are, and this island may be something like Japan, subject to quakes, or it may be that this one is merely a spasmodic tremor. Perhaps the great storm which brought us here was part of the disturbance of nature which ended up with the earthquake. We may have no more."

"And there may be one at any time," added Mr. Fenwick.

"Yes," assented Tom.

"Then let's get ready for it," proposed Mr. Damon. "Let's take all the precautions possible."

"There aren't any to take," declared Tom. "All we can do is to wait until the shocks come—if any more do come, which I hope won't happen, and then we must do the best we can."

"Oh, dear me! Bless my fingernails!" cried Mr. Damon, wringing his hands. "This is worse than falling in an airship! There you do have *some* chance. Here you haven't any."

"Oh, it may not be so bad," Tom cried to reassure him. "This may have been the first shock in a hundred years, and there may never be another."

But, as he looked around on the island, he noted evidences that it was of volcanic origin, and his heart misgave him, for he knew that such islands, created suddenly by a submarine upheaval, might just as suddenly be destroyed by an earthquake, or by sinking into the ocean. It was not a pleasant thought—it was like living over a mine, that might explode at any moment. But there was no help for it.

Tom tried to assume a cheerfulness he did not feel. He realized that, in spite of his youth, both Mr. Damon and Mr. Fenwick rather depended on him, for Tom was a lad of no ordinary attainments, and had a fund of scientific knowledge. He resolved to do his best to avoid making his two companions worry.

"Let's get it off our minds," suggested the lad, after a while. "We were going to get something to eat. Suppose we carry out that program. My appetite wasn't spoiled by the shock."

"I declare mine wasn't either," said Mr. Damon, "but I can't forget it easily. It's the first earthquake I was ever in."

He watched Tom as the latter advanced once more toward the wreck of the airship, and noticed that the lad limped, for his right leg had been cut when the *Whizzer* had fallen to earth.

"What's the matter, Tom; were you hurt in the quake?" asked the eccentric man.

"No—no," Tom hastened to assure him. "I just got a bump in the fall—that's all. It isn't anything. If you and Mr. Fenwick want to get out some food from the wrecked store room I'll see if I can haul out the gasolene stove from the airship. Perhaps we can use it to make some coffee."

By delving in about the wreck, Tom was able to get out the gasolene stove. It was broken, but two of the five burners were in commission, and could be used. Water, and gasolene for use in the airship, was carried in steel tanks. Some of these had been split open by the crash, but there was one cask of water left, and three of gasolene, insuring plenty of the liquid fuel. As for the water, Tom hoped to be able to find a spring on the island.

In the meanwhile, Mr. Damon and Mr. Fenwick had been investigating the contents of the storeroom. There was a large supply of food, much larger than would have been needed, even on a two weeks' trip in the air, and the inventor of the *Whizzer* hardly knew why he had put so much aboard.

"But if we have to stay here long, it may come in handy," observed Tom, with a grim smile.

"Why; do you think we *will* be here long?" asked Mr. Damon.

The young inventor shrugged his shoulders.

"There is no telling," he said. "If a passing steamer happens to see us, we may be taken off to-day or to-morrow. If not we may be here a week, or—" Tom did not finish. He stood in a listening attitude.

There was a rumbling sound, and the earth seemed again to tremble. Then there came a great splash in the water at the foot of a tall, rugged cliff about a quarter of a mile away. A great piece of the precipice had fallen into the ocean.

"I thought that was another earthquake coming," said Mr. Damon, with an air of relief.

"So did I," admitted Mr. Fenwick.

"It was probably loosened by the shock, and so fell into the sea," spoke Tom.

Their momentary fright over, the castaways proceeded to get their breakfast. Tom soon had water boiling on the gasolene stove, for he had rescued a tea-kettle and a coffee pot from the wreck of the kitchen of the airship. Shortly afterward, the aroma of coffee filled the air, and a little later there was mingled with it the appetizing odor of sizzling bacon and eggs, for Mr. Fenwick, who was very fond of the latter, had brought along a supply, carefully packed in sawdust carriers, so that the shock had broken only a few of them.

"Well, I call this a fine breakfast," exclaimed Mr. Damon, munching his bacon and eggs, and dipping into his coffee the hard pilot biscuit, which they had instead of bread. "We're mighty lucky to be eating at all, I suppose."

"Indeed we are," chimed in Mr. Fenwick.

"I'm awfully sorry the airship is wrecked, though," spoke Tom. "I suppose it's my fault. I should have turned back before we got over the ocean, and while the storm was not at its height. I saw that the wind was freshening, but I never supposed it would grow to a gale so suddenly. The poor old *Whizzer*—there's not much left of her!"

"Now don't distress yourself in the least," insisted Mr. Fenwick. "I'm proud to have built a ship that could navigate at all. I see where I made lots of mistakes, and as soon as I get back to Philadelphia, I'm going to build a better one, if you'll help me, Tom Swift."

"I certainly will," promised the young inventor.

"And I'll take a voyage with you!" cried Mr. Damon. "Bless my teaspoon, Tom, but will you kindly pass the bacon and eggs again!"

There was a jolly laugh at the eccentric man, in which he himself joined, and the little party felt better. They were seated on bits of broken boxes taken from the wreck, forming a little circle about the gasolene stove, which Tom had set up on the beach. The wind had almost entirely died away, though the sea was still heaving in great billows, and masses of surf.

They had no exact idea of the time, for all their watches had stopped when the shock of the wreck came, but presently the sun peeped out from the clouds, and, from knowing the time when they had begun to fall, they judged it was about ten o'clock, and accordingly set their timepieces.

"Well," observed Tom, as he collected the dishes, which they had also secured from the wreck, "we must begin to think about a place to spend the night. I think we can rig up a shelter from some of the canvas of the wing-planes, and from what is left of the cabin. It doesn't need to be very heavy, for from the warmth of the atmosphere, I should say we were pretty well south."

It was quite warm, now that the storm was over, and, as they looked at the vegetation of the island, they saw that it was almost wholly tropical.

"I shouldn't be surprised if we were on one of the smaller of the West Indian islands," said Tom. "We certainly came far enough, flying a hundred miles or more an hour, to have reached them. But this one doesn't appear to be inhabited."

"We haven't been all over it yet," said Mr. Damon. "We may find cannibals on the other side."

"Cannibals don't live in this part of the world," Tom assured him. "No, I think this island is practically unknown. The storm brought us here, and it might have landed us in a worse place."

As he spoke he thought of the yacht *Resolute*, and he wondered how her passengers, including the parents of Mary Nestor, had fared during the terrible blow.

"I hope they weren't wrecked, as we were," mused Tom.

But there was little time for idle thoughts. If they were going to build a shelter, they knew that they must speedily get at it. Accordingly, with a feeling of thankfulness that their lives had been spared, they set to work taking apart such of the wreck as could the more easily be got at.

Boards, sticks, and planks were scattered about, and, with the pieces of canvas from the wing-planes, and some spare material which was carried on board, they soon had a fairly good shack, which would be protection enough in that warm climate.

Next they got out the food and supplies, their spare clothing and other belongings, few of which had been harmed in the fall from the clouds. These things were piled under another rude shelter which they constructed.

By this time it was three o'clock, and they ate again. Then they prepared to spend the night in their hastily made camp. They collected driftwood, with which to make a fire, and, after supper, which was prepared on the gasolene stove, they sat about the cheerful blaze, discussing their adventures.

"To-morrow we will explore the island," said Tom, as he rolled himself up in his blankets and turned over to sleep. The others followed his example, for it was decided that no watch need be kept. Thus passed several hours in comparative quiet.

It must have been about midnight that Tom was suddenly awakened by a feeling as if someone was shaking him. He sat up quickly and called out:

"What's the matter?"

"Eh? What's that? Bless my soul! What's going on?" shouted Mr. Damon.

"Did you shake me?" inquired Tom.

"I? No. What—?"

Then they realized that another earth-tremor was making the whole island tremble.

Tom leaped from his blankets, followed by Mr. Damon and Mr. Fenwick, and rushed outside the shack. They felt the earth shaking, but it was over in a few seconds. The shock was a slight one, nothing like as severe as the one in the morning. But it set their nerves on edge.

"Another earthquake!" groaned Mr. Damon. "How often are we to have them?"

"I don't know," answered Tom, soberly.

They passed the remainder of the night sleeping in blankets on the warm sands, near the fire, for they feared lest a shock might bring the shack down about their heads. However, the night passed with no more terrors.

The Other Castaways

"Well, we're all alive, at any rate," announced Tom, when the bright sun, shining into his eyes, had awakened him. He sat up, tossed aside his blankets, and stood up. The day was a fine one, and the violence of the sea had greatly subsided during the night, their shack had suffered not at all from the slight shock in the darkness.

"Now for a dip in old Briney," the lad added, as he walked down to the surf, "I think it will make me feel better."

"I'm with you," added Mr. Fenwick, and Mr. Damon also joined the bathers. They came up from the waves, tingling with health, and their bruises and bumps, including Tom's cut leg, felt much better.

"You did get quite a gash; didn't you," observed Mr. Fenwick, as he noticed Tom's leg. "Better put something on it. I have antiseptic dressings and bandages in the airship, if we can find them."

"I'll look for them, after breakfast," Tom promised, and following a fairly substantial meal, considering the exigencies under which it was prepared, he got out the medicine chest, of which part remained in the wreck of the *Whizzer*, and dressed his wound. He felt much better after that.

"Well, what's our program for to-day?" Mr. Damon wanted to know, as they sat about, after they had washed up what few dishes they used.

"Let's make a better house to stay in," proposed Mr. Fenwick. "We may have to remain here for some time, and I'd like a more substantial residence."

"I think the one we now have will do," suggested Tom. "I was going to propose making it even less substantial."

"Why so?"

"Because, in the event of an earthquake, while we are sleeping in it, we will not be injured. Made of light pieces of wood and canvas it can't harm us very much if it falls on us."

"That's right," agreed Mr. Damon. "In earthquake countries all the houses are low, and built of light materials."

"Ha! So I recollect now," spoke Mr. Fenwick. "I used to read that in my geography, but I never thought it would apply to me. But do you think we will be subject to the quakes?"

"I'm afraid so," was Tom's reply. "We've had two, now, within a short time, and there is no way of telling when the next will come. We will hope there won't be any more, but—"

He did not finish his sentence, but the others knew what he meant. Thereupon they fell to work, and soon had made a shelter that, while very light and frail, would afford them all the protection needed in that mild climate, and, at the same time, there would be no danger should an earthquake collapse it, and bring it down about their heads while they were sleeping in it.

For they decided that they needed some shelter from the night dews, as it was exceedingly uncomfortable to rest on the sands even wrapped in blankets, and with a driftwood fire burning nearby.

It was noon when they had their shack rebuilt to their liking, and they stopped for dinner. There was quite a variety of stores in the airship, enough for a much larger party than that of our three friends, and they varied their meals as much as possible. Of course all the stuff they had was canned, though there are some salted and smoked meats. But canned food can be had in a variety of forms now- a-days, so the castaways did not lack much.

"What do you say to an exploring expedition this afternoon?" asked Tom, as they sat about after dinner. "We ought to find out what kind of an island we're on."

"I agree with you," came from Mr. Fenwick. "Perhaps on the other side we will stand a much better chance of speaking some passing vessel. I have been watching the horizon for some time, now, but I haven't seen the sign of a ship."

"All right, then we'll explore, and see what sort of an island we have taken possession of," went on Tom.

"And see if it isn't already in possession of natives—or cannibals," suggested Mr. Damon. "Bless my frying pan! but I should hate to be captured by cannibals at my time of life."

"Don't worry; there are none here," Tom assured him again.

They set out on their journey around the island. They agreed that it would be best to follow the beach around, as it was easier walking that way, since the interior of the place consisted of rugged rocks in a sort of miniature mountain chain.

"We will make a circuit of the place," proposed Tom, "and then, if we can discover nothing, we'll go inland. The centre of the island is quite high, and we ought to be able to see in any direction for a great distance from the topmost peak. We may be able to signal a vessel."

"I hope so!" cried Mr. Damon. "I want to send word home that I am all right. My wife will worry when she learns that the airship, in which I set out, has disappeared."

"I fancy we all would like to send word home," added Mr. Fenwick. "My wife never wanted me to build this airship, and, now that I have sailed in it, and have been wrecked, I know she'll say 'I told you so,' as soon as I get back to Philadelphia."

Tom said nothing, but he thought to himself that it might be some time before Mrs. Fenwick would have a chance to utter those significant words to her husband.

Following the beach line, they walked for several miles. The island was larger than they had supposed, and it soon became evident that it would take at least a day to get all around it.

"In which case we will need some lunch with us." said Tom. "I think the best thing we can do now is to return to camp, and get ready for a longer expedition to-morrow."

Mr. Fenwick was of the same mind, but Mr. Damon called out:

"Let's go just beyond that cliff, and see what sort of a view is to be had from there. Then we'll turn back."

To oblige him they followed. They had not gone more than a hundred yards toward the cliff, than there came the preliminary rumbling and roaring that they had come to associate with an earthquake. At the same time, the ground began to shiver and shake.

"Here comes another one!" cried Tom, reeling about. He saw Mr. Damon and Mr. Fenwick topple to the beach. The roaring increased, and the rumbling was like thunder, close at hand. The island seemed to rock to its very centre.

Suddenly the whole cliff toward which they had been walking, appeared to shake itself loose. In another instant it was flung outward and into the sea, a great mass of rock and stone.

The island ceased trembling, and the roaring stopped. Tom rose to his feet, followed by his companions. He looked toward the place where the cliff had been. Its removal by the earthquake gave them a view of a part of the beach that had hitherto been hidden from them.

And what Tom saw caused him to cry out in astonishment. For he beheld, gathered around a little fire on the sand, a party of men and women. Some were standing, clinging to one another in terror. Some were prostrate on the ground. Others were running to and fro in bewilderment.

"More castaways!" cried Tom. "More castaways," and, he added under his breath, "more unfortunates on earthquake island!"

An Alarming Theory

For a few seconds, following Tom's announcement to his two companions, neither Mr. Damon nor Mr. Fenwick spoke. They had arisen from the beach, where the shock of the earthquake had thrown them, and were now staring toward the other band of castaways, who, in turn were gazing toward our three friends. There was a violent agitation in the sea, caused by the fall of the great cliff, and immense waves rushed up on shore, but all the islanders were beyond the reach of the rollers.

"Is it—do I really—am I dreaming or not?" at length gasped Mr. Damon.

"Is this a mirage, or do we really see people, Tom?" inquired Mr. Fenwick.

"They are real enough people," replied the lad, himself somewhat dazed by the unexpected appearance of the other castaways.

"But how—why—how did they get here?" went on the inventor of the *Whizzer*.

"As long as they're not cannibals, we're all right," murmured Mr. Damon. "They seem to be persons like ourselves, Tom."

"They are," agreed the lad, "and they appear to be in the same sort of trouble as ourselves. Let's go forward, and meet them."

The tremor of the earthquake had now subsided, and the little band that was gathered about a big fire of driftwood was calmer. Those who had fallen, or who had thrown themselves on the sand, arose, and began feeling of their arms and legs to see if they had sustained any injuries. Others advanced toward our friends.

"Nine of them," murmured Tom, as he counted the little band of castaways, "and they don't seem to have been able to save much from the wreck of their craft, whatever it was." The beach all about them was bare, save for a boat drawn up out of reach of high water.

"Do you suppose they are a party from some disabled airship, Tom," asked Mr. Fenwick.

"Not from an airship," answered the lad. "Probably from some vessel that was wrecked in the gale. But we will soon find out who they are."

Tom led the way for his two friends. The fall of the cliff had made a rugged path around the base of it, over rocks, to where the other people stood. Tom scrambled in and out among the boulders, in spite of the pain it caused his wounded leg. He was anxious to know who the other castaways were, and how they had come there.

Several of the larger party were now advancing to meet the lad and his friends. Tom could see two women and seven men.

A moment later, when the lad had a good view of one of the ladies and a gentleman, he could not repress a cry of astonishment. Then he rubbed his eyes to make sure it was not some blur or defect of vision. No, his first impression had been correct.

"Mr. Nestor!" cried Tom, recognizing the father of his girl friend. "And Mrs. Nestor!" he added a moment later.

"Why—of all things—look—Amos—it's—it can't be possible—and yet—why, it's Tom Swift!" cried the lady.

"Tom—Tom Swift—here?" ejaculated the man at her side.

"Yes—Tom Swift—the young inventor—of Shopton—don't you know—the lad who saved Mary's life in the runaway—Tom Swift!"

"Tom Swift!" murmured Mr. Nestor. "Is it possible!"

"I'm Tom Swift, all right," answered the owner of that name, "but how in the world did you get on this island, Mr. Nestor?"

"I might ask you the same thing, Tom. The yacht *Resolute*, on which we were making a voyage to the West Indies, as guests of Mr. George Hosbrook, was wrecked in the awful gale. We took to the boats and managed to reach this island. The yacht sunk, and we only had a little food. We are almost starved! But how came you here?"

"Mr. Fenwick's airship was wrecked, and we dropped down here. What a coincidence! To think that I should meet you here! But if you're hungry, it's the best thing in the world that we met you, for, though our airship was wrecked, we have a large supply of food. Come over to our camp, and we'll give you all you want!"

Tom had rushed forward, and was shaking hands with Mary's parents, so unexpectedly met with, when Mr. Nestor called out:

"Come over here, Mr. Hosbrook. I want you to meet a friend of mine."

A moment later, the millionaire owner of the ill-fated *Resolute* was shaking hands with Tom.

"I can't understand it," Mr. Hosbrook said. "To think of meeting other people on this desolate island—this island of earthquakes."

"Oh, please don't speak of earthquakes!" cried Mrs. Nestor. "We are in mortal terror! There have been several since we landed in the most terrible storm day before yesterday. Isn't it awful! It is a regular earthquake island!"

"That's what I call it," spoke Tom, grimly.

The others of the larger party of refugees now came up. Besides Mr. and Mrs. Nestor, and Mr. Hosbrook, there was Mr. and Mrs. Floyd Anderson, friends of the millionaire; Mr. Ralph Parker, who was spoken of as a scientist, Mr. Barcoe Jenks, who seemed an odd sort of individual, always looking about suspiciously, Captain Mentor, who had been in command of the yacht, and Jake Fordam, the mate of the vessel.

"And are these all who were saved?" asked Tom, as he introduced his two friends, and told briefly of their air voyage.

"No," answered Mr. Hosbrook, "two other boatloads, one containing most of the crew, and the other containing some of my guests, got away before our boat left. I trust they have been rescued, but we have heard nothing about them. However, our own lives may not long be safe, if these earthquakes continue."

"But did I understand you to say, Mr. Swift, that you had food?" he went on. "If you have, I will gladly pay you any price for some, especially for these two ladies, who must be faint. I have lost all my ready cash, but if we ever reach civilization, I will—"

"Don't speak of such a thing as pay," interrupted Mr. Fenwick. "All that we have we'll gladly share with you. Come over to our camp. We have enough for all, and we can cook on our gasolene stove. Don't speak of pay, I beg of you."

"Ah—er, if Mr. Hosbrook has no money, perhaps I can offer an equivalent," broke in the man who had been introduced as Barcoe Jenks. "I have—er—some securities—" He stopped and looked about indefinitely, as though he did not know exactly what to say, and he was fumbling at a belt about his waist; a belt that might contain treasure.

"Don't speak of reimbursing us," went on Mr. Fenwick, with rather a suspicious glance at Mr. Jenks. "You are welcome to whatever we have."

"Bless my topknot; certainly, yes!" joined in Mr. Damon, eagerly.

"Well, I—er—I only spoke of it," said Mr. Jenks, hesitatingly, and then he turned away. Mr. Hosbrook looked sharply at him, but said nothing.

"Suppose we go to our camp," proposed Tom. "We may be able to get you up a good meal, before another earthquake comes."

"I wonder what makes so many of them?" asked Mrs. Nestor, with a nervous shiver.

"Yes, indeed, they are terrifying! One never knows when to expect them," added Mrs. Anderson.

"I have a theory about them," said Mr. Parker, the scientist, who, up to this time had spoken but little.

"A theory?" inquired Tom.

"Yes. This island is one of the smaller of the West Indies group. It is little known, and has seldom been visited, I believe. But I am sure that what causes the earthquakes is that the whole island has been undermined by the sea, and it is the wash of great submarine waves and currents which cause the tremors."

"Undermined by the sea?" repeated Tom.

"Yes. It is being slowly washed away."

"Bless my soul! Washed away!" gasped Mr. Damon.

"And, in the course of a comparatively short time, it will sink," went on the scientist, as cheerfully as though he was a professor propounding some problem to his class.

"Sink!" ejaculated Mrs. Nestor. "The whole island undermined! Oh, what an alarming theory!"

"I wish I could hold to a different one, madam," was Mr. Parker's answer, "but I cannot. I think the island will sink after a few more shocks."

"Then what good will my—" began Barcoe Jenks, but he stopped in confusion, and again his hand went to his belt with a queer gesture.

A MIGHTY SHOCK

Tom Swift turned to gaze at Mr. Barcoe Jenks. That individual certainly had a strange manner. Perhaps it might be caused by the terror of the earthquakes, but the man seemed to be trying to hold back some secret. He was constrained and ill at ease. He saw the young inventor looking at him, and his hands, which had gone to his belt, with a spasmodic motion, dropped to his side.

"You don't really mean to say, Parker, that you think the whole island is undermined, do you?" asked the owner of the *Resolute*.

"That's my theory. It may be a wrong one, but it is borne out by the facts already presented to us. I greatly fear for our lives!"

"But what can we do?" cried Mrs. Nestor.

"Nothing," answered the scientist, with a shrug of his shoulders. "Absolutely nothing, save to wait for it to happen."

"Don't say that!" begged Mrs. Andersen.

"Can't you gentlemen do something—build a boat and take us away. Why, the boat we came here in—"

"Struck a rock, and stove a hole in the bottom as big as a barrel, madam," interrupted Captain Mentor. "It would never do to put to sea in that."

"But can't something else be done?" demanded Mrs. Nestor. "Oh, it is awful to think of perishing on this terrible earthquake island. Oh, Amos! Think of it, and Mary home alone! Have you seen her lately, Mr. Swift?"

Tom told of his visit to the Nestors' home. Our hero was almost in despair, not so much for himself, as for the unfortunate women of the party—and one of them was Mary's mother! Yet what could he do? What chance was there of escaping from the earthquake?

"Bless my gizzard!" exclaimed Mr. Damon. "Don't let's stand here worrying! If you folks are hungry come up to our camp. We have plenty. Afterward we can discuss means of saving ourselves."

"I want to be saved!" exclaimed Mr. Jenks. "I must be saved! I have a great secret—a secret—"

Once more he paused in confusion, and once more his hands nervously sought his belt.

"I would give a big reward to be saved," he murmured.

"And so, I fancy, we all would," added Captain Mentor. "But we are not likely to. This island is out of the track of the regular line of vessels."

"Where are we, anyhow?" inquired Mr. Fenwick. "What island is this?"

"It isn't down on the charts, I believe," was the captain's reply, "but we won't be far out, if we call it Earthquake Island. That name seems to fit it exactly."

They had walked on, while talking, and now had gone past the broken cliff. Tom and his two friends of the airship led the way to the camp they had made. On the way, Mr. Hosbrook related how his yacht had struggled in vain against the tempest, how she had sprung a leak, how the fires had gone out, and how, helpless in the trough of the sea, the gallant vessel began to founder. Then they had taken to the boats, and had, most unexpectedly come upon the island.

"And since we landed we have had very little to eat," said Mrs. Nestor. "We haven't had a place to sleep, and it has been terrible. Then, too, the earthquakes! And my husband and I worried so about Mary. Oh, Mr. Swift! Do you think there is any chance of us ever seeing her again?"

"I don't know," answered Tom, softly. "I'll do all I can to get us off this island. Perhaps we can build a raft, and set out. If we stay here there is no telling what will happen, if that scientist's theory is correct. But there is our camp, just ahead. You will be more comfortable, at least for a little while."

In a short time they were at the place where Tom and the others had built the shack. The ruins of the airship were examined with interest, and the two women took advantage of the seclusion of the little hut, to get some much needed rest until a meal should be ready.

One was soon in course of preparation by Tom and Mr. Damon, aided by Mate Fordam, of the *Resolute*. Fortunate it was that Mr. Fenwick had brought along such a supply of food, for there were now many mouths to feed.

That the supper (which the meal really was, for it was getting late) was much enjoyed, goes without saying. The yacht castaways had subsisted on what little food had been hurriedly put into the life boat, as they left the vessel.

At Tom's request, while it was yet light, Captain Mentor and some of the men hunted for a spring of fresh water, and found one, for, with the increase in the party, the young inventor saw the necessity for more water. The spring gave promise of supplying a sufficient quantity.

There was plenty of material at hand for making other shacks, and they were soon in course of construction. They were made light, as was the one Tom and his friends first built, so that, in case of another shock, no one would be hurt seriously. The two ladies were given the larger shack, and the men divided themselves between two others that were hastily erected on the beach. The remainder of the food and stores was taken from the wreck of the airship, and when darkness began to fall, the camp was snug and comfortable, a big fire of driftwood burning brightly.

"Oh, if only we can sleep without being awakened by an earthquake!" exclaimed Mrs. Nestor, as she prepared to go into the shack with Mrs. Anderson. "But I am almost afraid to close my eyes!"

"If it would do any good to stay up and watch, to tell you when one was coming, I'd do so," spoke Tom, with a laugh, "but they come without warning."

However, the night did pass peacefully, and there was not the least tremor of the island. In the morning the castaways took courage and, after breakfast, began discussing their situation more calmly.

"It seems to me that the only solution is to build some sort of a raft, or other craft and leave the island," said Mr. Fenwick.

"Bless my hair brush!" cried Mr. Damon. "Why can't we hoist a signal of distress, and wait for some steamer to see it and call for us? It seems to me that would be more simple than going to sea on a raft. I don't like the idea."

"A signal would be all right, if this island was in the path of the steamers," said Captain Mentor. "But it isn't. Our flag might fly for a year, and never be seen."

His words seemed to strike coldness to every heart. Tom, who was looking at the wreck of the airship, suddenly uttered an exclamation. He sprang to his reet

"What is it?" demanded Mr. Fenwick. "Does your sore leg hurt you?"

"No, but I have just thought of a plan!" fairly shouted the young inventor. "I have it! Wait and see if I can work it!"

"Work what?" cried Mr. Damon.

Tom did not get a chance to answer, for, at that moment, there sounded, at the far end of the island, whence the yacht castaways had come, a terrific crash. It was accompanied, rather than followed, by a shaking, trembling and swaying of the ground.

"Another earthquake!" screamed Mrs. Nestor, rushing toward her husband. The castaways gazed at each other affrighted.

Suddenly, before their eyes, they saw the extreme end of that part of the island on which they were camping, slip off, and beneath the foaming waves of the sea, while the echoes of the mighty crash came to their ears!

MR. JENKS HAS DIAMONDS

Stunned, and well-nigh paralyzed by the suddenness of the awful crash, and the recurrence of the earthquake, the castaways gazed spell-bound at one another.

Succeeding the disappearance of the end of the island there arose a great wave in the ocean, caused by the immersion of such a quantity of rock and dirt.

"Look out!" yelled Tom, "there may be a flood here!"

They realized his meaning, and hastened up the beach, out of reach of the water if it should come. And it did. At first the ocean retreated, as though the tide was going out, then, with a rush and roar, the waves came leaping back, and, had the castaways remained where they had been standing they would have been swept cut to sea.

As it was the flood reached part of the wreck of the airship, that lay on the beach, and washed away some of the broken planks. But, after the first rush of water, the sea grew less troubled, and there was no more danger from that source.

True, the whole island was rumbling and trembling in the throes of an earthquake, but, by this time, the refugees had become somewhat used to this, and only the two ladies exhibited any outward signs of great alarm, though Mr. Barcoe Jenks, Tom observed, was nervously fingering the belt which he wore about his waist.

"I guess the worst is over," spoke Mr. Fenwick, as they stood looking toward where part of the island had vanished. "The shock expended itself on tearing that mass of rock and earth away."

"Let us hope so," added Mr. Hosbrook, solemnly. "Oh, if we could only get away from this terrible place! We must hoist a signal of distress, even if we are out of the track of regular vessels. Some ship, blown out of her course may see it. Captain Mentor, I wish you and Mr. Fordam would attend to that."

"I will, sir," answered the commander of the ill-fated *Resolute*. "The signal shall be hoisted at once. Come on, Mr. Fordam," he added, turning to the first mate.

"If you don't mind," interrupted Tom, "I wish you would first help me to get what remains of the airship up out of reach of any more possible high waves. That one nearly covered it, and if there are other big rollers, the wreck may be washed out to sea."

"I can't see that any great harm would result from that," put in Mr. Jenks. "There isn't anything about the wreck that we could use to make a boat or raft from." Indeed, there was little left of the airship, save the mass of machinery.

"Well, it may come in handy before we leave here," said Tom, and there was a quiet determined air about him, that caused Mr. Damon to look at him curiously. The odd gentleman started to utter one of his numerous blessings, and to ask Tom a question, but he thought better of it. By this time the earthquake had ceased, and the castaways were calmer.

Tom started toward the airship wreck, and began pulling off some broken boards to get at the electrical machinery.

"I guess you had better give Mr. Swift a hand, Captain Mentor," spoke the millionaire yacht owner. "I don't know what good the wreck can be, but we owe considerable to Mr. Swift and his friends, and the least we can do is to aid them in anything they ask. So, Captain, if you don't mind, you and the mate bear a hand. In fact, we'll all help, and move the wreck so far up that there will be no danger, even from tidal waves."

Tom looked pleased at this order, and soon he and all the men in the little party were busy taking out the electrical apparatus, and moving it farther inland.

"What are you going to do with it, Tom?" asked Mr. Damon, in a low voice, as he assisted the young inventor to carry a small dynamo, that was used for operating the incandescent lights.

"I hardly know myself. I have a half-formed plan in my mind. I may be able to carry it out, and I may not. I don't want to say anything until I look over the machinery, and see if all the parts which I need are here. Please say nothing about it."

"Bless my toothpick! Of course, I'll not," promised Mr. Damon.

When the removal of most of the machinery of the wrecked airship had been completed, Mrs. Nestor exclaimed:

"Well, since you are moving that out of harm's way, don't you think it would be a good idea to change our camp, also? I'm sure I'll never sleep a wink, thinking that part of the island may fall into the ocean at any moment in the night, and create a wave that may wash us all out to sea. Can't we move the camp, Mr. Swift?"

"No reason why we can't," answered the lad, smiling. "I think it would be a good plan to take it farther back. We are likely to be here some time, and, while we are about it, we might build more complete shelters, and have a few more comforts."

The others agreed with this idea, so the little shacks that had been erected were taken down, and moved to higher ground, where a better outlook could be had of the surrounding ocean. At the same time as safe a place as possible, considering the frequent earthquakes, was picked out—a place where there were no overhanging rocks or cliffs.

Three huts were built, one for the two ladies, one for the men, and third where the cooking could be done. This last also held the food supplies and stores, and Tom noted, with satisfaction, that there was still sufficient to eat to last over a week. Mr. Fenwick had not stinted his kitchen stores.

This work done, Captain Mentor and Mate Fordam went to the highest part of the island, where they erected a signal, made from pieces of canvas that had been in the life boat. The boat itself was brought around to the new camp, and at first it was hoped that it could be repaired, and used. But too large a hole had been stove in the bottom, so it was broken up, and the planks used in making the shacks.

This work occupied the better part of two days, and during this time, there were no more earthquakes. The castaways began to hope that the island would not be quiet for a while. Mrs. Anderson and Mrs. Nestor assumed charge of the "housekeeping" arrangements, and also the cooking, which relieved Tom from those duties. The two ladies even instituted "wash-day," and when a number of garments were hung on lines to dry, the camp looked like some summer colony of pleasure-seekers, out for a holiday.

In the meanwhile, Tom had spent most of his time among the machinery which had been taken from the airship. He inspected it carefully, tested some of the apparatus, and made some calculations on a bit of paper. He seemed greatly pleased over something, and one afternoon, when he was removing some of the guy and stay wires from the collapsed frame of the *Whizzer*, he was approached by Mr. Barcoe Jenks.

"Planning something new?" asked Mr. Jenks, with an attempt at jollity, which, however, failed. The man had a curious air about him, as if he was carrying some secret that was too much for him.

"Well, nothing exactly new," answered Tom. "At best I am merely going to try an experiment."

"An experiment, eh?" resumed Mr. Jenks, "And might I ask if it has anything to do with rescuing us from this island?"

"I hope it will have," answered Tom, gravely.

"Good!" exclaimed Mr. Jenks. "Well, now I have a proposition to make to you. I suppose you are not very wealthy, Mr. Swift?" He gazed at Tom, quizzically.

"I am not poor," was the young inventor's proud answer, "but I would be glad to make more money—legitimately."

"I thought so. Most every one would. Look here!"

He approached closer to Tom, and, pulling his hand from his pocket, held it extended, in the palm were a number of irregularly-shaped objects—stones or crystals the lad took them to be, yet they did not look like ordinary stones or crystals.

"Do you know what those are?" asked Mr. Jenks.

"I might guess," replied Tom.

"I'll save you the trouble. They are diamonds! Diamonds of the very first water, but uncut. Now to the point. I have half a million dollars worth of them. If you get me safely off this island, I will agree to make you a quarter of a million dollars worth of diamonds!"

"Make me a quarter of a million dollars worth of diamonds?" asked Tom, struck by the use of the work "make."

"Yes, 'make,'" answered Mr. Jenks. "That is if I can discover the secret—the secret of Phantom Mountain. Get me away from the island and I will share my knowledge with you—I need help—help to learn the secret and help to make the diamonds—see, there are some of the first ones made, but I have been defrauded of my rights—I need the aid of a young fellow like you. Will you help? See, I'll give you some diamonds now. They are genuine, though they are not like ordinary diamonds. I made them. Will you—"

Before Tom could answer, there came a warning rumble of the earth, and a great fissure opened, almost at the feet of Mr. Jenks, who, with a cry of fear, leaped toward the young inventor.

Secret Operations

"Help me save this machinery!" yelled Tom, whose first thought was for the electrical apparatus. "Don't let it fall into that chasm!"

For the crack had widened, until it was almost to the place where the parts of the wrecked airship had been carried.

"The machinery? What do I care about the machinery?" cried Mr. Jenks. "I want to save my life!"

"And this machinery is our only hope!" retorted Tom. He began tugging at the heavy dynamos and gasolene engine, but he might have saved himself the trouble, for with the same suddenness with which it opened, the crack closed again. The shock had done it, and, as if satisfied with that phenomena, the earthquake ceased, and the island no longer trembled.

"That was a light one," spoke Tom, with an air of relief. He was becoming used to the shocks now, and, when he saw that his precious machinery was not damaged he could view the earth tremors calmly.

"Slight!" exclaimed Mr. Jenks. "Well, I don't call it so. But I see Captain Mentor and Mr. Hosbrook coming. Please don't say anything to them about the diamonds. I'll see you again," and with that, the queer Mr. Jenks walked away.

"We came to see if you were hurt," called the captain, as he neared the young inventor.

"No, I'm all right. How about the others?"

"Only frightened," replied the yacht owner. "This is getting awful. I hoped we were free from the shocks, but they still continue."

"And I guess they will," added Tom. "We certainly are on Earthquake Island!"

"Mr. Parker, the scientist, says this last shock bears out his theory," went on the millionaire. "He says it will be only a question of a few days when the whole island will disappear."

"Comforting, to say the least," commented Tom.

"I should say so. But what are you doing, Mr. Swift?"

"Trying an experiment," answered the young inventor, in some confusion. He was not yet ready to talk about his plans.

"We must begin to think seriously of building some sort of a boat or raft, and getting away from the island," went on the millionaire. "It will be perilous to go to sea with anything we can construct, but it is risking our lives to stay here. I don't know what to do."

"Perhaps Captain Mentor has some plan," suggested Tom, hoping to change the subject.

"No," answered the commander, "I confess I am at a loss to know what to do. There is nothing with which to do anything, that is the trouble! But I did think of hoisting another signal, on this end of the island, where it might be seen if our first one wasn't. I believe I'll do that," and he moved away, to carry out his intention.

"Well, I think I'll get back, Tom, and tell the others that you are all right," spoke Mr. Hosbrook. "I left the camp, after the shock, because Mrs. Nestor was worried about you." The place to which the airship machinery had been removed was some distance from the camp, and out of sight of the shacks.

"Oh, yes. I'm all right," said Tom. Then, with a sudden impulse, he asked: "Do you know much about this Mr. Barcoe Jenks, Mr. Hosbrook?"

"Not a great deal," was the reply. "In fact, I may say I do not know him at all. Why do you ask?"

"Because I thought he acted rather strangely."

"Just what the rest of us think," declared the yacht owner. "He is no friend of mine, though he was my guest on the *Resolute*. It came about in this way. I had invited a Mr. Frank Jackson to make the trip with me, and he asked if he could bring with him a Mr. Jenks, a friend of his. I assented, and Mr. Jackson came aboard with Mr. Jenks. Just as we were about to sail Mr. Jackson received a message requiring his presence in Canada, and he could not make the trip."

"But Mr. Jenks seemed so cut-up about being deprived of the yachting trip, and was so fond of the water, that I invited him to remain on board, even if his friend did not. So that is how he came to be among my guests, though he is a comparative stranger to all of us."

"I see," spoke Tom.

"Has he been acting unusually strange?" asked Mr. Hosbrook suspiciously.

"No, only he seemed very anxious to get off the island, but I suppose we all are. He wanted to know what I planned to do."

"Did you tell him?"

"No, for the reason that I don't know whether I can succeed or not, and I don't want to raise false hopes."

"Then you would prefer not to tell any of us?"

"No one—that is except Mr. Fenwick and Mr. Damon. I may need them to help me."

"I see," responded Mr. Hosbrook. "Well, whatever it is, I wish you luck. It is certainly a fearful place—this island," and busy with many thoughts, which crowded upon him, the millionaire moved away, leaving Tom alone.

A little while after this Tom might have been seen in close conversation with Mr. Damon and Mr. Fenwick. The former, on hearing what the young inventor had to say, blessed himself and his various possessions so often, that he seemed to have gotten out of breath. Mr. Fenwick exclaimed:

"Tom, if you can work that it will be one of the greatest things you have ever done!"

"I hope I can work it," was all the young inventor replied.

For the next three days Tom, and his two friends, spent most of their time in the neighborhood of the pile of machinery and apparatus taken from the wrecked *Whizzer*. Mr. Jenks hung around the spot, but a word or two from

Mr. Hosbrook sent him away, and our three friends were left to their work in peace, for they were inclined to be secretive about their operations, as Tom did not want his plans known until he was ready.

The gasolene motor was overhauled, and put in shape to work. Then it was attached to the dynamo. When this much had been done, Tom and his friends built a rude shack around the machinery shutting it from view.

"Humph! Are you afraid we will steal it?" asked Mr. Parker, the scientist, who held to his alarming theory regarding the ultimate disappearance of the island.

"No, I simply want to protect it from the weather," answered Tom. "You will soon know all our plans. I think they will work out."

"You'd better do it before we get another earthquake, and the island sinks," was the dismal response.

But there had been no shocks since the one that nearly engulfed Mr. Jenks. As for that individual he said little to any one, and wandered off alone by himself. Tom wondered what kind of diamonds they were that the odd man had, and the lad even had his doubts as to the value of the queer stones he had seen. But he was too busy with his work to waste much time in idle speculation.

THE WIRELESS PLANT

The castaways had been on Earthquake Island a week now, and in that time had suffered many shocks. Some were mere tremors, and some were so severe as to throw whole portions of the isle into the sea. They never could tell when a shock was coming, and often one awakened them in the night.

But, in spite of this, the refugees were as cheerful as it was possible to be under the circumstances. Only Mr. Jenks seemed nervous and ill at ease, and he kept much by himself.

As for Tom, Mr. Damon and Mr. Fenwick, the three were busy in their shack. The others had ceased to ask questions about what they were doing, and Mr. Nestor and his wife took it for granted that Tom was building a boat.

Captain Mentor and the mate spent much time gazing off to sea, hoping for a sight of the sail of some vessel, or the haze that would indicate the smoke of a steamer. But they saw nothing.

"I haven't much hope of sighting anything," the captain said. "I know we are off the track of the regular liners, and our only chance would be that some tramp steamer, or some ship blown off her course, would see our signal. I tell you, friends, we're in a bad way."

"If money was any object—," began Mr. Jenks.

"What good would money be?" demanded Mr. Hosbrook. "What we need to do is to get a message to some one—some of my friends—to send out a party to rescue us."

"That's right," chimed in Mr. Parker, the scientist. "And the message needs to go off soon, if we are to be saved."

"Why so?" asked Mr. Anderson.

"Because I think this island will sink inside of a week!"

A scream came from the two ladies.

"Why don't you keep such thoughts to yourself?" demanded the millionaire yacht owner, indignantly.

"Well, it's true," stubbornly insisted the scientist.

"What if it is? It doesn't do any good to remind us of it."

"Bless my gizzard, no!" exclaimed Mr. Damon. "Suppose we have dinner. I'm hungry."

That seemed to be his remedy for a number of ills.

"If we only could get a message off, summoning help, it *would* be the very thing," sighed Mrs. Nestor. "Oh, how I wish I could send my daughter, Mary, word of where we are. She may hear of the wreck of the *Resolute*, and worry herself to death."

"But it is out of the question to send a message for help from Earthquake Island," added Mrs. Anderson. "We are totally cut off from the rest of the world here."

"Perhaps not," spoke Tom Swift, quietly. He had come up silently, and had heard the conversation.

"What's that you said?" cried Mr. Nestor, springing to his feet, and crossing the sandy beach toward the lad.

"I said perhaps we weren't altogether cut off from the rest of the world," repeated Tom.

"Why not," demanded Captain Mentor. "You don't mean to say that you have been building a boat up there in your little shack, do you?"

"Not a boat," replied Tom, "but I think I have a means of sending out a call for help!"

"Oh, Tom—Mr. Swift—how?" exclaimed Mrs. Nestor. "Do you mean we can send a message to my Mary?"

"Well, not exactly to her," answered the young inventor, though he wished that such a thing were possible. "But I think I can summon help."

"How?" demanded Mr. Hosbrook. "Have you managed to discover some cable line running past the island, and have you tapped it?"

"Not exactly." was Tom's calm answer, "but I have succeeded, with the help of Mr. Damon and Mr. Fenwick, in building an apparatus that will send out wireless messages!"

"Wireless messages!" gasped the millionaire. "Are you sure?"

"Wireless messages!" exclaimed Mr. Jenks. "I'll give—" He paused, clasped his hands on his belt, and turned away.

"Oh, Tom!" cried Mrs. Nestor, and she went up to the lad, threw her arms about his neck, and kissed him; whereat Tom blushed.

"Perhaps you'd better explain," suggested Mr. Anderson.

"I will," said the lad. "That is the secret we have been engaged upon—Mr. Damon, Mr. Fenwick and myself. We did not want to say anything about it until we were sure we could succeed."

"And are you sure now?" asked Captain Mentor.

"Fairly so."

"How could you build a wireless station?" inquired Mr. Hosbrook.

"From the electrical machinery that was in the wrecked *Whizzer*," spoke Tom. "Fortunately, that was not damaged by the shock of the fall, and I have managed to set up the gasolene engine, and attach the dynamo to it so that we can generate a powerful current. We also have a fairly good storage battery, though that was slightly damaged by the fall."

"I have just tested the machinery, and I think we can send out a strong enough message to carry at least a thousand miles."

"Then that will reach some station, or some passing ship," murmured Captain Mentor. "There is a chance that we may be saved."

"If it isn't too late," gloomily murmured the scientist. "There is no telling when the island will disappear beneath the sea."

But they were all so interested in Tom's announcement that they paid little attention to this dire foreboding.

"Tell us about it," suggested Mr. Nestor. And Tom did.

He related how he had set up the dynamo and gasolene engine, and how, by means of the proper coils and other electrical apparatus, all of which, fortunately, was aboard the *Whizzer*, he could produce a powerful spark.

"I had to make a key out of strips of brass, to produce the Morse characters," the lad said. "This took considerable time, but it works, though it is rather crude. I can click out a message with it."

"That may be," said Mr. Hosbrook, who had been considering installing a wireless plant on his yacht, and who, therefore, knew something about it, "you may send a message, but can you receive an answer?"

"I have also provided for that," replied Tom. "I have made a receiving instrument, though that is even more crude than the sending plant, for it had to be delicately adjusted, and I did not have just the magnets, carbons, coherers and needles that I needed. But I think it will work."

"Did you have a telephone receiver to use?"

"Yes. There was a small interior telephone arrangement on Mr. Fenwick's airship, and part of that came in handy. Oh, I think I can hear any messages that may come in answer to ours."

"But what about the aerial wires for sending and receiving messages?" asked Mr. Nestor.

"Don't you have to have several wires on a tall mast?"

"Yes, and that is the last thing to do," declared Tom. "I need all your help in putting up those wires. That tall tree on the crest of the island will do," and he pointed to a dead palm that towered gaunt and bare like a ship's mast, on a pile of rocks in the centre of Earthquake Island.

MESSAGES INTO SPACE

Tom Swift's announcement of the practical completion of his wireless plant brought hope to the discouraged hearts of the castaways. They crowded about him, and asked all manner of questions.

Mr. Fenwick and Mr. Damon came in for their share of attention, for Tom said had it not been for the aid of his friends he never could have accomplished what he did. Then they all trooped up to the little shack, and inspected the plant.

As the young inventor had said, it was necessarily crude, but when he set the gasolene motor going, and the dynamo whizzed and hummed, sending out great, violet-hued sparks, they were all convinced that the young inventor had accomplished wonders, considering the materials at his disposal.

"But it's going to be no easy task to rig up the sending and receiving wires," declared Tom. "That will take some time."

"Have you got the wire?" asked Mr. Jenks.

"I took it from the stays of the airship," was Tom's reply, and he recalled the day he was at that work, when the odd man had exhibited the handful of what he said were diamonds. Tom wondered if they really were, and he speculated as to what might be the secret of Phantom Mountain, to which Mr. Jenks had referred.

But now followed a busy time for all. Under the direction of the young inventor, they began to string the wires from the top of the dead tree, to a smaller one, some distance away, using five wires, set parallel, and attached to a wooden spreader, or stay. The wires were then run to the dynamo, and the receiving coil, and the necessary ground wires were installed.

"But I can't understand how you are going to do it," said Mrs. Nestor. "I've read about wireless messages, but I can't get it through my head. How is it done, Mr. Swift?"

"The theory is very simple," said the young inventor. "To send a message by wire, over a telegraph system, a battery or dynamo is used. This establishes a current over wires stretched between two points. By means of what is called a 'key' this current is interrupted, or broken, at certain intervals, making the sounding instrument send out clicks. A short click is called a dot, and a long click a dash. By combinations of dots, dashes, and spaces between the dots and dashes, letters are spelled out. For instance, a dot and a space and a dash, represent the letter 'A' and so on."

"I understand so far," admitted Mrs. Nestor.

"In telegraphing without wires," went on Tom, "the air is used in place of a metallic conductor, with the help of the earth, which in itself is a big magnet, or a battery, as you choose to regard it. The earth helps to establish the connection between places where there are no wires, when we 'ground' certain conductors."

"To send a wireless message a current is generated by a dynamo. The current flows along until it gets to the ends of the sending wires, which we have just strung. Then it leaps off into space, so to speak, until it reaches the receiving wires, wherever they may be erected. That is why any wireless receiving station, within a certain radius, can catch any messages that may be flying through the air—that is unless certain apparatus is tuned, or adjusted, to prevent this."

"Well, once the impulses, or electric currents, are sent out into space, all that is necessary to do is to break, or interrupt them at certain intervals, to make dots, dashes and spaces. These make corresponding clicks in the telephone receiver which the operator at the receiving station wears on his ear. He hears the code of clicks, and translates them into letters, the letters into words and the words into sentences. That is how wireless messages are sent."

"And do you propose to send some that way?" asked Mrs. Anderson.

"I do," replied Tom, with a smile.

"Where to?" Mrs. Nestor wanted to know.

"That's what I can't tell," was Tom's reply. "I will have to project them off into space, and trust to chance that some listening wireless operator will 'pick them up,' as they call it, and send us aid."

"But are wireless operators always listening?" asked Mr. Nestor.

"Somewhere, some of them are—I hope," was Tom's quiet answer. "As I said, we will have to trust much to chance. But other people have been saved by sending messages off into space; and why not we? Sinking steamers have had their passengers taken off when the operator called for help, merely by sending a message into space."

"But how can we tell them where to come for us—on this unknown island?" inquired Mrs. Anderson.

"I fancy Captain Mentor can supply our longitude and latitude," answered Tom. "I will give that with every message I send out, and help may come—some day."

"It can't come any too quick for me!" declared Mr. Damon. "Bless my door knob, but my wife must be worrying about my absence!"

"What message for help will you send?" Captain Mentor wanted to know.

"I am going to use the old call for aid," was the reply of the young inventor. "I shall flash into space the three letters 'C.Q.D.' They stand for 'Come Quick—Danger.' A new code call has been instituted for them, but I am going to rely on the old one, as, in this part of the world, the new one may not be so well understood. Then I will follow that by giving our position in the ocean, as nearly as Captain Mentor can figure it out. I will repeat this call at intervals until we get help—"

"Or until the island sinks," added the scientist, grimly.

"Here! Don't mention that any more," ordered Mr. Hosbrook. "It's getting on my nerves! We may be rescued before that awful calamity overtakes us."

"I don't believe so," was Mr. Parker's reply, and he actually seemed to derive pleasure from his gloomy prophecy.

"It's lucky you understand wireless telegraphy, Tom Swift," said Mr. Nestor admiringly, and the other joined in praising the young inventor, until, blushing, he hurried off to make some adjustments to his apparatus.

"Can you compute our longitude and latitude, Captain Mentor," asked the millionaire yacht owner.

"I think so," was the reply. "Not very accurately, of course, for all my papers and instruments went down in the *Resolute*. But near enough for the purpose, I fancy. I'll get right to work at it, and let Mr. Swift have it."

"I wish you would. The sooner we begin calling for help the better. I never expected to be in such a predicament as this, but it is wonderful how that young fellow worked out his plan of rescue. I hope he succeeds."

It took some little time for the commander to figure their position, and then it was only approximate. But at length he handed Tom a piece of paper with the latitude and longitude written on it.

In the meanwhile, the young inventor had been connecting up his apparatus. The wires were now all strung, and all that was necessary was to start the motor and dynamo.

A curious throng gathered about the little shack as Tom announced that he was about to flash into space the first message calling for help. He took his place at the box, to which had been fastened the apparatus for clicking off the Morse letters.

"Well, here we go," he said, with a smile.

His fingers clasped the rude key he had fashioned from bits of brass and hard rubber. The motor was buzzing away, and the electric dynamo was purring like some big cat.

Just as Tom opened the circuit, to send the current into the instrument, there came an omnious rumbling of the earth.

"Another quake!" screamed Mrs. Anderson. But it was over in a second, and calmness succeeded the incipient panic.

Suddenly, overhead, there sounded a queer crackling noise, a vicious, snapping, as if from some invisible whips.

"Mercy! What's that?" cried Mrs. Nestor.

"The wireless," replied Tom, quietly. "I am going to send a message for help, off into space. I hope some one receives it—and answers," he added, in a low tone.

The crackling increased. While they gathered about him, Tom Swift pressed the key, making and breaking the current until he had sent out from Earthquake Island the three letters—"C.Q.D." And he followed them by giving their latitude and longitude. Over and over again he flashed out this message.

Would it be answered? Would help come? If so, from where? And if so, would it be in time? These were questions that the castaways asked themselves. As for Tom, he sat at the key, clicking away, while, overhead, from the wires fastened to the dead tree, flashed out the messages.

ANXIOUS DAYS

After the first few minutes of watching Tom click out the messages, the little throng of castaways that had gathered about the shack, moved away. The matter had lost its novelty for them, though, of course, they were vitally interested in the success of Tom's undertaking. Only Mr. Damon and Mr. Fenwick remained with the young inventor, for he needed help, occasionally, in operating the dynamo, or in adjusting the gasolene motor. Mrs. Nestor, who, with Mrs. Anderson, was looking after the primitive housekeeping arrangements, occasionally strolled up the hill to the little shed.

"Any answer yet, Mr. Swift?" she would ask.

"No." was the reply. "We can hardly expect any so soon," and Mrs. Nestor would depart, with a sigh.

Knowing that his supply of gasolene was limited, Tom realized that he could not run the dynamo steadily, and keep flashing the wireless messages into space. He consulted with his two friends on the subject, and Mr. Damon said:

"Well, the best plan, I think, would be only to send out the flashes over the wires at times when other wireless operators will be on the lookout, or, rather, listening. There is no use wasting our fuel. We can't get any more here."

"That's true," admitted Tom, "but how can we pick out any certain time, when we can be sure that wireless operators, within a zone of a thousand miles, will be listening to catch clicks which call for help from the unknown?"

"We can't," decided Mr. Fenwick. "The only thing to do is to trust to chance. If there was only some way so you would not have to be on duty all the while, and could send out messages automatically, it would be good."

Tom shook his head. "I have to stay here to adjust the apparatus," he said. "It works none too easily as it is, for I didn't have just what I needed from which to construct this station. Anyhow, even if I could rig up something to click out 'C.Q.D.' automatically, I could hardly arrange to have the answer come that way. And I want to be here when the answer comes."

"Have you any plan, then?" asked Mr. Damon. "Bless my shoe laces! there are enough problems to solve on this earthquake island."

"I thought of this," said Tom. "I'll send out our call for help from nine to ten in the morning. Then I'll wait, and send out another call from two to three in the afternoon. Around seven in the evening I'll try again, and then about ten o'clock at night, before going to bed."

"That ought to be sufficient," agreed Mr. Fenwick. "Certainly we must save our gasolene, for there is no telling how long we may have to stay here, and call for help."

"It won't be long if that scientist Parker has his way," spoke Mr. Damon, grimly. "Bless my hat band, but he's a *most* uncomfortable man to have around; always predicting that the island is going to sink! I hope we are rescued before that happens."

"I guess we all do," remarked Mr. Fenwick. "But, Tom, here is another matter. Have you thought about getting an answer from the unknown—from some ship or wireless station, that may reply to your calls? How can you tell when that will come in?"

"I can't."

"Then won't you or some of us, have to be listening all the while?"

"No, for I think an answer will come only directly after I have sent cut a call, and it has been picked up by some operator. Still there is a possibility that some operator might receive my message, and report to his chief, or some one in authority over him, before replying. In that time I might go away. But to guard against that I will sleep with the telephone receiver clamped to my ear. Then I can hear the answer come over the wires, and can jump up and reply."

"Do you mean you will sleep here?" asked Mr. Damon, indicating the shack where the wireless apparatus was contained.

"Yes," answered Tom, simply.

"Can't we take turns listening for the answer?" inquired Mr. Fenwick, "and so relieve you?"

"I'm afraid not, unless you understand the Morse code," replied Tom. "You see there may be many clicks, which result from wireless messages flying back and forth in space, and my receiver will pick them up. But they will mean nothing. Only the answer to our call for help will be of any service to us."

"Do you mean to say that you can catch messages flying back and forth between stations now?" asked Mr. Fenwick.

"Yes," replied the young inventor, with a smile. "Here, listen for yourself," and he passed the head-instrument over to the *Whizzer*'s former owner. The latter listened a moment.

"All I can hear are some faint clicks," he said.

"But they are a message," spoke Tom. "Wait, I'll translate," and he out the receiver to his ear. "*Steamship "Falcon" reports a slight fire in her forward compartment,*" said Tom, slowly. "*it is under control, and we will proceed.*"

"Do you mean to say that was the message you heard?" cried Mr. Damon. "Bless my soul, I never can understand it!"

"It was part of a message," answered Tom. "I did not catch it all, nor to whom it was sent."

"But why can't you send a message to that steamship then, and beg them to come to our aid?" asked Mr. Fenwick. "Even if they have had a fire, it is out now, and they ought to be glad to save life."

"They would come to our aid. or send," spoke Tom, "but I can not make their wireless operator pick up our message. Either his apparatus is not in tune, or in accord with ours, or he is beyond our zone."

"But you heard him," insisted Mr. Damon.

"Yes, but sometimes it is easier to pick up messages than it is to send them. However, I will keep on trying."

Putting into operation the plan he had decided on for saving their supply of gasolene, Tom sent out his messages the remainder of the day, at the intervals agreed upon. Then the apparatus was shut down, but the lad paid frequent visits to the shack, and listened to the clicks of the telephone receiver. He caught several messages, but they were not in response to his appeals for aid.

That night there was a slight earthquake shock, but no more of the island fell into the sea, though the castaways were awakened by the tremors, and were in mortal terror for a while.

Three days passed, days of anxious waiting, during which time Tom sent out message after message by his wireless, and waited in vain for an answer. There were three shocks in this interval, two slight, and one very severe, which last cast into the ocean a great cliff on the far end of the island. There was a flooding rush of water, but no harm resulted.

"It is coming nearer," said Mr. Parker.

"What is?" demanded Mr. Hosbrook.

"The destruction of our island. My theory will soon be confirmed," and the scientist actually seemed to take pleasure in it.

"Oh, you and your theory!" exclaimed the millionaire in disgust. "Don't let me hear you mention it again! Haven't we troubles enough?" whereat Mr. Parker went off by himself, to look at the place where the cliff had fallen.

Each night Tom slept with the telephone receiver to his ear, but, though it clicked many times, there was not sounded the call he had adopted for his station—"E. I."—Earthquake Island. In each appeal he sent out he had requested that if his message was picked up, that the answer be preceded by the letters "E.I."

It was on the fourth day after the completion of the wireless station, that Tom was sending out his morning calls. Mrs. Nestor came up the little hill to the shack where Tom was clicking away.

"No replies yet, I suppose?" she inquired, and there was a hopeless note in her voice.

"None yet, but they may come any minute," and Tom tried to speak cheerfully.

"I certainly hope so," added Mary's mother, "But I came up more especially now, Mr. Swift, to inquire where you had stored the rest of the food."

"The rest of the food?"

"Yes, the supply you took from the wrecked airship. We have used up nearly all that was piled in the improvised kitchen, and we'll have to draw on the reserve supply."

"The reserve," murmured Tom.

"Yes, there is only enough in the shack where Mrs. Anderson and I do the cooking, to last for about two days. Isn't there any more?"

Tom did not answer. He saw the drift of the questioning. Their food was nearly gone, yet the castaways from the *Resolute* thought there was still plenty. As a matter of fact there was not another can, except those in the kitchen shack.

"Get out wherever there is left some time to-day, if you will, Mr. Swift," went on Mrs. Nestor, as she turned away, "and Mrs. Anderson and I will see if we can fix up some new dishes for you men-folks."

"Oh—all right," answered Tom, weakly.

His hand dropped from the key of the instrument. He sat staring into space. Food enough for but two days more, with earthquakes likely to happen at any moment, and no reply yet to his appeals for aid! Truly the situation was desperate. Tom shook his head. It was the first time he had felt like giving up.

A REPLY IN THE DARK

The young inventor looked out of the wireless shack. Down on the beach he saw the little band of castaways. They were gathered in a group about Mr. Jenks, who seemed to be talking earnestly to them. The two ladies were over near the small building that served as a kitchen.

"More food supplies needed, eh?" mused Tom. "Well, I don't know where any more is to come from. We've stripped the *Whizzer* bare." He glanced toward what remained of the airship. "I guess we'll have to go on short rations, until help comes," and, wondering what the group of men could be talking about, Tom resumed his clicking out of his wireless message.

He continued to send it into space for several minutes after ten o'clock, the hour at which he usually stopped for the morning, for he thought there might be a possible chance that the electrical impulses would be picked up by some vessel far out at sea, or by some station operator who could send help.

But there came no answering clicks to the "E. I." station—to Earthquake Island—and, after a little longer working of the key, Tom shut down the dynamo, and joined the group on the beach.

"I tell you it's our only chance," Mr. Jenks was saying. "I must get off this island, and that's the only way we can do it. I have large interests at stake. If we wait for a reply to this wireless message we may all be killed, though I appreciate that Mr. Swift is doing his best to aid us. But it is hopeless!"

"What do you think about it, Tom?" asked Mr. Damon, turning to the young inventor.

"Think about what?"

"Why Mr. Jenks has just proposed that we build a big raft, and launch it. He thinks we should leave the island."

"It might be a good idea," agreed the lad, as he thought of the scant food supply. "Of course, I can't say when a reply will be received to my calls for aid, and it is best to be prepared."

"Especially as the island may sink any minute," added Mr. Parker. "If it does, even a raft will be little good, as it may be swamped in the vortex. I think it would be a good plan to make one, then anchor it some distance out from the island. Then we can make a small raft, and paddle out to the big one in a hurry if need be."

"Yes, that's a good idea, too," conceded Tom.

"And we must stock it well with provisions," said Mr. Damon. "Put plenty of water and food aboard."

"We can't," spoke Tom, quietly.

"Why not?"

"Because we haven't plenty of provisions. That's what I came down to speak about," and the lad related what Mrs. Nestor had said.

"Then there is but one thing to do," declared Mr. Fenwick.

"What?" asked Captain Mentor.

"We must go on half rations, or quarter rations, if need be. That will make our supply last longer. And another thing—we must not let the women folks know. Just pretend that we're not hungry, but take only a quarter, or at most, not more than a half of what we have been in the habit of taking. There is plenty of water, thank goodness, and we may be able to live until help comes."

"Then shall we build the raft?" asked Mr. Hosbrook.

It was decided that this would be a good plan, and they started it that same day. Trees were felled, with axes and saws that had been aboard the *Whizzer*, and bound together, in rude fashion, with strong trailing vines from the forest. A smaller raft, as a sort of ferry, was also made.

This occupied them all that day, and part of the next. In the meanwhile, Tom continued to flash out his appeals for help, but no answers came. The men cut down their rations, and when the two ladies joked them on their lack of appetite, they said nothing. Tom was glad that Mrs. Nestor did not renew her request to him to get out the reserve food supply from what remained in the wreck of the airship. Perhaps Mr. Nestor had hinted to her the real situation.

The large raft was towed out into a quiet bay of the island, and anchored there by means of a heavy rock, attached to a rope. On board were put cans of water, vhich were lashed fast, but no food could be spared to stock the rude craft. All the castaways could depend on, was to take with them, in the event of the island beginning to sink, what rations they had left when the final shock should come.

This done, they could only wait, and weary was that waiting. Tom kept faithfully to his schedule, and his ear ached from the constant pressure of the telephone receiver. He heard message after message flash through space, and click on his instrument, but none of them was in answer to his. On his face there came a grim and hopeless look.

One afternoon, a week following the erection of the wireless station, Mate Fordam came upon a number of turtles. He caught some, by turning them over on their backs, and also located a number of nests of eggs under the warm sands.

"This will be something to eat," he said, joyfully, and indeed the turtles formed a welcome food supply. Some fish were caught, and some clams were cast up by the tide, all of which eked out the scanty food supply that remained. The two ladies suspected the truth now and they, too, cut down their allowance.

Tom, who had been sitting with the men in their sleeping shack, that evening, rose, as the hour of ten approached. It was time to send out the last message of the night, and then he would lie down on an improvised couch, with the telephone receiver clamped to his ear, to wait, in the silence of the darkness, for the message saying that help was on the way.

"Well, are you off?" asked Mr. Damon, kindly. "I wish some of us could relieve you, Tom."

"Oh, I don't mind it," answered the lad "Perhaps the message may come to-night."

Hardly had he spoken than there sounded the ominous rumble and shaking that presaged another earthquake. The shack rocked, and threatened to come down about their heads.

"We must be doomed!" cried Mr. Parker. "The island is about to sink! Make for the raft!"

"Wait and see how bad it is," counseled Mr. Hosbrook. "It may be only a slight shock."

Indeed, as he spoke, the trembling of the island ceased, and there was silence. The two ladies, who had retired to their own private shack, ran out screaming, and Mr. Anderson and Mr. Nestor hastened over to be with their wives.

"I guess it's passed over," spoke Mr. Fenwick.

An instant later there came another tremor, but it was not like that of an earthquake shock. It was more like the rumble and vibration of an approaching train.

"Look!" cried Tom, pointing to the left. Their gaze went in that direction, and, under the light of a full moon they saw, sliding into the sea, a great portion of one of the rocky hills.

"A landslide!" cried Captain Mentor. "The island is slowly breaking up."

"It confirms my theory!" said Mr. Parker, almost in triumph.

"Forget your theory for a while, Parker, please," begged Mr. Hosbrook. "We're lucky to have left a place on which to stand! Oh, when will we be rescued?" he asked hopelessly.

The worst seemed to be over at least for the present, and, learning that the two ladies were quieted, Tom started up the hill to his wireless station. Mr. Damon and Mr. Fenwick went with him, to aid in starting the motor and dynamo. Then, after the message had been clicked out as usual Tom would begin his weary waiting.

They found that the earthquake shock had slightly disturbed the apparatus, and it took them half an hour to adjust it. As there had been a delay on account of the landslide, it was eleven o'clock before Tom began sending out any flashes, and he kept it up until midnight. But there came no replies, so he shut off the power, and prepared to get a little rest.

"It looks pretty hopeless; doesn't it?" said Mr. Fenwick, as he and Mr. Damon were on their way back to the sleeping shack.

"Yes, it does. Our signal hasn't been seen, no ships have passed this way, and our wireless appeal isn't answered. It does look hopeless but, do you know, I haven't given up yet."

"Why not?"

"Because I have faith in Tom Swift's luck!" declared the eccentric man. "If you had been with him as much as I have, up in the air, and under the water, and had seen the tight places he has gotten out of, you'd feel the same, too!"

"Perhaps, but here there doesn't seem to be anything to do. It all depends on some one else."

"That's all right. You leave it to Tom. He'll get an answer yet, you see if he doesn't."

It was an hour past midnight. Tom tossed uneasily on the hard bed in the wireless shack. The telephone receiver on his ear hurt him, and he could not sleep.

"I may as well sit up for a while," he told himself, and he arose. In the dimness of the shack he could see the outlines of the dynamo and the motor.

"Guess I'll start her up, and send out some calls," he murmured. "I might just happen to catch some ship operator who is up late. I'll try it."

The young inventor started the motor, and soon the dynamo was purring away. He tested the wireless apparatus. It shot out great long sparks, which snapped viciously through the air. Then, in the silence of the night, Tom clicked off his call for help for the castaways of Earthquake Island.

For half an hour he sent it away into space, none of the others in their shacks below him, awakening. Then Tom, having worked off his restless fit, was about to return to bed.

But what was this? What was that clicking in the telephone receiver at his ear? He listened. It was not a jumble of dots and dashes, conveying through space a message that meant nothing to him. No! It was his own call that was answered. The call of his station—"E. I."—Earthquake Island!

"Where are you? What's wanted?"

That was the message that was clicked to Tom from somewhere in the great void.

"I get your message 'E. I.' what's wanted? Do I hear you right? Repeat." Tom heard those questions in the silence of the night.

With trembling fingers Tom pressed his own key. Out into the darkness went his call for help.

"We are on earthquake island." he gave the longitude and latitude. *"Come quickly or we will be engulfed in the sea! We are castaways from the yacht* Resolute *and the airship* Whizzer. *can you save us?"*

Came then this query:

"What's that about airship?"

"Never mind airship," clicked Tom. *"Send help quickly! Who are you?"*

The answer flashed to him through space:

"Steamship Cambaranian *from Rio de Janeiro to New York. Just caught your message. Thought it a fake."*

"No fake," Tom sent back. *"Help us quickly! How soon can you come?"*

There was a wait, and the wireless operator clicked to Tom that he had called the captain. Then came the report:

"We will be there within twenty-four hours. Keep in communication with us."

"You bet I will," flashed back Tom, his heart beating joyously, and then he let out a great shout. "We are saved! We are saved! My wireless message is answered! A steamer is on her way to rescue us!"

He rushed from the shack, calling to the others.

"What's that?" demanded Mr. Hosbrook.

Tom briefly told of how the message had come to him in the night.

"Tell them to hurry," begged the rich yacht owner. "Say that I will give twenty thousand dollars reward if we are taken off!"

"And I'll do the same," cried Mr. Jenks. "I must get to the place where—" Then he seemed to recollect himself, and stopped suddenly. "Tell them to hurry," he begged Tom. The whole crowd of castaways, save the women, were gathered about the wireless shack.

"They'll need to hurry," spoke Mr. Parker, the gloomy scientist. "The island may sink before morning!"

Mr. Hosbrook and the others glared at him, but he seemed to take delight in his prediction.

Suddenly the wireless instruments hummed.

"Another message," whispered Tom. He listened.

"*The* Cambaranian *will rush here with all speed*," he announced, and not a heart there on that lonely and desolate island but sent up a prayer of thankfulness.

"WE ARE LOST!"

There was little more sleep for any one that night. They sat up, talking over the wonderful and unexpected outcome of Tom Swift's wireless message, and speculating as to when the steamer would get there.

"Bless my pocket comb! But I told you it would come out all right, if we left it to Tom!" declared Mr. Damon.

"But it hasn't come out yet," remarked the pessimistic scientist. "The steamer may arrive too late."

"You're a cheerful sort of fellow to take on a yachting trip," murmured Mr. Hosbrook, sarcastically. "I'll never invite you again, even if you are a great scientist."

"I'm going to sit and watch for the steamer," declared Mr. Damon, as he went outside the shack. The night was warm, and there was a full moon. "Which way will she come from, Tom?"

"I don't know, but I should think, that if she was on her way north, from South America, she'd pass on the side of the island on which we now are."

"That's right," agreed Captain Mentor. "She'll come up from over there," and he pointed across the ocean directly in front of the shacks and camp.

"Then I'm going to see if I can't be the first to sight her lights," declared Mr. Damon.

"She can't possibly get here inside of a day, according to what the operator said," declared Tom.

"Wire them to put on all the speed they can," urged the eccentric man.

"No, don't waste any more power or energy than is needed," suggested Mr. Hosbrook. "You may need the gasolene before we are rescued. They are on their way, and that is enough for now."

The others agreed with this, and so Tom, after a final message to the operator aboard the *Cambaranian* stating that he would call him up in the morning, shut down the motor.

Mr. Damon took up his position where he could see far out over the ocean, but, as the young inventor had said, there was no possible chance of sighting the relief steamer inside of a day. Still the nervous, eccentric man declared that he would keep watch.

Morning came, and castaways brought to breakfast a better appetite than they had had in some time. They were allowed larger rations, too, for it was seen that they would have just enough food to last until taken off.

"We didn't need to have made the big raft," said Mr. Fenwick, as Tom came down from his station, to report that he had been in communication with the Camabarian and that she was proceeding under forced draught. "We'll not have to embark on it, and I'm glad of it."

"Oh, we may need it yet," asserted Mr. Parker. "I have been making some observations just now, and the island is in a very precarious state. It is, I believe, resting on only a slim foundation, and the least shock may break that off, and send it into the sea. That is what my observations point out."

"Then I wish you wouldn't make any more observations!" exclaimed Mrs. Nestor, with spirit. "You make me nervous."

"And me, also," added Mrs. Anderson.

"Science can not deceive, madam," retorted Mr. Parker.

"Well it can keep quiet about what it knows, and not make a person have cold chills," replied Mary's mother. "I'm sure we will be rescued in time."

There was a slight tremor of an earthquake, as they were eating dinner that day, but, aside from causing a little alarm it did no damage. In the afternoon, Tom again called up the approaching steamer, and was informed that, because of a slight accident, it could not arrive until the next morning. Every effort would be made to keep up speed, it was said. There was much disappointment over this, and Mr. Damon was observed to be closely examining the food supply, but hope was too strong to be easily shattered now.

Mr. Parker went off alone, to make some further "observations" as he called them, but Mr. Hosbrook warned him never again to speak of his alarming theories.

Mr. Barcoe Jenks called Tom aside just before supper that evening.

"I haven't forgotten what I said to you about my diamonds," he remarked, with many nods and winks. "I'll show you how to make them, if you will help me. Did you ever see diamonds made?"

"No, and I guess very few persons have." replied the lad, thinking perhaps Mr. Jenks might not be quite right, mentally.

The night passed without alarm, and in the morning, at the first blush of dawn, every one was astir, looking eagerly across the sea for a sight of the steamer.

Tom had just come down from the wireless station, having received a message to the effect that a few hours more would bring the *Cambaranian* within sight of the island.

Suddenly there was a tremendous shock, as if some great cannon had been fired, and the whole island shook to its very centre.

"Another earthquake! The worst yet!" screamed Mrs. Anderson.

"We are lost!" cried Mrs. Nestor, clinging to her husband.

An instant later they were all thrown down by the tremor of the earth, and Tom, looking toward his wireless station, saw nearly half of the island disappear from sight. His station went down in collapse with it, splashing into the ocean, and the wave that followed the terrible crash washed nearly to the castaways, as they rose and kneeled on the sand.

"The island is sinking!" cried Mr. Parker. "Make for the raft!"

"I guess it's our only chance," murmured Captain Mentor, as he gazed across the water. There was no steamer in sight. Could it arrive on time? The tremors and shaking of the island continued.

THE RESCUE—CONCLUSION

Down to where the small raft was moored ran Mr. Parker. He was followed by some of the others.

"We must put off at once!" he cried. "Half the island is gone! The other half may disappear any moment! The steamer can not get here on time, but if we put off they may pick us up, if we are not engulfed in the ocean. Help, everybody!"

Tom gave one more look at where his wireless station had been. It had totally disappeared, there being, at the spot, now but a sheer cliff, which went right down into the sea.

The women were in tears. The men, with pale faces, tried to calm them. Gradually the earthquake tremor passed away; but who could tell when another would come?

Captain Mentor, Mr. Hosbrook and the others were shoving out the small raft. They intended to get aboard, and paddle out to the larger one, which had been moored some distance away, in readiness for some such emergency as this.

"Come on!" cried Mr. Fenwick to Tom who was lingering behind. "Come on, ladies. We must all get aboard, or it may be too late!"

The small raft was afloat. Mrs. Anderson and Mrs. Nestor, weeping hysterically, waded out through the water to get aboard.

"Have we food?" cried Mr. Damon. "Bless my kitchen range! but I nearly forgot that."

"There isn't any food left to take," answered Mrs. Anderson.

"Shove off!" cried Captain Mentor.

At that instant a haze which had hung over the water, was blown to one side. The horizon suddenly cleared. Tom Swift looked up and gave a cry.

"The steamer! The steamer! The *Cambaranian!*" he shouted, pointing to it.

The others joined in his exclamations of joy, for there, rushing toward Earthquake Island was a great steamer, crowding on all speed!

"Saved! Saved!" cried Mrs. Nestor, sinking to her knees even in the water.

"It came just in time!" murmured Mr. Hosbrook.

"Now I can make my diamonds," whispered Mr. Jenks to Tom.

"Push off! Push off!" cried Mr. Parker. "The island will sink, soon!"

"I think we will be safer on the island than on the raft," declared Captain Mentor. "We had better land again."

They left the little raft, and stood on the shore of the island. Eagerly they watched the approach of the steamer. They could make out hands and handkerchiefs waving to them now. There was eager hope in every heart.

Suddenly, some distance out in the water, and near where the big raft was anchored, there was a curious upheaval of the ocean. It was as if a submarine mine had exploded! The sea swirled and foamed!

"It's a good thing we didn't go out there," observed Captain Mentor. "We would have been swamped, sure as guns."

Almost as he spoke the big raft was tossed high into the air, and fell back, breaking up. The castaways shuddered. Yet were they any safer on the island? They fancied they could feel the little part of it that remained trembling under their feet.

"The steamer is stopping!" cried Mr. Damon.

Surely enough the *Cambaranian* had slowed up. Was she not going to complete the rescue she had begun?

"She's going to launch her lifeboats," declared Captain Mentor. "Her commander dare not approach too close, not knowing the water. He might hit on a rock."

A moment later and two lifeboats were lowered, and, urged on by the sturdy arms of the sailors, they bounded over the waves. The sea seemed to be more and more agitated.

"It is the beginning of the end," murmured Mr. Parker. "The island will soon disappear."

"Will you be quiet?" demanded Mr. Damon, giving the scientist a nudge in the ribs.

The lifeboats were close at hand now.

"Are you all there?" shouted some one, evidently in command.

"All here," answered Tom.

"Then hurry aboard. There seems to be something going on in these waters—perhaps a submarine volcano eruption. We must get away in a hurry!"

The boats came in to the shelving beach. There was a little stretch of water between them and the sand. Through this the castaways waded, and soon they were grasped by the sailors and helped in. In the reaction of their worriment Mrs. Anderson and Mrs. Nestor were both weeping, but their tears were those of joy.

"Give way now, men!" cried the mate in charge of the boats. "We must get back to the ship!"

The sea was now swirling angrily, but the sailors, who had been in worse turmoils than this, rowed on steadily.

"We feared you would not get here in time," said Tom to the mate.

"We were under forced draught most of the way," was his answer. "Your wireless message came just in time. An hour later and our operator would have gone to bed."

The young inventor realized by what a narrow margin they had been rescued.

"The island will soon sink," predicted Mr. Parker, as they reached the steamer, and boarded her. Captain Valasquez, who was in command, warmly welcomed the castaways.

"We will hear your story later," he said. "Just now I want to get out of these dangerous waters."

He gave the order for full speed, and, as the *Cambaranian* got under way, Tom, and the others, standing on the deck, looked back at Earthquake Island.

Suddenly there sounded a dull, rumbling report. The whole ocean about the island seemed to upheave. There was a gigantic shower of spray, a sound like an explosion, and when the waters subsided the island had sunk from sight.

"I told you it would go," cried Mr. Parker, triumphantly, but the horror of it all—the horror of the fate that would have been theirs had they remained there an hour longer—held the castaways dumb. The scientist's honor of having correctly predicted the destruction of the island was an empty one.

The agitation of the sea rocked even the mighty *Cambaranian* and, had our friends been aboard the frail raft, they would surely have perished in the sea. As it was, they were safe—saved by Tom Swift's wireless message.

The steamer resumed her voyage, and the castaways told their story. Captain Valasquez refused to receive the large amount of money Mr. Hasbrook and Mr. Jenks would have paid him for the rescue, accepting only a sum he figured that he had lost by the delay, which was not a great deal. The castaways were given the best aboard the ship, and their stories were listened to by the other passengers with bated breath.

In due time they were landed in New York, and Mr. and Mrs. Nestor accompanied Tom to Shopton. Mr. Damon, with many blessings also accompanied them, going to his home in Waterfield. Later it was learned that the other boats from the *Resolute* had been picked up, and the sailors and guests were all saved.

Of course, as soon as our friends had been rescued by the steamer, the wireless operator aboard her, with whom Tom soon struck up an acquaintance, sent messages to the relatives of the castaways, apprising them of their safety.

And the joy of Mary Nestor, when she found that it was Tom who had saved her parents, can well be imagined. As for our hero, well, he was glad too—for Mary's sake.

"I won't forget my promise to you, Tom Swift," said Mr. Barcoe Jenks, as he parted from the young inventor, and what the promise was will be told in the next volume of this series, to be called: "Tom Swift Among the Diamond Makers; or, The Secret of Phantom Mountain." In that Tom is destined to have many more surprising adventures, as is also Mr. Damon, who learned new ways to call down blessings on himself and his possessions.

And now, for a time, we will take leave of the young inventor and also of his many friends, who never ceased to wonder over Tom Swift's skill with the wireless.

16801691R00157

Made in the USA
Lexington, KY
11 August 2012